THE
EIGHTH
WARNING

THE EIGHTH WARNING

Book One of the Reclaimed Saga

SAM ODIORNE

www.samodiorne.com

First Edition: September 2021

Eighth Warning / Sam Odiorne
ISBN: 978-0-000-00-0000-0

10 9 8 7 6 5 4 3 2 1

For Delene,

who was brave enough to leave the Garden
and discovered she was Cern after all.

ONE

Hyatt's eyes scanned the dense and unwelcoming forest on either side of the trail as he walked, all his rational reasons for going out with the Line Team melting away as the branches above him seemed to blend into the consuming patches of darkness between them. The dawn light that filtered through the dense canopy of the Reclaimed should have driven back the shadows but it only seemed to deepen the contrast, building pools of light at odd distances in the thick forest that made the spaces between seem impenetrable and dangerous. His boots crunched the hard-packed earth of the path from Brathnee Garden to Vohk Bridge and he ran his thumb beneath the broad leather strap of his satchel, shifting it to rub unfamiliarly against a new swath of his shoulder. The sounds of the twelve members of the Line Team shuffling towards their day's task were louder than anything that came out of the forest, and he found himself wondering if it would be deathly still without their presence.

"I heard one of the Line Teams spotted a Skarren last week," Gorman said beside him, hitching his backpack higher on his lanky frame and cinching the straps tighter. "They spent a whole day hiding under the leaves until it left."

His companion's comment made Hyatt's stomach tighten and sent a wash of tingling tension through his shoulders, but he tried not to let it show. "That's bullshit. There are no Skarren in Brathnee. Who said that?"

"I dunno." Gorman shrugged. "Just something I heard."

He looked away from the eerie stillness of the forest to give Gorman a skeptical look. "You're just talking out of your ass – if there were Heirs in Brathnee, the whole garden would know, and you'd remember where you heard about it from."

The taller man didn't deny Hyatt's accusation and settled for a shake of his head, as if after two decades of friendship he had expected his story to slip past Hyatt's defenses and was consternated when it didn't. A crisp gust sliced through the branches beside and above them, needles and leaves rustling in a whispering hiss as they brushed against each other. Somewhere above the blanket of foliage, a low, dense cloud shifted in front of the sun, dimming the daylight and driving the warmth from the air around them. Hyatt shoved his fingerless gloves into his pockets and raised his shoulders so his neck could take advantage of the woolen collar lining of his leather jacket.

"Maybe. I don't know. Can you imagine, though? Out here working, and suddenly the sky goes black... wings a hundred feet across and talons like swords..." He trailed off to guilty silence as the Line Team leader drew closer to them, but not soon enough to avoid her notice.

"Hey, saplings – how about a little more shutting the fuck up and a little less trying to attract everything in the Reclaimed to us?" Jenna's voice was low and level, but every syllable carried the force of a battering ram as she looked briefly at Hyatt and then hard at Gorman. "There are no Heirs in Brathnee and it's a good fucking thing, because they'd rip our little security team apart in about one-tenth of a second. Now watch the damn brush."

Embarrassment and frustration made Hyatt's jaw flex and tighten – a bad report from the Line Team lead would be the opposite of the whole reason he was outside the Garden to begin with, sending rumors running through the city that he couldn't keep his mouth shut and put his team in danger. He forced himself to nod towards her in apologetic agreement and then stared a hole through the side of Gorman's head as Jenna extended her stride to check on the next pair of workers on the path ahead. Gorman took sudden and intense interest in the path before them and the opposite side of the forest, anything that didn't involve looking at him.

"Are you kidding me?" Hyatt growled when he was sure Jenna was far enough forward to avoid her coming back and reprimanding them again.

"What?" Gorman protested, though his voice was a whisper.

A dozen rebukes flooded into Hyatt's mind but they stumbled over each other and before he could land on the right one, the moment had passed, so he walked in aggravated silence. They passed one of the security workers, her flechette carbine suspended from a strap on her shoulder and her hand rested on the action of the short-barreled gun. For a moment he wished he'd been allowed to bring one of the restricted weapons, but he flashed back to how awful he'd been with one during the one class everyone had to take in Garden Defense during their Trade training.

He was sure he saw her smirk at him as he crossed her periphery before her eyes returned to searching the branches and the depths of the Reclaimed. "Great. I'm fucked."

Hyatt fought the urge to glance back at her and let her eye contact confirm she was amused by his helplessness. He imagined the slender woman shouldering her gun and the roar of the shot as it flung jagged metal flechettes through the brush at a Cern raider or wild beast, but his imagination expanded his view to see himself curled up in a terrified ball as she pivoted to fire again, and he sighed. Against his better judgment, he looked over his shoulder and met the gaze of the Security worker whose smirk expanded as she turned her attention to the wilderness.

Hyatt's eyes drifted again to the carbine and he wondered if he could even remember how to load it after the years since he'd held one, or pull it apart if it jammed.

The sun rose higher and broke free of the cloud masking it, pouring warmer and brighter daylight through the dense foliage. The pockets of shadow finally began to lose ground, as if drains had opened in the forest floor to funnel the darkness down beneath the blanket of dead leaves and fallen branches. While Gorman walked in silence to let Hyatt's frustration pass, Hyatt did his best to follow the instructions Jenna had given them – stay between the security workers, pay attention to the depths of the forest, keep twenty paces between pairs of workers, and don't make more noise than required. The rhythm of their footfalls and the height of the sun overhead marked the passage of time as they followed the winding trail that paralleled the knee-high conduit carrying the lines of the Brathnee network.

Beyond the nearest reaches of the wood line, the remains of buildings overgrown with moss and vines came into view. His pace slowed as he took in the open gaps where windows might have been, the jagged tops of shattered walls and rusted metal bars like skeletal remains of what might have once been a home or shop or library. In any space that fell victim to both pooling water and sunlight, patches of moss clung to the uneven surfaces. His eyes shifted to the pair of entwined saplings that rose from the center of what had been the largest room of the ground floor, tracking down from its fledgling canopy to where mushrooms and tall-stalked flowers grew in the ribbons of shade it cast. The pictures drawn by Brathnee artists did no justice to the majesty and the fear that the ancient building inspired.

"Seventh History," Gorman scoffed as if he'd seen hundreds of the buildings taken back by nature. "Probably not even early Seventh."

Hyatt tore his gaze from the building and as he turned towards his friend, he spotted Jenna making her way back through the Line Team on her constant patrol. "Gorman. Shut. The. Fuck. Up."

"I'm just..." he trailed off again, realizing his mistake too late as he locked eyes with the team lead walking right toward him. "Oops."

"Gorman, head to the front. Send Tyson back here." Her instruction left no room for debate and she waited until he picked up his pace to obey before falling into step beside Hyatt. "Tyson doesn't talk. Now we'll see if the problem is you, or your friend."

Hyatt turned to look at Jenna and his eyes riveted to the seven deep scars that escaped from beneath her blond hair. The parallel white lines traced counterclockwise behind her ear and along the right side of her neck, vanishing just before her windpipe. Wondering about their origin derailed his thoughts as he tried to weigh the merits of apologizing for his friend or explaining it hadn't been his fault, but he realized he was staring and jerked his gaze away with another rapid, silent nod. He could feel her eyes on him, that azure gaze that seemed to shred his skin and bone to see something deep inside him. After another ten paces, she nodded as if satisfied and continued her walk towards the back of the team.

Tyson joined him with an impersonal tilt of his head, adjusting the crossed straps of two satchels hanging at his side, and they matched paces. True to Jenna's promise, he made no sound beyond the faint rustle of his bags shifting and his boots disturbing the earth as they passed. For two hours they walked in silence, watching opposite sides of the road and the backs of the workers ahead of them to keep enough space between pairs. Alone with his thoughts, Hyatt dwelt on the team leader reprimanding him twice and the irrational thought that Gorman might have been right about Skarren stalking the Reclaimed around Brathnee Garden in search of workers stupid enough to leave the walls trying to impress a woman.

He was so lost in his thoughts that he ran into the arm Tyson extended to stop him in his tracks. The satchel at his side swung from the abrupt halt and he grabbed it to stop the contents from clanking and jostling as he looked around and saw the pair of workers ahead of him kneeling and hunching low. Hyatt's pulse began to race as a thousand terrible reasons the group might have stopped flooded his head in the form of bloody, fast-moving snapshots, and he let Tyson's fist around his sleeve pull him down to his knees. A moment later Jenna jogged between them, her boots making almost no noise as she headed for the front of the team. Minutes seemed to thicken and expand to terrifying lifetimes as Hyatt tried to make even his breathing quieter and fought the queasy feeling in his tightening stomach. The sound of his own heartbeat in his ears was bass and relentless.

One of the workers from the pair in front of them held up both their hands with their palms flat, touching their middle fingers together over their head to form a triangle, and Tyson let out a slow breath that seemed to take two dozen seconds to finish exhaling. Hyatt studied the tension in the man's face and when their eyes met, he shot Tyson his most confused expression. In reply, Tyson leaned forward and traced his finger in the dirt to write four letters that made the blood drain from Hyatt's face and hands.

Cern. No... no, no, no, no.... His lips felt numb and he pressed his palms to his knees to stop his fingers from trembling. *This isn't happening. There shouldn't be Cern here. This is Brathnee. This isn't real.*

Tyson reached over his head with the same gesture to alert the pair of workers behind him, and the pair in front of them gestured to move closer. Hyatt waited as Tyson looked back along the path to ensure the next pair had received the message, then rose to a half-crouch and started moving ahead. The thought of getting closer to whoever had signaled the alarm made Hyatt's stomach turn over again but he moved with Tyson, creeping ahead on the path until they were close enough to whisper. Jenna arrived moments later and grabbed each worker by the shoulder, turning them to face the direction she wanted them to watch and spacing them apart from each other until every direction was covered with security workers spaced between the Line Team.

When they were in a ring facing outward, the team leader moved from one to the next, relaying something in tones too low for Hyatt to make out. He cursed his luck for being the eighth person in the team leader's arc, each person before him giving Hyatt an opportunity to imagine a new version of bad news. When he felt Jenna beside him with her hand on his shoulder, he glanced over to catch her in the edge of his gaze before looking outward and leaving his ear close enough to her lips for him to feel her warm breath on his neck.

"Fifty paces ahead, Cern bones are hanging from trees and staked in the ground." Her voice was neutral, but the words still lanced through Hyatt's heart like icicles driven by a hammer. "Vohk Bridge is a hundred paces beyond that. The lead pair didn't see any Cern, but these weren't here on our last job out this way. Nod if you understand."

Hyatt nodded, ashamed of himself for the nervous speed his head jerked up and down but unable to help it. He hoped that the team leader was too close to him to notice the goosebumps that had broken out along his neck or the way his whole body tightened as she whispered the terrifying words in his ear.

"High Ranger says we still need to do the job, so we're going to go out there and repair the line," Jenna continued. "If we are attacked, stay out of the security worker's way. Use your knife, kill as many Cern as you can. Don't let them take any of the workers, and don't get taken alive. Nod if you understand."

Kill as many of them as you can?! Hyatt tasted bile in his mouth, but he nodded. *This can't be happening.*

"Watch your area and follow Tyson when he moves." She patted his shoulder twice, surprisingly hard for how little sound the gesture made. "We're going to be okay. Trust me."

The feeling of her hand on his jacket and her breath on his neck vanished and Hyatt knew she'd moved on to repeat the message, even though she made no sound as she passed behind him on the inside of the perimeter. He searched the forest in front of him with a new focus, trying to peer around the broad trunks and between the low branches in search of any human forms. With every rustle of bush or shift of shadow, he expected to catch a glint of metal or shift in the dark that would be the only warning of his imminent death. Hyatt felt his fingernails digging into his palms through the knit material of his gloves and forced himself to unclench his hands and take a deep breath.

It felt like a thousand years before Jenna finished her revolution around the ring and Tyson got up to move. Hyatt rose slowly, his legs cramped from the unfamiliar pose and the tension of knowing Cern could be skulking in every space hidden from view in the Reclaimed. He winced as his knee buckled and his satchel clacked and jostled before he could clutch it close, drawing a withering look from Tyson over his shoulder.

Damn it. He cringed apologetically and continued to follow Tyson.

The sight of bones, rawhide strands wrapped around their ends and suspended unevenly overhead, almost stopped him in his tracks. The charred and cleaned remains swung idly in the morning breeze, moving just a little too quickly to make out the markings carved on their surfaces. Sunlight glinted on their yellow-white surfaces, and less brightly on the faded tan ends where ligaments had been peeled or burned away. He slowed down to look up, transfixed by the macabre sight, until the worker behind Hyatt nudged him to keep moving.

The hanging bones had been frightening, but the clusters of fragments driven into the ground in a parody of wildflowers made Hyatt recoil in horror. On either side of the path, far enough in so they couldn't be missed in the thicket, two sets of bones seemed to spring up from the earth in tight rings around a central stalk. Twine lashed small, dark violet pennants to the bones in imitations of leaves and petals, the mid-weight fabric shifting and fluttering from their skeletal branches. He felt his gag reflex fire as he stared at them, cold terror washing through his veins as he forced himself to move between them while everything inside him wanted to turn and run the other way.

Jenna crouched just beyond the Cern bone markers and paused until Tyson reached them, then sent them on together with a point down the path and a pat on Tyson's back. Hyatt felt like her eyes lingered on him, judging the way his hands were shaking and his chest rose and fell in shallow breaths, and knowing he deserved her critical assessment made it even worse. He gritted his teeth and fell into place beside his assigned partner, hoping Gorman had dealt with the display worse than he did.

As soon as Vohk Bridge came into view, Jenna passed between him and the side of the path. He stared after her stocky, muscular frame, noting how none of her gear made a sound as it shifted around her, and wondered where she found the endless endurance to move up and down the length of the Line Team hour after hour. Watching her pass bigger and smaller workers without ever seeming out of breath or in a hurry made him focus on the ache in his shoulders from his satchel and in his thighs from the hike from Brathnee Garden. He couldn't tell if he envied her, or resented her.

He gathered with the other workers in a loose cluster around Jenna, who set down her pack and rested her boot on it as she hooked her thumbs in her belt and regarded the team. "Okay Line workers – and saplings – you can talk here. We don't know why the Cern marked this area, but it means they think they own it and we don't want to be here when they come back to check their lines so work quickly and get it right the first time."

"Assignments." She looked across the crowd and made eye contact with each one of the assembled workers to ensure she had everyone's undivided attention before continuing. "Security workers, both ends of the bridge. Line workers, get on the bridge, find out how bad it is – I want to know how long it will take to repair the line, right-fucking-now."

Two of the men and women armed with flechette carbines posted on the near end of the bridge, and two others set off at a jog to secure the far end. Tyson and three other workers picked up the packs they'd set down and moved towards the line conduit on the bridge. Hyatt watched them go before looking back over his shoulder at the forest edge and the hanging bones above the path, but the sound of Jenna's voice drew his attention back to her.

"Structure workers, get down the banks – I want to know if the bridge is damaged or just the line and conduit." Her eyes swung to Gorman and then to Hyatt, and it seemed to him like she lingered on the two of them longer than the rest of the team. "Saplings, you're splitting up. Gorman, get up on the bridge and help the Line workers. Hyatt, go with the Structure workers, do whatever they tell you to."

Hyatt glanced over at his friend – as much trouble as Gorman had caused on the trek from the Garden, he was the only person Hyatt knew on the team and he expected they'd be working together. The lankier man met his gaze with a shrug and adjusted his pack again before heading towards the bridge. When Hyatt looked back at Jenna, she was staring at him as if he should have already left, and he hurried to get out of her line of sight down the muddy bank with the other workers.

By the time he reached the bottom, the five Structure workers were climbing beneath the bridge to inspect the supports. He moved their way, gasping in shock as he stepped in the river and the frigid water instantly numbed everything from his ankle to the sole of his foot. With a growl and a shake to shed the water from his boot, he worked his way along the marshy grass and mud. When he reached the nearest worker, the willowy woman glanced down at his exhausted face and laughed before turning her attention back to the pillar in front of her.

"First day in the Reclaimed?" she asked without looking at him again, running her hand along the smooth stone surface.

Hyatt hated that it was obvious, but he couldn't argue. "You're all so... capable. Jenna is..."

"Capable?" she finished for him, smirking at her echo of his chosen word. "Don't try to keep up with her, just do as she says. She's the best – you're lucky to have her on your first trip out."

"First and last," Hyatt muttered, shifting the strap of his satchel. "What makes her the best?"

The Structure worker reached into her pocket, produced a piece of chalk, and made a mark on the support. With a look to her left and right to see who else was within earshot, she leaned a little closer to Hyatt. When he didn't lean in, she took a half-step to close the space between them.

"Jenna used to be Cern." She emphasized the statement with a solemn nod, then turned back to the pillar.

"She..." Hyatt stared at the shaved side of the worker's head beneath her braid as all the things he didn't know about life beyond the Garden avalanched into his brain. "She what-the-fuck?"

Before she could answer, a staccato crack roared and echoed off the surface of the water. A moment later, one of the line workers plummeted from the bridge above and splashed into the water, a frothy rush of crimson trailing behind the man's body on the surface. Everything seemed to slow down like Hyatt was seeing the whole world underwater, and then another crack rang out above the bridge.

TWO

"**G**et down!" Jenna's voice called out, and before he could react, the Structure worker slammed into his chest and knocked him into the mud.

Time sped up for Hyatt again and the air was filled with shouting. He fought the strap of his satchel to get it up over his head and off his shoulder, the mud making every motion feel heavier and resisted by the earth itself. Over and over, the unfamiliar crack filled the air, and another Line worker fell from the bridge into the frozen, rushing water.

"What is that?" Hyatt shouted at the woman beside him who was crawling on her belly up the bank to seek protection beside the bridge's end.

"I don't know!" she shouted back. "Get behind something!"

"From what direction?" Hyatt protested, but had no idea if she heard him or not.

Leaving his satchel in the mud, he followed the Structure worker's example and dragged himself up the wilting grass and dark earth by his forearms. A strange whizzing sound passed over his head and he buried his face in the mud, the taste of minerals and grit coating his lips. The realization that he could have been at his factory job in Brathnee Garden if he hadn't wanted to impress Stella rose unbidden in his mind, but the sight of a Cern raider running low across the embankment towards him erased that and every other thought from his head.

"Cern!" he screamed in a pitch that mortified him to hear in his own ears, his shaking hands pulling at the straps that held his knife in his sheath.

Hyatt forced himself to his knees as the Cern raider reached him, and he threw himself back down on the bank as she swung a four-foot cleaver over him in a vicious slash. He planted his boots for traction but the mud gave way beneath them and Hyatt began sliding towards the water, his free hand clawing at the grass to stop himself from ending up in the river. The raider brought her evil weapon down in an arc and he rolled over to avoid it, mud splattering his forehead and cheek as the blade embedded in the ground inches from his nose where his neck had just been. He cringed as she jerked her weapon free, knowing he had no chance of avoiding the next slash, and cried out as the Structure worker dove over him and collided with the Cern.

Hyatt climbed to his hands and knees, turning to face the two fighters. The Cern raider was on her back, her hand grasping or the handle of her weapon as the Structure worker straddled her, slamming her elbow into the raider's face over and over with a primal scream. He threw himself on the pinned woman's arm and kicked her weapon further down the bank, but looked up to see the Structure worker catch a swinging fist to the temple and sprawl away.

"Kill her!" she shouted, rolling to a stop in the mud.

The Structure worker struggled frantically to grab for the Cern woman's legs before the raider could get up. Hyatt lunged and threw himself across the prone raider, his chest pinning her to the ground   beneath him as she thrashed in the mud like a fish caught on dry land. She tried to worm out from under him, her arms and knees battering his frame, and every time he tried to lift his knife and bring it down on her, the Cern woman punched at his ribs or face.

"Fucking stab her!" the worker yelled again, her whole body wrapped around the raider's legs in a struggle to hold them together and down.

Hyatt smashed the raider's next swing away and planted his knee on her bicep, pinning it in the mud. Her other hand swung and caught him in the ear before he could stop it, and his vision swam. With a grunt of exhausted effort he swung his leg over her, straddling her body so he could fend off her free hand with one hand arm? and raise his knife with the other. At the top of his swing, he froze as their eyes met, her mint-green irises shining with a ferocious and defiant pride he hadn't expected and her bloodied lips parted in a primal joy he couldn't understand.

"Stop!" he shouted at her, his knife still poised above his shoulder to plunge down and end her life. "Stop fighting! Stop!"

The Cern raider laughed at him and spat, wet dirt and warm blood spraying his face. He clenched his eyes closed and shook his head as if thrashing it back and forth could dislodge the crimson spatter on his cheeks. He brought the knife down, and the feeling of the metal deflecting off bone and sliding to a stop in meat and tendon almost made him vomit. Her body spasmed and her breath sounded wet, and when he looked down blood was bubbling from her lips and leaking from the side of her neck where his knife was buried to the handle.

"Oh my- fucking.... Oh, fuck-" Hyatt dry heaved, half crawling and half scrambling off her to rest on all fours while his sternum spasmed and threatened to empty his stomach into the mud beside the raider.

A shadow fell over Hyatt's head and formed an outline in the dirt under him and realities battered him like wind in a taut sail – he was too exhausted to keep fighting, he couldn't do anything about whoever was standing over him, and he didn't care if he lived as long as that moment ended. He collapsed on his side, nearly nesting himself against the writhing Cern raider, and squinted up against the blinding daylight to see how he would die. His gaze focused on the silhouette of the Cern cleaver, black as night except for the wicked curve of the blade that glinted blindingly white.

"Move, sapling!" Jenna's voice crashed over him as her hand closed around his collar and tugged hard, rolling him down the embankment in the mud.

He spat out the mud that collected on his lips, dug his hands in before his slide could land him in the river, and looked up in time to see the weapon in Jenna's hand arc in a perfect circle that severed the Cern raider's head with brutal elegance. She stepped over the dead body and the Structure worker still holding the dead woman's legs, and he followed her form until it was flanked by two more Cern raiders squaring off with her.

The sight of Jenna with the Cern blade held low and ready, her knees half-bent and her head turning back and forth to regard her enemies, burned away the fatigue and fear that paralyzed him. Hyatt crawled back up the bank in a frantic scramble until his hand found the grip of his knife and he yanked hard to free it from the headless corpse, then struggled to his feet as the layers of caked mud tried to weigh him down. He staggered towards Jenna, who had begun turning the weapon over in her hand with a dull woosh as it swung.

"Who burns on the pyre tonight?" she snarled, a clot to her words Hyatt hadn't heard before. "Whose child gets their new skin today?"

He'd almost reached Jenna when the two Cern raiders roared and charged, their unbridled rage stalling his step with surprise and fear. The team leader swung upward with a vicious slash and opened the raider from his navel to his chin, the Cern's momentum carrying a body no longer alive into a facedown pile on her right. She spun and used the momentum of her whirl to bring the blade around horizontally, and the other raider lowered his weapon to block it but underestimated the sheer force of the swing. It ripped the weapon from his hand and sent it careening up the bank. He only had a moment to register that it was gone before Jenna rained hack after hack down on his neck and shoulder, driving him to the ground with a relentless storm of strikes that sprayed the raider's blood in every direction as he collapsed. When he lay lifeless on the bank Jenna stopped, her body heaving with deep breaths and her arms coated to her elbows in blood. From the other side of the bridge, a flechette carbine fired twice.

She turned to regard Hyatt and the Structure worker, her eyes glittering through the mud and spattered Cern blood on her forehead and temples. "Stay here, stay low. Don't die."

Without waiting to see if they obeyed her command, the team leader trudged with grim determination towards the sound of the shots. Hyatt collapsed to his knees and then fell onto his side, his head laying in the cool mud and his eyes fixing on the dead raider closest to him before they unfocused and stared through the bodies to a distant place. He didn't look up but didn't resist when the Structure worker knelt beside him and turned his chin to meet her eyes, squinting as she studied his pupils.

"Are you hurt, or are you scared?" she asked, and when he didn't respond, she opened her hand and slapped him with the back of it. "Hey, answer me. Are you injured, or just 'cussed?"

"I think... I think I'm okay," Hyatt mumbled, wincing as her slap began to warm in his cheek.

The worker's fingers released his chin and his head dropped onto the ground. "If you think you're fine, then you're fine. Listen – no more shots. We're alive."

A part of Hyatt's brain that was functioning knew she was right – he couldn't hear any more of the unfamiliar, louder shots or the sounds of the flechette carbines firing – but that region of his mind seemed detached from the parts that moved his body or worked through things. He forced himself to roll onto his back and nod, and realizing how hard that was let shame and embarrassment start seeping in to fill the cracks in his thoughts. The sinking viscous mortification met his rising bile and his gag reflex fired again, but he swallowed hard and nodded again to prove he could. At the sound of running boots he turned to spot a Line worker crossing the bank to them, slipping and almost following as he jogged across the slippery bank.

"Jenna wants to see everybody under the bridge. Come on."

The determination Hyatt had just mustered bled from him like the open wounds of the bodies beside him, the thought of moving was more than he could bear. His brain told him to follow instructions but his body refused until the Structure worker wrapped her slender, strong fingers around his wrist and pulled. His own hand closed around her arm more from reaction than intended and as he pulled back, he almost dragged her into the mud with him. She caught her balance and he stumbled to his feet. Together they followed the Line worker along the bank until they reached the pillar Hyatt had been by when the attack started. From beside them and the other side of the bridge, the rest of the Line team drew closer until they formed a crescent moon in front of Jenna. Hyatt spotted Gorman as he joined the group, a welt by his hairline and cradling his hand to his chest.

He watched the team lead look them over, composed and comfortable with the shaft of the Cern raider's weapon in her hand, as if the fight that had almost killed them all had been nothing more than an inconvenience. He felt sure she was counting survivors, though there was no nod of her head movement of her lips to give substance to his thought. When she'd made eye contact with each of the six people still standing, Jenna ran her free, bloodstained hand through her hair and knocked loose clods of mud that landed silently on the soft earth beside her boots.

"The Line still has to be repaired," she said, as if she was commenting on the weather. "Line workers, get back on the bridge and finish the repair. Structure workers... worker, assess the bridge. Let me know if it's compromised. Sapling, Hyatt – come with me."

Hyatt wondered how every realization about life beyond Brathnee Garden was somehow followed by an even worse realization. He looked around at the remaining workers and saw what he hadn't before, a grim resolve in the dimness of their gazes and jaws strengthened by locking them again and again. Some looked tired, some looked determined, and Gorman looked terrified.

"Now." Jenna didn't change her tone, but it was clear she wasn't used to repeating herself.

The direction broke the workers free of the roots that held them in place. Hyatt glanced at the Structure worker as she made her way closer to the pillars that held the bridge up, and he almost stumbled as one of the Line workers bumped into him on his way to the top of the embankment. When it was only Gorman and Hyatt left, he crossed the trampled mud to Jenna.

"Let's go." Jenna gestured vaguely towards the side of the bridge where Hyatt had fought with the Cern raiders. "We're going to look for our dead, and then we'll search the raiders. Nod if you understand."

Hyatt started to follow Jenna down to the edge of the water, but Gorman grabbed the sleeve of his jacket to slow him down and let the team leader get a few feet ahead of them. "Are you okay?"

He didn't have any idea how to answer that, so tugged his arm free of Gorman's grip and carefully crept down the muddy bank towards Jenna with Gorman working to stay by his side. He felt his friend still looking at him. and shrugged, the best he could do.

"You're shaking," Gorman pressed.

Hyatt's boots fought for traction in the treacherous mud and by the time he reached the water's edge, Jenna was up to her hips in the river and dragging the Cern weapon back and forth through it. He ignored Gorman's remark and waded in after her, looking around in the shallows but unsure what to do. The bite of the coursing water was instant and cut straight to his marrow, and he locked his jaw to keep his teeth from chattering as he took another step and the river rose above his knees.

"You're not going to find them," Gorman called from the bank, pacing the edge just beyond where the water began. "They fell from the middle of the bridge – they're miles from here by now!"

"You could learn something from Hyatt, Gorman." The team leader didn't spare him a look, her eyes fixed on the surface as she worked the weapon through the water like an oar. "It doesn't matter if we find them. It matters that they were worth looking for. Worth getting wet for."

Amidst the horror of the fight and his shame at being afraid, the bubbles of pride that streamed upward inside Hyatt surprised him. The corner of his lip started to turn up and he fought it, leaning further over the water in case Jenna looked back and thought he wasn't taking the search seriously. He took another step into the water and felt the bitter cold rise another inch along his thighs.

"That's insane!" his companion protested, a squeak breaking his words at their peak. "I didn't live through a Cern attack just to die of hypothermia – no thank you!"

Jenna opened her mouth to reply but paused as the end of her weapon bit into something. She tucked the handle of the weapon through her belt and leaned forward, diving beneath the water for a moment before resurfacing with the head of a dead Line worker caught in the crook of her arm like she was choking him. She started dragging the body backwards towards the shore and Hyatt splashed deeper, meeting her with the water up to his navel. The team leader turned and Hyatt ducked under the dead man's arm, and together they pulled him towards the bank. The corpse's legs dragged in the mud and made him feel like he weighed twice as much, water-weeds clinging to his pants, but they made it to the bank and dumped him onto the mud with a heave. Gorman scurried closer, dropping to a knee beside the body while Jenna tugged at his clothing and turned his head from side to side to inspect him.

She stopped when she found the hole in his chest, just beneath his collarbone. With a frown, she pressed her finger into the gap and moved it around, and her frown deepened as she pulled it back and shook her hand absently. The wind caught them and Hyatt's teeth let a single chatter escape before he clamped his jaw closed again, hoping she hadn't heard it.

"Get him up the bank. Save anything his family might want - we're planting him here." Jenna turned and waded back into the river, droplets from her drenched hair cascading around her to rejoin the rushing water.

Hyatt watched her go, the water rising up her legs as she pulled the Cern blade from her belt and began sweeping the river again. "She's... unbelievable."

Gorman scoffed, grabbing the corpse's shoulder. "She's full of herself. I heard she used to be the pack-master of a Cern pack, but she got exiled for being too dangerous even for Cern."

He ripped his gaze away from Jenna and picked up the dead body from the other side, grunting with effort as he and Gorman dragged the lifeless form up the bank to the waiting grass. By the time they set him down, Hyatt was out of breath. He sank to his knees and looked back at the team leader in the river, her focus entirely on finding any more workers, then turned his attention to the body.

"Jenna's Haleu now, just like us." He was irritated with Gorman, but the bite in his words surprised him a little. "She follows the Seven Warnings, earns her place in the Garden, and probably saved our lives today. I don't care who she used to be."

Gorman's mouth moved in a mimicry of Hyatt's last sentence, his hands patting the pockets and belt of the body between them. "Stella will be so disappointed you've found someone else to dream about. I don't know if she'll ever recover."

"What is that supposed to mean?" He snapped at his companion, glaring at him while he frisked the corpse's legs and felt around the top of his boots.

"Jenna is so strong, and so brave, and so amazing," Gorman mocked, his words loaded down with honey. "Have you asked her if she's paired yet?"

"I am not paired." Jenna's silent walk and the sun driving her shadow away had given them no warning of her approach, and she stood over them with one thumb in her belt and the other hand resting her weapon on her shoulder.

They both blanched at her sudden appearance, Gorman turning intense focus to the dead Line worker's collar while Hyatt turned shades of carnation and squinted up at the team leader. She didn't move, one half of her form consumed by daylight and the other half darkened by contrast but her visible blue eye staring directly at his. He tried to look away but couldn't, the twist of his head halting as her gaze held his until she turned towards Gorman.

"Hyatt would make a very good pair. He keeps his mouth shut, he works hard, and today he killed a Cern raider." Her voice had the same level tone she'd used on the trail, stripping the compliment of any warmth while letting the implied insult coat Gorman's dry skin in frost.

His companion's head snapped towards him in alarm at the mention of the kill, but shifted back to his work under the relentless weight of Jenna's direct attention. "No, I agree. He'd make a great pair."

"Sapling, don't forget his arm-braid." The team leader stared at him a moment more as if she was daring him to follow his concession with another protest, then nudged Hyatt's leg with the toe of her boot. "Hyatt, come with me."

As he struggled to his feet, he realized that was the second time she'd call Gorman a sapling and him by his name. Jenna had already started walking and he scrambled to catch up, a dozen questions rattling in his head like his teeth were still trying to. The sun and his body heat had warmed the water in his clothes to a bearable temperature and he wiped his face with both hands, smearing dirt and blood along his cheeks as he tried to remove some of it. They reached the three dead Cern raiders and Jenna paused, looking all three over as if deciding something.

"I didn't kill her." He'd meant to say it clearly, but when he heard it in his own ears, he realized he'd barely whispered it and tried again. "I didn't kill her, I just stabbed her. You killed her."

"You gave her a wound that would have killed her, and she could no longer fight." Jenna flicked her wrist to bat away his argument and started toward the beheaded raider. "If she had done it to you, she would have said she killed you. I just cut the space between. Hyatt, there are many people who will take credit for what you do without sharing it – don't throw it away when it's given."

She crouched and reached into the bloody opening of the raider's neck and found something to grab onto, then hauled the body up to a sitting position and stripped the raider's battered leather jacket from her shoulders and arms with two savage yanks. The sight made Hyatt's stomach turn over and his saliva tasted like copper, warm and eager to be spit from his mouth. He swallowed hard and hoped he wasn't making a pathetic face as Jenna turned to him and thrust the jacket at him, punching him in the chest with it clenched in her fist while blood dripped from her other hand. His arms came together reflexively and he realized he was clutching the worn leather in his hands as she let go of it.

"What?" he asked blankly, feeling like an idiot.

"You cut her out of it – it's yours." She paused, and something cloudy and conflicted moved across her eyes like morning mist on a lake. "That means the world to five generations of Cern and a sixth that would have someday worn it – treat it like it. If you lose that jacket, I'll kill you."

He'd heard people make threats that were idle or exaggerated, but nothing in her tone or her unsettlingly direct eye contact made him think she was being hyperbolic. "Okay. I will. Yes."

She held his gaze and she squinted a little with one eye, calculating whether or not she'd made a grave mistake. After a moment, her eye widened again and she nodded as if the scales had tipped in Hyatt's favor, and she turned towards the bridge. Uncertain if he was supposed to follow, he tucked the jacket under his arm and hurried to keep up. As they drew closer to the bridge, Hyatt saw the last surviving Structure worker turn to spot them and her head visibly tipped down to fix on the jacket, tracking it with her whole upper body until he and Jenna left her line of sight. He pulled it tighter to his side, listening to the creak of the thin leather, and knew when he got back to Brathnee Garden he would need to find someone to explain it to him.

They passed the bridge and as they moved down the far bank, Jenna paid no mind to the dead Security workers or Structure workers. She moved with purpose, the way she always seemed to, even strides and no variation from whatever destination she knew she was going to reach. Hyatt was the same height as the team lead but still found himself stumbling to keep up. She didn't stop until she reached the base of a tree, another Cern crumpled at the base with seven five-inch steel flechettes embedded in his face. Jenna loomed over the body and for a moment Hyatt thought she was going to stomp the metal shards deeper into the dead man's skull, but instead she looked up into the branches of the tree.

"Can you climb, Hyatt?" she asked without taking her eyes off the lower branches.

He tried to recall the last time he'd climbed a tree, but whenever it was, it had been a much smaller tree and without dead bodies strewn around its trunk. He stared up in the direction Jenna was looking, trying to spot what she could see, but couldn't make out anything other than leaves and branches.

"I can try?" His answer was more question than statement, but he moved closer to the tree.

"Here." Jenna turned her back to the tree and bent her knees like she was sitting in a chair, bracing against the broad trunk. "Step on my leg, then my shoulder. You should be close enough to grab the branch."

Hyatt almost paused but stopped himself, unwilling to question the team leader's strength or endurance. He set the Cern jacket on the ground beside her and gingerly placed his boot on the top of Jenna's thigh, leaned forward, and slowly added more and more of his weight until he could spring off her leg to step onto her shoulder. She didn't move under his pressure and made no sound as he pushed off, standing on one leg and grabbing the tree for balance as he reached for the branch. His fingertips grazed it, but nowhere near close enough to wrap his hand over.

"I can't reach it," he grunted, straining his arm for another inch of height.

Instead of answering, a low growl escaped Jenna as she began to straighten her legs. The shift of her shoulders under Hyatt almost unbalanced him and he pinwheeled with his free arm while the other clung to the trunk, the bark catching and dragging against his jacket's sleeve. Unwilling to miss his chance to live up to the team leader's expectation, he forced himself to stop swinging his arm and reached up until he could slide his hand over the branch.

"I've got it!" he shouted, letting go of the trunk and lunging to close his other arm around it.

His legs scrambled up along the tree, showering Jenna in scraps of bark that broke away under his boots. Just as his arms began to ache, he was able to cross his legs over the branch, and he grunted with effort as he worked his way around the circumference of the limb until he was laying on top of it. A firm breeze shook the leaves around him, and it felt good washing over him.

He paused to catch his breath and shake his arms to chase the burn from his forearms and shoulders, then leaned his head to the side so he could see Jenna. "Now what?"

"Look up," she called up to him. "Can you see it?"

As Hyatt shifted and contorted himself to get a better view, the branch beneath him creaked. An image of himself smashed upon the ground with a dozen bones broken flashed through his mind and he shook his head to clear it. His knuckles were white as he gingerly moved until he could look up. He saw it immediately – the stock of a weapon like a flechette carbine but with a longer barrel and a wide leather sling anchored to the foregrip and the butt. He leaned into the trunk and rose slowly until his fingers found the brass buckle of the sling, and he walked his fingertips higher and higher until he could get purchase on it. Hyatt tugged hard and the weapon dislodged from the little branches pinning it in place, and it plummeted past him before he could grab ahold of it.

"Look out!" he shouted at the same time the weapon landed on the ground with a clatter, ejecting a magazine from its underside on impact.

He expected Jenna to snap at him, but no reply came from the ground. He shifted to sit on the branch and looked down again, gauging how much it would hurt to jump down from his height. The idea of breaking his leg so far from the Garden shot a spike of fear through his chest. He wiggled his toes in his boots and his hands pressed harder against the branch on either side. With a half-breath that he held, he pushed off the branch.

Hyatt hit the ground and tumbled, rolling to a stop as the wind was knocked out of him. When his momentum stopped, he lay on his back and tried to gulp air that his lungs refused to take in. He let out a wheezing exhale and rolled onto his stomach before fighting up to all fours and then struggling to his feet. With a shake of his head, he turned until he saw Jenna, who was lost in her inspection of the weapon.

"What is it?" he asked, favoring his left leg for his first few steps as his hip twinged before straightening and joining Jenna.

She didn't answer immediately, her bloodstained fingers exploring the parts of the weapon as if she was learning through her fingertips. Her thumb slid under a latch and she lifted it, then grabbed the stock and pulled hard. It separated from the weapon's barrel and it came apart in two pieces. Jenna discarded the stock and tipped the barrel towards the sky, looking through the near end like a spyglass. Hyatt saw her shoulders tighten and her knuckles go white, and she lowered it slowly.

"Is that what made that cracking sound?" Hyatt tried again.

"Take a look." She held the barrel out to him, her hand clutching it at the center.

He couldn't explain his aversion to taking it from her, but the thought of taking it in his hands filled him with dread. He looked at her hesitantly, but she just nodded toward the metal tube, thrusting it closer to him. Hyatt locked his jaw and grabbed it gingerly with both hands, feeling the weight of it. Recalling what the team leader had done, he pointed one end towards the sky and brought the other end in line with his eye. His vision tracked the silver grooves that spiraled in mild counterclockwise arcs along the interior from the near end to the barrel's tip, and he felt his heart seize in his chest.

"Holy fuck!" He cried out as he dropped the barrel.

The part of the weapon landed on an exposed root and made a dull clang as it bounced, then rolled to a stop in the pale, damp grass. Jenna picked it up and grabbed the other part, fitting together and jostling them until the barrel slid into place and locked with a click. Hyatt stared at it and when she slung it over her shoulder, his eyes stayed on it.

"Is that..." he began, but the rest of his words turned dry and blew away from his lips like dust.

"a Turning Weapon," she finished for him, her tone flat as if she'd seen thousands of them before.

"Holy fuck," was all he could manage again.

"Get your jacket, Hyatt.," she replied. "Let's go."

As Jenna walked toward the bridge, his eyes stayed on the weapon over her shoulder and he almost called after her that he was already wearing his jacket. He opened his mouth but stopped before a sound escaped. He tore his gaze from the weapon and hurried to the base of the tree to collect his Cern jacket, then jogged to catch up with Jenna. She hadn't broken stride and he came alongside her just before they reached the bridge.

"Line worker, I need a handset!" she called, her gaze sweeping over Gorman seated on the bank and the Structure worker moving purposefully her way. "Sapling, help the workers plant the Haleu bodies. Leave the Cern for their pack to get."

Suddenly without a purpose for the first time since the Cern attack, Hyatt felt helpless and awkward. He cast about for anything to occupy him. The idea of planting the dead workers made his stomach tense, but it looked like everything else had been done while he'd been with Jenna – discarded satchels had been collected nearby, the last of the surviving workers were moving away from the repaired Line on the bridge, and Cern weapons were piled haphazardly with Haleu knives and carbines in the grass.

"The bridge isn't damaged," the Structure worker said as she approached, gesturing over her shoulder at it with her thumb.

"The moss on the supports is untouched and there aren't any cracks in the spanners."

"Good," Jenna replied, nodding in approval and accepting a handset from the Line worker who joined them. "Grab weapons and follow me. You too, Hyatt."

He followed the two workers to the pile of discarded arms and picked up one of the Cern blades. The shaft slipped against his wet gloves and he tried to peel them off, but with the weapon in one hand and the Cern jacket under his other arm, he couldn't get traction on them. With a consternated frown he tried to drag one of his wrists against his hip to tug at the knit fabric, but the damp glove refused to submit to the clumsy effort.

Hyatt looked back and saw that Jenna hadn't waited for any of them. He dropped the weapon and the Cern jacket, stripped his gloves and the woolen-collared coat he'd worn from Brathnee Garden, and tossed them in a pile in the grass. His fingers curled around the collar of the Cern jacket and he shook it hard, then slipped into it. He was surprised how much better it fit than his own and he rolled his shoulders to settle it into place, picked up the Cern weapon, and jogged after the team leader. His haste infected the other two workers and he heard them running behind him, and Jenna glanced back at the sound of three pairs of boots approaching behind her as they caught up.

Her eyes moved down Hyatt's form from his pupils to the buckle of his belt and then back up until her unyielding gaze met his above the first hint of a smile on her lips. She smacked him on his back between his shoulders as he fell into step beside her, the two workers finding their pace a step behind on either side. Hyatt fought the goofy grin that threatened to ruin the crest of her silent approval, lava-like joy washing through his veins.

Together they reached the square box at the Line juncture where the forest began. Jenna dropped to one knee and turned the lever that held the face of the box closed, and it creaked from lack of use as the thin metal panel swung open. Inside, a row of three horizontal ports waited above a series of red toggles in a row below. The team leader's fingers slid down the cable dangling from the handset until they found the coupling, and she pressed it over the center port with a quarter-turn to lock it in place.

"Keep your eyes open," she told them as she flipped the first and seventh toggle into the up-position. "If you see anything that didn't come from the Garden with us, kill it."

The thought of having to repel another group of Cern raiders cooled the happiness that lingered from Jenna's treatment of him, and suddenly the jacket on his back didn't seem to fit so well. He turned his back to her, searching the edge of the Reclaimed.

"This is Jenna, at Vohk Bridge. Connect me to the Gloratt," she said behind him.

Hyatt remembered working the Switches when he learned the trades as a youth, but he'd never been asked to connect anyone to the High Ranger's seat of power. In the long pause while the distant Switch worker rearranged cables and toggles to obey the team leader, he looked from one tree to another for the skulking forms of Cern reinforcements. Every rustle of branches made him turn and try to spot where the sound came from.

It seemed like a year before Jenna spoke again. "High Ranger, we've lost six workers. We're planting the ones we can here... but there's a problem. You should send for an Iron."

THREE

Hyatt didn't remember most of the walk back to Brathnee Garden. After the first hour, the adrenaline of the fight had run its course, and a desperate fatigue crept into his body. By the time the walls of his home came into view, all he could think of was his bed. He didn't look up at the white arch as they crossed from the Reclaimed to the safety of the Garden and he could only mumble appreciative responses to the Security workers who welcomed them home. Jenna said something about them having done good work and not dying, and he felt like his legs were going to give out underneath him by the time she let them go.

As he stumbled through the streets to his dwelling, a random thought bubbled up in his foggy mind that he would have looked drunk if not for the mud and blood that caked his hands and face. The door to his home felt like it weighed fifty pounds as he worked the latch and put his shoulder into it to force it open, and it was all he could do to lean the Cern blade in the corner before collapsing onto his bed on his back. His mattress was overdue for replacement and a dry chuckle escaped his lips as he remembered finding it uncomfortable days before. Hyatt was certain he would be blissfully unconscious in the space of a single blink.

He had no idea how long he'd been asleep when a fist pounding on his door woke him with a start, and he growled in incoherent protest. "No. Go away."

His visitor knocked again, three more thuds that shook the door in its frame. Hyatt growled and swung his legs over the side of his bed, letting his head hang for another moment before sitting upright and then standing with a grunt. He staggered to the door, surprised and aggravated that laying down had made his legs and shoulders hurt more instead of resting them. The daylight as he pushed the door open made him squint and confirmed his suspicion that he hadn't been asleep nearly long enough.

The teenage boy outside took one look at him and staggered backward, Hyatt's first reminder that he was still spattered with the marks of his first Reclaimed trip and still wearing the Cern jacket. "Hyatt?"

"Yeah, I'm Hyatt. What do you want?" He tried not to snap at the tense boy.

"Jenna sent me to get you. She said you need to meet her at the Gloratt." The words tumbled from the boy like a rockslide. "She said you need to come right away."

He'd been ready to claim his Rest Hours and send the boy running, but the mention of the Gloratt raced through him like caffeine and mixed concern and disbelief into his reluctance. Hyatt leaned against the door's frame and rubbed his face, the grains of dirt trapped between his palm and his cheek tearing at him like sandpaper.

"She said that?" he asked, still struggling to shake off the claws of sleep.

"She said 'Get Hyatt from the Vohk Bridge job. Tell him he needs to be at the Gloratt right now.' You're..." he hesitated, his gaze walking up from Hyatt's bare wrist where an arm-braid would have been to the crossed, thick stitching on the forearm of his jacket. "Are you from the Vohk Bridge job?"

He sighed and nodded to the boy, still squinting in the offensive daylight. "I'm on my way. You can go. Thank you."

The runner's relief was palpable as he turned and walked hurriedly away. Hyatt glanced back into his unlit dwelling and wondered if he had time to wash his face and hands, but he abandoned the idea almost immediately. With a heavier sigh, he started towards the highest point in Brathnee.

Hyatt found Jenna waiting for him at the last intersection before the High Ranger's building, leaning against a signpost and cleaning the dirt from beneath her fingernails with a jagged flechette. The Turning Weapon slung over her shoulder, and just the sight of it replaced the fog of sleep still clinging to his consciousness with alert tension. She locked eyes with him and he realized she had seen him before he had seen her, but she returned her attention to carving the dark earth from her fingertips. Her very presence made him want to quicken his pace to avoid keeping her waiting, but the way his muscles ached gave him just enough delay to resist the urge. By the time he reached her, she'd finished her work and tucked the steel sliver into the bag on her hip.

It felt inadequate to say hello, but no other word fit in his mouth and he had no idea why she'd called for him. "Hi again?"

"Come with me." She pushed away from the signpost as he approached, frowning and dusting the dried dirt from the front panels of his jacket before turning and walking towards the Gloratt.

Hyatt stepped up to walk beside her. "Sorry, I didn't have time – I mean, I did, but I went to sleep, I didn't know I..."

She didn't answer him or interrupt, letting his explanation run out of fuel on its own. Hyatt fell silent as other residents of Brathnee passed them on the road, their eyes clinging to the pair while trying and failing to be discreet as they passed. The furtive looks from his fellow Haleu and the open stare from a young girl they passed made Hyatt feel unpleasantly visible and he grit his teeth, glancing to Jenna for guidance on how to react and finding none on her unconcerned features.

"Where are we going?" he asked to break apart his anxiety. "I mean, I know where we're going, but why are we going there- why am I going there with you?"

Jenna slowed and bent down to pick up a piece of debris in the road, then changed direction to deposit it in the collection bin at the street's edge. "The sapling said you were trying to impress a woman so she would pair with you. Meeting the High Ranger is impressive. I'm rewarding you for doing good work on your first time in the Reclaimed."

He didn't know what to make of the jumble of feelings her reply caused – pride at having done well, embarrassment at his motivation being called out so plainly, and relief that she wasn't about to tell the High Ranger he was unwelcome on future jobs. Another, more insidious feeling crept through him, a gnawing concern that her awareness of his interest in Stella would make her take him less seriously as a possible pair.

What the fuck is that? Fractured shards of explanation blew apart in his brain like the charges of the Demolition workers. *What the hell, stop acting like a spring bee!*

He shook his head to physically clear the thoughts and feelings jumbled inside it and studied the other side of the road, lined by a row of elms that divided the walkway from the park beyond. Sunlight got caught in the hanging moss that weighed down the broad branches. In the fields behind the trunks, paired men with their arms linked watched three children chase each other across the short, dark grass.

"You already gave me a jacket," he finally replied, shoving his hands into his pockets so the sleeves bunched around his wrists.

"You earned the jacket. You gave it to yourself." There was no trace of humor in Jenna's voice. "This, I'm giving to you."

It seemed to Hyatt that she was splitting hairs, but he didn't want to seem ungrateful, so he changed the subject. "What is the High Ranger like?"

She reached into her shirt-pocket and produced an herb-twist, and as she bit into it, the scent of mint and ginger flooded the air between them. She ground the part she'd broken from the end of the snack between her teeth, turning over his question as they walked. Hyatt waited as patiently as he could until she'd sapped the flavor from the bite and spat the tacky remains to the side.

"You've seen him speak. He's just like that in private. Quieter, but the same." She took another bite and pushed the remainder back into her pocket, talking around the piece in her mouth as she talked to him. "He's good for Brathnee. I like him."

"Do you know him well?" Hyatt pressed.

She shrugged non-commitally, the cuff of her sleeve rising just enough to bare the Master Security arm-braid knotted around her wrist. "Not really."

Well enough to call him and tell him what he should do, though. He caught himself wondering how a Cern-turned-Haleu became close to the leader of one of the Nine Gardens but decided not to dig into something she had no interest in discussing. "Do you think the Iron will be there?"

Hyatt watched the question register with Jenna like he'd asked her to cut her own arm off. Her shoulders flexed and her skin tightened at the corners of her eyes, and her fingers curled into fists. She spat out the remains of her second bite and it seemed to Hyatt that it was more emphatic than her last. He had no idea why the question upset her and focused on the outline of the Gloratt at the end of the road.

"Yes." Her voice was sharper. "The Iron arrived this morning."

The rational part of him didn't want to risk making her angry, but the confused part of Hyatt teamed up with the part of him that was nervous about the upcoming meeting to overpower his reservations. "Didn't you tell the High Ranger to call for the Iron?"

"Remember on the road to Vohk Bridge, when you weren't allowed to talk?" She replied.

Hyatt frowned but said nothing as he walked beside her through the fringes of shadows from the lampposts that lined the avenue. Her form persisted in his periphery, and he tried to reconcile the savage warrior he'd seen at the bridge with the powerful and purposeful but calm woman beside him, tracing an apex-predator gene through both versions of Jenna he'd encountered in the last day. There was something in the way she moved that tightened his stomach and made his heart rise in his chest, and she gave him a sideways glance as if she could taste the change in his body on the mid-day air.

"You don't want to Pair with me, Hyatt," she said, matter-of-fact. "You think you do because like the idea of me, because I'm something you can't find in the Garden – and because I saved your life."

His frown had escaped him, but her flat remarks restored it. "I don't— I mean, I didn't—"

She waved her hand, brushing away his poorly formed protest. "It's okay. Go home, scatter yourself to the idea – then go get your Garden girl. You're not like me, and you would spend all five years of our Pairing wishing you were. It would mulch you."

Hyatt wanted to argue, but there was such certainty in her voice that the words bore into him like spears of irrefutable fact. He shrugged helplessly and looked out across the Garden, searching for anything to commit his attention to that wasn't the fascinating woman beside him, but he found the standard too high for anything in his view to overcome.

"I'm not going to scatter about you." He shoved his hands in his pockets and gave her a sideways glare, before turning his attention to the Gloratt ahead.

"Okay." Jenna didn't sound any part convinced.

Together they reached the seven stairs that ascended from the street's surface to the Gloratt, broad steps with the Seven Warnings carved into their stone faces beneath their nosings in chiseled letters. Hyatt lingered a moment to let Jenna lead the way, looking up at the two Security workers posted on either side of the top step, and fell in step behind her. Neither moved as Hyatt and Jenna passed between them and continued up to the cylindrical building ahead where two more guards stood beside the large wooden doors.

"Is the High Ranger expecting you?" The shorter guard asked as they moved closer to block the door.

Jenna smiled, a dangerous expression that thinned the air around them and dared the guards to hold their ground. "Yes."

If they had more questions, neither voiced them. The two guards pulled the wooden doors open and Hyatt followed Jenna into the round anteroom beyond. He took in the cream-colored walls, the curved benches on his left and right, and the bowed door on the far wall flanked on either side by blue-white lights in black metal cages. The shape of the room and the placement of the lights drove their shadows behind them and bent them in strange arcs. Jenna rapped on the door and it swung open silently, and she led the way into the main hall.

Like the building and the anteroom, the hall was round with a domed ceiling that made it seem larger than it was. Hyatt wished he could pause longer to take in the tall pillars that paralleled the outer edge of the room and the paintings that covered the walls behind them, but the oval table that stood at the center of the room and the Garden leaders gathered around it demanded his focus. At the far end, the High Ranger stood in front of his chair. On his left, the Garden planner sat with a dozen pages scattered across the table, and on the opposite side the Garden provisioner leaned forward in his chair and rested his head on his open palm. All three wore the mint and ivory colors of Brathnee, sturdy trousers and loose, layered shirts, but the fourth person seated beside the Garden planner stood out against their uniformity.

The woman's blood-red curls looked like living fire against the shoulders of her dark gray jacket, but it was her posture that Hyatt noticed first. While the Garden planner and provisioner sat forward in their clean clothes and spoke in quiet tones before the High Ranger who loomed over them with his arms crossed, the one he guessed was the Iron reclined back in her chair with her knee-high boots crossed at her ankles and her unfocused eyes staring up at the frescoed dome above. Something about her reminded him of Jenna, though he couldn't place what it was.

As his companion stepped forward, the woman rolled her head towards them without lifting it from the back of her chair until her temple rested against it and her eyes fixed on them. Her motion stopped the conversation between the High Ranger's counsel and the leader of the Garden lifted his head to look their way. Jenna walked towards the close, narrow end of the table, her thumb hooked under the sling of the Turning Weapon over her shoulder, and Hyatt took longer steps to stay beside her. The red-haired woman pushed her chair back and rose, turning to face them with her hand resting on the handle of a weapon at her belt that Hyatt hadn't noticed while she was seated.

"Jenna, first of Brathnee, once of Whitefall Pack," the High Ranger said in a quiet, clear voice, gesturing first to one woman and then the other, "Delores, Iron of the Eastern Reach. You know my counselors, Master Planner Argus and Master Provisioner Trayvor."

Without breaking her stride, Jenna unslung the weapon and tossed it onto the large table. It connected stock first and clattered as the barrel crashed down, sliding across the pale wood until it stopped just beyond the Iron's reach. The sudden sound made the Garden planner flinch but he stopped himself from unsettling his chair, and the Garden provisioner leaned away in his seat as if the sound could somehow hurt him. The High Ranger kept his focus on Jenna instead of following the weapon across the table, something calculated but impenetrable in the way he looked at her.

"Whitefall Pack roams north of Relcora Garden," Delores said as she took two steps along the table's edge to stand beside the weapon. "Did you come through Fennan Pass?"

Jenna stopped and rested her palms on the table, ignoring the Iron's question. "High Ranger, two of your workers set aside their arm-braids to help us repair the line at Vohk Bridge – Hyatt killed a Cern raider when we were attacked and recovered this Turning Weapon in the aftermath. He is a great rainfall of your Garden."

The High Ranger walked slowly around the table, passing behind the Master Planner. His boots thudded heavily on the wooden floor as he drew closer, and Hyatt realized he had no idea if he should shake the man's hand or bow or stand straighter. The leader of the Garden stopped in front of him and regarded him evenly for a moment.

"I don't think we've met, Hyatt. How are you braided?" the High Ranger asked.

Hyatt opened his mouth to answer but his voice cracked and he cleared his throat, then tried again. "I'm a Journeyman Artist from here, orange and white, with seven green threads from my mother's roots."

The High Ranger's gaze slipped lower to take in the Cern jacket, as dirty as the moment Jenna had stripped it from its previous owner and handed it to him. His eyes moved back up slowly to meet Hyatt's and he put his hand on Hyatt's shoulder, squeezed it, then patted him twice. Hyatt stood still, and in his periphery, he could see Jenna's eyes sparkle with bemusement as his discomfort.

"The artist who kills Cern warriors and brings us a violation of the Third Warning," the High Ranger replied, neither compliment nor insult. "Four Security workers dead and here you are, a Cern jacket and a... paintbrush?"

It took Hyatt a second to realize he'd been asked a question. "I... I carve, High Ranger, stone and wood. I'm a sculptor."

The leader of Brathnee Garden smiled and his hand dropped from Hyatt's shoulder. "Is that what you'll do now, work in the statuary, or make game pieces for children? Is that jacket a story to tell little Brathnee sprouts, or did some of the Reclaimed get into your blood?"

He had no idea how to answer the most powerful man in Brathnee, in front of his counsel and the Iron and the most formidable woman he knew. He glanced at Jenna, who shook her head to tell him he was on his own. Hyatt's saliva tasted like copper and his heart rose up to lodge in his throat.

"I don't know yet, High Ranger," he replied.

"That is a good answer." The High Ranger pat his shoulder again, then turned to Jenna. "Was it an isolated raid, or do the

Cern plan to claim the edge of Brathnee? Master Argus wants to expand the garden towards Vohk Bridge, but we don't need to go as far as the river. I won't start a war with Moss Wall Pack over space we don't need."

Jenna frowned as she considered the question, then shrugged. "They claimed it in bone, but defended it poorly. They are seeing what they can get away with."

"If they take the bridge, we lose the mines to the north," Master Trayvor called from his seat, but stopped as the High Ranger waved away the remark without turning towards him.

"What do you recommend?" he asked.

As Hyatt watched them talk, he wondered if it was Jenna's Cern history or the Master Security braid on her wrist that made the High Ranger place so much stock in her advice, or if they had another history together that made him believe in her. He tried to recall a time when anyone had put so much faith in him but none came to mind. His thoughts drifted to Stella, and he was certain she would pair with a man with that kind of respect from important leaders of the Garden.

"It depends on why they're so far east," Jenna answered raising and lowering her open hands like she was weighing options. "Send a Master Speaker to talk with them, see what the Bridge means to them, and if you can reach an understanding. We left them their bodies unplanted – there should be no grudge from the loss."

The High Ranger turned and walked back along the table's edge. As he passed two of the chairs, he grabbed the tops of their high backs and dragged them backward, leaving them open for Hyatt and Jenna. The idea of sitting down at the table where the choices about Brathnee's future were made terrified Hyatt and he felt his hands begin to sweat. He wiped them against his trousers and walked unsteadily behind Jenna to the chair further from the head of the table, taking a seat before it occurred to him to wonder if he should have waited for the High Ranger to sit first. He was relieved when Jenna collapsed into the chair beside him like she owned it.

Across the table, Delores picked up the strange weapon on the table and turned it over in her hands. Hyatt watched the deft way her fingers moved over the stock and barrel and he couldn't help but notice the similarities to how Jenna had held it when she first picked it up. She released the magazine from beneath it and detached the barrel with two distinct clicks, then set the stock back down and hefted the barrel in her hands. Her thumb moved over the strange, miniature markings on one side of the tube and her eyes closed, as if she could see with her fingertips.

"The turns are on the inside," Jenna said, her voice entirely devoid of warmth.

The Iron's eyes didn't open and her thumb slid back and forth over the ridges of the little markings again. Every interaction in the room added another dozen questions to Hyatt's thoughts and he hated being unable to ask them. He folded his hands in his lap and absently mimicked the Iron's motions, one thumb sliding back and forth between the joints of the other.

Instead of looking through the metal tube, Delores set it down on the table so gently it made no sound. Her hands rested over it, and Hyatt wasn't sure if it was to keep control of it or to stop it from rolling, but he felt better knowing the Turning Weapon was in the hands of someone who could be responsible for it. The High Ranger leaned back in his chair and regarded her patiently, waiting for the Iron to speak. When she didn't, he returned his focus to Jenna.

"Tell me about the attack, and the weapon."

In her direct, unambiguous way, Jenna recounted the attack. As she described the bones hung from the trees and driven into the ground, Hyatt watched the Iron tap the pads of her fingers against the barrel in varying patterns like she was playing a woodwind instrument. Children's stories of Irons with mystical Gifts crept into his mind and even though he pushed them down, a part of him expected Delores' fingertips to begin glowing or the air around her to begin crackling with power. Instead, all he saw was the shift behind her closed eyelids as her pupils darted back and forth like she was asleep, causing her lashes to shiver almost imperceptibly.

Beside him, Jenna described the beginning of the ambush on the Line Team, and she didn't pause when the Iron opened her eyes. As the team leader told the High Ranger about the Cern that came from both sides and the Turning Weapon fired from the trees, Delores grabbed the collar of her jacket and peeled it back off her shoulders. She shifted in her seat to shed the leather shell and left it crumpled between herself and the back of her chair. Hyatt caught himself staring at the sleeveless shirt she wore beneath it and looked up to see her staring back at him across the table with an eyebrow raised, and a flash of panic shot through him. He turned quickly towards the High Ranger who was giving Jenna his undivided attention, but when he glanced from the corner of his eye at Delores, she was still regarding him with an expression he couldn't place between curiosity and amusement.

"When it was done, we planted our dead and used the Line to reach you," Jenna finished.

The High Ranger waited to be sure she had no more to tell, then asked, "Were there any strange signs? Any... omens?"

Hyatt had always known the risks of any of the Seven Warnings being broken but as he looked at the dissembled weapon and tried to imagine how it could bring about the end of humanity, it seemed both more and less real than his lessons as a youth had taught him. As terrifying as it had been, it was impossible to fathom the scattered pieces of the Turning Weapon heralding the extinction of mankind. His imagination ran wild, summoning images of dark clouds rolling across the sky and raining fire that lit the Reclaimed in an unstoppable blaze that burned the Nine Gardens to ash.

As difficult as it was to fathom, the hint of amusement in Jenna's voice surprised Hyatt. "No, High Ranger. I don't think the Ninth History began today."

The leader's eyes hardened a bit but the change in his expression didn't cause Jenna to back down, so he turned to his counselors. "Jenna still believes like the Cern, that we Garden-dwellers misunderstand the Warnings. She doesn't believe in the end-of-times, which gives her nothing to fear, which is why she fights so bravely."

"Oh, I believe in the Ninth History," she disagreed with her trademark candor. "I just don't think a spiraled bullet begins it."

The High Ranger waved his hand to bat away the semantic argument, and Hyatt had the impression he and Jenna had worn that path together dozens of times before. It only compounded his curiosity about their history. He looked from one to the other, but nothing in their expressions gave away any secrets. The topic gave neither of the High Ranger's counselors a safe way ahead and so they nodded at his statement and said nothing, Angus busying himself with the papers in front of him.

"I'll go to Moss Wall Pack and find out where it came from," Delores broke the uneasy quiet. "I can escort your Master Speaker, if you plan to send one."

Before the leader could answer, the door at the back of the hall opened and four workers joined them with covered trays and open platters. They moved wordlessly, long knit robes whispering around their legs and masking their footfalls as they flanked the tables. Scents of cooked meat and roasted vegetables with spices filled the chamber and the shape of the room trapped it around them, and Hyatt's stomach growled at the sudden reminder he hadn't eaten since before dawn. The workers placed the trays at even intervals on the table and as they slipped from the room, identically dressed workers took their places to deliver plates and tableware to everyone seated there.

"Please, eat," the High Ranger insisted, gesturing broadly at the provided food.

As they passed the trays and loading savory slices of red meat and portions of chopped and roasted vegetables, the workers slipped from the room and closed the door. The first bite of charred shallots made Hyatt's mouth water as the sweet juices hit his dry tongue and he fought the urge to moan in enjoyment. Beside him, Jenna's fork and knife tore at a slab of meat and the gristle crunched as she ground it between her molars.

As they ate, a question nagged at Hyatt. Once it appeared in his mind, he couldn't shake it, and looked around the table to see if anyone else would pick up the conversation where it left off. Everyone seemed focused on eating and the question began to grow and expand inside him until it was too heavy to keep in. With another bite of the roasted vegetables, he leaned closer to Jenna.

"How will the Master Speaker get back to the Garden?" he asked quietly, chewing on the skin of a squash that had refused to be swallowed with the meat of it. "Will the Iron escort them back, too?"

"I don't depend on Irons." Her reply was jagged, saying a dozen caustic things in the spaces between her words. "We'll send workers, to see them there and back."

He wondered if her hostility was a Cern thing, but the High Ranger's table didn't feel like the place to ask, so he added it to the list of things he'd find someone to explain to him later. As he picked up his table knife to sever a strip of the steaming meat on his plate, the surreal nature of his day crashed over him again – he seemed a lifetime away from the day before when his biggest concern was whether to carve a mantle statuette from hardwood or soft pine.

"Thank you, Iron Delores," the High Ranger replied as if there had been no break between the red-haired woman's question and his answer, "I know just the Speaker to send with you, and a few workers too. Is tomorrow morning too late?"

The Iron shook her head and swallowed, pausing to breathe in the spices that lingered on her tongue, and exhaled with contentment. "Tomorrow will be fine."

The matter resolved, the High Ranger turned his attention back to his counselors. As plates began to clear and not be refilled from the platters, workers appeared through the back door of the chamber to collect them. The leader of the Garden said nothing to formally end the conversation but Hyatt was certain his reason for being in the Gloratt was over and when Jenna pushed her chair back to rise, he followed suit. Delores stood as well, drawing an openly aggressive look from Jenna, and he thought for a moment the two women would brawl in the High Ranger's hall. Instead, Delores turned and walked towards the antechamber.

"Cern slayer," the High Ranger called from behind them as they reached the door, and Hyatt looked back to find him still seated but with his attention on them. "You are a great rainfall for our Garden. I expect I will hear your name again."

Hyatt tried to make words, but they all seemed to have strange shapes and odd edges in his mouth, so he inclined his head in what he hoped was a less awkward appreciation of the compliment than it felt. Jenna pushed the door open and he hurried from the chamber behind her, disappointed and relieved to be out of the room all at once. His companion said nothing as they descended the stone steps to the road below and he looked around to spot the Iron, but she'd already vanished from view.

"Where did she go?" he asked Jenna, sweeping the road and parks again in case he'd overlooked her. "We were right behind her!"

Jenna's lips curled like she was trying to scrape a bitter flavor from her tongue against the roof of her mouth. "Better for both of us she's gone."

FOUR

Hyatt thought sleep would bring an end to the insanity of his day, but instead he found himself alone on Vohk Bridge. Instead of the low rush of the river as it coursed through the Reclaimed, the surface was completely placid and reflected an obsidian sky broken only by moonlight and pinpoint stars. The weight in his hand drew his attention and he looked down at the bloody knife he was holding, and the Cern raider's lifeless body sprawled across the bridge's broad planks beneath his feet.

Her hand locked around his leg like a vice, fingers digging into his calf just below his knee with searing pain. Hyatt's leg buckled as she yanked down hard and suddenly he was on top of her, staring into her pale green irises from an inch away while blood oozed from the wound in her neck.

"Give it back," she hissed, the moisture of her breath sticking to his lips and her hands closing around his throat.

He choked and spasmed, planting one hand on the bridge and the other on her face as he tried to push up and away, but he couldn't break her impossibly strong grip around his neck. Panic flashed through him as he realized he couldn't breathe and he lifted his hand from her face, closed it into a fist, and slammed it back down. It felt like punching a rock and her nose made a wet crunch, but she didn't let go.

"It's mine!" she snarled as her knees rose up on either side of him, the extra effort causing the fatal stab wound in her neck to spurt fresh red blood. "Give it to me!"

He pulled back and hit her again, as hard as he could. When he lifted his hand again her face was disfigured, her cheekbone collapsed and her slender nose displaced to the right. More blood covered the Cern woman's mouth and throat, and the greens of her eyes started to bleed outward across the whites of her eyes. His vision swam and he gasped for air that couldn't make it past her hands to his lungs, and his body spasmed as the world went dark.

Hyatt bolted upright in his bed and his hands flew to his throat to break a grip that no longer held him, and he gulped air into his burning chest. Sweat on his forehead built enough mass to break free and trailed down his temple, and his hands shook. He shook his head and looked at the clock on the far wall.

Nine o'clock. I don't fucking think so. He stumbled up from his bed to the back room and pulled the chain that started water streaming from the twin showerheads, spattering him with lukewarm droplets that warmed and intensified to a rushing stream.

The stone wall felt cold and safe against his shoulders and he relaxed against it, enjoying the contrast before the steam and his body heat brought it into equilibrium. As the shower coursed over his skin, he felt the vivid images of his nightmare blur and break apart until all he could recall clearly were the Cern's eyes staring directly into his. The memory made him shiver and he tipped his head back to let the water crash over his face, as if it could rinse the image from his mind like scraps of food from a plate.

One look at his bed told him he wasn't ready to go back to sleep and risk another fight to the death with the Cern raider, so he dressed quickly. As he buckled his belt, he turned and saw his two coats hanging on pegs by the door, the faded canvas of his old jacket absorbing the dim light from his kitchen while the

Cern jacket reflected it. He reached out for his canvas jacket, but his fingers lingered on the woolen collar as his eyes were drawn to the other one.

"Fuck you," he muttered out loud as he grabbed the Cern jacket.

The main roads that ran between his home and Hoenbeck's Assembly were lit with streetlights that shown down in soft apricot light. He wondered as he passed through their pools of illumination if he should have called Gorman, but he decided not to stop at the Line junction box and continued on. A man and woman walking together smiled as they crossed paths and he waved to an old man sitting in a wooden chair in front of his house, but the street was mostly empty.

Compared to the nearly abandoned streets of Brathnee Garden, the common room of Hoenbeck's Assembly was full of life. Workers gathered around tables or stood in clusters in the open space, while still others refilled their cups from the four rows of spigots protruding from the back wall. He searched the room and his suspicions were confirmed when he saw Gorman lingering by the taps talking animatedly with a man and a woman with Apprentice Clerical braids around their wrists. Hyatt picked up a mug from the table by the door and headed towards him. Hyatt filled his cup from the closest tap and worked his way into the cluster between Gorman and the man he was terrifying with his story.

"... must have been thirty of them," he heard Gorman saying. "They came from everywhere, even from the river, rising up out of it and crawling up the bank with knives in their teeth. Our Security workers didn't stand a chance – they cut them down like weeds."

"That's awful," the woman said, her face two shades paler.

Gorman noticed Hyatt beside him and had the character to look embarrassed as he cleared his throat. "Lauren, Rojas, this is Hyatt. He was at the Vohk Bridge massacre with me."

"The Vohk Bridge *massacre?*" he repeated, trying to stop his skepticism from leaking into his voice before turning to the other two workers who had become fascinated with his jacket. "Great to meet you, Lauren, Rojas. Could I have a minute with my friend?"

Lauren looked a bit disappointed and Rojas seemed like he'd been waiting for an opportunity to escape Gorman's story, but they both smiled and drifted away into the crowd. Hyatt took a sip of the thick amber mead in his cup and waited until the other two were out of earshot before turning to his friend. Gorman looked down at the surface of his drink.

"What are you telling people?" Hyatt demanded, his voice low but insistent.

"What? The attack was a big deal – everybody's already talking about it." Gorman scoffed.

"Yeah, but they weren't there." He looked around and everywhere saw workers leaned together and talking in low tones, he imagined them repeating Gorman's version of events. "You were. You know what happened."

Gorman shrugged it off as if the truth were irrelevant. "I'm starting a conversation, okay? We all need to be talking about Cern attacks. Moss Wall Pack ambushed helpless Brathnee workers – you and me – and tried to kill us. Besides, this is the coolest thing that's ever going to happen to us. The real question is, why aren't *you* telling the story to *her?*"

He followed the direction of Gorman's nod and saw Stella immediately, honey-golden hair framing her heart-shaped face. She was leaned forward across one of the communal tables but her head was tipped back, laughing at something one of the five workers near her had said. The unexpected sight of her made his heart clench, but he realized as his eyes clung to her that his chest didn't tighten as much as it usually did and his brain only waded in mist instead of filling up with fog.

Hyatt stepped beside Gorman so he could keep his eyes on the beautiful woman. "Or, we walked past obvious Cern markings into a place they claimed, and they fought to drive us out of it."

"Are you seriously defending them?" Gorman snapped at him, glad to be on the offensive. "There are Haleu planted on that riverbank, Hyatt."

"I know that." He watched Stella turn to the worker beside her and rest her hand on his arm in a casually flirtatious touch Hyatt would have killed for, and wondered why the pang he felt was so faint. "I'm just saying, you could tell it how it happened."

"Nice jacket." There was no mistaking Gorman's retort for a compliment as he sipped his drink and walked towards another table to find someone else willing to listen to his story.

Hyatt took a step to follow Gorman and mitigate his version of the attack as best he could, but as he looked past him to the door, he saw Iron Delores framed against the night sky. Her silhouette bled into illuminated definition as she stepped into Hoenbeck's Assembly, shadows receding from her features and draining into the creases in her jacket slung by two fingers over her shoulder. Around the room, boisterous voices and bursts of laughter faded to murmurs and whispers like someone had put a lid on a boiling pot. Seemingly oblivious to the change, the Iron picked up a cup and headed across the room towards the wall of taps. Their eyes met and he knew it was too late to look away, and she changed her path through the crowd, other workers parting before her confident stride with mumbled apologies.

As Delores crossed the room, Hyatt searched his periphery for Jenna, imagining the possible catastrophe of the team leader with a head full of drink and strong opinions winding up face to face with the Iron. He didn't spot the woman's high braid but was still unable to let go of the breath he hadn't realized he'd been holding as Delores stopped in front of him.

"The fabled Cern-slayer of Brathnee," she said in a parody of naivete, her eyes sparkling with amusement. "The story goes you held your own against three raiders, all bigger than you. Cut them down, one after another, 'til you wore enough blood to fill a grown man's body."

He felt the blood rush to his face until it felt as thick as leather and his eyes throbbed. "I stabbed one raider – I'm not even sure I killed her. And I haven't told any stories."

"No?" She cocked her head and raised an eyebrow.

It felt like nobody in the room was looking directly at him, and everyone in all of Brathnee was staring him down in their periphery. "I fought, I walked, I went to the Gloratt, and I slept... and I just got here. I haven't talked to anybody."

Hyatt's insistent tone was too much for Delores' affected expression and a smirk broke through, the glint in her eyes growing to a fully amused glow. "You're not the type, anyway. What should we drink?"

Finally able to breathe, he fought the urge to shiver as the tension leaked from his shoulders and stomach. "Bottom row on the left. Cardamom mead is good. Great, I mean. It's really, really good."

She nodded and threw her arm around his shoulders, guiding him towards the taps. Hyatt looked around helplessly, first at Gorman who was standing with his mouth open across the room, and then something he'd never seen before – Stella's eyes tracking him as they moved, her fingers absently tucking a stray lock behind her ear as she saw him notice her looking. His body felt as if it was moving without his brain's permission, drifting across the room like the seeds of a dandelion on a summer breeze.

She let go of him to pour a drink from the tap, watching the dark amber fluid fill her cup. "Have you decided on an answer to the High Ranger's question?"

Hyatt's mind raced, but he couldn't recall being asked one. "Huh?"

"Are you going back to making statues and toys?" she asked.

The Iron was standing close enough to him that turning to face him put them closer than he expected, as close as paired Haleu, and the memory of his dream and the dead Cern raider's eyes so close to his came flashing back to him. He took an involuntary step back before he could stop himself, and Delores lifted her glass in the space between them to take a sip.

"Oh- that. I don't know. Yes?" he replied.

Delores' chin rose in a short, jerking motion as she sent her mouthful of mead to the back of her throat and swallowed it in a single gulp. "Is that a question?"

"Yes," he replied more forcefully, but then faltered. "I mean, no – no it's not a question. Yes, I'm going back to sculpting. I am."

Delores nodded, looking around the room. Hyatt followed her gaze and realized that for all the people he hadn't thought were watching them, a lot of them looked further away as she turned towards them. He saw Stella glance his way again, but when she saw him, she turned back to the woman sitting across the table from her.

"Okay," she said before draining her cup and setting it on the bar beside them. "Good luck."

The way she patted his shoulder felt more like a punch than a kind gesture, and he watched her cross the room towards the door. She'd barely reached the exit when Gorman appeared beside him like a ghost. Hyatt ignored him, watching the Iron disappear into the night, until his friend stepped directly into his line of sight.

"And... what the fuck was that?" he asked, his eyes as big as radishes.

"It was nothing," Hyatt replied, walking towards the taps with his friend clinging to him like a shadow.

"Nothing?" he protested. "How do you know the Iron of the Eastern Reach?"

Until that moment, he'd forgotten that Gorman didn't know about his trip to the Gloratt or meeting the High Ranger. The moments between their return to Brathnee Garden and his arrival at Hoenbeck's tumbled around his brain like rocks in a polisher and rather than try to string them together, he decided to skip all of it.

"I don't. She asked me what to drink, and I told her." Hyatt poured another round of the cardamom mead into his cup and headed towards the long communal tables.

Gorman grabbed his shoulder from behind and spun him around, hanging onto his jacket so Hyatt couldn't keep outrunning his questions. "She definitely knew you. Try again."

He grabbed his friend's hand and physically removed it from his jacket. "Let it go."

Gorman opened his mouth to press the issue but closed it without a word. Something changed in his face, a hardness at being insulted, and threw his hands up in mock surrender. Hyatt watched as he turned and walked away, then sighed as he realized he'd have to mend bridges with his friend later. He took a gulp of his drink to wash that problem down the road.

"Hi there," Stella's voice said from over his shoulder, taking him by surprise.

He turned and found himself closer to her than he'd ever been before. She was taller than he thought, her blue eyes looking down into his beneath the jagged bangs that drifted across her eyebrows. Hyatt felt the familiar swell of desire, but it felt as watered down as when he'd spotted her across the room and realizing it made everything better and worse at once.

"Hi," he replied.

She smiled as if he'd said something much smarter, absently tracing her finger under her exposed bra strap to adjust it against her shoulder. "It's... Hiram, right?"

He tried not to let her getting his name wrong look like the sledgehammer to his confidence that it was, covering his faltering expression with his glass and giving himself time to swallow before replying. "It's Hyatt. No big deal."

"Oh – I'm so sorry!" she looked genuinely surprised. "I thought it was Hiram."

You know it's not. Years of trying to dream up ways to make Stella notice him evaporated. He couldn't put his finger on why, but the idea that he'd risked a trip beyond the Garden and almost died to get her attention felt like the most foolish thing he could have done.

The pause stagnated and she spoke to restart the conversation, tucking her hair behind her ear again. "I was just thinking, we don't know each other really well, and maybe it would be fun to change that... really get to know each other, you know?"

She touched his arm to emphasize her point, but it was impossible for him to ignore it was the same gesture she'd used earlier with the worker standing beside him. The realization that it had nothing to do with him, that he meant nothing to her, had taken hold and Hyatt couldn't shake it. Even as she smiled at him in hopeful certainty, he realized she would never see him the way he wanted her to. The understanding felt like sandbags rested on his shoulders and tied to his legs.

"Yeah, maybe," he lied.

Her smile brightened and a flush touched her angular cheekbones, and she bounced on her toes a bit in excitement. "Yeah? Okay – okay, great! Let's meet tomorrow then, maybe at the park by the exchanges?"

"Maybe. I'll come find you," Hyatt answered.

"Okay, perfect! I'm excited! Don't forget, okay?" Her smile faded a little as she met his gaze, adding gravity to her request.

He smiled back and hoped she didn't realize that it was because a day before it would have been absurd that anything could have kept him from keeping his date with Stella. "I won't forget."

She turned on the balls of her feet and moved back towards her table, the hem of her skirt swaying just above her knees. Hyatt watched her go, admiring how pretty she was, and struggling to reconcile the changes in his thoughts. The suddenness of it bothered him and he wondered how he could go from so certain about Stella as his only choice for a pairing to uninterested in going on a date with her. He lifted his cup towards his lips, then paused and looked down at it as if the mead was to blame and set the partially filled drink down on the bar beside the Iron's abandoned cup.

What the fuck is wrong with me? He stared after Stella's long legs and beautiful hair until she sat down with her friends, then looked across the room to Gorman who was regaling two men with his version of the fight at Vohk Bridge.

He made his way through Hoenbeck's Assembly, lost in his thoughts and barely noticing the way people shifted to let him pass or trailed him with their gazes. When he reached the door he stopped, turning to look back across the room. The feeling that everyone wanted to talk about him and nobody wanted to talk to him dropped on his heart like a bale of hay, capping the emotionally draining day with an overwhelming loneliness, and he pulled the Cern jacket closer around himself.

Why don't I belong here?

FIVE

Hyatt hung his jacket on the peg beside his door and traced his fingers down the sleeve, letting his fingertips bump over each of the outsized threads that crisscrossed between the cuff and the elbow. He twisted the fabric in his hands, looking over the patches and rivets and lacing in the half-light of his home. Jenna's words came back to him and he wondered what she'd meant when she'd talked about Cern generations, how she'd known there were five represented in the jacket's markings, or that a young Cern would have inherited it. The symbols made no sense to him and Hyatt wondered how many he didn't even know to wonder about.

He let go of the jacket and took a woozy step towards his bedroom, his drinks at Hoenbeck's finally taking hold of him. His stagger caught him at the doorway between his living room and his bed, and he paused to lean against it while the floor shifted back and forth like a raft on the water. He blinked twice and fumbled with the buttons of his shirt, fighting the first one to get it to open, when a knock at his door startled him and almost caused him to fall over.

His visitor knocked again and he caught himself against the opposite side of the doorway. "Okay, hang on. I'm coming. Hang on."

Hyatt shuffled back toward his front door, resting a hand against the wall and taking a deep breath to steady himself. His exhale smelled like fermented honey and stung his vision, and he blinked again before pushing the door open.

"Oh wow," Iron Delores drawled, looking him up and down before holding up a stoneware bottle for him to see. "I guess you don't need this."

"I, um..." Hyatt shook his head, and the motion set his vision swimming again. "Why are you here?"

Even through his haze, he realized he was being blunt, but he was too deep in his cup to muster more than a frown by way of apology. He stepped out of the doorway and waved his hand, hoping she took his meaning. Delores stepped inside and pushed the door closed behind her. He cast around for what to do next and his watercolor vision settled on the table in his kitchen, so he led the way there and pulled a chair out for his visitor. Delores settled into it, set her bottle on the table, and began to shed her jacket as Hyatt found his own seat on the near side.

"Nuh-uh," he slurred, wishing in a moment of clarity that he was on his way out of a drunken stupor instead of descending into one. "Clothes on, lady."

Delores threw her head back and laughed, a full-throated and surprised sound that filled the home, but nodded amicably as she pulled her jacket back on over her shoulders to comply. "Okay. Clothes on."

An alcohol-soaked thought warned him that he'd misinterpreted something, but it wasn't able to struggle through his mind to become a permanent part of his consciousness, so he nodded in satisfaction instead. Together they sat in silence in his kitchen. The Iron regarding him evenly while his eyes floated between her and the table and the door she'd come in from. Time seemed spongy to Hyatt and he blew out a breath through his closed lips in hopes of expelling some of the mead that packed his head with cotton.

"May I help?" she asked, laying her open hand on the table, palm up.

Hyatt's brow furrowed in confusion, but he reached forward and put his hand in hers. He felt her fingers curl up around the edge of his palm and index finger, and it seemed like he could feel every individual ridge of her fingerprints. He focused on how cool she seemed to the touch and the feel of the muscle beneath her skin, and his vision dialed in on the white crescents of her fingernails. Through her thumb resting on the back of his knuckles, he could feel her even pulse.

He started as he realized he could see clearly, and jerked his hand back like hers had grown fangs and bit him. "What the fuck!"

The Iron shook her head and shushed him, a soothing sound that implied he'd done nothing wrong but demanded he stopped all the same. "Give me your hand."

Alarm bells fought for dominance with the alcoholic fog in his head, but he slowly reached back across the table. Delores caught his fingers against her palm as her own curled back into place and her thumb found the same spot between his third and fourth knuckle. A primal panic raced through him and insisted he yank his hand away again, but he resisted it and stared at their joined grips as if she might suddenly squeeze hers closed and crush his hand to powder.

"You're okay," she assured him, a soothing lilt to her words. "I need to tell you something, and I need you to be able to hear it when I say it, okay?"

The cotton packed between his temples continued to recede, amplifying the surreal moment, but he nodded. "I can hear you. What are you doing to me?"

She smirked at his implication and shook her head. "I'm not *doing* anything. I'm just helping you focus."

"But you're..." with his emerging clarity, a wave of mortifying realization slammed into him. "Fuck... did I tell you to put your clothes on?"

She laughed again. "That's not important right now. I came here to tell you something. We need to talk."

Suddenly, Hyatt wished he was as drunk as he'd been a moment before. Something in her words anesthetized his embarrassment and confusion, replacing them with undiluted foreboding. He tried to pull his hand back but the Iron tightened her grip and refused to release it. His inability to pull free of her lined his panic with a steel core and he stared across the table at her, his pupils shrinking even in the dim light of his home.

"When I leave for Moss Wall Pack tomorrow, you're coming with me," The Iron said, holding his eye contact as firmly as she held his hand, "and you're probably never coming back to Brathnee Garden again."

"No, I am not," he laughed nervously, but the sound faltered as Delores neither released his hand nor looked away. "Why? I don't want to do that!"

"You don't?" she asked, and he couldn't tell if she was teasing him or not.

"No, I don't." He tried to add emphasis to his denial, but as the sound of his voice filtered through his impaired condition, he heard himself sounding more pathetic than resolute. "Why can't I come back? I hate that part the most!"

"We are all subject to Sklodowska's will, Hyatt," she replied, her voice overly soothing as she squeezed his hand in reassurance. "You have the rare benefit of having it laid out for you."

He scowled and tugged his hand harder, and he wasn't sure if he was forceful enough or if she let his fingers go, but his momentum slammed his shoulders against the backrest harder than he had expected. As if she was an anchor and he was a drifting ship, the room seemed to rock around him as the floor slanted and threatened to dump him out of his chair. His alarm combined with the renewed vertigo and he felt his throat swell and his saliva turn sickly warm, and he was almost certain he was going to vomit. Hyatt clamped his hands over his mouth and turned sideways in his chair, doubling over to hang his head over his knees.

The sound of Delores' chair sliding across the floor filled the kitchen, and her footfalls on the hardwood were soft. Hyatt felt her hand on the nape of his neck and focused on the feeling, his eyes closed and his breathing shallow. When his throat stopped clenching and spasming, he lowered his hands to his knees and pushed with more effort than it should have taken to straighten himself in his chair.

"Is this because of the bridge?" he asked, ashamed of the way his voice cracked and the wetness he felt in his eyes as he looked up at the Iron standing over him. "That's not me – I wasn't brave! I was terrified! I don't even remember... it was all so fast, and I was so scared – I'm not a fighter. I'm still afraid! I see her when I close my eyes, and I..."

Hyatt's words choked him and realized he was rambling, and nothing in the Iron's face told him that anything he said changed anything. Somehow that made it worse – if she'd been amused, or irritated, or concerned, it would have validated the nauseating churn of feelings inside him, but she just stared at him with an attention devoid of judgment that made him feel small and foolish and alone.

"Please don't make me go with you," he started again, his voice barely a whisper. "Tell me I don't have to go."

Delores took her hand off the back of his neck and grabbed the back of her chair, dragging it closer. She sat down, close enough that her knees settled between his like the teeth of a zipper and their faces were two handspans apart. Hyatt licked his lips and stared at the floor between his feet, mortified at the feeling of a hot tear burning a path down his cheek.

"I didn't choose this for you. If I could set aside your fate, or do this for you, I would." A note had crept into the Iron's voice, the barest wisp of something melancholy and empathetic around the edges of her words. "I won't make you come with me, but you'll come anyway. Now that She has decided you have a role to play in this History, you're caught in a current... you can swim with it or you can be dragged beneath, but it will carry you downstream all the same. Choose to swim, Hyatt."

He shook his head, trying to reject what she said, but the motion made his skull throb and set the world atilt again. He didn't want to cry, but thinking about the possibility was enough to send another tear streaking down his face. Bursts of panic shot through him and he crushed his eyes closed to lock them out, his teeth grinding and his jaw locked tight.

"Please..." he said again, unable to formulate what he was asking for beyond a relent to the way he was feeling.

Delores sat quietly with him, offering no reply. Hyatt couldn't look at her, but in the mostly dark room as time slipped by, something changed for him – her presence was reformed by the silence to be a comfort instead of the source of his distress. He found himself grateful to have someone there as his life changed without his permission, even if it had been the Iron who had delivered the news. His breathing slowly steadied and his pulse started to balance, and he swallowed hard to clear the taste from his mouth.

"I think... I think I want to sleep." He lifted his head to look at her. "Can I please go to sleep?"

She held his gaze for a moment, then nodded. "Yeah, you can sleep. Go lay down."

Hyatt nodded like they had reached the end of a long negotiation and finally come to terms that he could accept. He stood and Delores rose with him, adjusting her jacket and tucking her chair neatly against the table. As Hyatt crossed the room to the front door, he felt more exhausted than he had been after the fight at Vohk Bridge, more exhausted than he ever remembered being in his life. The hinges of his front door squeaked softly as he opened it, and Delores stopped just outside to look up at the blanket of stars that greeted her.

He'd almost closed the door when the sound of her voice made him pause. "Choose to swim, Hyatt."

He nodded even though she couldn't see him and pushed the door closed, separating himself from the Iron with a distinct click. Alone in his home, he let out a ragged, shuddering breath and leaned against the door as his legs threatened to give out under him. The distance from his front door to his bed seemed a thousand miles long and he trudged with steps half their normal length, peeling off his shirt and leaving it on the floor where it landed. His fingers opened his belt and his trousers but he lacked the ambition to remove them, and settled for collapsing face down on his bed and plunging into welcome unconsciousness.

When Hyatt woke, everything was quiet in his home. His eyes opened and he stared at his bedroom wall, his muscles sore from processing the evening's drinks and his body conformed to his mattress like only motionless sleep could cause. He knew that moving would shift the oily feeling in his stomach and bring the dull throb radiating from the base of his skull to life and so he lay still. He knew as long as he didn't get out of bed, he would be okay.

Focusing on his headache brought to mind the memory of Delores' hand on the back of his neck and he started, pushing himself up from his bed and immediately regretting it. His stomach turned and the pounding in his brain doubled, but he fought through it to stumble into his kitchen. His chair was still at the angle he'd left it and the one Delores had occupied was tucked in neatly, giving substance to the growing dread that he hadn't dreamt up the Iron's visit.

"No… no no no no…" he moaned, leaning back against the wall, and wincing as the back of his head connected with it to a shower of painful sparks in his brain.

Hyatt rubbed his head, willing himself to believe the night before had been a mortifying, irrational dream brought on by his trip outside the Garden. With only the starlight outside his window to navigate by, he felt his way along the counter to a pitcher and a metal cup, and the water burbling from one into the other sounded like rolling thunder. He winced as the cold water woke his taste buds and he held it in his mouth until it warmed, then swallowed and felt it jolt his sedentary blood into motion.

Did I agree to go with an Iron to a fucking Cern camp? Fragments of a memory, his unlit home and the Iron of the Eastern Reach seated at his table, rained on his consciousness as he carried his metal cup towards the shelf of knick-knacks in his living space.

He set the cup down and reached for one of the six carvings on the shelf, a miniature Skarren the side of his fist from his Heirs of the Reclaimed set, and the condensation from his fingertips darkened the stone where he touched the wing of the statuette. He'd never planned to see one in person and didn't know anyone who had, and the thought of comparing his rendering to a real Skarren was enough to make his fingers tremble.

I'm not going. He shook his head as he returned the carving to its place on the shelf between the Drashvoy and the Veshtrue carved from the same stone, as if he could physically reject a fate that felt more and more certain as the last traces of sleep left him. *I'm absolutely not going – there's no way. Why would I go?*

SIX

The first rays of daylight broke over the walls of Brathnee Garden like water flooding over a dam and beside the gate, Hyatt watched the streetlamps fade and wink out. A pair of songbirds spiraled around one of the posts and lit upon the rim of the lamp, quizzically inspecting the lightless bulb as if they didn't turn off every morning as the sun's glow took over their responsibilities. He watched their wings flutter almost too quickly to see as they rose in the air and landed again, like they could switch the lamp back on by perching on the perfect spot. The sounds of the Garden waking up filled the air, and he wondered if it was the last time he would hear the familiar melody.

Down the main road that spanned from the gate to the Gloratt, the Iron walked towards him with a small entourage in tow. He squinted and shielded his eyes from the sun, trying to make out who else had been coax or coerced into traversing the Reclaimed, but he only recognized Delores. Her gait struck him – the others in her little group walked less comfortably under the unfamiliar weight of their packs, but she moved with the same easy confidence that she'd possessed since he first met her. The Iron's boots seemed to land more comfortably on the street and the way her hair bounced and shifted reminded him of leaves in a breeze.

Delores smiled as she drew close, nodding in approval. "You chose to swim."

Hyatt had spent two hours standing by the Brathnee Garden gate, deciding if he was making the right decision, and wished he'd spent some of it coming up with something clever to say. Instead, he nodded in response and accepted her handshake. He caught the looks on the faces of her assembled team, curiosity at her easy recognition of them, and wondered how many had been the recipients of late-night visits to tell them they had sacred callings. Hyatt's eyes moved to the arm-braids he could see and found himself unsurprised that there were no Master Security or Master Hunter workers among them.

Without the Iron leading for them to follow like the tail of a comet, the group milled around like the Still Stars caught in her orbit. Hyatt counted six heads plus the Iron and as they spoke to each other, he tried to place them. The Master Speaker, in their mid-fifties, was easy to spot by their umber-and-beige braid laced with several generational threads. Three of the other workers wore jackets that covered their wrists and though he knew their faces like everyone else in Brathnee Garden, he couldn't place their names. They carried similar packs and two-foot, shallow-scalloped blades in leather sheaths, and their similarity made him guess they knew each other and had prepared for the trip together. Another worker had a flechette carbine slung over her shoulder and a bandoleer of extra magazines dangling over her worn and patched pack. The last worker wore a Journeyman Provisioner arm-braid and a pair of bladed fighting-sticks strapped to the side of her outsized pack. Hyatt's hand drifted absently to his hunting knife as he finished his silent inspection and suddenly, he wished he'd thought to find something more formidable.

The Iron made no gesture or noise to get everyone's attention but by the end of her first word, everyone had fallen silent and turned towards her. "We are traveling through the

Reclaimed to reach Moss Wall Pack. I am not your leader, but I know the way and if you stay near me, I will try to keep you safe. I have no idea where Sklodowska will take me after Moss Wall, so for those who need to return to Brathnee Garden, remember the way so you can travel quickly and quietly.

"I don't know what kind of reception we will have from the Cern... everyone who leaves the gate with me needs to know and accept the risks. Do what your High Ranger has asked of you, make good choices, and with any luck your place in the Eighth History will go on for many more years. Nod if you understand."

Hyatt was struck by Delores' use of words Jenna had spoken to him and to Gorman over and over on his first trip outside the walls. As the Iron made eye contact with every member of their team and watched them nod solemnly, he wondered if there was more meaning to them than simple acknowledgment. When she looked at him, he nodded and felt a burst of confidence as she nodded back with the smallest tilt of her chin.

The Iron moved closer to the gate and turned back to face them when she could see everyone at once. "We don't have to be silent because we're looking to find Cern, but don't let your conversations distract you from your surroundings. There are more dangerous things in the Reclaimed than raiders, and they don't obey boundaries drawn by the Haleu. Don't kill anything you don't have to."

She nodded to the Security workers at the gate, who threw the toggles on the large boxes that made the gate machinery work. The central latches pivoted away from each other and the large doors retracted along the rusted metal rails that held them, a sound between a squeak and a grind that ended with a metallic clunk as they collided with their stops. Seeing the road beyond the wall and the Reclaimed encroaching on it from both sides had always sent a cold wash through Hyatt and knowing he was going to be walking along it made his whole body tense, but he swallowed hard and fell into step behind the Iron as they headed towards the yawning opening.

On either side, workers lingered to watch the band of travelers move towards the world not protected by the walls of the Garden. Some watched with curiosity, others with envy, and still others with concern, and seeing them made Hyatt recall all the times workers headed into the Reclaimed had seen him watching their departure. He wondered what his face had said to them as the last thing they had seen as they departed.

Just before Delores crossed the threshold, a young boy darted towards her. The child wouldn't have reached her in time so she slowed her step to a lazy stroll, giving the youth's pumping legs time to carry him to her side. He arrived out of breath and his hair tousled, grabbed her jacket with one hand, and stared up at her expectantly.

Hyatt stepped within earshot as the boy thrust his free hand upward, clutching a burlaps pouch knotted with twine. "Iron, I have this for you!"

She crouched beside the boy and accepted the little pouch, her fingers tugging at the knotted string until it came loose. Hyatt wasn't close enough to see into the bag but Delores looked inside and then threw her head back with a laugh before she caught herself and fought to suppress a smirk that would not be denied.

"Thank you, sprout." She brushed the boy's hair back from his forehead, her words brimming with amusement. "This is very thoughtful."

Clearly pleased with himself, the boy darted back towards the edge of the road. Delores stood and retied the string, then tucked the pouch into her pocket. With a single glance back at the team, she resumed her walk through the gate that separated the Garden from the world beyond. When the last member of the group had crossed the threshold, the squeaking growl of the gates filled the air and the doors closed behind them. Everyone slowed to watch the gate wall of the settlement.

The Iron waited a moment to let them experience their transition in their own way, then started walking. "Let's go."

As they started their hike, Hyatt quickened his step to move closer to Delores, but faltered as he drew near. A sense of dichotomy crashed into his thoughts like a falling tree, uncertain whether he should see her as the nearly mythical Iron of the Eastern Reach or the fellow Haleu who had shared a vulnerable moment with him in his home before dawn. Unbidden, Jenna's voice came to mind, her blue eyes dark like evening storm clouds as she warned him not to rely on the Iron. He slowed his pace to let her move further ahead, and smiled at the worker with the flechette carbine over her shoulder as she caught up with him.

"Hey, I'm Omolara," she said, nodding towards the Iron's back ahead of them as her voice took on a skeptical note. "Friend of yours?"

He replied with an obligatory chuckle, though he wasn't sure if she was trying to be funny. "We go way back – all the way to twenty hours ago. I'm Hyatt."

Omolara pursed her lips and widened her eyes, a parody of being impressed. "Wow. Basically cradle-paired."

He'd hoped the conversation would flow naturally, but he still couldn't tell if she was being serious or making fun of him. "What? No. Um, I'm not paired. I mean—"

The woman smiled with her whole face, a broad expression that raised her cheeks and widened her nose. "You must be the backup in case something happens to the Master Speaker."

The direct jab broke the tension for Hyatt and he abandoned his explanation, letting out a shaky laugh. He shrugged helplessly and turned to scan the Reclaimed for signs of trouble, a convenient reason to look away as heat rose in his cheeks. They walked quietly together, listening to the thrushes chirp and flutter across the chasm in the canopy that left the sky visible over the road.

As they walked, Hyatt started to notice how different the Line Team trek had been. He glanced back at the loose scattering of workers, no team lead walking up and down the road to make sure they kept enough distance from each other or stayed quiet as they moved. Casually loaded packs made soft rattles and swishes that would have incensed Jenna, but the Iron either didn't notice or didn't care. The walk to Vohk Bridge had been tense, but by the time Delores' signaled for them to take their first break, Hyatt had become accustomed to the shift of his gear and begun to enjoy the hike.

The Iron set her pack down. "Stretch if you need to, and if you're getting hot or your straps are irritating you, take the time to fix them. I'll be moving again soon – if you're coming with me, be ready."

Hyatt thought back to the last thing she'd said before leaving the Garden, how egalitarian it had felt when she said she wasn't the group's leader, but looking around the Reclaimed on either side it seemed suicidal to abandon her company. He moved to the side of the trail to where the workers with matching gear were piling their packs together and set his down beside theirs, then took a seat on it and stretched his legs.

"Is that an artist braid?" the closest member of the trio asked, looking pointedly at Hyatt's wrist.

"Yeah – I'm a sculptor. Journeyman Artist Hyatt." He pulled his canteen from the side-pouch of his pack and unthreaded the top, then took a sip.

"Tayo," the worker replied, jerking his thumb toward the other two. "Pippa, and Aleks. Apprentice Hunters."

"And I'm Vamerie," the provisioner offered as she walked up on his other side, tossing her pack carelessly on the ground with a clatter.

"Nice to meet you," he said, replacing his canteen in his pack. "Any of you done this before?"

Hyatt fought the urge to wince as the Hunters exchanged hesitant glances, looking like none of them wanted to be the first to admit they'd never been on a Hunt. He cleared his voice and searched for a way to let them off the hook, when Vamerie spoke.

"I went on a provision run to Ceojic Garden once, a year ago," she said, taking a seat on top of her pack like Hyatt had and kicking her legs out to cross them at her ankles. "Made it all the way there and back, no trouble on the road."

The Hunters took seats on the ground and leaned back against their packs, splayed out like the spokes of a wheel, and Aleks replied, "You were lucky. There are Heirs in Ceojic."

"Maybe, but we didn't see any," Vamerie shrugged.

While the four of them debated the existence of massive monsters that roamed the Reclaimed, Hyatt glanced over his shoulder to look for Delores. She was seated on a log at the very edge of the path, facing the Master Speaker and Omolara who rested on their packs and leaning toward her in a closed cluster. He wondered what they were talking about, and if him walking up to them would make them fall quiet and stare at him expectantly. Uncertain, he returned his focus to the four workers near him, who seemed happy to ignore him as they argued over the wingspan of Skarrens.

"Hyatt," Pippa asked, tucking their short hair back behind their ear, "don't take this the wrong way, but... what are you doing here?"

Fuck if I know, he thought. "I'm headed to Moss Wall Pack."

Pippa furrowed their brow, squinting at him. "Yeah, but why? Are you trying to learn how they make their bone-flowers?"

"Or are you joining the Cern?" Tayo tacked on, grinning at the absurdity of it, but his smile faltered as he reached out and touched Hyatt's sleeve. "That's a... that's a Cern jacket."

Tayo's recognition of the jacket changed the posture of the other two Hunters. They leaned a little closer, looking him over with calculating, speculative eyes. The sudden attention made Hyatt uncomfortable and he shifted his weight on his pack, looked down, and fidgeted with the straps of his pack.

"Wait a minute, I think I heard about you – are you the artist that killed four Cern at Vohk Bridge?" The excitement in her voice gathered momentum as she talked, her words coming quicker and more clearly. "I heard you drowned one while she begged for her life!"

Hyatt opened his mouth to protest, but Aleks cut him off. "That's some weeds. I heard the same story, but he found a Turning weapon. You know it's weeds because Cern don't beg – they don't care if they die. It's just some Line Workers making up stories, so they seem like better pairings."

Tayo and Pippa mumbled their agreement and Vamerie studied Hyatt for a moment, then shrugged. "I never got why jobs that risked dying made people think they were better pairs. When I pair, I want someone I can count on."

Hyatt's wrestled with wanting to set the record straight, cursing Gorman for his version of events that spread like wildfire, and being grateful to be out of the spotlight. The four workers dove into a conversation about what made for a good pairing and he sat quietly, listening to them debate while Tayo dropped subtle hints in Vamerie's direction that he was unpaired and worth considering.

"I'm leaving now," Delores interrupted, standing in the middle of the road flanked by the Master Speaker and Omolara.

Hyatt stood and struggled into the straps of his pack, proud of himself for being the first of the five of them to be ready to move. The Iron had been as good as her word and the three of them were fifteen paces ahead on the road by the time he started to walk, and he glanced behind him to see the hunters and provisioner still getting their packs adjusted. He picked a moderate pace to avoid losing distance from the Iron and allow the others to get started, sighing wryly as he once again found himself trapped between two groups he didn't feel like he belonged with.

He watched Omolara ease her pace, letting the Iron and the Master Speaker move ahead, and quickened his to meet her. When he reached her, she settled in beside him and matched his stride. He watched one side of the road and she watched the other as the mid-morning sun bent the shadows into new shapes and the canopy trapped the heat beneath the expansive branches.

"I've never met any Cern before," she said, glancing at his jacket before turning her focus to the trees on her side. "I mean, I've seen the traders with their Security escorts when they've come to Brathnee, but I've never... met one. What are they like?"

The question jarred him, a request for expertise that he didn't think he had. "I don't know... the one who tried to kill me wasn't very nice, but they can't all be like that. I think they just thought we were in their lands or something."

"Aren't we going right into their lands right now?" she asked.

Hyatt immediately regretted his phrasing but couldn't argue with her logic. "I guess we are, yeah."

Omolara's chuckle was dry and she shifted the sling of her weapon on her shoulder. The road turned west and narrowed, the trunks of the trees on either side larger than they had been near the Garden. Taller grass and thicker brush made the Reclaimed look less passable, walling them in. Hanging moss weight down the branches, and black and green lichen clung to the boulders that dotted the landscape.

"Do you believe in all of..." Omolara trailed off for a moment, then nodded at the Iron, "that?"

Hyatt followed her gaze to Delores, watching the rise and fall of the Iron's shoulders and the gentle shift of her pack as she walked, her face in profile as she talked with the Master Speaker. "I think she believes in it, and the High Ranger believes in her, so..."

"So?" his companion pressed, unwilling to let him off the hook that easily.

"So... I don't know," he admitted quietly, glancing over her shoulder to see how closely the hunters and provisioner were following. "I guess I never thought about it very much. Does it feel like there might be something bigger out there? Sure. Does the Iron have a direct link to a divine presence that guides her? I don't know."

And that's why you're walking through the Reclaimed to a Cern pack with the promise of never going home. Hyatt felt a tide of frustration rise in him and looked down at the trail so Omolara wouldn't think she caused it. The sun was nearly overhead, turning the amorphous shadows on the trail into little blobs and the darkness on the edges of the road push further away, seeming to widen the route.

"And the Gifts?" Omolara asked, looking at him with something indiscernible in her eyes. "Do you think the Irons can do magic?"

The memory of the Iron in his home came back to him. He knew he would sound crazy if he described it, and he wasn't ready to talk about the reason he was on the team, so he contented himself with a helpless shrug. Omala nodded like she'd expected him to avoid committing to an answer and looked out into the forest.

"I'm going to fall back with the others, get to know them a little better. Want to come?" she asked.

"Nah, I'll walk alone for a while," Hyatt replied. "Have fun."

She slapped him on the shoulder and slowed her pace, lingering on the road as he moved ahead. Alone with his thoughts, he listened to the birds moving in the branches and the sound of the wind rustling the underbrush, and wondered for the thousandth time since leaving Brathnee Garden what he was doing on the road through the Reclaimed.

SEVEN

"Do you know what that is?" the Iron asked as Hyatt caught up with her, pointing to the Line box on the side of the road.

"It's a junction box to call back to Brathnee," he replied, confused by the question.

"It's the *last* junction box on this road." She lowered her arm and fell into step with him. "This is the edge of Brathnee... we're in Ceojic."

Hyatt looked back as they passed the box and realized she was right – the knee-high conduit that carried the Line ran back towards the Garden and four posts beneath the box held it up, but the Line didn't continue forward along the road. There seemed to be no change in the hard-packed earth of the path ahead and the Reclaimed looked no more inviting than it had for the first section of their trip, but something about continuing out of Brathnee felt like losing clothing and layers of skin. He caught sight of the Master Speaker, Omolara, Aleks, and Vamerie walking together, lost in conversation, and none of them looked over at the junction box as they passed it. Behind them, Pippa and Tayo walked together and each watched a side of the trail.

"Hey... can I ask you something?" he asked quietly.

"Sure." Delores absently tucked her mess of curls back behind her ear, so her crimson locks lay on top of her pack.

"In my home, at the table..." Hyatt stumbled over what he was trying to say, rejecting the first three versions of how to reach his point, "how did you... how was I sober?"

The Iron smiled like she knew the punchline to a joke Hyatt was starting to tell but wanted him to finish telling it anyway. "What do you mean?"

"You know what I mean," he replied, his voice low but firm. "Did you... do something to me?"

"Hyatt, you were drunk and needed to focus. I gave you something to focus on. That's all," the Iron replied, though the shine in her eyes made him think there was much more to it. "I didn't do anything to you."

"Okay, different question – are Irons allowed to lie?" he asked, giving her a sideways glance as he looked ahead to another bend in the path.

"Really?" She laughed and looked him over as if seeing him for the first time. "What do they say about Irons in Brathnee?"

Hyatt felt like he'd stumbled into a spiderweb with no way to extract himself. He cleared his throat and kicked a loose rock off the path, wishing he could disappear into the brush like the skipping stone did. The feeling of the Iron's eyes on the side of his head told him that he wasn't going to get away without an answer, but he waited to reply until the silence gained enough mass to tip over.

"Well, um... just things, you know? Like..." he searched his mind for any of the scraps of stories about Irons that might be true and hoped he was right. "Like, you don't answer to High Rangers, and you're chosen by the Iron before you... and that you hunt people who ignore the Warnings..."

"...and we can't die, and we hear the voice of Sklodowska, and we do magic? That we're born in the Low Flowers, and we eat babies left in the Reclaimed?" Delores picked up the list, amusement tangled around each statement, but the humor was swallowed by perfect seriousness as she said, "It's all true."

Hyatt flinched in horror, stepping further away from the Iron. "You eat babies? Baby Haleu?"

"Would it be better if it was baby Cern?" The smirk spread across Delores' face like a sunrise and she winked at him. "Okay, maybe not all of it is true."

Hyatt laughed uneasily. He was about to ask which parts weren't true when she reached out to stop him with a hand on his chest. No sound warned him of danger and he hadn't seen anything out of place, but he froze all the same as a jolt of fear drove curiosity and fascination out of his mind.

"There," she said quietly, pointing the broken bones driven into the ground like spikes beneath the wilting leaves of ferns that lined the edge of the road.

He leaned on his only other experience outside the walls of Brathnee Garden and looked up, fighting a gasp of surprise as he saw white bones with indiscernible carvings strung between branches. While the Cern markings near Vohk Bridge had dangled like stalactites in plain view, the bones overhead were strung horizontally like ribbons and easy to miss amidst the leaves. Hyatt felt familiar foreboding in his neck and joints as the Iron started walking again, and he fell into step behind her but his eyes clung to the bones above.

"Now what?" he asked.

"Now we wait until they find us," Delores replied, "or keep walking until we find a trail to their camp."

Hyatt had no idea how he imagined meeting the Cern, but leaving the road never occurred with him. The thought of stepping off the network of roads between the Nine Gardens terrified him and he stared at the side of the path like it was the edge of a precipice. Images of Heirs descending from the branches to dismember them and living trees impaling them on broken branches as vines ripped them apart flashed through his mind.

"Of course," he said. "Great."

The path curved down a gentle slope and veered north, and he slowed his pace. Delores continued ahead without a glance or a word like she was a piece of a machine, moving at a set rhythm independent from the world around her. Omolara and the Master Speaker had also fallen back, but as Hyatt lingered, Aleks and Vamerie caught up with him. Vamerie offered him an herbtwist, shrugged when he declined, and popped the end between her teeth.

"I don't think this is Brathnee anymore," Aleks said, shifting her pack.

"We're in Ceojic," Hyatt replied, grateful to have something useful to say, "but this area is claimed by Cern."

"What?" Aleks' eyes snapped to Hyatt in alarm and then out toward the forest, his hand floating closer to the grip of his weapon. "How do you know?"

"Iron Delores pointed out the last Brathnee junction box and the bone markings when we crossed them. We've been in Moss Wall Pack territory for a little while."

"I think he's right," Vamerie agreed. "I think this hill is in Ceojic."

That's what I just said. Hyatt frowned and almost vocalized the thought, but decided it wasn't worth it.

They walked together, watching the sides of the path as they moved down the mild slope. Something changed as they moved and Hyatt tried to place it, looking closer at the trees and the leaves for what seemed off, but came up with nothing. Vamerie seemed to pick up on it too and curled her fingers around the dangling ends of the fighting sticks strapped to her pack, moving closer to the edge of the road as if she could see deeper into the Reclaimed from there.

"It's the birds," Aleks said softly, moving between them. "They've stopped."

As soon as the Apprentice Hunter said it, Hyatt knew he was right – no song of the breeze through the branches had lost the harmony of birds chirping and the scurry of small game across fallen leaves. He glanced back to see the two groups of travelers behind them picking up their pace to close the distance, and knew they'd noticed too, and as he focused on the road ahead, he saw Delores slowing down.

"Is this bad?" Hyatt asked, looking from Vamerie to Aleks.

"Maybe not," Aleks reasoned, though his hand stayed close to his weapon. "It could just be a wildcat or a wolverine."

Hyatt tried to keep the alarm from his voice, but he couldn't help himself. "In what world is a wolverine not bad?"

"In the world where there are much worse things in the Reclaimed," Pippa answered for Alex, joining them. "It could be *just* a wolverine."

The clusters formed by the team melded into a loose pack as they reached Delores, who was standing in the road with her arms crossed. As they approached, she pointed off the right side of the path between two massive birch trees. At first Hyatt couldn't see what she was pointing at, but as he squinted, a stone staircase covered in moss with a tree growing from the center of the top step came into view. The eerie structure seemed to start and end nowhere, with no room around the landing and only fragments of a wall clinging to their right side, and stopping at a broken doorway that led into open air. He couldn't help but imagine stepping through it and plunging to the broken shards of rock on the forest floor below, his legs and neck broken like twigs on the jagged edges.

"How old is it?" he asked no one in particular, his voice barely louder than a whisper.

Delores stepped off the path, her tall boots disappearing to her mid-calf in the wild grass. "Sixth History, probably. Come on."

"Wait – we're not going over there, are we?" he protested before he could stop himself.

The Iron didn't answer, and embarrassment rushed through him at asking a stupid question, compounded by the frustration that he was embarrassed much more often than he was used to and didn't like it. As he stood at the edge of the path and watched her walk into the Reclaimed, the three Apprentice Hunters spread out and passed him in crouching walks that made them seem to bleed into the foliage. He gritted his teeth and tried to step over the edge of the road to follow, but his body refused to obey his mind's demands.

"Come on," Omolara said, resting a hand on his shoulder reassuringly before stepping into the grass. "We're safer with her than we are alone on the road."

He knew she was right and looked up and down the road in both directions, but the idea of crossing the threshold into the Reclaimed paralyzed him. The Master Speaker stopped beside him and stroked his short, graphite gray beard, watching the rest of the team weave between the bushes and trunks. The silence seemed to swallow even the movements of their companions.

"I once met a Keeper who specialized in the Sixth History," they began with a professorial tone that accompanied a straightening of their posture, "and he believed that the Ones Before covered all of this in cities and destroyed all of the Reclaimed. He said you could walk for days without seeing a tree. Hard to imagine, isn't it?"

Hyatt looked at the sprawling forest and the mysterious stairs, the only structure in sight, and tried to imagine it shaved bare like the High Ranger's head. "I can't."

"Maybe it's just a story," the Master Speaker ceded with a slight tilt of his head, "but it gives me heart. If apprentice workers could brave the Reclaimed and drive it from the land, surely the Carver of Cern can walk a hundred paces into it, right?"

He stiffened at the older man's nickname for him, but couldn't argue his point. Hyatt watched the Master Speaker step off the trail and grit his teeth. He edged closer to the side of the road until the toes of his boots touched the swaying grass, clenching his fists until his fingernails bit into his palms and his knuckles were as white as ice.

"Maybe they were just really fucking stupid," he muttered under his breath as he took a step and planted his sole in the Reclaimed.

With every step he moved faster, anxious for the safety of the group, until he was almost running when he caught up with Omolara and the Master Speaker. He forced himself to slow down and walk with them towards the stone staircase to nowhere, focusing on his breathing and the shapes of the apprentice hunters fanning further out to surround the structure. Omolara smiled at him and threw her arm around his shoulder as they walked, and he smiled with gratitude for her presence.

Delores stood on the second and third step of the curved staircase, her bare hand resting on the moss that clung to the shattered remains of the wall beside her like her fingertips could unlock the stone's secrets. Aleks, Pippa, and Tayo settled in a triangle around the perimeter and Hyatt wondered what hunter skills they employed as they listened to the quiet and observed the bushes and branches, but decided it would be better to ask when they were finished. Instead he stood with Omolara and the Master Speaker near the base of the stairs, watching the Iron as she ascended the staircase one step after another.

When she reached the top stair and the tree that grew from it, she knelt down. It seemed to Hyatt that she stayed that way for an hour, while every direction he wasn't facing threatened to let monsters appear to devour him. He looked suspiciously at roots that broke the forest floor and tried to remember if they were exactly where he'd seen them last or if they'd crept closer.

"See? Nothing to worry about out here." Vamerie said, nearer to him than he'd expected.

Hyatt whirled at the sound of her voice and almost fell over as his heel sunk in the softer earth, and the hunter struggled to suppress her smirk.

Catching his balance, he shook his head. "We didn't die in the first minute. That's not the same thing."

"Are you sure you're the artist who killed four Cern raiders?" she asked, winking as she stepped by him and keeping pace with the other hunters who were shifting clockwise in a methodical motion.

"No, definitely not!" Hyatt called after her.

He would have missed her chuckle if not for the perfect quiet of the Reclaimed. At the top of the stairs, the Iron stood and pressed her palm to the sapling that struggled skyward in front of her, then moved down the steps much faster than she'd climbed them. When she reached the bottom, she joined them.

"The Moss Wall Pack encampment is that way," she threw her thumb over her shoulder, pointing deeper into the forest. "Probably not more than four hours."

No... no no no... Hyatt felt the blood draining from his face and hoped it wasn't as obvious to the three people closest to him as it felt to him. "Four hours deeper into the Reclaimed?"

Omolara put her arm around his shoulders again and gave him a sympathetic smile, but instead of reassuring him, it made him feel small and made of cotton. He nodded and smiled back so that she'd release him, then shoved his hands into his pockets and studied a distant point on the ground as if the leaves could arrange themselves to give him an alternative to a suicide trek into the Reclaimed.

The Master Speaker touched Omolara's arm and led her away, and the Iron stepped into his vision and lifted his chin with her finger until their eyes met. "Choose to swim."

"I hate swimming." His whisper hardened with a vehemence that surprised him, but it gained momentum and he leaned into it. "I didn't ask to be here – I should be at the artist's patch, carving statuettes right now! This is insane!"

"You are here because Sklodowska-" Delores began.

"Fuck what Sklodowska wants!" he snapped, cutting her off with words like a slashing knife.

Overhead, a carrion bird screeched and against the backstop of absolute silence, it sounded deafening. Hyatt looked up and spotted the wings of the bird as it spiraled. His heart seized in his chest and he looked back at the Iron, but she was looking up at the broad arcs of the bird's flight as well. When she looked down and saw his face, she burst out laughing.

"Relax," she managed between her chuckles, "She doesn't care if you get angry with her."

The twang of a bow echoed off the trees, and the carrion bird began a twirling plummet to the earth. In one movement and as if they had magically all been shot by the arrow that killed the bird, the three hunters threw themselves on the ground and landed like lifeless corpses. Hyatt rushed towards the side of the stairs and crouched against the cold stone, hoping the wall was between him and the direction of the shooter. Omolara and the Master Speaker joined him, and a moment later Vamerie reached him too.

Alone in the open at the base of the stairs, the Iron turned slowly with her eyes narrowed in calculation. She slipped her pack from her shoulders and rested her hand on the handle of the weapon at her hip as the bag hit the forest floor. The wicked hiss of another arrow whistled through the air inches from her ear and vanished in the distance, but Delores didn't flinch.

"My name is Delores, Iron of the Eastern Reach," she called out in a clear, strong voice. "I have the right to be heard, by the Iron Accords of the Seventh History, and these Haleu are under my protection. Reveal yourselves, Cern!"

Hyatt recoiled from the sound of her voice, and he felt his brain melt as he heard her words and wondered what she was thinking. He shot wild, disbelieving eyes at Omolara who threw back a helpless throw of her hands before unslinging her carbine and wrapping her arm through the sling to pull it close to her shoulder.

The silence seemed to last forever as Hyatt envisioned a volley of Cern arrows impaling Delores and leaving them alone in the Reclaimed, hours from Brathnee Garden. He pressed himself to the stone, trying to quiet his breathing. Omolara swung her weapon upward and aligned her eye with the sights as she swept them over the near trees in search of raider silhouettes.

"Your Accords don't promise safety for your companions," a voice called out, and Hyatt panicked as he realized it came from a tree just beyond the stairway.

As quietly as he could, he pulled his knife free of its sheath. The memory of the Structure worker shouting at him over and over again to kill the raider on the riverbank bubbled up in his mind and he felt his blood rush in response, the blade shaking in his hand as adrenaline ripped through him. He guessed the tree was twenty paces away and wondered if the Cern had seen him yet, or if he could run fast enough to surprise him.

"Are you trusted to make enemies with an Iron on behalf of the Moss Wall Pack?" She called back like she was calling a bluff, walking slowly in the direction the arrows had come from. "Do you want to explain to your pack-mates why every Iron in the Nine Gardens is coming for you?"

Hyatt lost sight of her as she walked by one of the hunters laying prone and still in the grass, and being unable to see her wound the tension in his chest a turn tighter. He nudged Omolara and pointed to the tree that hid the Cern man, and she stepped behind him to point her carbine at it. When no answer came from Delores' challenge he crept along the wall, crouched, and then bolted for the trunk.

Everything seemed to happen in slow motion for Hyatt. When he was halfway across the space between the stone steps and the tree, he broke a branch under his boot. One step further, the shadowed form of a Cern man melted away from the tree in front of him. Omolara fired immediately and he swore he could feel the four-inch steel flechette slice through the air over him before they buried deep into the soft wood of the tree. The Cern man instinctively recoiled behind the trunk at the sound of the shot and by the time he peered around the tree again, Hyatt was slamming into him at full force.

His sense of slowed motion ended and everything was a chaotic blur. Hyatt felt blow after blow land on him and couldn't tell if they were fists or knees as the Cern man struggled underneath him, flailing in surprise and a desperate need to survive. He swung wildly and felt his knuckles connect but couldn't tell if he hit the Cern in his face or chest or ribs. A snarl of pain was the last thing Hyatt heard clearly before something hard hit him in the ear and sent him sprawling across the forest floor.

"Hold! Stop!" Delores shouted, and suddenly someone's hands were on Hyatt's shoulders, dragging him to his feet and backward away from the scrambling Cern man.

The world came back into focus and Hyatt gasped for air, spitting dirt from his lips. Omolara's arm had slid around his throat but loosened as he relaxed, and he pushed himself away from her. In front of him, the Cern man scrambled to his feet and took a few steps back. Hyatt stared at the Cern and watched him recognize that jacket he was wearing, a spark of understanding in his dark eyes.

Delores was walking towards Hyatt and Omalara, flanked by a man and a woman with bows tucked under their arms. "Put your weapons away. We're not fighting these Cern today."

Omolara uncoiled the sling of her carbine from around her arm and lowered her carbine, but her knuckles were still white around the grip like she planned to snap it back to her shoulder and fire. In front of them, one of the Cern sneered at her, daring her to violate the Accords and spark the fight again. Hyatt watched the raider he'd struggled with back slowly towards one of his companions, and Hyatt slid his knife into its sheath but kept his fingers curled around the handle. The hunters had risen from their prone positions and Hyatt caught sight of them as they walked towards the Iron, hands resting on the hilts of their blades.

"This is Rellah and Veckram, sentries for Moss Wall Pack," Delores explained as the rest of the team drew closer, making eye contact with each one to ensure they heard her. "They'll show us to the camp. Get your packs, and keep your weapons stowed."

Hyatt kept his eyes on the Cern he'd tackled and saw him stare daggers back at him. He wondered if the man was subordinate to the sentries and imagined that Cern blade plunging into his back while they walked through the Reclaimed. The unknown dangers of the forest combined with the familiar dangers of Cern raiders, and made Hyatt feel like their plan was pure suicide.

"Don't worry, little weeds. Nobody's going to rip your roots out while the big, bad Iron is protecting you," Veckram tacked on, a condescending snarl tugging at his upper lip. "Do as you're told like good little compost piles, and you'll make it back to your quaint Gardens."

The idea that moments ago he and his companions had been fighting for their lives, and because the Iron said so they were suddenly not supposed to fight anymore, seemed insane to Hyatt. He was terrified at the prospect of the battle continuing but couldn't fathom how they could switch from mortal enemies to guests of the Cern pack in the blink of an eye. Across a space small enough to cross in six paces, the raider he'd tried to kill said with his eyes that he was just as strained to accept the new terms.

"Let's get our packs," Omolara urged him quietly, rubbing her shoulder where the stock of the carbine had kicked.

He swallowed his protest and followed her back to the edge of the stairs. As they crossed the space, he looked up at the eerie doorway that arched over the top step and the sapling that grew up beneath it. Daylight punched through the openings between the tree's leaves and seemed to glow against the trunk and glint against the edge of the last step. As he shouldered his pack, he kept his eyes on the tree and the doorway, unsure of what he expected to happen but unable to look away.

"Who builds steps to nowhere?" Omolara asked as if she had read his mind, looking up at it.

"Who follows Cern through the Reclaimed to their camp?" he countered, bitterness edging around his words.

She nodded, taking his point, even as she stepped by him to head towards the Iron. "Who is afraid of everything outside the Garden, but is still the first to attack a Cern?"

The jab surprised him and he jogged to catch up with her so he could look at her face as he replied, "Who risks shooting their friend for a chance to stick a Cern full of flechettes?"

Omalara smiled and nudged him with her elbow. "Who said we're friends?"

EIGHT

After three hours of walking through the Reclaimed, Hyatt couldn't have found his way back to the road if his life depended on it. He couldn't tell if the jagged path the Cern laid out was to confuse the Haleu walking with them or to avoid the deep gashes and jagged rock faces, but he felt certain they turned in every direction of the compass and that they passed the same fallen oak and massive granite boulder over and over. When he realized he had no idea where he was, Hyatt focused on the constant in his environment – the three Cern leading their way.

The man he'd tackled wore a jacket like the one Jenna had given Hyatt, but he was no closer to understanding the symbols and secrets that made it unique than he'd been at Vohk Bridge. The man said nothing as he walked and moved with a lumbering gait, less nimble than the Cern raiders he'd met before. He walked beside the Master Speaker near the back of the column but seemed to pay no attention to the forest around him, interested only in the Haleu he was escorting. When he caught Hyatt looking in his direction, his eyes narrowed and his lips tightened, and Hyatt was certain he had made an enemy.

Rellah walked in the middle of the pack, her Cern blade slung upside down across her back and her bow tucked under her arm. The ash-and-indigo fletchings of the arrows in her hip quiver shifted as she walked, blending into near camouflage in one moment and then flaring bright as sunlight snuck around her arm to catch on the incandescent blue feather. Something about the way she moved reminded him of Jenna, a comfortable confidence crossed with the predatory fluidity of a cat. Her attention was divided between the Reclaimed on every side, the Haleu closest to her, and the Iron.

Veckram and Delores walked side by side at the front of the column and it looked to Hyatt like they were discussing something important, but he was too far back to make out the subject or tone. He wondered if it was a coincidence or a choice that they walked with their weapons outboard from each other, Delores' left hand resting idly on the hilt of her blade and Veckram's bow tucked under his right arm. The Cern man walked like he knew where he was going and his dark gray hair seemed to absorb the light that filtered through the canopy above.

When they reached a divide in the terrain, the left descending into a valley and the right rising up a hill with a cliff dividing them, they slowed to a stop and Delores gestured for the Haleu to join her. The three Cern sentries arrayed themselves behind her as if she were a tree and they were shadows cast from her trunk. Hyatt remembered seeing Jenna hook her thumbs in her belt when addressing the workers and affected the same pose, cocking a leg and keeping his arms tucked to his sides. Through the tension and anxiety of being lost in the Reclaimed and in the company of Cern, a surprising feeling of confidence streamed upward in him like bubbles in a bog, and he made a mental note to do things that made him feel brave and stable whenever he could.

"Look at you," Tayo said beside him, his gaze running up and down Hyatt before focusing on the Iron, "looking like this is just another day in the Garden."

He didn't know if it was a compliment or a jab and looked to the other side, only to catch Pippa nodding with approval as they slid their fingers under the straps of their pack. Their acceptance meant more to Hyatt than he expected and he fought a grin, feeling foolish for caring, and turned his attention to Delores only to find her looking directly at him with a bemused expression that deflated him immediately.

"Veckram tells me this is the heart of Moss Wall Pack. The Master Speaker and I have business with the Pack leaders," she nodded to the Master Speaker, who nodded once in return, "and the rest of you will be asked to stay together with Rellah. You will need to turn in your packs and your weapons, but I have Veckram's word that they will be returned to you when you leave. Remember that you are far from your homes and guests in theirs."

Delores' last sentence sounded more like a warning than friendly advice and sent a tingle of apprehension down Hyatt's spine, and the fact that they would have to disarm caused the hunters to tense so obviously that it felt like the air between them had been strung tight like a bowstring. She paused to be sure everyone had a moment to process the information.

"Your lives are yours, but you'll live them longer if you do as Rellah says while you're here," she finished, then turned to Veckram. "After you."

Hyatt watched the Master Speaker move through the crowd to Delores' side, and they walked up the hill together. He fought the surge of anxiety as he wondered if he would ever see her again. The Reclaimed seemed to encroach closer on him from every side, and the reality of being on his own with the Cern crashed over him. He took a deep breath and fought the toxins of fear by looking around at the rest of the team and committing to the fact that he wasn't as alone as he felt.

"My name is Rellah, and if we are very lucky, I will never know any of your names," Rellah lifted an arrow four inches in her quiver, and when she let it fall back into the sheath, it landed with a click. "Stay together, and where I can see you. If I can't see you, I can't keep you away from my pack-mates... and they are not as welcoming as me."

Their Cern escort turned to walk down the hill, and Omolara leaned closer. "Wasn't she the one who shot at the Iron twice?"

Hyatt shrugged and shuffled forward with the rest of the Haleu. "That might have been Veckram."

Her chuckle was uneasy, and it brought him a bit of comfort to know he wasn't the only person tense under the circumstances. "Nah, he doesn't look like he can shoot. It was definitely her."

A loose rock slipped under Hyatt's boot and tumbled down the slope ahead of him, and he reached out to balance himself as he found his footing. "The shooter *did* miss twice."

The grade steepened and they abandoned the conversation to focus on using roots and embedded rocks as makeshift steps. Beside them, the ascending cliff face glittered as filtered sunlight caught on flecks of mica between the patches of moss. They passed the first Cern structure, part tent and part foliage. In front of it, three men sat in a half-circle playing a game that involved flipping darts into the air, so they landed on a board between them. Hyatt watched them as he walked, the gleaming tip and fletched end turning end over end before burying in the soft plank on the ground.

Rellah came to a stop in front of a similar tent and pointed to the shaded earth beneath the stretched pavilion. "Packs and weapons, here."

The unorganized mass filtered towards the tent like water to a drain, and one by one they dropped their packs. Vamerie and Omolara set their weapons in the dirt, and behind them, Pippa and Aleks leaned their blades against one of the logs inside the tent that looked like they were used as chairs. Tayo followed suit, but as he stepped from the tent, Rellah's hand moved in a rapid blur and caught the end of a knife coming out of his boot. Tayo felt it move and spun, his hand closing around her wrist, but Rellah stepped behind him and swept his legs out from under him. Tayo's shoulders hit the dirt with a solid thud and Rellah followed him to the ground, her knee between his legs and his stolen own? knife's blade resting across his throat. Tayo started to sit up and felt the edge bite into his skin, and he collapsed backward with his hands open in surrender. She lifted the knife, flipped it over in a deft motion, and drove it savagely downward.

Hyatt didn't realize he'd stepped forward to help the apprentice hunter, and he didn't see the blade bypass Tayo's ear and drive through the collar of his shirt to pin him to the earth. Rellah drew and knocked an arrow with the same uncanny speed she'd taken Tayo's knife, rising as she drew it back. His next clear thought was freezing as he found himself staring at the wicked blades of her arrow's tip at full extension, two feet in front of him and pointed at his sternum. His tongue went dry and his lungs locked, unwilling to breathe in and make his chest rise even a fraction of an inch closer to the arrow that could end his life.

Rellah's eyes shifted up from the length of the arrow to his and when she was sure he understood the cost of interfering, she swung downward to point her bow at Tayo's mouth. "I am not even a raider, you stupid Haleu compost. There is nothing you could do with that knife to stop one of my pack-mates from fileting you with it while your friends watched. Now, tell me it was an eating knife."

"What?" Tayo stammered, turning his face away from the arrow's tip as if he could escape it.

The string of Rellah's bow creaked as she pulled against it. "Say it."

"I don't – it was an eating knife!" He tugged his shoulders, trying to dislodge the knife that staked him to the ground, but it held fast.

She slanted her aim away from him and slowly relaxed the draw of her bow. "I believe you. Someone help him up."

Hyatt watched her un-nock her arrow and return it to her quiver as Pippa and Aleks rushed to his side to wrench the knife from his shirt and lift him to his feet. Pippa didn't make eye contact as she held the knife out towards Rellah and looked relieved when the Cern woman took it from her. The three hunters moved together toward the rock wall and the rest of the travelers followed suit, finding seats where they could rest their back against the stone. Hyatt headed for a space between the hunters and Omolara, and as he moved, he felt Rellah's eyes on him.

"I don't think she liked you stepping up for Tayo." Omolara inched closer to him as he sat down and nodded toward their sentry.

He followed her gesture to where Rellah was leaning against a tree, looking right at him, and jerked his gaze away to face Omolara. "You think?"

"She's coming over here," she warned him, inching away across the dirt.

"Hey, get back here..." he whispered, each word louder, but gave up when forced to pick between continuing and risking anyone else noticing his desperation.

Omolara stared off into the encampment and pretended she hadn't heard him. Hyatt looked up and saw Rellah walking toward him just as his companion had warned. He settled for picking up a rock and chucking it at Omolara's leg to punish her for her treachery, then tilted his head and squinted at the Cern woman walking toward him with the sun blinding him from behind her. When Rellah was halfway to him she grabbed a log by the knob of what had been a branch and dragged it behind her, the muscles in her arm like coils of rope.

She dropped the section of tree trunk in front of Hyatt and took a seat, resting her forearms on her thighs and leaning forward to study him. Rellah's eyes started on the bridge of his nose and moved down to his chest, then out to his left shoulder and back across his Cern jacket to his right. Her head turned as she looked down along his sleeve, all the way to the cuff, then slowly back up to meet his eyes.

"Where did you get your jacket, Haleu?" she asked, her voice disarmingly curious and her gaze full of something much sharper.

Almost every fiber of his being wanted to break eye contact with her but he managed not to flinch and in that moment, he felt a thread of steel laced up through his center that surprised him. He paused for the space of a breath, his lips parted as a word was going to escape between them, but no sound slipped through and he settled for staring back at her.

"I asked you a question, compost." She leaned a little closer and her tone sweetened to something sticky and unpleasant. "How did you come by your Cern jacket?"

"I killed the woman wearing it." It felt like someone else was saying the words and hearing them leave his mouth fascinated and horrified him at the same time. *What the fuck was that?*

The flare of Rellah's eyes would have been almost imperceptible without the way it made her dark lashes tremble, the barest hint of surprise against the backdrop of her utter control. A slanted beam of light caught on the metal wire coiled three times through the cartilage on the top of her left ear and

Hyatt squinted again as it momentarily blinded him. When his eyes adjusted, she was still staring right at him.

"I don't believe you. Tell me how." Rellah pulled an arrow from her quiver and pinched it just beneath the head, turning it slowly and studying the blades as they rotated.

Hyatt watched the shining steel edges of the blades reflect against the Cern woman's pupils, linear gleams that passed by one after another. A metallic taste tinged the edges of his tongue and his chest felt tight as his heartbeat started to thud harder. He could barely make out Omolara in his periphery, but he could tell that on the other side of him, the three hunters watched the exchange with rapt attention and tried to read their lips.

"I stabbed her in the throat, here." Hyatt reached across his body to press his fingers into the hollow behind his collarbone, holding it there until Rellah looked up at him before letting his hand fall back to his lap. "She fought even after I stabbed her, but she lost a lot of blood all at once. Then..."

Hyatt paused, visions of Jenna picking up the woman's dropped weapon and using it to sever her neck breaking violently into his memory. Rellah stopped rotating the arrow in her hands, resting it across her knees and covering it with her hands.

"Then... what?"

Then Jenna cut her fucking head off. He swallowed hard and fought a wave of nausea that churned in his gut. "Then, she died."

The silence that followed his sentence felt like trying to breathe through wet wool. Hyatt wondered if she would drive that arrow through his eye with another lightning-fast gesture and as her knuckles whitened around its shaft, he thought she was going to. He felt his palms start to sweat and fought the desire to wipe them on his pants. In a random, panic-inspired moment he couldn't understand, he wondered what Gorman was doing at that exact moment while he waited for Rellah to move or speak.

A pair of Cern walked by as the moment drew out, comfortable gaits that looked like they had grown used to living in the Reclaim and no longer feared its terrifying mysteries. They studied their line of Haleu travelers with curiosity and distrust until they spotted Rellah, then turned to talk to each other as they continued on their way. Overhead, a carrion bird cried out again, and Hyatt wondered whether it was the same one from the steps or if a new one had sensed an imminent opportunity to feed. Finally, Rellah slipped her arrow back into her quiver.

"That jacket belonged to Shelara. I knew her." She reached out and tapped two yellow stitches that wrapped over the cuff of his left sleeve like the wire coiled over her ear. "These are her boys, Kendek and Liyek. They would want to know how she died. Shall I send for them?"

A wash of ice ran through Hyatt's blood, and for a split second, he wished she had shoved the arrow through his iris instead. He could feel hot tears glazing his eyes and welling behind his lashes, threatening to spill over and trace mortifying trails down his face. A shadow danced over his face as a branch swayed between the sun and him.

"I don't want to tell them that," he said softly, looking away from Rellah for the first time.

Her brow creased, and he couldn't tell if it was confusion or disapproval. "Why? Was she... no. I knew Shelara. She wasn't afraid – not of you. Not of anything."

Hyatt wiped at his cheek even though none of his tears had escaped, then shook his head to clear the memory of her mint green eyes staring up at him in defiant pride. "No, no at all. She was... she took on two of us. I was just... I got lucky. She could have killed us both."

"Then... what kind of human being denies children closure?" Rellah asked, an edge creeping into her voice. "Do you spit on sprouts in your Gardens?"

The cocktail of panic, fear, regret, and confusion swirled inside Hyatt and he thought he was going to vomit. "What are you talking about? I don't want to tell them I killed their mother! That's not going to make it better!"

Rellah glared at him and stood, and for a moment Hyatt thought she was going to stop her boot through his head against the cliff face. She started to turn but spun back, jabbing her finger at him like she was driving a knife.

"You are exactly the kind of Haleu I'd expect an Iron to bring here. Fuck you both," she snarled.

Rellah pivoted and stormed off towards the tent where their gear was stored. As soon as she was under the pavilion, his fellow travelers converged like waves crashing in on him from both sides.

"What did you say to her?" Aleks demanded.

"She was fucking angry!" Vamerie piled on, looking to make sure the Cern sentry wasn't coming back. "What did you do?"

"What did she want?" Pippa asked, jostling past Tayo to be sure Hyatt heard them.

Before he could answer the barrage of questions from the others, the sound of running feet breaking leaves and branches drew their attention. From up the hill, a Cern girl was moving as fast as her legs would carry her, arms pumping furiously and chestnut hair flapping wildly around her. She was halfway past the Haleu when she turned sideways and bent her knees, tearing a trail through the dirt to slow herself down.

She almost lost her balance and pinwheeled wildly, as she changed directions towards them. "Rellah!"

The Cern sentry emerged from the tent and caught the full force of the girl as she slammed into the larger woman, almost bowling her over. Rellah spun to let the girl's momentum carry her by and snatched her by her collar as she flew by, and the runner's legs flailed like a rag doll before the sentry set her down on her feet. Out of breath, the girl doubled over and gasped for air.

"Pack-master wants to see you up top," she gasped out, looking up through her bangs at Rellah without standing, "and the one they call Hyatt, too."

Rellah turned slower than the planet beneath her feet to look at Hyatt at the center of the cluster of his fellow travelers. Her animosity bloomed back to life in her eyes and she walked toward him, stepping over the long she'd been seated on before and crossing her arms as she glowered down at him.

"You're Hyatt, aren't you?" There was no question in her voice.

Hyatt dusted himself off and struggled to his feet, keeping his back to the cliff. "Yes."

"Of course you are," she sighed. "Get your pack and your little knife. Hurry up."

He felt her eyes on him and tried to hurry, but his leg had fallen asleep where he sat and he almost collapsed on his first step away from the wall. He clamped his hand around his thigh to brace it and limped forward, moving as quickly as he could toward the tent where their gear was stashed, but his pace was slow enough to realize that none of the Haleu had risen to help him and he found himself resenting them for it. The knowledge that whatever fate the pack-master had in store for him was his alone chilled him like a snowfall and he tried not to glare at his companions as he shouldered his pack. His knife settled into the empty sheath on his belt. While he adjusted his straps and tied the retaining strap around the handle of his little weapon, Rellah stared at him.

"Let's go," she barked at him, gesturing for Hyatt to head up the hill with a quick movement that sowed no patience or kindness.

He started the walk up the slope with the Cern sentry behind him. From that direction, the slender trunks of the elms and birches looked sparse and melancholy. He hadn't noticed on the way down that the low branches of the trees had been cut away intentionally, but he studied the cleft wood where limbs had been as he climbed. As he passed close to one he reached out, tracing his fingers over the smooth surface where the shoulder-high branch had been removed in a single slice of something sharp.

"Why does my pack-master know your name, Hy-att?" Rellah's voice behind him stretched his name to three syllables like she was rolling it around her mouth to taste the full flavor of it.

Hyatt had no idea, so didn't answer. The loose leaves under his boots gave way and he slipped a little, and Rellah seized the moment to shove his pack. The force of her impact sprawled him forward and he landed hard on his chest. His hands did nothing to break his fall but tear open as they hit the ground, branches pulling at his soft skin. He sucked a breath through his clenched teeth and climbed to his feet, shaking his hands to fade the sting of the abrasions.

"Climb." Rellah's voice was flat and took no responsibility for his fall. "Maybe your Iron has traded your life for a favor from the pack-master. Maybe we've been called so he can watch me kill you."

Is that a real thing? His mind latched onto the thought and he imagined himself facing off with the Cern sentry in a fight to the death, himself laying on the ground with a dozen arrows stuck in his stomach and chest like one of the cushions Master Stitchers used to hold needles. A rational thought tried to fight through, insisting that she wouldn't have told him to bring his things if the plan was to kill him, but the panic in his heart argued that his instructions were just to tire him out so she could kill him more easily. As if siding against him, his pack seemed to get heavier with each step.

"Why do you hate me?" he replied, desperate to replace the morbid thoughts in his head with anything else. "Is it because I'm Haleu?"

Rellah laughed, a dry chuckle that sounded perfectly matched to her personality and implied Hyatt had said something ignorant. "That would be reason enough. Or it could be because you killed Shelara, or because you brought an Iron to my home. Or because you denied her children her death-story. Or it could be your stupid face. I haven't decided yet, Hy-att."

Her answer flooded him with an impotent frustration that felt trapped inside him, a pressurized feeling he had no way to vent. He rounded the corner at the edge of the cliff and continued to climb, anger fueling him and making him march faster on the uneven ground. The edge of the precipice blocked the sun and stretched the shadows of the trees all the way across the forest until they blended together, melting into the edges of Cern tents and swallowed by the low bushes between larger trunks.

"At least if I get killed, I won't have to listen to your fucking voice anymore," he snapped back, too late to have much impact and more hateful than he'd expected. *What the fuck is wrong with me?*

Rellah just laughed and climbed the hill behind him. Her boots made almost no sound as they rose and fell against the earth, and Hyatt realized he couldn't hear the shift of her arrows in the quiver or even the soft hiss of her bow grazing against her side as she carried it – if he hadn't known she was there, she could have vanished like a ghost in the Reclaimed.

The hilltop rounded over. Ahead of them, a larger tent stood against the distant, pale sky with only a handful of trees behind it to break up the horizon. On logs inside, Iron Delores and the Master Speaker sat on a log across from a hulking man with a shaved head. Hyatt started to quicken his step, but Rellah set her hand on his shoulder to stop him. With no idea what she was doing, he let her set his pace. They were a dozen paces from the tent when Delores looked up and saw him, then turned back to the man Hyatt assumed was the pack-master.

You'd better not be making a deal to let them murder me, he thought, a bitter scowl tugging at his mouth. *That had better not be Sklodowska's fucking plan for me.*

As they finished crossing the hill to the Pack Master's tent, Hyatt suddenly wished he hadn't yelled at the Iron. In six paces, he ran through every reason he did and did not believe in the tenets of Sklodowska and the Irons who abide them, until skepticism and doubt were whipping around inside him like a hurricane. Delores and the Cern man rose from their seats and stepped out of the tent to face Rellah and Hyatt, and the sentry by his side let go of his shoulder.

"Still swimming," she said, more statement than question, and a smirk tugged at the corner of her mouth.

"Still swimming," he answered anyway.

"So... you are the toy-carver who stabbed Shelara to death at Vohk Bridge," the man said, his voice like gravel covered in mud and his mint-green eyes looking him up and down as if deciding how many steaks Hyatt could be cut into.

He opened his mouth and turned to look at Delores for help, who was still watching him with her glittering eyes and hint of a smile. Hyatt slowly turned back to face the much larger man, tilting his head up to meet his eyes.

"Yeah... I did that," was all he could manage.

The pack-master reached out and closed his hands around the open flaps of Hyatt's jacket, the leather creaking in his boulder-sized fists. He gave it a shake, a single gesture that seemed to strain the ligaments in Hyatt's shoulders and elbows and spine in every direction all at once. As the Cern man let go, he thought he might collapse in a puddle of disconnected bones and muscles, but somehow he kept his feet.

"It looks good on you, Journey-man Hy-att." The slap that accompanied the compliment nearly knocked him off his feet. "It will be good to you until you are cut out of it."

From the corner of his eye, he saw Rellah lower her head for a moment before looking up again, and realized he'd received some kind of praise or approval from the Cern man. "Thank you, pack-master."

Hyatt hadn't realized the Cern man had been smiling until he saw the corner of his mouth turn down in faltering acknowledgment, but the pack-master said nothing. The quiet gave him just long enough to wish someone had written a book on Cern customs before the Iron cleared her throat.

"The Master Speaker has more business with pack-master Jethrek, and the others will see him back to Brathnee when they finish, but your time and my time here is done. We're leaving for Ceojic Garden, and Rellah is coming with us to represent Moss Wall's interests." She turned to Rellah. "We'll wait for you on the road – meet us there when you have your instructions and your traveling gear."

Rellah turned and spat, the projectile from her lips hitting the earth hard enough to leave a divot in the dirt. If Delores was impressed or offended, it didn't show through the bemused expression on her face. The Iron started down the hill and nodded to Hyatt as she passed, and he stumbled to keep up with her. A shadow passed over him and without the telltale call to go with it, it took looking up through the canopy of the forest and spotting a wingspan to know it was the same carrion-bird circling.

When they were out of earshot from Rellah and the packmaster, he grabbed Delores' sleeve. "I'm not going to Ceojic Garden!"

She let him hang on to her sleeve, and suddenly he felt like a little kid nagging at his parents about something ridiculous. Hyatt uncurled his fingers and as he stumbled again, he wondered how she walked so effortlessly through the woods while he felt like he was hurrying to keep up. There was no sound behind him but he knew Rellah didn't need to make any to appear within arm's reach so he looked back, relieved not to find her murderous glare inches away.

"Why are we going there?" He asked, realizing too late as Delores smirked that he'd changed his position from refusal to a search for rationale. "What does Ceojic Garden have to do with the ambush on Vohk Bridge?"

"Go say your goodbyes to the Brathnee workers, if you need to. You're not likely to see any of them again," she replied.

It wasn't an answer, but the gravity of the Iron's caustic remark crushed his need for an explanation to dust. Delores lingered at the bottom of the hill and inclined her head towards the base of the cliff where his Brathnee companions sat together.

Hyatt hesitated, suddenly unsure of what to do, but as he looked past them to the Cern that guarded the tent where their weapons and packs were piled, he realized he had no choice.

"Get your things," Rellah growled at him as she passed on her way toward the tent. "Let's not keep the rotted Iron waiting – I'm looking forward to forgetting your names."

NINE

It was an hour into Delores' and Hyatt's walk from the Moss Wall Pack to the road between the Gardens of Brathnee and Ceojic before she said anything that sounded like an explanation or a goal to him. Until she spoke, he'd resigned himself to staring at every shifting shadow and swaying bush – without the protection of the other travelers, everything he couldn't immediately see seemed more dangerous. As he stepped over exposed roots and followed the Iron around depressions filled with standing water, he dwelled on how every new moment seemed more dangerous than the last and wondered how long that would continue.

"The Cern who attacked you weren't Moss Wall Pack – at least, not anymore." The Iron stepped around a tree trunk like it was obstructing a specific line she was trying to walk. "They'd been Severed, banned from staying in Pack spaces. He was a little evasive about the reason but when he last saw them, they were headed towards Ceojic Garden, and they didn't have a Turning Weapon with them."

"So they got it from the Garden?" Hyatt's brow furrowed and he shook his head, rejecting it out of hand. "That doesn't make any sense."

Delores spared him a glance before focusing on the way ahead. "No?"

"No. It doesn't." Hyatt turned it over in his mind as he talked, and every new word was more concrete. "There is no way the Garden wouldn't have turned over a Turning Weapon to the

Keepers, and they definitely wouldn't have given it to a Cern. There's... no, it's impossible. No way."

The Iron nodded as he spoke, seeming to take in his points. "So if they didn't have it here, and they didn't get it there..."

The unasked question lingered between them and as Hyatt searched the gaps between the branches above for another glimpse of the bird that seemed to be following them, he tried to fill in the space left open. The sun had passed its apex and shone from behind them, striking the foliage at just the right angle to bring a hundred shades of green and yellow to life while deepening the shadows that stretched out in front of them across the forest floor.

"Maybe they ambushed Keepers carrying it?" He darted his eyes towards the Iron to validate his theory, but she wasn't looking his way. "And if they did... the Garden might have heard about the attack... so we're going there to look for a lead."

From a step ahead, Delores looked back over her shoulder at him. "That's a really good idea. Let's do that."

"They didn't ambush your Keeper weeds, Hy-att," Rellah said from just a step behind him, close enough that she could grab him by the back of his collar.

"What the fuck!" Hyatt jumped and spun around, almost falling into the nearby bush. "Don't do that!"

"We don't bother your strange little packs of scavengers," she continued as if she hadn't almost scared him to death, walking by him to take up a place beside Delores. "They're off-limits."

He hurried to catch up and almost asked what Rellah meant, but realized she disliked him so much she preferred the Iron's company to his and decided not to make things worse. He fell into step behind and between them, trying to ignore the soreness in his shoulders from the weight of his pack and the reality of how far they would have to walk to the Garden. The soles of his feet felt hot in his boots, and he noticed for the first time that one of his laces was fraying, and the thought of it snapping consumed him until the carrion bird overhead called out again to steal his attention.

"I hate this," he muttered to himself, tugging at the straps of his pack to adjust how it rode on his back.

The three of them walked together quietly for the next hour. To Hyatt, the Iron seemed completely at ease, taking in the Reclaimed with a comfortable awareness but unafraid of anything it held. By comparison, the tension and animosity that poured from Rellah radiated in waves. Delores didn't seem to notice, but it was powerful enough to make Hyatt feel like it was a gale-force wind. He had no idea how the Iron either didn't notice it or didn't mind, and the thought of finishing the walk to Ceojic Garden filled him with dread.

They got just close enough to see the road when Delores slowed to a lingering stop. At the same time, Rellah bent her knees a little and looked up through the branches above, her hand settling on the end of an arrow in her quiver. Hyatt opened his mouth to ask what was happening, when a violent downdraft buffeted him and knocked him off his feet. He landed on his back and the air left his lungs in a heaving gasp, and they refused to refill as he tried to suck breaths through his open mouth.

"What the... fuck was..." he wheezed when he could force sound from his throat, his eyes bugging from their sockets.

Rellah rushed to brace her back against the broad trunk of an elm and somewhere between where she started and where she stopped, she'd knocked an arrow. Delores stood in the open and drew the weapon on her hip, the sound of sliding steel echoing off the trees all around her as the blade broke free of its sheath. Hyatt only caught a glimpse of the wide weapon and the section of vicious-looking teeth just above the handle before another down-gust slammed into him and knocked him flat again.

"Lay still!" Rellah shouted as she drew her bowstring back and pointed it skyward, her voice falling to a whisper. "Come here, Skar…"

She didn't finish the word but as Hyatt spread his arms and legs across the forest floor and nestled his chest and cheek into the dirt, the thought coated his heart in frost all the same. *Skarren!*

The shadow that passed over them covered thirty paces of ground, and the sound of flapping wings rumbled like thunder. It shook every branch as far as Hyatt could see and whipped at his jacket like sheets on the clothesline. He could feel the leather strain across his shoulders as if the gusts were trying to shred it against his body. He crawled closer to the nearest tree and wrapped his arms around it, looking over his shoulder and trying to catch a glimpse of the massive creature.

The rumble of the Skarren's wings was replaced by the deafening roar of branches and treetops shattering. Splintered limbs plunged down all around them, embedding in the ground. They fell like deadly rain destroying lower branches and leaves before slamming into the earth. Hyatt pressed himself to the tree trunk and covered his head with his hands as if his jacket could stop one of the massive, sharp spears from tearing through him and killing him instantly. Amidst the roar, he heard the thwack of Rellah's bowstring.

He didn't know how long he cowered against the tree before he realized the danger had passed, but when he looked up, Delores was sheathing her weapon. In a jagged ring around her, broken branches with springs like deadly thorns stuck upright in the ground. Rellah's bow was lowered but not at rest beside her, and her other palm rested over the remaining arrows on her quiver.

"Is it dead?" Hyatt's voice was hesitant and strained.

Rellah's eyes stayed focused on the sky as she turned, but slowly she finished lowering her weapon and she shook her head. "If it was dead, it would have shook the ground when it landed... even a baby like that one."

Even through the chaos and his panic, incredulity still managed to punch through, and he spun away from the trunk with his eyes wide. "That was a baby? That was... a baby!"

Delores grabbed one of the embedded branches with both hands and wiggled it back and forth until she could pull it out of the ground, then tossed it aside. "Yes. Three, at the most."

He walked towards her but flinched and looked up as something shifted in the trees above him. When he recovered, Rellah was headed toward the Iron as well. The three of them converged in the carnage of the Skarren's low pass through the treetops. Hyatt focused on the cracked and fragmented ends of the branches still stuck in the ground, imagining the sheer force required to snap limbs five and ten inches in diameter. Deep lines carved through the bark around the broken wood to reveal white wood green with sap, and he couldn't envision the talons that made those carvings.

"Now what?" Hyatt traced his finger along one of the deep slashes in the branch closest to him.

"Now, we keep moving to the Garden," Delores replied, and Rellah nodded in agreement.

He looked back and forth between them, unable to comprehend what they were saying. As they turned to start walking towards the road, he stood still and stared after them. By the time he broke himself free of where he was rooted they were ten paces ahead, and he rushed to collect his pack from where he'd dropped it.

"We just... keep going?" His words came out between gasps as he caught up with Delores and Rellah. "With that thing still up there?"

The Iron smiled at his utter shock but said nothing, and Rellah shrugged. "That thing was always up there, Hy-att. Nothing has changed, except you are afraid now, and that has not changed either. You are afraid of everything."

Rellah's casual delivery of her disinterested assessment of him somehow made it hit harder than if she'd been condescending or hateful. Hyatt bristled but it faded on a wave of helplessness – he wanted to argue but couldn't, and he wanted to fight but he knew she would kill him without breaking a sweat. He settled for stomping harder as he walked, but that made him feel like a petulant child so after a few paces he stopped that too.

"Fear keeps us alive," he muttered in half-hearted protest. "It stops us from doing stupid things."

Neither of the women answered him and he walked quietly behind them. The stairway to nowhere appeared and Delores said something to Rellah who scoffed, but he couldn't hear what it was. His eyes lingered on the doorway at the top of the stairs and the carrion bird sitting on the sapling that grew from the step. The bird seemed to notice him and stared back with one black, beady eye, its head moving in little, twitchy motions to keep him in sight. He wondered what the corpse-feeder knew that he didn't.

They reached the road and Hyatt looked left as if he could see the walls of Brathnee Garden where the road disappeared, but he followed Delores and Rellah as they turned right. They walked quietly as the sun disappeared behind the treetops and started to dye the sky shaves of peach and lilac. The wind got colder and seemed to cut lower across the earth, slipping beneath the branches and clinging to the ground as it turned over dead leaves and shook the bushes on either side of the path. Hyatt pulled his jacket tighter against the chill.

They had walked for hours and the light was almost gone when Rellah slowed down and nodded to the side of the road. "We should camp."

"How far is it to Ceojic Garden?" Hyatt called after Rellah, who hadn't waited for confirmation before stepping off the path.

"About two days' walk," Delores replied as she passed him.

The Iron's words hit him like a sledgehammer. "Two days?"

Delores didn't turn around but held two fingers up over her shoulder. Hyatt sighed and tromped off the path after them. Rellah led the way to a space thirty paces away from the road and set her pack down. Seeing her offload her pack made Hyatt's own backpack feel twice as heavy and he grunted in relief as the straps slipped from his shoulders, the bag hitting the ground with a careless thud. As he knelt down beside it, he cast furtive glances at his companions to see what he should do next. Rellah was unrolling a blanket that looked like it had been made for sleeping on the ground, and Delores had begun collecting branches in a pile. He rifled through his bag until he felt his blanket at the bottom and tugged on it until it came free, dumping socks and gloves on the ground as he fought with it. When he'd laid the blanket out, he looked over the scattered contents of his pack that seemed so important when he left home, but instead looked like extra weight he'd never find use for. With a sigh, he hurried to shove the rest of his things back into his pack and hoped neither Delores nor Rellah had noticed his clumsiness.

Hyatt's last waking memory was the first waft of smoke from the fire Delores had made, and then the exhaustion and fear of the day washed over him like a broken dam and dragged him under. He didn't dream or move, and woke facedown with an arm completely asleep and the wrinkles of his blanket creased into his cheek and forehead. He groaned as Delores nudged him and opened one eye to see her crouched beside him.

"We're leaving soon. You should eat something." She waited until he groaned in acknowledgment and tried to roll onto his side without success, then moved out of his periphery.

Hyatt tried again to roll over and winced as sharp sparks exploded through his arm. He settled for dragging his pack closer and fishing around with his functioning hand until he found a ration wrapped in waxed paper. Tearing it open, he bit into the tacky, caramel-soaked bread and sighed in satisfaction as the flavor hit his tongue. He flexed his other hand a few times to drive blood back to his fingertips and lifted his head to find the other two. The Iron was snuffing out the little fire by kicking dirt over it and Rellah was eating strips of meat from a rolled cloth in her hand. When she saw him look her way, she rolled her cloth around the rest of her meat strips, shoved them in her pocket, and walked over to him.

"You sleep too much." Rellah's voice was flat and she shoved an open hand towards him with such authority that Hyatt had reached up to grab it before he realized what he was doing.

The Cern woman pulled hard and he was propelled to his feet, barely getting them under himself as she let go. He rubbed his shoulder where the force of her pull had almost dislocated it and squinted in the first light of pre-dawn as she returned to where she had been sitting. Rellah had already rolled up her blanket and strapped it to her pack. By the time he'd crushed his blanket into his pack and fastened the straps, Delores and Rellah were ready to move.

With the Iron walking ahead, Rellah settled into a purposeful stride beside him. "Everything you do is slow and soft and afraid. Tell me again how you killed a Cern raider?"

Sleep crusts still clung to the corners of his eyes, and he squinted them closed as he wiped them from his face with a grumble. His legs, still sore from the day before, ached in anticipation of the walk ahead. The idea of spending the whole time with Rellah harassing him made the distance to Ceojic Garden twice as far.

"Why are you here?" He asked instead of answering her. "The Iron said the Turning Weapon wasn't yours."

Something passed over Rellah's eyes, and Hyatt couldn't tell if it was surprise or irritation, but it was gone when she spoke. "Jethrek knows it wasn't ours, but the High Ranger could say anything when the Iron gets there."

"So, you're his... representative?" Hyatt was glad his misdirect worked, and he was happy to keep the focus on her.

"His arbiter," she corrected, her tone sharper than he expected.

"So what happens if the High Ranger says it was yours?" he pressed. "Do you have proof?"

"I have the Pack Master's word." Nothing in her words suggested she saw any difference between what Hyatt had asked and how she replied.

Hyatt walked a little further in silence, trying to wrap his mind around Rellah's statement. The sun began to warm the ground and throw long shadows across the road. Ahead of him, Delores walked with her hands in her pockets as if she had no cares in the world. He wondered how many times she'd walked the roads between the Gardens.

"Have you ever been to Ceojic Garden?" He asked Rellah.

She scoffed like he'd said something stupid. "I'm not a trader, Hy-att."

He puzzled over that for a minute. "Only traders go to the Gardens?"

Rellah turned slowly towards him until their gazes met, a cold smile tugging at the corner of her mouth. "It's the kind of Cern visit your Haleu settlements prefer."

The look in her eyes and the hint of a smirk around her lips felt like a bucket of cold water and nails dumped over his head. He could feel her staring at him after he looked away, and they walked silently beside each other toward the next bend in the road.

TEN

The walls of Ceojic Garden seemed to appear suddenly as Hyatt crested the hill to stand beside Delores, who had come to a stop at the high point of the road. The way ahead sloped down the hill and the settlement spread out across the valley. He expected to feel a cascade of relief at the sight of the pennants fluttering above the towers on either side of the gate, but looking down at the wide gates made him feel a kind of apprehension he hadn't prepared for.

Rellah stopped on Hyatt's other side and closed one eye, held up one thumb so it covered one of the towers, then dropped it to her side with a dry chuckle. "Only Haleu would set up a camp within bow-range of the high ground. Fucking compost."

Delores burst out laughing, throwing her head back and then doubling over. Hyatt watched the woman who had walked into a Cern arrow barrage and stood in the open under a Skarren attack come apart at the seams at a joke he didn't understand, and was pretty sure Rellah hadn't meant to tell. The Iron looked up at Hyatt and the expression on his face redoubled her fits of laughter, and she almost fell over.

Rellah tried to cling to the look of disgust on her face, but the Iron's laughter was infectious. A smile spread slowly across the Cern's face, fighting for every inch of ground, until her grin was wider than her eyes. The Iron gasped for air as the moment passed and dried a tear of laughter from the corner of her eye, shook her head, and started down the hill.

"She's fucking rotted." Rellah's voice sounded like she was saying something complimentary and her smile didn't change, but she stared at Delores' shoulders as the Iron moved down the slope. "Even for an Iron."

Rellah started down the hill as Hyatt's mind tried to catch one of the dozens of thoughts that her comment sparked. He hurried after her to keep pace, wincing as his pack jostled and the strap dug into his shoulder. The loose rocks shifted under his boots and he slid before finding traction. Rellah rolled her eyes at him without breaking her stride.

"Irons aren't Haleu. Why do you hate her?" He noticed the Cern was walking with slanted steps to control her movement on the steep slope and tried to imitate her.

She gave him another look that made him feel like he'd said something stupid but didn't answer him. Together they made their way down the grade until it began to level out. The trees on either side seemed to change, with fewer arrow-straight trunks launching skyward and more low and sprawling limbs dotted with small white flowers. A pair of thrushes wove and turned between the trees, wings humming as they flapped too fast to see.

Enough time had passed that Hyatt wasn't sure what Rellah was talking about when she spoke. "Are you that dumb, Hyatt?"

"What did I do now?" he snapped back.

"Do you know how many Cern that woman has cut down?" Rellah shook her head. "You could fill one of your stupid gardens with them."

Hyatt found himself looking at the back of Delores' jacket before he realized what he was doing. She'd plucked one of the white blossoms from a low branch and held it under her nose as she breathed it in, then discarded it with a twirl of the stem. The petals pinwheeled slowly over the edge of the road to the floor of the Reclaimed where it landed stem-first, then tipped over to lay on its side.

"Her?" he asked, trying to envision it.

"Probably," Rellah shrugged as if the specifics were irrelevant. "The Iron of Water-Edge murdered every woman able to carry a child in the Western Reach Pack – they lost an entire generation. The Iron of the Broken Mountain killed every Cern in the Black Shore Pack – even the children. That's who they are – Sklodowska's little butchers."

As she talked, Hyatt watched Delores. With her plucked flower gone, she walked with the same carelessly confident stride she'd had since he'd met her. One hand rested comfortably on the handle of her weapon and the other swung in gentle, idle motions like branches in a soft breeze. The morning light made the stray locks from her loose braid turn shades of heated metal, pale yellow and burnt orange whispers in the air around her. Moments before it would have looked almost spiritual to Hyatt, but with Rellah's words in his mind, it looked like a halo of destruction.

"That can't be right." Hyatt shook his head.

"Why do you think your High Rangers defer to their Irons?" The Cern countered. "Why do the nine most powerful Haleu alive listen when they talk?"

"Because the Iron Accords—" he started to reply, but the words sounded hollow in his own ears.

"And how did eleven Irons get ten Gardens and twelve Cern packs to agree to every one of their demands?" she cut him off.

"Nine Gardens." Hyatt realized it was a strange detail to focus on, but the only one he was certain about.

"Yeah, now." Rellah's voice managed to be condescending and pointed at the same time.

Delores slowed down as they neared the gate, turning back to see how far away the pair were. "Are you ready?"

Rellah smiled again, an expression devoid of warmth, and Hyatt waved as they closed the distance. "Ready."

Delores reached within her jacket and unclipped the three metal plates that hung from her belt like a ladder. Hyatt watched her hold them up as she approached the gate, the light glinting off the three flat silver panels that identified her as an Iron. Moments later, the giant locking mechanism on the gate shifted and the doors began to part. By the time they reached the threshold, the massive barriers were open and two people were walking towards them with knee-length black jackets furling around them.

"Lady Iron, your visit is unexpected," the taller one said as he pulled his hood back to reveal a shaved head and hazel eyes, pausing before he continued, "but always an honor. I'm Arter. Ceojic Garden welcomes you."

"I'm Delores, Iron of the Eastern Reach. Thank you, Arter." She walked up to him and looked him over, taking in the twin fighting sticks tucked in his belt and the Journeyman Security braid just beyond the end of his cuff. "And it's just Iron. The Lady part is unnecessary."

He cleared his throat. "Of course. My apologies. Who are your companions?"

The Iron took a step back and gestured to them both. "This is Rellah of Moss Wall Pack, arbiter for the pack-master. This is Hyatt, once of Brathnee."

Hyatt nodded as she began to introduce him, but blanched and shot her a confused look as she finished her statement. *Once of Brathnee? What the fuck?*

The shorter Security worker had been studying the jackets Rellah and Hyatt wore, and as Delores finished speaking, she leaned closer to study Hyatt's features. "You're Haleu?"

"Yeah," he replied, glaring at Delores. "First of Brathnee, seven roots deep."

The Iron rolled her eyes and started walking, and the two Security workers hurried to flank her on either side. Rellah and Hyatt followed them over the threshold. The gates rumbled like a rockslide as they started to close behind them. When the gates met it sounded like a peal of thunder. Hyatt couldn't help looking back at them and was startled to realize he felt more trapped than safe. He told himself it was because he didn't know Ceojic Garden. As they walked he noticed two Apprentice Security workers leave the gate ahead of them, and knew the whole settlement would know an Iron had arrived.

Rellah leaned closer as they walked behind the Iron and the two guards. "Notice how your warriors keep their eye on the Iron, and not the Cern raider."

"It's an honor," he hissed back at her. "Shut up."

She shrugged and slapped him on the shoulder. "Hang on to that."

They moved through the garden and Hyatt took in the sounds of the new space, the shuffle of carts and the hum of livestock milling in their penned spaces. Workers on their way to their assemblies and workspaces looked them over as they passed, and Hyatt imagined what they saw, two road-worn people in Cern jackets and an Iron in the company of two of their own Security workers. It made him wish there was a place to wash the dust and dirt from his face and hands, but another part of him that didn't care attached himself to that unfamiliar thing inside him that felt trapped by the Garden walls.

"High Ranger Kestianne is managing Garden affairs at one of our assemblies," Arter volunteered. "Would you like to wait for her at the Gloratt?"

Delores shook her head. "Take me to the assembly. I'd like to see her right away."

Rellah shot Hyatt a meaningful look, but he ignored her. They crossed through the Garden to a large structure. As they drew closer, sounds of rising and falling voices and bursts of laughter became clearer. Lights through the windows shifted as people moved back and forth inside. When they reached the door, Arter turned to block the way.

"If you'd wait a moment, Iron Delores, we'll let her know you are here," he said.

"I am absolutely sure she already knows." Delores laughed and stepped around him, patting him on his shoulder. "Leave your packs outside."

Arter opened his mouth to mount a counterargument, but before he could, the Iron was through the door. Hyatt shrugged at the Security worker helplessly as he dropped his pack against the wall and followed her inside. He blinked as his eyes adjusted to the dimmer light of the space.

Dozens of Ceojic workers churned and jostled in the assembly beneath a scattering of caged bulbs hung from the ceiling at uneven heights. The rustle of papers formed a persistent murmur, and Hyatt noticed most of the people near him held crushed sheets of paper in their hands. He couldn't make out any singular voice amidst the rising and falling voices, but suddenly everyone was erupting in laughter again. It felt frenetic, positive, and aimless.

From the moment the first Ceojic worker noticed Delores, a ripple spread through the crowd. The shifting masses continued to jostle except near them, where the workers became more still and parted to create a path through the large, crowded room toward the center. The Iron walked through the aisle that appeared before her until the inner edge broke and she was standing before a woman about her height facing away from her. Hyatt lingered in her wake and wondered if the crowd would collapse back together.

"High Ranger, I'm Delores, Iron of the Eastern Reach," she said.

The woman was halfway into a sip from a cup in her hand and looked up at Delores' voice. Her eyes lit with the spark of recognition and she raised a finger to ask the Iron to wait, then stepped on a wooden box and rocked it under the sole of her boot to ensure it was stable. Satisfied, the High Ranger stepped up onto it, so she stood a head above the rest of the assembled workers.

"Ceojic, we have an important guest, one of our own, come home!" she called out, lifting her cup and her open hand to quiet the crowd, and waiting for the roar to fade to a murmur. "It's been nearly a year since an Iron joined us in the Garden, and much longer since one came from as far as the Eastern Reach. Give us the room, would you?"

The sound in the assembly shifted as she spoke and fell to a hushed murmur as they filtered around Hyatt on both sides like he was a stone in the middle of a river. Rellah leaned against the wall beside the door and matched gazes with anyone who looked at her until they either looked away or disappeared through the doorway. As the last dozen workers were slipping from the large room, the High Ranger stepped down off the box.

"I heard you'd been Whispered for," Kestianne said, the showmanship gone from her voice as she shook hands with Delores, then pulled her in for a crushing hug. "They must have had a hell of a time finding you."

"And you... High Ranger of Ceojic. How did that happen?" the Iron shook her hand twice and then let it go.

"I'm a likable woman." The High Ranger shrugged. "Is it too much to hope that you're here because you've heard another name Whispered?"

Delores smiled and shook her head. "No, my time as an Iron isn't over just yet. A Cern raid in Brathnee turned over a breach of the Second Warning, and the path to it led me here. I'm hoping you can tell me where some Severed Cern got their hands on a Turning Weapon."

Kestianne's eyes widened and she took a step backward. "You think it came from here?"

The Iron met her gaze for a long moment before responding. "Did it?"

"No, of course not!" The High Ranger raised her voice, and Hyatt couldn't tell if it was anger or disbelief that fueled her. "We were little sprouts together, Dee! Do you really think we're over here breaking Warnings? Trying to start the end of the world?"

The Iron let the High Ranger's remark hang in the air, and Hyatt began to realize it was one of her favorite tactics – she let the silence eat away at the edges of a sentence until it lost something and became manageable. It reminded him of campfires, blazes burnt down to coals by letting the air devour the branches without adding any fuel. Rellah pushed away from the wall to join him, her boots thudding softly across the wooden floors until her shadow was merged with his.

"Gardens can be planted with intention, but there's no helping what grows in their shade," Delores replied. "No, I don't think you or your council has a stash of Turning Weapons. I'd like to talk to some of your people, see if we can pick up the trail."

The High Ranger visibly relaxed as she nodded and gestured to the room. "You can use this assembly. Anything you need – tables, food, housing. I'll find a Provisioner to see to you and your... friends? Traveling companions?"

The Iron followed Kestianne's gaze to Hyatt and Rellah, and she smirked. "Something like that."

Hyatt stepped forward and offered his hand. "I'm Hyatt, first of Brathnee. It's an honor to meet you, High Ranger."

"I've heard good things about the Line network you're building in Brathnee." Kestianne shook his hand, nodding in approval. "Maybe someday it will reach Ceojic Garden."

Rellah looked the High Ranger up and down like a prospective opponent. "Your warriors let me come in here with my bow. You should fire them. Or kill them."

Kestianne raised her eyebrow. "I'll take that into consideration. Who are you?" "I'm Rellah, arbiter for Moss Wall Pack." She hooked her thumb in her belt, a pose that reminded Hyatt of Jenna on the Line-repair mission. "The weapon wasn't ours, and I'm here to deal with anyone who says it was."

"Well, let me put your mind at ease, Rellah. No group of Cern came to Ceojic Garden together, Claimed or otherwise. We had a trader three weeks ago and two more, a few weeks before that. None of them came in with a Turning Weapon." She turned to Delores. "I'm certain of it."

"Good." Rellah's nod was curt, more confirmation than gratitude.

The door to the assembly creaked and a man appeared. He made eye contact with the High Ranger and gestured to her. Kestianne held up a finger for him to wait and turned to look over the three companions, her eyes clouded like she was trying to make sure she hadn't forgotten anything. She looked to

Delores last and gave her a quick hug, then stepped back and cleared her throat.

"Iron of the Eastern Reach, we in Ceojic recognize the Accords. The Garden welcomes you. One of my Provisioners will be here shortly. Sklodowska guide you, and all of us." The High Ranger's voice had become more formal but as she passed the Iron, she closed her hand into a fist and bumped her knuckles against Delores' hand with a half-wink.

They turned to watch until the door closed behind her, leaving them alone in the large room lit with more than a dozen canary-yellow lights. Delores moved to the edge of the room and grabbed one of the tables pressed against the wall, pulling it behind her to the center of the room like an Apprentice Hunter dragging a slain penny-deer. The two dragging legs made a scratching, vibrating sound as they slid across the wooden floor, and the other two made an unsatisfying thunk as Delores dropped them. She stepped back and studied the placement in relation to the door, turned it a little by bumping one end with her hip, and then stripped off her jacket and tossed it on the near end.

"Well Rellah – you did what Jethrek sent you to do," she said, absently rubbing her shoulder where her pack had been before hopping up on the table. "Your work is done."

The Cern frowned in uncertainty and considered the Iron's statement, turning to pace through the length of the assembly. The shadows from the caged lights passed over her in bands and her fingers curled and uncurled around the handle of her bow in a rhythmic pattern, and Hyatt wondered if it matched her pulse or her breathing. When she reached the end of the room she turned and walked back along the same line but didn't answer Delores.

"I have this really good feeling that I've done what Sklodowska wants from me," Hyatt said without making eye contact with the Iron, "so I'll just join up with the next worker-team headed to Brathnee and go with them."

Delores let her legs swing back and forth from the edge of the table as she leaned back on her hands. "Okay."

He opened his mouth to mount a protest to whatever she was going to say, but her reply registered just in time to stop him. "What?"

"I told you that you will never see Brathnee again." She shrugged. "If you want to race to your harvest, the road is straight from one Garden to the next. I'm going to stay here and see what the workers of Ceojic have to say, and for what it's worth, I think you should too – but I told you before we left that I wasn't going to make you."

Hyatt felt her looking straight at him as she spoke, that direct and focused attention that Jenna, Rellah, and the Iron all seemed to have that made him feel naked and obliterated fog and shadows inside him until the truth had nowhere to go. Part of him was terrified under it and another part bristled in frustration, but there was something else in him too, a craving to be seen that unanchored things he felt were solid. He turned to meet her eyes and she didn't change anything at all, staring back at him with no more and no less intensity than when he'd been looking for anything else to focus on.

"Okay. I'll stay. I still have no idea what I'm doing here," he said softer than he intended to.

"Choosing to swim," she replied, a smirk tugging at the corner of her mouth.

Rellah stopped beside them and looked at both of their faces, her frown deepening in exasperation before settling her attention on Delores. "I am staying too. Until you know where it came from, anyone you meet can tell you it came from my pack, so my work is not yet done."

"Okay, so we're all staying." The Iron replied. "Let's get some chairs, three on each side of the table, and find out where this Turning Weapon came from."

She climbed off the table and they all moved to the edges of the room to collect chairs. Hyatt picked up one and then noticed that Rellah had managed to grab two without letting go of her bow, so he grabbed a second one waddled back to the center table with one under each arm. They had just finished arranging the seats around the table when the door to the assembly opened again. A short, stocky man in a knee-length black jacket stepped inside and blinked as his eyes adjusted.

"Excuse me... which one of you is the Iron of the Eastern Reach?" he asked, his voice higher than Hyatt expected it to be.

Rellah scoffed at the possibility she could be an Iron, but Delores ignored her, stepping towards the man. "I am. You can call me Delores."

"I'm Master Provisioner Walsei. I've sent for three beds, afternoon meals, and writing materials for you and your friends. What else can I get for you?" As he spoke, an older boy stumbled through the door with Rellah's and Hyatt's packs in tow and set them against the wall.

"That's good for now," Delores replied as the boy scurried outside and appeared moments later with the third pack. "Can you put out word that we want to talk to anyone with knowledge of a Warning breach, or anything unusual in Ceojic Garden over the last month?"

"Of course," he replied with a partial bow from his waist. "If you need anything else, I have three Apprentice Speakers working shifts in a chair outside. They can fetch me or my pair, Master Provisioner Garson, at a moment's notice."

Delores thanked him and he made a partial bow again, then turned and left. The older boy followed behind him and pulled the door closed. When they were gone, Rellah moved to her pack and looked it over to ensure it hadn't been opened and everything was still there. When she was satisfied, she stalked back to the group.

"So... now what?" Hyatt asked, looking from one to the other and back.

The Iron walked around the table so she could take the middle seat facing the door. "Now we wait and see what Sklodowska sends us."

ELEVEN

"The Warnings say no capturing people, but Josref locked me in my room and wouldn't let me out." The little girl across the table had an earnest tone and sincere eyes. "I was in there until evening meal!"

Hyatt fought to stop from smirking and beside him, Delores nodded gravely. On her other side, Rellah had a fixed scowl that hadn't changed during the reports of the last dozen workers. The young girl across the table sat very upright and looked very cross.

The Iron studied the ceiling in a parody to consideration, then held up a finger. "The Warning prohibits incarceration. It sounds to me like you were just trapped. Trapped is bad, but not a breach of the Warnings. Go home. Tell Josref the Iron forbids him from trapping you in your room."

The little girl grinned and stood up. "Thank you, Iron!"

She skipped from the room and the door closed behind her, and Rellah stood up in a huff. "Sibling rivalries. Workers missing shifts. Crops growing badly. This is a waste of time."

Delores leafed through the sheaf of papers in front of her, her eyes darting in short, quick movements over the notes she'd taken. "No time is wasted if this is where we're supposed to be."

Rellah scoffed and waved her hand to dismiss the remark. She started to pace again, making use of the length of the hall. Hyatt didn't want to agree with her, but nothing he'd heard all afternoon had touched on the origin of the Turning Weapon.

He wondered what was going through Delores' head behind her content half-smile.

The door opened and a lanky man stepped through, his longcoat over his arm. He made his way to the middle seat across from the Iron and gestured to it in askance. When she nodded, he slid the chair back and took a seat. Rellah stomped over to the empty seat beside Delores and sat down, crossed her arms, and leveled a skeptical look at the newcomer.

"Hello, Iron. I'm Apprentice Shipper Tohger," he said, an awkwardness in his voice as he tried to decide where to begin.

"Hi, Tohger," she replied, her smile broadening with warmth. "What would you like to tell me about?"

"It's just... well, it's probably nothing. It's just... you're looking for where a Turning Weapon came from, right?" He cleared his throat. "That's what Keepers do, right? Destroy the Turning Weapons?"

"It's one of the things they do, yes," she replied, leaning a little closer. "Why do you ask?" "Well, about a month ago, there was a Keeper here recruiting workers. I think he was from the Cloi south of here. Anyway, he said it was for a destruction job, but none of them have come back."

The Iron etched her pen across the top page of her papers and when she reached the end, she paused, tapping the point against the last character as she thought it over. "How long do jobs for Keepers usually take?"

"Not more than a week." He replied.

Hyatt tried to imagine a month outside the protective walls of the Garden. He flashed back to everything that had happened since Vohk Bridge. He expected a wave of nausea and cold fear at the idea of it but felt nothing beyond a tension in his bones that didn't feel like terror.

"How do you know none of them came back?" Rellah asked, her fingertips tapping a quiet rhythm on the edge of the table.

"My pair John was with them. When he didn't come home, I started asking around. None of them came back," Tohger replied.

"Maybe they got killed," she shrugged.

"Rellah!" Hyatt snapped, leaning forward to look around Delores at her. "Stop!"

The Cern matched his posture and her eyes flared. "What did you say to me, weed?"

The knife-edge in her words set Hyatt back a breath, and by the time he mustered a response, Delores intervened. "Both of you, relax. Tohger, I'm sorry your pair is missing. Thank you for telling us about this – I'll let you know if I hear anything."

The lanky man stood. "Thank you, Iron."

She followed him to the door and said something to the apprentice seated outside, then closed the door behind her. Rellah was still staring at Hyatt as the Iron made her way back to the table, but looked up when Delores put both palms on the table across from them.

"That's enough for a day. We're all tired and in a new place. We'll sleep on it and start again tomorrow." She looked at Rellah and then Hyatt. "Rest. Reset."

At the suggestion of rest, Hyatt felt exhaustion crash over him that he hadn't realized he'd been holding back. He rubbed his eyes and tipped his head back over the backrest of his chair, took a deep breath, and let it out slowly. With a groan of effort, he rolled himself off the chair to his feet and walked towards the beds provided by the Master Provisioner. He was grateful the High Ranger had given them the Assembly to work and sleep in, and the mattress and blanket at the side of the room seemed to pull at him like an undertow.

He had just closed his eyes when he heard the bed beside him creak. He wasn't sure how he knew it was Rellah without opening his eyes, but the sound of her arrows clacking together as she slung her quiver over one of the headboard's posts confirmed it. Her proximity made him feel more exposed than he expected and he pulled his blanket tighter around himself, rolling away from her as he heard her shedding her clothes. He crushed his eyes closed, surprised by the imagination of Rellah undressed, and fought to dispel them as he felt the lights in the assembly go out. Moments later, the bed on Rellah's far side shifted as the Iron flopped down on it.

Hyatt opened his eyes, and he was standing on the center of Vohk Bridge under a clear midnight sky. He could taste the cold air and he fumbled for his knife, but the sheath on his belt was empty. He looked down as if he could will it into existence and felt along his belt, but it was gone.

"Looking for this?" Shelara's voice crooned from behind him.

Hyatt whirled and she was there, limping across the bridge with the handle of his knife protruding from her neck. Her mint-green eyes shone as bright as the stars over them, as if they created a light of their own, and stayed fixed on Hyatt as she staggered towards him.

This isn't real. He balled his hands into fists and winced as his fingernails bit into his palm. "You're not real."

"I'm not real?" Shelara's lips parted in a grin and a stream of blood ran from the center of her bottom lip, drizzling onto her shirt. "Then what are you? No home, no family, no friends... what are you?"

Her words hit like arrows and he staggered backward a step, bracing himself against the bridge's railing. "I have a home! I'm first of Brathnee!"

"Once of Brathnee," she sneered, and though she looked like the Cern raider he killed, her voice was Delores' words. "You can never go home."

Shelara reached up and grabbed the handle of the knife protruding from her neck. Hyatt lurched at her with a wide swing but her free arm entangled his and then they were locked in an embrace. He was so close he could hear the slick, crunching noise as she pulled the blade from beneath her collarbone and through the meat of her chest and shoulder. He felt the edge pull his jacket open and press into his side, and he screamed.

"Hyatt!" Rellah whispered over his face, shaking him. "Wake up!"

His eyes snapped open and he flailed, swinging at Rellah. She deflected his arms without any effort and slapped him once, hard, stunning him. He caught his breath and blinked, realized he was looking up at Rellah, and heaved a sigh as he settled back against his pillow. She sat on the edge of his bed and grabbed his chin, turning his head toward her and down and prying at his upper eyelids to force them open. He spasmed and reached for her hands but she smacked it away again, looking at his eyes for a long moment before releasing him.

"Sometimes the dead stick to us," she said softly.

Hyatt blinked to stop the sting in his eyes, Rellah forcing them open compounded by unexpected welling of tears at her gentle tone. He forced himself to nod so she knew he had heard her, and hoped she couldn't see the streaks on his face in the dark.

"The best thing to do is give them lots of company," she continued with a half-smile. "Let them play with each other and leave you be."

There was a compassion in her grisly advice that made Hyatt's heart clench unexpectedly, and he nodded again. Rellah pressed her hand to his face again and turned his head away from her, and he let his cheek rest against the pillow where she put it. He felt the bed shift as she stood and padded quietly back to her own, and closed his eyes to try and sleep.

Hyatt woke without dreaming again to the sound of Delores preparing her pack for travel. His muscles felt heavy with sleep, as if neither his nightmare nor his words with Rellah were real. He looked to Rellah's bed and saw it was empty as well, and pushed himself upright with a grunt.

"Good, you're up!" Delores said when she caught his gaze. "We're leaving for the Cloi, as soon as Rellah gets back."

"We are?" He asked, pulling his pack closer and fastening the straps. "Why?"

"The visit from the Keepers, the missing workers..." Delores pulled her weapon from her sheath and looked it over, then drove it back into its home. "That's the path. We'll find what we're looking for there."

Hyatt nodded and started to reply, but his attention was stolen as the door opened and Rellah walked in. The opening of her jacket showed she had forgone her shirt and he flashed back to the silhouette of her sitting naked on the side of his bed, and immediately found himself studying the rafters of the assembly.

"Here, Hyatt." She shoved a warm package of waxed paper into his hands, then lobbed a second one to Delores who caught it. "Eggs and charred meat, fresh."

He unfolded the top and picked up a clump of the scrambled egg, devouring it as Delores shed her jacket and pulled her woven shirt over her head. As she did, he noticed scars down the right side of her ribs that he hadn't seen before. He flashed back to the lines on Jenna's head and suddenly the space between her world and his seemed like a giant chasm again, but the flavor of the salted breakfast erased every thought but the way his mouth watered.

"This is amazing," he said with his mouth still full.

"Your Provisioner called it onion-salt," Rellah replied off-handedly, picking up a pack that she'd closed before heading out. "He gave me some for the trail. I think he wants to pair."

Delores' laugh at Rellah's theory was wry as Hyatt devoured a strip of charred brisket. "No time for pairing. The Rail leaves for Leshtara Garden in an hour and the Provisioner has promised us space. We should be able to jump off near the Cloi and save a lot of time."

"The Rail? Leshatara?" Hyatt jammed the last of his eggs into his mouth and stood, crumpling the wax paper into a ball. "How long have you been awake?"

"Since right after you went back to sleep," Rellah answered for her, shooting the Iron a sideways glare.

"I wake when She tells me and go where She says," Delores replied with a shrug, then took a bite of the meat in the wax package she was holding. "This really is good."

As Hyatt stood and hefted his pack onto his shoulders, he made a commitment to not always be the last person ready to go. Delores led the way out into Ceojic Garden, where the Apprentice Speaker with the morning shift pulled his hood back and greeted her with a half-bow. He led the way through the shops and houses to the working assemblies. Hyatt found himself walking beside Rellah and behind the Iron again, and uncrumpled his wax-paper ball to offer her what was left of the charred meat. She looked at it and then at him, then shrugged and grabbed the strip. He tossed the paper into one of the fire barrels between shops and she swallowed the strip of brisket in two gulps, then nodded to him in something that might have been mistaken for gratitude by anyone else. Hyatt took it as the conclusion of a transaction.

After almost an hour of walking, they turned a corner and spotted what looked like another gate. Hyatt looked over his shoulder and turned around to get his bearings, then took a few steps to catch up to Delores.

"Is that a second gate?" he asked.

The Iron smirked at his surprise. "It is."

"Like... out of the garden?" He tried again, certain he misunderstood.

"If that surprises you, you're going to love the Rail." She patted him on the shoulder. "Brathnee has the Line – Ceojic has the Rail."

Confused, he walked with her as the buildings on either side were replaced with stacks of packaged goods held together by nets. Workers moved between the stacks with check-sheets and extra nets over their shoulders. The Apprentice Speaker led them between the piles of goods towards a worker near the back who was watching a team of workers load boxes onto a massive wooden platform.

"Master Rauld?" the young man called as they got closer, making the supervisor turn toward them.

They crossed their arms and looked over the apprentice and the three travelers in their wake, settling on Delores. "I'm Master Railworker Rauld. You must be the Iron my workers are missing shifts to stand in line for."

She smiled, and Hyatt could almost see the worker's attitude wash off her. "I don't know if I must, but I am."

Rauld nodded but their mouth turned into a frown and as they narrowed their eyes at her, their charcoal eyeshadow caught the morning light and filled their features with judgment. "The Provisioner explained that we won't be slowing down, right?"

"We understand," she assured them. "What are you using on your eyelashes?"

They didn't quite smile, but the corner of their mouth rose to neutral. "The Journeyman Petaler gave it to me. They called it Latch."

"It really works," she beamed. "Where do you want us?"

They stared at her for a moment, then nodded toward the platform. "Load between the second and third brown lines. Don't unhook any straps."

Delores nodded to them and headed toward the platform with Rellah a step behind her. Hyatt waited until they were a few paces ahead and then turned to the Master Railworker.

"Hey... how fast does the Rail go, exactly?" He asked quietly.

"Don't worry," they replied, turning toward one of the nearby stacks of goods. "The Rail barely moves at all."

Hyatt let out a breath he hadn't realized he'd been holding. "Sounds like a long trip, but better that way. Thanks, Master Rauld."

The Railworker didn't reply and Hyatt jogged to catch up to Delores and Rellah, reaching them just as they stepped over a small gap onto the wooden platform. Across the surface, stacks of netted boxes were anchored to the platform by metal hooks that latched to round eyelets screwed to the surface, holding them in neat rows. Every four rows, a dark brown band spanned the platform. Between the second and third band, a series of straps attached to bolts and nothing else, and Hyatt watched as the Iron looped one over her shoulder. He found a space near her and another free strap, leaned back against a nearby net, and pulled the strap up over his arm.

"Will we need these?" he asked, giving it a tug to see how firmly it was anchored to the platform. "Master Rauld said the rail barely moves."

Rellah started chuckling and when he looked at her, it turned into the first full-throated laugh he'd heard from the Cern.

TWELVE

The wind roared around Hyatt, snapping at the straps of his pack so fast they hummed like a thrush's wings. "I hate this!"

On either side of him, Delores and Rellah sat with their backs to stacks of goods with their heads tucked to their chest and their retaining straps pulled across their bodies. The platform underneath them shook violently as it rocketed along the rails beneath it, and the sound was deafening. Leaves and dirt pelted them.

"What?" Rellah turned her head and pressed it against her knee as she shouted the question at him.

In the aisle between the netted cargo, a Railworker with a scarf wrapped over their nose and mouth walked along the platform grabbing handfuls of netting to stabilize themself. Hyatt watched them pass and decided to add heavy gloves and goggles to the things he carried in his pack. The wind consumed the sound of the worker's boots but Hyatt looked up when he saw them stop in their row and tried to nod when the worker gave him a little fist-pump.

The worker kept moving and Hyatt tucked his head between his knees. The rattling platform under him made his legs feel numb and his spine like it was trying to rattle apart, and the retaining strap he clung to bit into his shoulder. The rail turned and he leaned his shoulders into it, shifting his weight to counterbalance the way the platform slanted underneath him until it leveled out again.

A tap on his shoulder made him lift his head and he saw Rellah waving her arm towards the edge of the platform, while the Railworker stood over her making the same gesture. *Oh, you've got to be fucking kidding me...*

He turned towards Delores and tapped her hard the arm to get her attention, and her mess of crimson locks lifted to let her eyes focus on him, then Rellah, then the Railworker. She smiled and slipped the strap on her arm down to her hand, pulling against it to rise to her feet. She slipped her arms out of her pack and let it land on the platform, and Hyatt quickly did the same. He felt Rellah's hand curl into the collar of his jacket and reached for the Iron, latching onto her collar. She started walking towards the edge and he followed, Rellah in tow.

As Delores squared herself with the edge of the platform, Hyatt leaned into her and shouted in her ear, "This is the worst of all your ideas, Iron!"

She didn't answer, but Hyatt felt Rellah's other hand on his shoulder as she climbed past him to grab the Iron's jacket. With a tug to propel herself forward and a hard jump, she cleared the edge of the platform and vanished. Delores steadied herself by the boxes on her side and grabbed Hyatt, pulling him forward while he clung to her back and arm.

"I hate this!" He yelled as she shoved him, hard.

Hitting the ground felt like how he imagined flechettes must feel jerking to a stop in a tree trunk. He bounced and tumbled, and it seemed like his bones were trying to explode out of him in every direction while also tumbling end over end. The world was upside down and when he came to a stop he lay on his back, gasping for air that wouldn't come, with his legs and arms spasming. His head pounded. When he tried to sit up, his whole body screamed in protest, so he collapsed back onto his shoulders and stared up at the canopy of the Reclaimed.

Hyatt had no idea how long he lay on the forest floor, but suddenly Rellah was above him. She was shouting something at him but he couldn't hear her over the bell in his head clanging a monotone note that drowned out every other sound. He blinked and worked his jaw, trying to get it to pop, and with a rush of air he could suddenly understand her, though the ringing continued like an accompanying symphony.

"you almost didn't make it!" she finished, gesturing across him.

He turned where Rellah pointed and fewer than two paces from him, jagged metal posts overgrown with moss stuck out of the ground at a wicked angle. In a flash he saw himself impaled on the four-inch-wide spikes, his lifeless body crumpled and suspended in mid-air. The thought chilled him and he rolled away from them instinctively, pushing himself up to all fours while Rellah dropped into a sitting position beside him. A dry heave racked him and he thought he was going to vomit, while the Cern pulled an herb twist from her pocket and took a calm bite.

"You don't want to do that," she said while chewing. "Eggs smell very bad the second time."

He grimaced at her and sat back on his heels, taking a deep, shuddering breath and willing his nausea to subside. "Thanks."

"No problem." She held out her half-eaten herb-twist.

Hyatt took it without a second thought, biting off a section and letting the ginger mix with his saliva before swallowing. He reached to pass the remainder back to her but she waved it off, savoring the piece in her mouth, and he gratefully took another bite. From ahead of them, Delores appeared carrying their packs under her arms and wearing her own.

"You both made it," she said as she dropped their packs near them, set down her own, and sat on it. "That's great. Anybody hurt?"

Hyatt rocked his neck from side to side to check for injuries. "Just some bruises, I think."

"Good. We're about five hundred paces from the Cloi – it would be a long way to walk with a broken leg." Delores brushed chunks of dirt and leaves from her legs, then dusted her hands together.

Seeing his moment to not be the last to move, Hyatt stood and grabbed his pack even though his back and shoulders still ached from his jump from the Rail. He was adjusting his straps when Rellah picked up her pack and caught his eye, and he suddenly knew something in his face gave his thoughts away.

"Oh yeah?" she said, raising an eyebrow at him as she shouldered her pack.

"What?" He tried and failed to keep his tone neutral. "I'm just- what?"

The Cern shook her head, but Hyatt thought for sure he saw a smile tug at the corner of her mouth. Delores looked at them both and behind her eyes, gears turned, but she said nothing. Instead, she headed away from the Rail into the Reclaimed, her hand on the hilt of her weapon. Hyatt followed and glanced back, unable to help himself.

"You coming?" he asked, fighting a smirk of his own, but Rellah just shook her head again.

Hyatt moved quietly through the Reclaimed and the deeper they walked, the more he began to notice stone structures low to the ground and eroded by time and overgrowth. In places nearly hidden by brush, renegade metal and gray rock rose from the forest floor towards the canopy above. There was not enough remaining to tell if the remnants were once all one structure or several, but they held his attention as he followed the Iron and wove between the gnarled trunks of the old trees.

The amount of light that filtered through the branches overhead changed, drawing Hyatt's attention from the outcroppings of ruins. Ahead, the trees parted around an ancient building that looked more intact than any Hyatt had heard stories of, three floors high and larger than any of the assemblies in Brathnee. Vines climbed the walls and slender branches extended through the openings that windows had once closed. The entire outside of the first floor was consumed in gray and mint-colored moss, and nothing moved in the windows or around the outside of the building.

Delores slowed to a stop and knelt beside a large tree, Hyatt's first indication something might be wrong. He lowered his stance to a skulk and crept closer until he was two arms' length from the Iron and stopped, kneeling and slipping his pack off his shoulders. When it was quietly resting on the forest floor, he curled his fingers around the handle of his knife and waited. Out of the corner of his eye he saw Rellah, swinging wide around them as quiet as a shooting star, an arrow already knocked on her bow. Delores glanced back and gestured for him to come closer, and he left his pack where it lay as he moved beside her.

"There should be flickering light in those windows," she said, her voice calm and quiet. "Cloi are always lit, day and night."

He focused on the edges of the window openings and saw what she saw – shadows began at the edges of the sill and no light shifted on the stone. Only the branches that reached through the openings moved. Hyatt had no idea what to expect from a Keeper sanctuary, but memories of every time the Reclaimed had been silent and still filled him with a gnawing dread.

"Wait here," Delores said, rising to her feet.

As the Iron walked towards the front door of the ancient structure, Hyatt moved closer to the tree and waited. Her first steps were cautious but as she left the shade of the gnarled rowan tree, they gained confidence until she was walking with her casual and comfortable stroll like she was back in the Garden, one hand on her weapon and the other in her pocket. Even as the knot in his stomach tightened, he wondered at the audacity with which the Iron faced danger.

As Delores reached the door he looked for Rellah, but she wasn't where he'd seen her last. It took a moment for him to look up and spot her on a branch twenty feet up in the air and he couldn't figure out how she'd reached it, but the sound of the Iron opening the door drew his attention back to the building. With a smile and a gesture to wait, she stepped through the doorway and vanished from view.

Hyatt realized he was holding his breath and let it out slowly, watching the doorway. His gaze darted to one window, then another, then back to the door, looking for any sign of movement. Time seemed to stretch out as he waited, listening for the sound of clanging steel or the clatter of furniture being overturned. When Delores reappeared and waved her arm, Hyatt felt like he'd been waiting an entire day. He grabbed his pack and the Iron's and started for the door.

Halfway between where he'd crouched and the door, the smell reached him – a stale odor that carried a waft of hyacinths and bitter herbs. The air seemed not just still but stuck, like invisible sap had found a way to stagnate in suspension. He'd smelled death before, but never so thick. Hyatt curled his lip, his mouth trying to protect his nose, but he pressed forward until Delores held out a hand to stop him.

"It's bad in there," she warned him. "Probably worse than anything you've seen."

When she was sure he'd heard her, she lowered her arm and headed back inside. Rellah caught up with him and dropped her pack outside the door, but pulled a scarf from a side pouch and wrapped it around her nose and mouth. With a look that told him he was an idiot for not having one, she motioned for him to move, and Hyatt headed inside to avoid blocking the doorway. Passing the threshold of the door multiplied the scent and he gagged, leaning against the wall as he fought to breathe.

He could tell that the destroyed timbers and scattered books on the ground floor had once been rows of shelves, but more than two-thirds of them had been overturned. Bodies in cream-colored Keeper robes were scattered across the floor, some caught under the fallen shelves and some draped over them. In between the mostly complete corpses, stray limbs sat in dried pools of blood atop stacks of books. In the center of the room, a slender tree with a twisted trunk grew towards a hole in the ceiling, and three bodies were tied to it with throats cut and chests slashed apart. The sight was a horror Hyatt was unprepared for and he tried to look away, but with every new direction he turned, there were more sprays of red and dismembered parts. Stairs on the back wall climbed to a second floor and half a dozen bodies lay face-down on the steps, killed from behind as they tried to climb to safety.

Rellah stepped over a broken board from a destroyed shelf and ducked under a collapsed ceiling beam before coming to a stop and turning slowly to take it all in. She pulled an arrow from her quiver and slid the tip inside the jagged sleeve of a severed arm, lifting it until the blood that anchored it to a book cover started to lift it too, then set it down.

"The Ram..." she whispered, her voice the closest thing to afraid that Hyatt had heard since he met her.

He couldn't imagine what could have done the damage he saw and tried to speak, almost threw up, and then tried again. "Who the fuck are the Ram?"

Delores took a step onto the stairs and drew her weapon, the blade whispering as it slipped from its sheath. "The Ram are a Cern legend. They don't exist."

By the time the Iron had found her footing through the pile of bodies that blocked the stairs, Hyatt had reached the bottom of the steps and Rellah had begun to climb a broken shelf that led to the remains of the second floor through a collapsed section of wood and stone. He pulled his knife from its sheath and was immediately reminded of how useless it was, and when he began looking among the corpses for something better, he realized there was nothing to find.

"They were unarmed," he breathed, a new level of unspeakable horror dawning on him. "They never had a chance. Who could... who could do this?"

He followed in Delores' wake, stepping gingerly between the akimbo limbs of the corpses that blocked the center of the stairs. A broad band of daylight poured through the hole in the roof, down through the open center of the second floor, to light the scattered books and dead bodies on the ground below. The second floor looked like little more than a broad walkway that clung to three of the four walls, each home to a row of bookshelves that had been destroyed.

Across the opening, Rellah scrambled over the lip of the broken stone and rose to her feet. "There is no one left. We should go."

Hyatt lingered by a window at the top of the stairs and leaned outward, trying to breathe clearer air before continuing upward. His boot caught the cover of a book and sent it tumbling over the edge of the steps, and it landed on a broken shelf below with a rustling thud. He stared after it, then looked at the damage to the rails that ringed the second floor and the places where the construction had broken apart. Everything seemed at once perfectly still and on the edge of collapse.

The Iron ignored Rellah's remark, walking slowly amidst the carnage and the debris with her eyes moving from one place to the next. Hyatt didn't know what she was looking for but did the same, stepping onto the second floor and trying to focus on each severed arm and every overturned shelf individually. He hoped whatever they were searching for would become obvious when he saw it, but the further he walked, the more the destruction seemed to blend into a grisly mural.

"The Cern say a secret group called the Ram hunt and kill Keepers who abandon their calling and Irons corrupted by the service of Sklodowska," Delores' voice was absent as she knelt next to a dead Keeper and rolled her onto her back. "Someone wanted this to look like a Ram purge, but it wasn't, because the Ram aren't real."

As Rellah stepped on a broken shelf, it creaked and threatened to snap, so she shifted her weight off her lead foot and went around it. "Irons like being at the top of the food chain. They don't like thinking there is something else out there."

Across the panorama of death, Hyatt caught sight of something that glinted in the daylight. He considered the explanations from Delores and Rellah as he plotted his course through the piles of books and obstacles of smashed shelves, uncertain of who to believe. That realization hit him with a jolt as he stepped up onto a long board that spanned the distance like a balance beam, and he silently marveled at how much his worldview had changed with less than a week outside the walls of the Garden. The thought that he would weigh the words of a

Cern and an Iron unsettled him. He reached out his arms to maintain his balance as he walked heel-to-toe along the beam and wondered if it was better or worse that he was unsure.

Hyatt reached the glinting metal, half-hidden by a book cover and pinned beneath a broken board. He slipped his knife under the board and pried with it, shifting corpses and other broken shelves in the tapestry, until he could see the three linked metal bars spattered with blood that lay underneath. The shock of it made him stumble backward and he dropped his knife.

"Delores..." he said tentatively, collecting his weapon and sliding it under the board again.

By the time he had the beam lifted, the Iron was beside him. She reached into the cavity and grabbed the cold metal, pulling it free, and Hyatt dropped the debris with a crunching sound. His chest felt tight as he stood and faced her, not knowing what to say as her eyes moved over the symbol of an Iron in her hand. She slid her thumb over the fine patterns engraved on the flat side of the center metal band, her eyes unfocused.

"What is it?" Rellah called from the opposite balcony, making her way through the debris toward them.

Hyatt opened his mouth to reply and then caught himself. Instead, he took a step back and looked around for anything else to focus on. Rellah scrambled over a bookshelf and stepped between two seated corpses with massive gashes in their skulls, grabbing the railing for stability as she turned the corner to approach. She was two paces away when she saw what Delores was holding.

"This belonged to the Iron of the Great Crater." She folded the flat bars over on themselves until they stacked neatly and slid them between her sheath and one of the straps that wrapped around it. "I'm glad you found it, Hyatt. Let's keep looking."

Rellah and Hyatt stood motionless as she moved past him, headed for the stairway. He looked to the Cern, who looked back at him with an indiscernible expression before nodding for him to follow her. With a nod of his own, he turned and stepped over the lower half of a Keeper still wrapped in his long robes and climbed up onto the balance beam again. Rellah headed back the way she'd come, working through the debris to the hole in the floor with careful but confident steps. By the time Hyatt reached the bottom of the steps, Delores was standing in the middle of the room and turning in a slow circle to take everything in. The spotlight of sun made open books and torn pages wash white, but the light felt colder to Hyatt, and he rolled his shoulders to settle his jacket closer around himself. He didn't know what to say so he stood still, watching the Iron.

"What are we looking for?" Rellah asked as she hopped off the slanted board that had served as her makeshift stairs, breaking the silence.

"I..." she began, but faltered and paused, closing her eyes for a moment. "I don't know. I don't know where to go from here."

Without any further explanation, she moved to the door of the ancient building. Hyatt stared after her until she was gone and then started making his way through the bodies and debris, while Rellah took a seat on the edge of the shelf she'd been climbing. As he passed her, she tipped her head back and stared at the opening in the ceiling, as if an answer would reveal itself in the daylight and the swaying branches above it. Hyatt stepped out into the Reclaimed and looked around for Delores, spotting her just as she stepped out of the clearing around the Cloi and into the underbrush beyond.

He walked slowly, letting her keep her lead, and paced himself by searching the forest in every direction. The hanging, stagnant scent of death still lingered despite a breeze that shook the lower branches and rustled the bushes, as if it were too stubborn to be blown away by such a paltry effort. He wondered if the birds and game knew the smell and knew to stay away, and wished for even the squawk of the carrion bird that had stalked them at the Moss Wall Pack encampment, anything to break the stillness that filled all the space around him.

Hyatt found Delores seated cross-legged on the ground, her weapon across her knees and her head bowed over it. He stopped a few paces from her and felt suddenly like he shouldn't be watching her, as if she were changing clothes or relieving herself, but something kept him rooted in place. Her mess of curls hung down like curtains around her features, the longest of her locks nearly brushing her hands where they covered the handle and midsection of the strange blade she carried. It reminded him of the way she'd held the Turning Weapon at Brathnee Garden. Hyatt looked around for a place to rest and moved closer to a nearby tree. He was about to sit down when an arrow screamed through the air beside him, and a bone-rattling screech of pain and anger came from twenty-paces away.

"Veshtrue!" Rellah was running full tilt towards them from the Cloi, her scarf pulled up over her nose and mouth, and didn't slow down as she loosed and fired another arrow past them. "Veshtrue!"

Hyatt's heart hit the roof of his mouth like the upward swing of a hammer and he spun wildly, searching for movement, and there it was – four yellow eyes beneath the knobby brow, leathery skin, and jagged scales of an Heir. "Delores!"

The Iron didn't move, but the Veshtrue did. The beast extended its four legs to rise from its prone position, saplings snapping and brush flattening around it as it opened its six-foot wide jaws to show two rows of teeth the size of Hyatt's dagger. It moved four paces closer in a sinusoidal movement, faster than he would have guessed it could, and Hyatt caught sight of two indigo-fletched arrows in the Veshtrue's shoulder. Another twack from Rellah's behind him made a third blue feather blossom between the first two and the beast roared, its forked tongue lashing back and forth in its open mouth.

Hyatt felt like his boots were rooted in place and his blood had turned to ice. He saw the Veshtrue see him and its spiked tail swept back and forth as its claws clenched in the forest floor, tilling trenches of earth as it prepared to strike. His knife shook in his hand and he nearly dropped it as he stared back at the flat yellow eyes of the enormous creature, and he knew with certainty that he was going to die.

"Climb, you fucking compost!" Rellah screamed at him.

THIRTEEN

The Veshtrue lunged and Hyatt jumped for the lowest branch near him, but the beast's skull caught him mid-air. His body flipped end over and crashed into a bush, branches cracking under the force of his impact and thorns tearing at his jacket and neck. Pain exploded through his back and shoulders and he tried to pull himself free, but every direction he tried to move seemed resisted by another strand of the dense thicket.

"Don't breathe its breath!" Rellah roared from somewhere nearby, and he heard her bowstring twack again, followed by another gurgling roar from the Veshtrue. "Hey! Over here!"

The enormous beast swung the front half of its torso to fix four yellow eyes on Rellah, who stood her ground and knocked another arrow but as it stepped it refocused on Hyatt caught in the bushes. He thrashed against the thicket that refused to let him go and it felt like he was making it worse by struggling, but the sight of the scaled monster the size of a building bearing down on him left him no choice. He yanked at his arm savagely, trying to free it, but the brush held fast. An arrow embedded in the beast's head just behind its eye socket and it snarled, changing directions with terrifying speed and snapping at Rellah.

"That's right, you fucking fossil!" she shouted, that same Cern war-joy Hyatt had seen on Shelara's face radiating from Rellah's eyes as she pulled another arrow from her quiver.

As she drew her next shot back, the Veshtrue spun in place and lashed with its tail. The arrow went wild and embedded in a nearby tree as one of the spikes on the beast's tail caught Rellah in her side, punching through her jacket. The Cern cried out, more roar than scream, and the Veshtrue snapped its tail the other direction. The momentum ripped the spike from Rellah and flung her through the air until she slammed against a tree trunk with an audible crack and slumped over its roots.

"Rellah!" Hyatt screamed, adrenaline coursing through him.

He twisted in place and the thicket began to give way, dropping him to his knees as the Veshtrue turned with a predatory fluidity to focus on the Cern's crumpled form. Her arms and legs writhed in the dirt, struggling to get themselves under her, but the best she could do was crawl another inch from the stalking beast. Hyatt shook his shoulders to free himself of his jacket and fell forward, scrambling in the dirt and stumbling towards the Veshtrue's flickering tail. His knife was lost and he had no idea what he would do when he reached it, but he rushed towards it so desperately that he could barely keep his feet under him.

"Hey!" he shouted at it, "Leave her alone!"

"Hyatt!" Delores' voice called out, "Catch!"

His body was forward of his feet, careening towards the Veshtrue, and he looked up to see the Iron's weapon flipping through the air end over end. He flailed for it and had only a moment to register surprise that he'd grabbed the handle instead of losing his arm to the pinwheeling blade before he lost his balance and rolled across the ground. He forced himself back to his feet and kept running, grabbing the handle with both hands and raising it over his head.

The Veshtrue rose up and opened its jaw as Rellah rolled onto her back, pulled the last arrow from her quiver, and shoved it upward into the beast's torso so hard that the shaft snapped. "Fuck you!"

Hyatt reached the tail of the beast and jumped over the first spike of its tail, then ducked under a second one. He spun as he reached the Veshtrue's back leg and slashed into its calf as hard as he could, and a violent reverberation shot through the weapon to his bones as the blade hit bone. He yanked hard and fell over backward as the weapon came free, the lower serration of the blade ripping fist-sized chunks of meat from the Veshtrue. The leg gave out and it screamed, whirling toward him, and he found himself staring up at gnashing jaws wide enough to bite him in half or swallow him whole.

"Oh fuck," Hyatt stammered, crawling backward from under the Veshtrue as best he could across the uneven ground.

All four of the monster's eyes fixed on him and it exhaled wet breath from its nostrils. Hyatt tried to hold his breath and clamped his eyelids shut to stop the droplets from getting in his eyes, and waited for the feeling of the Veshtrue's knife-sized teeth slicing him to ribbons. His fingers uncurled from the handle of the Iron's weapon as his mind committed to being eaten, and he wondered why he'd ever left Brathnee Garden- in a burst of irrational thought, he doubted Stella or Gorman would ever hear what happened to the Journeyman Artist stupid enough to wander the Reclaimed with an Iron.

A sound like a peal of thunder filled the air and a smell like burning ozone engulfed Hyatt, and he could tell through his closed eyes that the Veshtrue's massive head was no longer between him and the sunlight filtering through the canopy above. He blinked and coughed, opening his eyes to see the hundreds of shades of green and yellow that made up the leaves between him and the sky, and he had never been so happy to be alive. A brilliant flash of violet and evergreen blinded him like he'd stared directly into a sun made from jade and amethyst, and he passed out.

Hyatt felt himself shaken awake and opened his eyes to see Delores kneeling over him. He tried to open his mouth, and the effort to do so made every joint from his toes to his neck ache like his tendons were made of lava. He tipped his head back and gasped for air, his lungs searing and his heart pounding four times faster than he'd ever felt. His body spasmed in rejection of the air and the movement, and Delores let go of his shoulder.

"You have to get up." Her words were matter-of-fact, insistent but almost unconcerned. "The Veshtrue won't stay gone, and we can't be here when he gets back. I need you to stand up."

Hyatt nodded, though he had no idea how he was going to be able to. The Iron stood and reached for his arm. Lifting his own to grab her hand felt like trying to lift a tree trunk off his body. Her hand closed around his wrist and he had the space of a breath to realize how bad being pulled up was going to hurt, and then he was being propelled to his feet. Hyatt grit his teeth to stop himself from crying out and he wobbled as Delores released him. He took a staggering step to get his balance and his head started throbbing.

Delores dug in one of the bags that hung from her belt and handed him a wad of paper bound at the top with wire. "Breathe this in through your nose. It'll help."

Hyatt wanted to ask what it was, but every fiber of his aching body told him to do as she said and so he untwisted the wire as Delores walked towards where Rellah lay on her back. With a glance at the black powder inside and a skeptical look at the receding Iron, he pressed the packet beneath his nose and breathed in as hard as he could. It felt like someone had poured fuel into his brain, let it run down to his heart, and then lit it on fire, and he dropped the packet and wire as his eyes bugged out. A moment later the blazing sensation was replaced with dripping frost like the aloe-salve Petalers gave out for burns.

"What the fuck..." Hyatt shook his head back and forth to dislodge the feeling of drizzling slime in his throat and chest and realized it didn't hurt to twist his neck back and forth. "What is this stuff?"

He realized she couldn't hear him and started her direction, amazed that his legs and back no longer hurt – instead, they felt stronger and more rested than he'd felt since he left Brathnee Garden. He walked faster and then started to jog, his body feeling better and better with every step. By the time they reached Delores and Rellah, it was as if he hadn't been beaten and battered by the Veshtrue. He felt strong, certain, and confident.

Delores grabbed Rellah's jaw and turned her head back and forth, then pressed her fingers to the side of her throat. "She's alive."

Hyatt knelt beside her and peeled her jacket back, exposing the deep puncture in her side that oozed dark red blood in spasming pulses. Her scarf had fallen around her neck and Hyatt snatched it from her, wadding it into a ball and shoving it into the open wound.

"She won't be for long. Give her some of what you gave me!" He felt the cloth saturate in his hands and folded more of the scarf into the wound, trying to stem the bleeding.

"It doesn't work like that." Delores pulled her weapon and slid it under Rellah's shirt with the blade up, cutting it down the center with a single tug.

She peeled the fabric away from Rellah and frowned, then stood and walked briskly toward the tree where she'd left her pack. The scarf began dripping blood as Hyatt pressed it harder against the hole where the Veshtrue's spike had impaled her, and he cursed under his breath. He looked at the unconscious Cern's face as panic built in him, a slow but unrelenting restlessness that needed to act without any way to release it.

"Iron!" He shouted, trying to keep the urgency from his voice. "We need to do something or she is going to die!"

Delores didn't answer, but she walked back to his side with the same purposeful stride and knelt beside him. "Hold her legs."

She held a metal tube in her hand, and she unthreaded the cap. Hyatt moved aside and slung a leg across Rellah's knees, settling his weight on her. Delores pulled the scarf away from the wound and tipped the open tube down, pouring a pale blue powder onto the open wound. It started to sizzle and pop as it hit the blood oozing from the opening, and Rellah arched her back as she opened her eyes and screamed. Her legs flexed under Hyatt as she tried to kick and climb out of her own skin to escape the burning sensation, but the Iron poured the rest of the powder from the tube all over the Cern's exposed side anyway.

Rellah tried to claw at the hole in her side but Delores grabbed her wrists, pulling her arms up over her head while she struggled. The powder began to caramelize over the wound and slowly her violent thrashing subdued, and she passed out again. Satisfied, Delores let go of her and stood.

"What was that? What else do you have in your pack?" Hyatt squinted up at her.

"We'll divide her pack up between us," she replied, ignoring his question. "See if you can find it."

Hyatt lingered at Rellah's side, reluctant to leave her, but the idea of the Veshtrue returning and tearing them apart overcame his need to stay with the unconscious woman. He tried to recall if Rellah had been wearing her pack she had come running from the ancient building and as he looked toward it, he was almost certain she hadn't. With a last glance at the Cern, he picked up his jacket from the bush nearby and set off for the ancient building.

By the time he returned with Rellah's pack, Delores had collected the Cern's bow and Hyatt's knife. "Here."

She held it out to him by the blade and Hyatt dropped Rellah's pack before accepting it, then shoved it into his sheath and worked on opening the pack's straps. "Thanks. Where are we going now?"

"The Great Crater is about an hour..." the Iron paused, looking down at Rellah, "or two, south of here. The Iron was here when the Cloi was destroyed. Maybe they'll know what happened, and where the Turning Weapon came from."

Hyatt felt a dozen concerns start to bubble up inside him before evaporating, and he wondered if he was getting better at living in the Reclaimed or if the black powder that cured his body was suppressing his fear. That thought worried him more, but it too melted away like ice in mid-day sun. As he pulled Rellah's clothes from her pack and shoved it into his own, only one fear was strong enough to hold its ground against his newfound confidence.

"Did the Veshtrue come from the south?" He asked, holding up a bandoleer full of smoke grenades with a shake of his head before shoving them into his bag.

"I don't know," Delores admitted, "but it left to the east. We shouldn't run into that one again."

"That one?" Hyatt felt like her words had slammed him to a stop from a full sprint.

The Iron started to respond but Rellah's eyes fluttered open as her head turned to look up at them. Her body squirmed against the forest floor as she tried to find traction and Hyatt slid his arm under hers, giving her something to pull against as she struggled to her feet. As soon as the Cern was able she pulled away from him but winced as the effort to do so strained her side where the powder had turned mud-brown and hardened.

"Veshtrue are pack beasts," she answered through clenched teeth, shrugging out of her jacket. "There are at least two more of them nearby."

Hyatt thought about how little the three of them had been able to do against one Heir and knew that three of the massive, scaled beasts would have torn them to pieces. "Let's hope they're in the east."

"I'm out of arrows, too." Rellah grabbed one of her shirts from the top of Hyatt's pack and pulled it on over her head. "You can hope we don't run into anything at all."

She put her jacket back on and shouldered her empty pack, then tucked her bow under her good arm. Somewhere near, a bird song floated between the branches, and Hyatt took it as a good sign that for the moment, no giant beasts lay in wait to murder them. Delores picked up her gear and started walking south, and he grabbed his pack and followed.

"Rellah is hurt and out of arrows, the Cloi was destroyed... is this going as badly as it feels like it is?"

She smirked at him. "This is probably a good time to tell you that the Herocaine I gave you is going to wear off in about an hour, and you're going to wish you were dead."

FOURTEEN

Hyatt ducked under a branch and worked his way around a giant root that broke the ground as high as a fallen log, every step feeling like the bones in his knees and spine were splintering to pieces. As the Herocaine faded, the shadows cast by twisted trunks and hanging vines seemed more sinister, and every new sound reminded him that the land he was crossing belonged to the Heirs and he was an unwelcome guest. The Reclaimed had grown thicker and harder to traverse over their first hour of walking, the ground more broken by outcroppings of gray stone and the underbrush denser.

Rellah had walked silently beside him since they'd begun, a tightness to her features that Hyatt hadn't seen from her before. At first, he thought it was pain from the injury but the further they moved through the forest, the more he believed there was something else wearing at her. His eyes strayed again to the empty quiver at her side, wondering if it was her vulnerability that haunted her.

"Ask," she said without looking at him, wincing as she grabbed onto hanging moss from a large branch to help her climb a steeper grade.

"What?" Hyatt hadn't realized he'd been staring and looked away, found a rock to use as a handhold, and scrambled up to the next flat space. "I didn't – I just... are you okay?"

The slope continued upward and Rellah grunted as she forced her legs to climb, grimacing as the exertion sent bolts of pain through her side. "That's what you wanted to ask, Hy-att? If I'm okay?"

Hyatt realized it was a dumb question and hearing her use his words with her derogatory drawl made him like an outsider again, compounding his frustration and embarrassment. He focused on scaling the slope beside her. The ground was solid but constantly shifted between a steep hike and a climb, forcing them to move from one resting place to another between mantling rock shelves and using saplings to pull themselves up. Ahead, Delores moved like a seasoned climber, each handhold seeming to appear where she needed it and never truly stopping as she shifted directions to continue up and onward.

The Iron crested the incline first and stood silhouetted against the pale blue afternoon sky. Beyond her, the broken sickle-shape of the moon hung low over the horizon as though it had forgotten to hide from the sun. Hyatt couldn't help the sense of wonder he felt looking up at Delores, hand on her weapon and more silhouette than detail between the trees. The last hundred paces between him and the crest looked treacherous, but he was excited to see what he thought she could from the top.

Rellah noticed the look on his face as she grabbed another young tree and pulled herself forward to the next place she could stand. "It could have been an Iron that did that, at the Cloi."

He turned to her and almost lost his footing, catching himself against an outcropping of stone and pushing himself against it to rest the thousand parts of his body that hurt. "That's not possible."

Rellah leaned back against the nearest tree and tipped her head back until it touched the smooth bark. She absently pressed her hand against the open wound in her side through her shirt as she took a deep breath, then looked over at Hyatt again.

"No?" There was something bitter in her eyes. "What drove the Veshtrue away?"

Hyatt opened his mouth to reply, but he paused as he searched his mind for an answer. The reality of it seemed to slip from one shadow to the next, refusing to be caught. He flashed back to the feeling of Delores' blade in his hands, the jarring impact as it bit into the bone of Veshtrue's leg, and staring up at the double row of razor-sharp, gnashing teeth. When it came to him, the memory of the blinding jade and amethyst blast resurfaced so intensely that it felt like a dozen needles driven through his irises. He squeezed his eyes closed as tight as he could and pressed his palms against them.

"That's what I thought." Rellah leaned forward and mantled onto the next rock. "She did it."

He shook his head to clear the memory and kept climbing, staying abreast of her as they looked for handholds. "She's the reason you're still alive."

They reached the top of the slope together. The crest was five paces across and dropped off sharply into a crater where no trees grew, fractured rock and raw dirt forming the walls of the round depression. Hyatt stepped to the edge and looked down the steep face of the crater's edge, following the jagged terrain until it started to curve. From the center, a blanket of blue spread along the cracks of the earth and around the rock formations, as if someone had poured frost-blue liquid into the bottom of the bowl and let it expand along whatever paths gave the least resistance. At the heart of the field of blue, an unlit fire pit in front of a lone building sent a spindle of smoke skyward.

'What... caused this?" he asked, unaware he was saying it aloud until he heard his own voice.

"No one knows," Delores checked the straps of her pack and then tossed it down the slope, watching it tumble and bounce along the side of the crater until it slid to a stop. "Older than our known Histories. They say the Keepers found one of the Warnings here."

"I've seen the Low Flowers before," he said, taking in the expansive blanket of light blue petals that shone in the afternoon light. "There's a patch that a Master Petaler tends in Brathnee Garden, so mothers who follow the faith can birth their children within them... but I've never seen so many before."

"They grow wild here, and in every Hold of an Iron. My home in the Eastern Reach was overgrown with them when I arrived." Her eyes unfocused and a wistful look crossed her features. "We're a long way from there now, Journeyman Artist."

He nodded, and it crashed over him how much his life had changed since he left Brathnee. Hyatt unslung his pack and dropped it over the edge like the Iron had, and it ricocheted off a rock and fell through the open air before reconnecting with the crater wall. As it caused rocks and pebbles to cascade in its wake, he imagined each one he could make out was something he used to be certain of – his want for Stella, the safety of the Gardens, his fear of the Cern, and his place in the world. His bag tumbled to a stop a few paces from the Irons.

"Do you know this Iron?" Hyatt unwound the clasp of the braid around his wrist and tucked it into the pocket of his Cern jacket, closing the zipper to trap it in.

"No, but I know of him." Delores' fingertips grazed the Iron artifact still tethered to the outside of her sheath. "I think he'll be able to tell us what happened, and maybe help Rellah too."

She took a seat on the edge of the crater and turned sideways as she pushed away from the rim, sliding on her hip and shoulder on the steep slope. Hyatt stared after her, dumbstruck, as she gained momentum and left a trail of upturned dust and showering rock behind her. He hadn't given any thought to how they would get to the building at the heart of the crater, but as the Iron hit a rock that refused to move and started her body tumbling, he couldn't believe there was no better way.

"Your Haleu women birth children in fields of flowers?" Rellah asked, watching the Iron roll to a stop below.

"The Low Flowers are sacred to Sklodowska. Being born in them blesses you – it means you can be called to be an Iron, and that good things will happen in your life—" he began, then stopped himself. "Do you really not know this?"

Rellah rolled her eyes as she took off her empty pack and smashed it flat, then sat down on it with her legs overhanging the rim of the crater. "Cern have no use for strange Haleu gods and rituals."

He sat down beside her, watching Delores dust herself off and walk across the crater floor towards where their packs had tumbled to a stop, and willing to delay his own slide down the steep slope. "What do Cern believe?"

He expected a quick, sharp response, but Rellah fell silent. He opened his mouth to apologize, but the words wouldn't form for him and he closed it again, waiting for her to reply. She leaned forward over the crater's rim and scraped her boot against the rough terrain to test for traction, sending a shower of dirt and pebbles down the severe drop.

"Cern believe if you're wounded by an Heir, you've been Claimed. It means you can't go home to your pack." Her words were flat, tinged with bitterness and sorrow, but without a quality that invited sympathy. "When an Heir breaks our skin, it does something to our blood – it tells our bodies not to heal, poisons our minds, and draws other Heirs to us. We can't risk being passed to other members of the pack... or to children."

He suddenly wished he'd said something when the moment struck him, because sitting in silence in the wake of her statement seemed to make the moment thicken around them. He didn't know if he should reach out to touch Rellah for comfort or say something funny to break the tension that built like a wall between them. Down in the crater, Delores had reached her pack and was looking it over for damage.

"I can't go home either," he said, quiet but loud enough to be sure she heard him.

Rellah didn't answer him right away, and he wondered if he'd said the wrong thing. They sat side by side on the rim of the crater, watching the Iron put her pack on and walk towards the cleft rock that had stopped Hyatt's bag from tumbling further. In the air high above the field of pale blue flowers, a small hawk tucked its wings to dive before stretching them to full expansion and driving in a lazy, counterclockwise arc.

"You're right, it could be worse. I could be you," she said at last.

Hyatt stiffened in anticipation of the sting of her words but found no steel core to the flung insult. He looked over at her, and she was looking at him with a faint expression that borrowed from the glint in her eyes to hint at a smile without actually forming one with her lips. There was something mutual and close there, and it made the marrow in his bones tingle, just before she pushed him off the edge.

He flailed as an instinct, looking for something to grab onto, but the slope was too steep and his arm dragged across the dirt without finding purchase. A rock caught his hip and rolled him over. Hyatt kicked with his legs, looking for anything to slow his tumble, and when his boot found a crack in the earth, he flipped end over end and started somersaulting towards the bottom of the crater.

It seemed like he fell for hours before friction drained his momentum and let him come to tumbling to a stop. He climbed to his knees and looked up at the straight, almost graceful line of dust trailing behind Rellah sliding down the bank on her hip and forearm with her pack underneath her. The hawk took note of their movement, swooping and circling overhead to decide if they were a threat or a meal. Hyatt made his way over to where Rellah was trying to pick herself up off the crater floor, struggling to rise to her hands and knees.

"Get up, come on – you're no good to us laying in the dirt," he said as he walked up.

The words left Hyatt's lips chased by a spike of panic. Half his brain screamed that he was insane to talk to her like that, but as she looked up through the hair that had fallen in front of her eyes, she was wearing the same rumor of a smile in the lack of tension beneath her cheekbones. She straightened her jacket and picked up her pack, walking towards him with the kind of purpose that made every muscle in his body tense like he was bracing for her impact.

"Careful, Haleu," she murmured, her words heavy with something dark and sticky that he couldn't place, "you didn't think to ask if I was okay. You're starting to sound like Cern."

She walked by him as his jaw fell open and as he turned to stare at her back, he saw Delores crossing the basin toward them. The Iron tossed his pack towards him and it landed in the dirt with a muted jangle.

"Let's go see if he's home." She turned towards the field of ice-blue flowers as Hyatt shouldered his backpack. "This way."

Hyatt followed her and as they crossed the barren earth towards the Low Flowers, he noticed the blanket of petals wasn't as complete as it looked from the crater's rim. Narrow paths wove through the field between the tiny blossoms like bloodshot veins in an eyeball, as if worn in place by little animals running the same routes over and over. Delores walked along one of the paths like a cat, the careful placement of her boots avoiding any disturbance to the delicate petals on either side.

He tried to step into the impressions left in the dirt by Delores' boots, the uneven weight in his pack shifted and almost toppled him over. He reached out on both sides to balance himself and teetered on the edge of his boot, until he felt Rellah's had on his pack to stabilize him. Once he had both feet planted, he shifted his pack back and forth to try and center it. The scent of the Low Flowers, like a saltwater breeze and clean cotton, rose up to meet him as he followed the little dirt path behind the Iron.

They got closer to the building at the center of the basin and the circling hawk plunged headfirst towards the structure's chimney, spreading its wings at the last moment to halt its plummet. With a ruffling flutter, the bird landed on the stone chimney and watched them. Hyatt stared back at it, watching it move inch by inch along the stone in search of the best vantage point to watch all three of them. When the narrow wisp of smoke began to contaminate the smell of the pale blue blossoms and interfered with the hawk's view of Rellah, it hopped back the way it had come to see around it.

"That bird doesn't trust us at all," Hyatt muttered back at Rellah, nodding toward it.

She scoffed. "We walked in from a direction no one should come from, tumbled down the hill, and started walking his way. I wouldn't trust us either."

Delores reached the inner edge of the field of flowers and slowed her stride as she reached the fire pit, holding her hand out to gauge how much heat radiated from the black and ash-gray coals. Hyatt instinctively did the same as he drew near the large circle of rocks that contained the smoldering charcoal but had no idea what the faint warmth meant and dropped his hand to his side. Somehow from behind him, Rellah read the entire course of his thoughts and chuckled at him, causing more heat to rise in his neck than he felt from the smoke and char beside him.

The building walled in the space around the fire pit on three sides, forming a courtyard with the ring of stones and thread of smoke at its center. At the back of the space, the awning of a porch covered the last ten feet to the double doors that stood ajar. The first step creaked as Delores put weight on it and she paused, listening. Hyatt stood still too, except his eyes that shifted from one pillar to another, taking in the ashen stain of the wood and the dingy mold that clung to their tops where they joined with the awning. After a moment Delores set down her pack and slowly, smoothly drew her blade from her sheath. With the point low, barely missing the steps, she climbed the next four steps to the broad timbers of the porch.

Rellah joined Hyatt at the bottom of the stairs. The walls that framed the courtyard on either side held windows with panes of amber glass and Hyatt squinted as he tried to see through them, but the shadow of the roof's overhang and the lack of light from inside made it impossible. Instead, it felt like the windows could see into him.

"This feels like a place we shouldn't be," Rellah murmured, not quite under her breath and not quite to Hyatt.

Delores slid the tip of her weapon into the space between the open doors and pressed the flat of the blade against the left one, and its hinges whined softly as it swung inward. No light bled out of the building onto the porch at her feet and she kept her arm extended as she moved her sword to the inside of the other door, pulling it further open. Overhead, the hawk took off and launched skyward, as if it had lost interest in them.

The Iron stepped over the threshold into the quiet building and Hyatt shed his own pack, then started up the stairs. He felt the weathered board sag as it groaned under his weight and hurried to climb to the porch, each stair complaining as he crossed it. The porch seemed sturdier by comparison, and he noticed some of the boards seemed newer than the steps were. Behind him, the bottom step creaked as Rellah started after him.

"Hello?" Delores called out as she crossed the line between outside daylight and inner darkness. "Anyone home?"

Hyatt paused in the doorway, looking over his shoulder at the row of unlit windows that seemed to be waiting with bated breath to see if he would follow the Iron inside. Rellah caught up to him in his moment of hesitation and turned slowly to stand with her back to him, facing out across the courtyard towards the rim of the crater beyond. Though she was out of arrows and wounded, something about her watching out for them made him feel safer.

In a moment of realization that crashed over him like a falling tree branch, Hyatt pulled his knife from its sheath and handed it to Rellah. "Here."

She looked over her shoulder at him and then half-turned towards him, her eyes tracking down from his face to the weapon in his hand. Her hand reached halfway across the space between them and then hesitated for the space of a breath, the first time he had ever seen her do anything without absolute confidence. The pause vanished so quickly Hyatt wasn't sure he hadn't just imagined it, and her fingers grazed his knuckles as she wrapped her hand around the handle. The touch caused a strange tingle through his forearm and his stomach turned over.

What the fuck is that about? He silently admonished himself, letting go of the handle and feeling her contact with his skin break as she pulled the knife from his grip. "You'll probably be better with it, even with a hole in your side."

Rellah turned the little weapon over in her in her hand and tossed it gently, letting the handle connect with her hand gently. "This is a terrible knife, Hy-att."

Her memory of a smile and her tone shot another spike of chaotic feelings through his sternum and robbed him of a clever response, so he shrugged helplessly and stepped over the threshold into the center section of the building. As his eyes adjusted he saw it wasn't as dark as it appeared from outside, with broad bands of light carving stripes across the room until they hit a wall or furniture. Delores had stepped beyond a curio and around a table with six chairs, her weapon still drawn.

"Iron?" she called out again. "I'm Delores, Iron of the Eastern Reach. I have your Bushehr... are you here?"

Hyatt reached for the wall inside the door and felt the toggle box for the building's light, but when he pressed the round button and felt it thunk into position, nothing happened. He pressed the off-button and then the on-button again, but the lights across the rafters of the central room remained unlit. With a frown, he walked along the closest path he could guess to the one Delores had taken.

The Iron moved through the corner of the central room, a sitting space with a low table in the center covered in loose papers. As she rounded the corner she broke into a run and Hyatt lost sight of her. He rushed after her with a curse under his breath, but stopped short in the doorway of the next room when he saw her kneeling beside a man slouched over a writing desk with a pool of blood expanding in every direction from beneath his chair. As Delores moved, he caught sight of a crude splint tied to the man's shin and the pearl-white glint of bone protruding through his pant leg.

She slid her hand into his salt-and-pepper hair and clenched tight. "Iron! Hey – hey, I need you! Wake up!"

Hyatt took in the amount of dried blood on the floor working backward from the large crimson stain under the slumped man towards the trail he hadn't noticed on his way through the central room. The sheer amount made him certain the man was dead.

"Iron, this is not your time and place!" she shouted in his ear, then picked up his head from the worn desk and slammed it back down so his forehead and nose connected with the hardwood with a crack that made Hyatt wince. "You have not been released from your duty – wake up!"

The man in the chair didn't respond or move, and Hyatt started towards them. "Delores, he's..."

His words dried on his tongue and he stopped as the man sat bolt-upright and gasped for air like he'd surfaced in a lake after minutes underneath. He tried to look around with his hair still clenched in Delores' hand and when he saw her, he leaned away but she pulled him back before he could tip over in his chair.

"You're okay! Hey – you're okay! You're here – you're alive!" she shouted at him as he swung at her arm in an unsuccessful bid to free himself from her grip. "Take it easy!"

The man's chest rose and fell in large heaves but he stopped thrashing against her grip, nodding to acknowledge her. Hyatt fought to breathe as part of his brain told him he'd just seen Delores bring a man back to life, while the rest of his rational thought peppered his consciousness with dozens of alternative explanations. His hands started shaking and he gritted his teeth, trying to retain control of his nervous system while it viscerally rejected the situation he was in. With a staggering step backward, he leaned against the doorway and clung to the edge of the opening for stability.

"I'm Iron Delores," she said in the same tone she'd used in Hyatt's home in Brathnee to pull him out of a drunken stupor. "You're okay. Breathe."

With her free hand, she sheathed her weapon and pulled the three linked bars from straps around her scabbard. Delores set them on the table and pulled them with her fingers as she released them, laying them out at full extension on the crumpled paper underneath them. The man in the chair reached for them, and Hyatt saw for the first time that his forearm was bent in the center at an unnatural angle and three of the man's fingers were no more than bloody sockets in his palm. The remaining finger and thumb rested on the center bar and he exhaled, a sound between content and relief as he dragged them closer to him.

"Iron... your place in Sklodowska's plan is almost fulfilled," Delores said, rising to her feet as the man looked up at her. "I need to know what name was Whispered to you, and what happened at the Cloi."

FIFTEEN

"Rellah, the Iron wants us both," Hyatt called from the central room as he wrestled with the back of three of the chairs at the table, trying to find a way to carry all three in a single trip.

Her acknowledgment was the toss of one pack and then another through the door, and they landed with muted thuds. Hyatt stumbled, off-balance with two chairs under one arm and one under the other, bumping the legs against doorframes and the wall, until he could set them down between the writing desk and the bed that occupied the far end of one of the building's wings. As he drew closer, he caught sight of torn gashes through the front of the man's shirt, with blood caked over his chest and stomach. Hyatt couldn't imagine what it had taken to make it back to the crater from the Cloi in his condition, and trying sent a shiver down his spine.

"... but we didn't see it," the man was saying to Delores, shaking his head and leaning on his broken arm against the desk to support it.

Delores took a seat in one of the chairs and Hyatt took the next one. As the injured man coughed, his lips spattering with blood, Rellah made her way into the room and settled into the last chair. The man at the desk licked his lips and took a shaky breath, steeling himself to continue.

"First, your name," Delores coaxed him, "and the Whisper you heard."

He nodded and his jaw worked to reply, his first two efforts producing no sound before he coughed again and spoke. "My name is... Sawmet... Iron of the..."

"... Great Crater," she finished for him. "I know this is hard, but you can rest soon. What was the Whisper?"

He blinked, his eyes welling with tears, and Hyatt couldn't tell if it was the pain of his mortal injuries or the reality of his own impending death that caused them, but the man continued to try and answer Delores' questions. "The name is... Adeben... I think, in Ceojic."

"Okay. I'll find them." She put his hand on her shoulder and glanced over at Rellah. "In my pack, in one of the outside pockets, there's more herocaine. Can you get it?"

"I'll get it," Hyatt interjected as Rellah started to rise and winced as the motion strained the large wound in her side, but she shoved his shoulder and set him back in his seat.

"I can do it." The edge in the Cern's voice was back and her knuckles were white against the edge of her chair as she pushed herself upward.

A sliver of consternation tried to slip into Hyatt's mind, but there was no room for it amidst the confusion and disbelief at the revival of Iron Sawmet. Rellah limped from the room as he turned his focus back to the two Irons, wondering how the man was even upright. Delores' hand had moved to his knee and she had leaned forward to meet his eyes in his slouched posture, and the man's free arm crossed in front of his stomach like he was stopping his intestines from falling out.

"What happened at the Cloi?" she asked, firm but gentle.

Even from where Hyatt sat, he could see Sawmet's pupils retract to pinpoints as the memory of the carnage flooded back, but he nodded like he knew he needed to answer her. "One of the Keepers... he's rotted. The others didn't... he was..."

His sentence broke up into a coughing fit that spattered Delores with speckles of blood from his lips. Rellah reappeared with a packet of crumpled paper between her fingers and tossed it to Delores, the wire closure glinting in the banded light from the windows as it arced through the air. She caught it and unwound the silver, twisted metal, then held the open packet underneath Sawmet's nose. He breathed in through his nose and tipped his head back, and Hyatt could taste the memory of the bitter numbness in his own throat as he watched the wounded man internalize the medicine. The feeling made him remember how much his whole body hurt and the sensations came rushing back, and he wished Delores had enough herocaine to give him another dose.

Iron Sawmet let a shaky breath out through his open mouth and flexed his fingers as if he was surprised he could feel them, then shook his head and continued. "The other Keepers called for me because one of their own had been hiding things he listed on their register as Destroyed... Turning Weapons, Untethered Communications, Storage Cells. They found a cache of them while he was out on a trip to the Sixth History ruins to the east."

Rellah adjusted in her chair, and something in her posture looked as condescending as she sounded. "So they called you to come murder their little lying thief."

Sawmet turned his shoulders towards her like he was going to argue, but the motion opened a wound across his stomach and fresh blood turned his torn shirt red and wet. Delores shot Rellah a warning glare and squeezed the wounded man's knee to pull his attention back to her. He clenched and unclenched his fingers again and Hyatt saw his fingertips shake as he did, the power of the medicine fighting for dominance over the effects of massive trauma.

"The runner said they found notes in his room – pages and pages of drawings and unfinished lines about an Eighth Warning. When the Keepers confronted him, he lost his mind, they said. Killed two of the Keepers, grabbed what he could carry, and left the Cloi." Sawmet paused and drew another shaky breath that caused his chest to shudder. "Delores, I'm... I'm so tired."

"I know," she replied, inching closer until she was sitting on the edge of her chair and her forehead was almost touching his. "You're almost done, Iron. The end of your path is right there. Tell us what happened at the Cloi."

"I'd just made it to the Cloi, to the library upstairs, when the screaming started... they were everywhere, a dozen Veshtlings and people in duffel coats, bandanas over their faces and bands in their hair... I've never... I've never seen anything like ..." The wounded man braced his hands on his knees to steady himself, and his words slipped through his grit teeth as the light from the windows caught the sheen of sweat on his forehead. "I woke up pinned under a shelf, and a Keeper's corpse. They must have thought I was dead. I have... somewhere..."

Sawmet lifted a hand to gesture across the room, but Delores touched his wrist and pressed his hand back down to his knee, where she left her palm on top of it. "It's okay. We'll find it after. If you can do one more thing for me, you can rest and I promise I'll take care of it, okay?"

He nodded, and echoed, "One more thing."

Delores nodded to Rellah who was still reclined in her chair, her features taut from the constant pain of her wound and betraying her otherwise languid position. "Can you tell her she is going to be okay?"

Hyatt thought it was impossible for the man to look more worn down, but his shoulders slumped forward and his eyes were glassed over as he turned to look at Rellah. "Show me."

"I don't need help." With a mistrustful look at Delores, she peeled back her jacket and lifted her shirt to expose the crusted shell over her round, three-inch wide puncture wound. "It's healing."

"No, it's not." Sawmet shook his head.

He tried to stand but his broken leg refused to support him and he fell forward, landing on his knees in front of Rellah with a thud that made Hyatt wince before he remembered that it would have felt like nothing with herocaine running through him. Sawmet grabbed the edge of Rellah's chair with one hand to steady himself and reached forward slowly with the other one like he was trying not to spook a wild animal, and she didn't pull away as he rested his palm over the wound. Rellah stiffened at his touch and grabbed the back of her chair with a vice-grip to stop herself from pushing him away.

"It's stopped bleeding out, but it's still bleeding in." The injured Iron's words were labored, forced out one at a time in a sentence that wanted to fall apart but held together by the force of his will. "But it will stop now. You're going to be okay... nod if you understand."

Hyatt felt a strange tension building in his shoulders and back as he watched their eyes meet and Rellah nodded, Sawmet's words echoing back through his memories to each other time he'd heard them spoken. There was no flare of light or waft of scent to tell him something had changed, but Hyatt was suddenly certain that Rellah would recover. He searched her face to see if she caught the same feeling, but if she did, it didn't register in her eyes.

Sawmet's hand withdrew from Rellah's skin and he planted it on the chair beside her leg, pushing with both arms in an effort to stand. His forearms shook with the effort and Delores stepped past Hyatt to help him, easing herself beneath his arm and straightening up so he could lean against her.

"Can you... can we go out into the Low Flowers?" he asked her, a pleading note tinging the end of his request and a bead of sweat tracing down the side of his neck. "I'd like to be there."

Delores nodded and looked across Sawmet's arm over her shoulder, but Hyatt stood and spoke before she could. "I'll wait with Rellah."

He pulled his chair out of the way to make room and the two Irons made their way towards the corner and the central room beyond, Sawmet leaning heavily on Delores. Hyatt looked down and was surprised to see Rellah had fallen asleep, her head leaned against the backrest and her lips parted. He looked around helplessly until his eyes fell on the tight-knit blanket on the bed and he grabbed it, gave it a shake, and lay it over the sleeping woman's form. She didn't stir as the surprisingly soft fabric settled over her shoulders, and Hyatt realized it was the most peaceful he'd seen her look since they met. In the next room, the double doors creaked as the Irons passed the threshold onto the porch.

Hyatt moved to the window, dragging his palm across the closest pane to clear the layer of dust built up on the amber glass. Outside, Delores and Sawmet reached the bottom of the steps and passed the far side of the firepit, smoke no longer rising from the dark center that looked like a deep black void through the tinted glass. He was surprised to feel hot tears brimming at the corners of his eyes and blinked to drive them away as distance stripped detail from the two Irons and turning them into silhouettes as they reached the far edge of the courtyard.

He moved along the row of windows to the far end of the room, brushing the cobwebs and film away from the glass. Five paces into the field of Low Flowers, Sawmet dropped to his knees and sat back on his heels, tipping his head back to look up at the open sky. Hyatt expected the tension in his body to fade with Rellah asleep and the herocaine limiting the wounded Iron's pain, but he felt like a wire was strung through his spine as tight as the string on Rellah's bow. His eyes were riveted to the two Irons, and it felt like his stomach was filling up with molten metal as he watched Delores draw her weapon and a glint from the sun run down the length of the blade.

Wait... no no no no... Hyatt pressed his hand harder against the warm glass.

The silhouette of Delores pressed the flat of her blade against the back of Sawmet's head, and it tipped forward to hang over his knees and stare at the ground between them. Like a woodcutter splitting logs, she raised her weapon in an arcing motion that seemed to stall and its apex before coming down almost too fast to see. Hyatt thought he heard the man's head land in the bed of flowers, but he knew that was impossible. He couldn't look away as Delores nudged his arm with her knee, and Sawmet's headless body collapsed on its side amidst the pale blue petals.

Delores started back towards the courtyard, her weapon swaying casually by her leg and her stride as carelessly confident as Hyatt had ever seen. The ease of it felt like a bucket of ice water dumped over his head and he watched her walk. She disappeared from view as she crossed the porch and entered the building, and when she reappeared in the sitting space at the far end of the room, her weapon was back in her sheath.

"What the fuck–" he stopped himself as he caught Rellah's sleeping features in his periphery and started again, his voice an urgent whisper. "What the fuck did you do?"

Her forehead creased in confusion, and realization was barely breaking across her features as she passed Hyatt on the way to the desk where Sawmet had been sitting. "His role in Her plan was complete. Look for anything that looks like it came from the Cloi."

"She told you that?" Hyatt felt something new building in him, an outrage that rose through him like steam. "You heard Sklodowska's voice in your head just now and she told you to walk him out into the Low Flowers and cut his fucking head off?"

Delores settled herself into Sawmet's vacant chair and picked up the nearest stack of papers, her eyes rapidly shifting over the lines of the top page before cycling it to the back of the pile. "Maps, notes... if the Iron grabbed it from the Cloi in his condition, he must have thought it was important. We'll collect it all in the sitting space. Maybe we can figure out where that Keeper is going."

He stared at the back of her head, dumbfounded. If she felt his eyes boring a hole through her skull, she didn't give any indication as she flipped through the next few pages in her hands. In the silence, whispered memories of everything Rellah had said about Irons swirled around him like a tornado. His attention shifted to Delores' fingertips, still flecked with blood from what he'd witnessed, as she set aside the sheaf of papers and pushed around the scattered pages on the desk in front of her. Hyatt couldn't place why the fact that she hadn't wiped her hands off seemed so unsettling to him, but she couldn't stop staring at the little crimson specks on her knuckles.

"You just... you just killed him." He didn't know what else to say or whether he was saying it to her – the words just fell out of his mouth like they'd reached a tipping point and gravity pulled them into the poorly lit room.

Delores' hands stopped moving shuffling the papers in front of her and she sighed, then turned in her chair to face Hyatt. Her eyes were slightly narrowed as they fixed on his, glinting in critical assessment. There was no warmth in her gaze, only calculation.

"You're not swimming anymore, slayer-of-Cern. I need you to choose to swim." The light from the window made her hair look like spun copper.

"You don't even–" he started.

"Hyatt, listen." The change in Delores' tone was almost imperceptible, but it cut through his protest like her blade had cut through Sawmet. "There is a Keeper out there with everything it takes to start the Nineth History. After we stop him, we can have a long talk about my methods. In the meantime, I will coax, coerce, kill, fuck, build, or burn down whoever or whatever I have to on my way. Choose to swim."

He opened his mouth to start again, but no sound came out, and he closed it again. Satisfied, Delores turned back to the mess of documents on Sawmet's table. He ran his hands through his hair and looked around until he settled on a book stuffed with extra pages on the nightstand by the bed. The edges of the loose papers were wrinkled and torn, stained with blood. He carried it to the low table amongst the chairs in the corner and dropped it.

In one of the chairs, he spotted a metal buckle like the ones on his pack that adjusted the length of the straps. With a frown, Hyatt moved around the back of the chair and spotted a backpack with the top slashed open and a strap missing, discarded in the narrow space between the chair's arm and a bookshelf. Around the bottom of the bag, the floorboards were marked by dried splotches of blood. He picked it up and the way it shifted in his hand told him it wasn't empty, so he took a seat and pulled it open. Inside, he found two leather folios with pages jammed hastily between their covers.

He pulled the folders out of the pack and put them on the low table, but the feeling of weight still in the bottom of the back drew his attention back to it. He reached inside and felt a loose flap of fabric, sewn down on three sides, covering a rectangular object. Hyatt's fingers felt along the edge of the flap and tipped the bag until he felt cool metal against his fingertips. He shook the pack until he was able to grab the edge of the box and pull it free from under the flap.

Delores appeared over his shoulder with papers and books in each hand. "Find anything?"

Hyatt uncurled his fingers from around the metal box hidden in the pack and gestured to the table with his free hand, easing the bag back onto the floor and out of sight with the other. "Maybe. A couple folios full of paper – I haven't gone through them yet."

The Iron moved around the table to one of the other chairs and set her books down, pulling the top leather folder closer to her. As she opened it and began pulling apart the pages inside, he felt his pulse quickening and wondered why he hadn't told her about the other thing in the bag. He tried to mask it by grabbing the other folder and pulling it onto his lap. Inside, a dozen sketches covered pages creased by the folder's binding and crushed at the edges by being carried in the damaged pack.

The silence felt incriminating, so Hyatt spoke to fill it. "There are only seven Warnings. What did the Iron mean, Keeper notes about an eighth one?"

"I don't know." Delores' eyes never left the rows of text on the pages in front of her. "The Keeper believed it enough to kill two people and steal Warning breaches, though."

Hyatt shuffled through the sketches, looking at one and then the next. Each one reminded him of his Trades training, started but unfinished drawings he'd crumpled and thrown into a firepit for having the wrong perspective or too much tremble in his lines. Tiny blotches on each page looked like the artist had absently tapped their pen while deciding what detail to add next, a reckless mistake no qualified Apprentice Artist would have made. He flipped the pages over and found the backs blank, a waste of paper no teacher would have allowed.

The Iron closed the folio in front of her. "Nothing here says where the Keeper is headed. Trade?"

"Sure." He closed the folder and passed it across the low table to her. "Nothing here either though, just drawings. Bad ones."

As he opened the folio Delores had discarded, she opened his and started flipping through the pages inside. "Sawmet thought it was important."

Her mention of the dead Iron brought Hyatt's thoughts riveting back to the memory of her blade catching the sun just before it swept down and severed Sawmet's head from his body. He couldn't focus on the words scrawled in uneven rows and jagged, slanted letters across the crumpled paper. His fingers tightened around the leather binding of the folio and he tried to clear this head, but his eyes strayed to the handle of the sword protruding from her sheath and it was a lost cause.

"Maybe Sklodowska can tell you why." His shoulders tensed at the sound of bitterness in his own voice, but he forced himself not to take It back.

She looked up from the folder and he expected to see a hard, hostile look in her eyes, but instead she looked at him with amused disbelief. "How far you've come from Brathnee."

"I..." His resolve failed him, and the rest of his sentence faded to a trickle and dried up into helpless silence.

Delores tossed the folio on the table and it landed with a padded thud. She put her hands on the upholstered arms of her chair and pushed against them as she stood, helping herself to her feet. Hyatt looked up at her, squinting in the angled shaft that washed across his face from the nearest window, and wondered if she was going to laugh or take two steps and punch him.

"You know what? You're right." Her eyebrow arched and her lower lip protruded as she nodded, then shrugged. "I'll go ask Her."

He watched, speechless, as she turned and walked towards the front door. She didn't look back or say anything. Even through the waves of alarm and caution that crashed over Hyatt, he marveled at the way she moved like she was always exactly where she was supposed to be and never seemed to be in a hurry. She disappeared from his view, the door opened and closed, and the porch creaked as she crossed it.

"You are not who I thought you were, Hy-att first-of-Brathnee," Rellah said from behind him.

His heart jumped and slammed against the roof of his mouth as he whirled around in his chair, almost tipping it over. Rellah stood leaning against the doorway that joined the corner sitting area to the side room beyond, her arms crossed and staring at him with a look of curious consideration.

"Once of Brathnee," he muttered, turning back to the table to hide the rush of blood to his face and let the back of his head deflect some of the intensity in Rellah's eyes. "First of who-the-fuck-knows. I don't know where I belong anymore."

She walked around the table and in Hyatt's periphery, he saw her settle into a different chair than the one Delores had chosen. She leaned back into it, kicking her boots onto the table on top of the scattered documents, and reached her arms up over her head in a giant stretch. When she finished she set her hands on the armrests, tipped her head back against the chair's back, and closed her eyes again.

"Good. You're one step closer to free." She didn't open her eyes as she said it, but the corners of her mouth turned upward in a genuine smile and her chest rose and fell in a deep breath.

He didn't know what to say to that, so went back to looking at the pages in the folio he held. The lines of text were no more complete than the drawings had been, sentences that dropped mid-thought and others that began the same way. Some of them had characters Hyatt didn't recognize, words that were key to understanding whatever the Keeper had been trying to figure out but in a language Hyatt had never seen.

"None of this matters." He closed the folder and tossed it on top of the one Delores had discarded. "There is no eighth Warning. The Keeper will die out there in the Reclaimed, and that will be that. We know where the Turning Weapon came from – it's over."

He hadn't been talking to Rellah and wasn't surprised when she didn't answer him. With a furtive glance her way, he slipped his hand between the open folds of the damaged backpack beside the chair until his fingers felt the metal box at the bottom. He traced his fingertips over the outside, feeling for anything that fastened it to the bag, then wrapped his hand around it and pulled it free. It was twice the size of his palm and cold to the touch, and the brushed metal surface diffused the light that caught against it when he held it up to study it.

He turned it over and his blood flushed cold as he saw three radiating arcs engraved in the center of the device and he almost dropped it, fumbling it twice like a fish trying to escape capture, before he clamped both hands around it and trapping it against his thighs. The scuffle was enough to draw Rellah's attention and her eyes opened, rolling her head towards him.

"What is it?" She asked without sitting up.

His hands shook as he grabbed the front and bottom of the object, pushing them in opposite directions and forcing it to slide open until it clicked. "I think it's an Untethered Communicator."

SIXTEEN

Rellah leaned forward and rested her forearms on her thighs, craning to see the device mostly obscured by Hyatt's hands. "How do you know what it is?"

He held it up for her, pointing to the engraving on the back. "This is a danger mark from the Seventh History – sculptors learn them in the Trades so we can make historical busts more realistic. There's one with the dot in the middle and three wedges widening away, the one that looks like two triangles side by side with roots coming from the middle, the one that looks like three crescent moons connected by a circle in the middle, and... this one."

She cocked her head. "It doesn't look dangerous."

He wanted to agree with her on a rational level, but a lifetime of obeying the Warnings made him feel imperiled by just touching it. He pushed on the two halves of it, but it refused to close. With a growing sense of dread, he turned it over and looked for a mechanism to release it. Rellah watched him fiddle with the device, offering neither suggestions nor critique. Hyatt didn't know what he pressed, but suddenly the lock released and the two halves slide back together to form a rectangle again.

"Are you going to tell the Iron about it?" Rellah asked.

He started to slide the two halves apart again slowly, watching the tracks in the device to see where it locked. "Breaches of the Warnings are an Iron's business. I have to."

She leaned back in her chair again, shifting her hips and kicking her boots back up on the table in search of the most comfortable position as she closed her eyes. Hyatt felt the device try to engage and stopped, sliding the top back and forth on the track and looking underneath it to see if he could find the catch. He pulled and it locked, and he felt the edges of the bottom click. With a squeeze and a push, the top began to slide again. Satisfied, he closed it and set it gently on the table in front of him, as if it might explode if he dropped it.

While he was leaning forward, his eyes refocused on Rellah's boots and moved slowly up her crossed legs, that same tingling clench starting in his stomach. He didn't understand his reaction to her and there was nothing particularly alluring about her trail-worn pants, but as his gaze moved up over her thighs to her ridged belt and the sliver of skin between the top of her pants and the bottom of her shirt, he felt his mouth get dry and his palms dampen.

"Hyatt."

His head jerked up to look at her and she was staring back at him evenly. "Um... uh-huh?"

"We are never going to pair. You know that, right?" Her words tilted up at the end like a question but left room for only one answer from him.

"Yeah- yeah, no. Of course not. I know." Hyatt looked around at the bookshelves against the walls and the papers on the table between them, anything to focus on that wasn't her direct gaze. "I wasn't thinking that."

"No?" she asked, retracting her boots from the low table and planting them on the floor. "You were just thinking about fucking?"

"What?" He choked out, feeling panic expand in his chest like ants pouring out of an anthill, scrambling out along his arms and up into his throat. "No!"

"Uh-huh." She rose to her feet, wincing from the exertion, but not as much as she had been.

Hyatt stood too because he felt like he was supposed to, even though he had nowhere in mind to go. "It's not like – I mean, you don't... we found out where the Turning Weapon came from, straight from someone who saw it. You're done – you don't have to stay here. Neither of us do."

She stared at him with that look she used to give him, the one that told him he'd said something stupid, then shook her head. "You're a dead weed, Hyatt. Even rain couldn't grow you."

Rellah stalked by him towards the common room and he stared after her with no idea what he'd done or said, his mouth open with no words escaping until she reached the far end of the common room and turned into the wing they'd yet to explore. *What was that about?*

Hyatt moved into the side room where they'd found Sawmet, determined to give Rellah the space she'd installed between them. Instead, he hovered next to the window by the writing desk, searching the crater beyond until he spotted Delores. The Iron was kneeling in the field not far from where Sawmet's body lay, her weapon free of her sheath and buried in the earth and her forehead rested against the handle. Hyatt hadn't expected her to take him seriously, but watching her kneel amidst the Low Flowers made him feel like he was intruding on something private.

Hyatt lingered just long enough to be overcome by the sense that he was seeing something he shouldn't and then turned to the desk, looking over the things Delores hadn't taken into the sitting room. He could immediately tell why – the writing on the remaining pages was in a different script than the notes from the Keeper, more fluid and upright and with none of the words in other languages. The paper was uncrumpled and none of the edges were torn. He wondered if they were Sawmet's notes or someone else's.

"Either way, not what I'm looking for," he muttered aloud to himself, pushing them aside.

He sat on the edge of the dead Iron's bed and closed his eyes, rearranging in his mind everything that had happened since the Cloi and trying to see a picture in the pieces. Delores seemed determined to continue hunting the Keeper and he understood why, but it seemed futile with the Keeper chasing something that didn't exist, by himself in the Reclaimed. Hyatt flashed back to the Veshtrue and the close call with the Skarren before that – if Cern raiders didn't kill the Keeper, an Heir would.

"Fucking eighth Warning compost," he muttered, running his hands through his hair and shaking his head to fight the rising tide of exhaustion that threatened to pull him under. "Out here chasing ghosts, risking our lives because the voices in her head say so..."

The band of light across the floor in front of him brightened as the sun slipped lower in the sky. He watched the glow increase like a miniature sunrise, then eased himself over onto his side on Sawmet's bed. The thin, lumpy mattress was surprisingly soft and seemed to pull him into it, and he closed his eyes against the first physical comfort he'd felt in days. Every part of his body ached or lanced with discomfort and the mattress below him seemed to amplify them by contrast.

Hyatt didn't remember falling asleep but when he opened his eyes, no daylight filtered through the windows across the room. He rubbed his eyes and rolled onto his back, feeling his tendons and cartilage protest as his shifting bones pulled and twisted them. The chill of the air burned as he breathed in through his nose and dried his tongue as he exhaled.

"Good, you're awake," Iron Delores' voice reached him.

He opened his eyes and blinked, adjusting to the darkness in the room. The Iron sat at the foot of the bed, her silhouette a different shade of black against the wall beyond. With a grunt, Hyatt pushed against the mattress to force himself into a sitting position.

"How long was I out?" He wiped his face with his palm, grimacing as it dragged the grime of travel across his nose and cheek.

"Five hours." Delores' reply was a statement of fact and hid no judgment in the spaces between her words.

"What? Sorry, I..." His words stalled as he swung his legs over the side of the bed and leaned forward to rest his head in his hands. "I guess, I..."

The Iron waved away his apology, and her weapon's sheath slapped softly against her thigh as he stood. "We all need to sleep. Grab your pack – we're going."

He nodded without looking her way or saying a word, and listened as her diminishing footfalls told him she had left the room. The grip of being sedentary gave ground in Hyatt's body as he struggled to lift himself from the mattress, and he stomped his feet to return blood flow to them before putting on the boots he didn't recall removing. His thoughts and memories broke free of the webs of sleep and he remembered everything – Delores beheading Sawmet, searching the building for clues, and the Untethered communicator in his pack. He turned to look after her and wondered if he should tell her about it, but she had vanished into the unlit depths of the building.

With a last look around the dark room, he made his way through the sitting room and the central chamber to the front door. Rellah was sitting on the porch steps outside and Delores was in the courtyard beyond, poking at the ashes of the cold fire pit with the tip of her blade.

Seeing Rellah, chewing on an herb-twist with her legs akimbo and her pack resting on the step beneath her, made Hyatt's back and shoulders tense as he remembered her stalking away from him hours before. He slowed his stride but she heard the sound of his boots on the old wood floor and looked over her shoulder at him, then reached out at arm's length to offer him the bottom part of the half-eaten snack. Confused, he closed the distance between them and took it with an appreciative nod.

"You look stupid when you sleep," she said as he let go of the wrapping around the bottom half of the snack, squinting up at him in the dark.

"Thanks?" he replied, biting off the end of the chewy, minty bar before handing it back.

Rellah nodded as if conceding that she'd done him a favor by telling him, and folded the wrapper over the end of the herb-twist.

Hyatt moved down the steps past her and she stood, pulling her pack closer to her. They joined Delores by the firepit and he looked up at the stunning blanket of stars that scattered across the sky, the first time he'd seen it unobstructed by the canopy of the Reclaimed and undiminished by the lights of Brathnee Garden. As he watched, four pinpoints of light across the sky raced in long white arcs across the black velvet backdrop of the night sky.

Rellah saw the look on his face and leaned closer to say for his benefit, "Metal stars that break apart and rain to earth. They fall on weak people to punish them for hesitating in life."

She sounded serious, but Hyatt couldn't tell if she was messing with him. He glanced at her and she nodded solemnly, and he squinted at her in response.

"That's not true." He said, less than half-certain he was right.

She just shrugged and adjusted the straps that held her bow to the side of her pack. With a shake of his head, Hyatt turned to Delores who was sheathing her blade and shifting the belt it hung from around her hips.

"Where are we going?" he asked, looking out across the field of Low Flowers until they vanished in the darkness and trying to imagine scaling the crater wall with only starlight to see by.

She nodded in the direction of the sliver of white moon that shone to Hyatt's left. "We're going to find and kill the Keeper, and end this."

Hyatt didn't know what to say. The matter-of-fact way she talked about murdering another human flushed ice water from his heart to his fingertips and make his thighs tighten. He glanced at Rellah who was nodding her assent, neither excited nor deterred by the Iron's declaration, but there was something in the smoothness of her cheek and the lack of tension in her lips that told him Rellah found familiarity in the brutal clarity of their goal. He expected seeing the two of them aligned in lethal purpose to redouble the frost in his lungs, but the look on Rellah's face sent a wash of warmth through his chest and throat instead. His reaction confused him and made him feel closer to her at the same time, which only compounded his bewilderment.

Get it together, Hy-att, he told himself sternly, but winced as he realized he'd reprimanded himself in her voice. *Shit.*

"Okay... so, that's the plan." It sounded surreal, hearing his own words agree to the plan, but he pressed through. "How do we find the Keeper?"

Rellah reached inside her jacket and produced a fistful of papers, the incomplete sketches Hyatt had looked through in one of the folios. "Here - when you line up the inkblots on the sides of the paper, they form a complete image. Take a look."

Squinting, Hyatt shuffled through the pages of half-complete drawings until he could trap the blotched near the bottom edges together. Careful to keep them aligned, he turned his back to the moon to get the most light on the surface of the images. As soon as he saw the amalgam of lines and shapes, he felt dumb for not having seen it earlier. The four pages in his hands formed a map with two recognizable landmarks – Ceojic Garden and the destroyed Cloi. Other markers he didn't recognize adorned the rest of the pages, but the edges of three pages formed a circle around another space on the map.

"I wish we had an artist to figure this out for us," Rellah drawled beside him, the teasing hint creeping into the consonants of her speech. "It might have been faster."

"I'm a sculptor," he muttered absently, his eyes moving over the remainder of the landmarks and trying to guess what they could represent. "Is the circle where we're going?"

The Cern grabbed the pages from him in an aggressive snatch, and she looked irritated with him as she folded them back inside her jacket. "Yes. The Iron knows the place."

"You do?" Hyatt turned to look at her, resisting the urge to ask Rellah what he'd done wrong.

Delores nodded and adjusted the strap of her pack. "It's a ruin, an old one. Sklodowska showed it to me when I was communing – I've been there before, years ago."

Rellah rolled her eyes at the Iron's claim of divine communication but didn't say anything, and Hyatt asked, "Are you sure that's the place?"

Delores nodded. "We'll find the Keeper on his way there, or reach it first and wait for him to arrive. Either way, it's the place. I'm sure... aren't you? Can't you feel your place in Her plan pulling you towards it, like a river's current?"

Something in her voice laced alarm through Hyatt's nerves, a note that fell somewhere between feverish delirium and the kind of absolute certainty that humans weren't meant to feel. He didn't realize he was clenching his fists until his knuckles began to ache from the exertion, but uncurling his fingers did nothing to alleviate the tension in the rest of his body. Delores' eyes seemed to shine in the starlight.

Without waiting for him to reply, she started walking toward the edge of the courtyard. He glanced at Rellah and then followed, and felt gratitude as she fell in step behind him. They kept the Iron close enough to follow but far enough ahead that the darkness swallowed the details of her form. A crisp breeze rustled the delicate petals of the Low Flowers around their boots as they moved through the crater's basin.

"She left out the fact that we'll be passing through Skarren territory and lands claimed by the Cleft Rock Pack on our way," Rellah offered quietly, "which makes me wish I had more arrows. Or one arrow. Or any arrows."

He wasn't sure if she was blaming him for not collecting her arrows while she was bleeding to death from a Veshtrue wound, but committed to blowing past the possibility. "How's your side?"

The Cern was quiet for a moment and the only sound was their boots and the shifting of the flowers, and he was about to say something to fill the space when she replied. "It's a lot better."

"Good. I'm glad you didn't die," he said, at a loss for what else to say.

She sighed. "Every time I think you're starting to act Cern, you go Garden like a weed."

The mixture of shock, embarrassment, and offense her remark filled him with was almost drowned out by how surprised he was at the strength of his reaction, and it completely robbed him of a response. They left the outer edge of the Low Flowers and the ground beneath their feet became more hardened and sterile, loose rocks shifting under their boots and nothing growing from the cracked, dry earth. Ahead, the crater's floor began sloping almost imperceptibly upward, and the rim of the giant depression started stealing more stars from the lowest parts of the sky.

Delores slowed her steps and then stopped, glancing back at them. "Ready to climb?"

SEVENTEEN

Climbing the wall of the canyon was even harder than Hyatt expected and by the time he collapsed on the flat ground beyond the rim, he was exhausted and coated in grime. He dropped to his knees and the weight of his pack carried him forward onto his face, and he made no effort to rise until Rellah nudged him in the side with the toe of her boot. He reluctantly planted his hands in the dirt and pushed himself back up to his knees, then sat back on his heels and took a deep breath.

"I'm glad you didn't die," the Cern called over her shoulder without breaking her stride on Delores' trail.

Hyatt's lip turned up in a sarcastic grimace and he climbed to his feet, his thighs screaming in protest, and he trudged forward. Ahead, the familiar stands of trees rose to create an uneven horizon with their canopies. Their blended silhouette broke apart into individual trunks and thatched branches as they moved closer, moonlight punching through the gaps between like razor blades. Low clouds blotted out swaths of stars, leaving the remainder to light their way as they crossed the rocky and barren ground towards the edge of the Reclaimed.

As the ground turned softer and the trees seemed to reach higher, the realization that he was looking forward to reaching the entangled thicket crept through him like cold honey. He looked up at the branches and felt the absence of terror like the memory of a missing limb, made real by the sudden thought that he hadn't missed Brathnee Garden in days. As the limbs and leaves overhead cast stripes of shadow across his face, he didn't know if he should feel relieved at becoming accustomed to the Reclaimed or concerned at the things he was losing in the process.

He caught up with Rellah, whose stride had taken on a lazy comfort like she was home and free from danger. "Do you know much about the... what did you call them? Cleft Rock pack?"

When she replied, her words were matted with her accent like she was pulling them from the shadows and trailing webs of darkness in their wake. "Cern learn the names and regions of other packs like we learn the names of Gardens and the Timeless Markers. I've never met any of them, if that's what you're asking."

Her reply gave Hyatt more questions than answers, but he was reluctant to risk collapsing the conversation by asking for something she hadn't volunteered in her answer so he changed directions. "Were you born Cern?"

Rellah's head turned towards him and the stripes of moonlight made her skeptical glare look even harsher. Hyatt opened his mouth to try to talk through whatever he'd said to provoke her, but stopped himself as a look of realization crossed her features.

"Cern don't divide our pack like that. To you Garden people, once-of and first-of are things that matter." She paused as if considering a more nuanced answer, then visibly discarded it with a shake of her head. "Cern are Cern from their first day in the pack, whether they are born that way or choose to earn acceptance. There's no before, no also. It's just Cern."

Hyatt walked quietly beside her, trying to understand the meanings of what she said. Lost in his thoughts, the tip of his boot caught an exposed root and he stumbled, cracking fallen twigs and rustling leaves as he tried to recover. The noise brought a look back from Delores, but when she saw he was upright, she pressed forward through the Reclaimed without a word.

"I don't know if the Skarren heard you," Rellah drawled. "Want to maybe bang your pack against that tree trunk a dozen times?"

He didn't know why the slightest criticism from her made the organs in his torso contract and wither, but it was enough to make him swallow hard in hopes of relieving it. His cheeks red, he shook his head in response and focused on his footsteps to ensure he didn't break any more branches.

"Hey," she said after a dozen more steps.

"Yeah?" Hyatt didn't look up from the makeshift trail Delores was creating through the thickening underbrush.

"You didn't apologize." She stepped over a low branch and then ducked under another one, her pack avoiding contact with either one by some miracle. "Do more of that. It's better."

He didn't know what to say, so he said nothing. They walked through the Reclaimed, following the Iron's lead. The forest was quiet except for the rustle of branches as a cold night wind shook them. Behind them, the stands of trees closed with the night sky to block the open space and the crater from view, and the air around them hung scents of stale timber and dry sap. Hyatt alternated his focus between the ground just in front of his boots and the silhouette of Delores shifting in the darkness ahead.

Under the canopy and within the density of the thick forest, the darkness began to dissipate before the sun broke the horizon. It reminded Hyatt of the way shadows grew and extended, light ebbing in around his periphery and subtly assassinating the dark patches between leaves and underneath low branches. As they walked, dawn surrounded them like sap dripping from the trees.

The first warmth reached Hyatt's fingers as the morning breeze slipped over the forest floor.

Delores slowed to a lingering stroll and then stopped, her gaze sweeping the treetops above. Hyatt closed the space between them until he was a stone's throw behind her and searched the depths of the forest for whatever had caused her to pause. He felt Rellah appear beside him more than he heard her and glanced over at her before continuing his sweep of the spaces between the trees.

"What is it?" she asked, her voice low.

He shook his head. "I don't know."

Rellah tipped her head back and breathed in through her nose, a long inhale that filled her lungs, then frowned as her jaw tightened. "Skarren."

Hyatt's eyes turned skyward in alarm and he sniffed the air, trying to pick up whatever had alerted the Cern woman, but he couldn't tell the difference between the normal scent of the Reclaimed and the telltale sign of the monstrosity. Without thinking about it, he stepped closer to the trunk of the nearest tree. As another wash of morning breeze passed over him, he felt his pulse begin to climb. Seconds seemed to stretch like toffee and the silence of the Reclaimed thickened around him until he thought he would drown in it.

As if nothing had happened, Delores started walking again. Hyatt shot an alarmed look at Rellah, who shrugged as if it was no big deal, but as she resumed her stride there was a tension to it that wasn't lost on him. He fell into step behind her and his eyes focused on the bow strapped to the side of her pack, a dire reminder that she had no arrows to fire with it. Daylight seemed to take on a bleak quality, more white and less yellow, as they walked single file towards the Iron's destination.

"If a Skarren attacks..." Hyatt began, just loud enough for Rellah to hear.

"we all die," she finished for him.

"Great," He muttered.

Twice more when Delores stopped to inspect the branches above her, Hyatt's heart clenched like a vice closed around it. Each time, after a blood-chilling series of moments in perfect silence, she started walking again. Rellah seemed at peace with the walk and with the pauses to search for the giant beasts, and the fact that it didn't bother her grated at Hyatt like sandpaper on his nerves.

He sped up his pace to walk beside her, careful to not disturb any branches and start their conversation at a disadvantage. "How do you get used to it?"

"What do you mean?" Rellah pulled an herb-twist from her seemingly never-ending supply as the first blinding sliver of true sunlight broke the horizon behind them.

"We could die out here at any moment... but you live out here. All the time. How?" He felt like he was explaining it in clumsy terms, but couldn't find better ones.

The Cern woman's face adopted the ghost of a smile Hyatt had come to take as a sign of encouragement, and his heart fluttered as clumsily as his words had tumbled from him. "There are... maybe eight things out here that can kill us – Skarren, Veshtrue, other Cern, Garden weeds, running out of water, running out of food, the cold, and Irons."

Hyatt waited until it was clear she thought she'd given him a whole answer before speaking. "... and?"

"And," she continued, "everything else out here tries to keep us alive. Shelter. Cover. Water. Edible plants. The wind, to warn us nearby danger. Light to see by. Darkness to hide us while we sleep. Fallen limbs to burn. Herbs for medicine. Ruins to camp in. Things to climb, so we become strong and see far. We don't have to be afraid of the Reclaimed – it's on our side."

Before Hyatt could process what she said, the Iron stopped again. Instead of looking up, she knelt down. The wash of cold through his blood continued to amaze him at the diverse ways fear could feel as it raced through him. He crouched and waited while Rellah crept closer to the Iron, and when they both stood, he rose and joined them. Ahead, six sun-bleached bones with iconography carved into their shafts had been strung between two saplings like a sideways ladder.

"There, too," Rellah said softly, pointing upward to five bones lashed together in a star formation, adorning the gap between two diverging branches.

"Can you read those marks," he asked her, his voice barely a whisper.

She shook her head. "All the packs use different markings. I could maybe figure it out if we stayed here long enough, but—"

"But we're not staying," Delores interrupted. "We're a few days' walk from the ruins on the map. We'll get to the other side of pack space, rest, and then find the Keeper."

Hyatt had ceased to differentiate between the draining sensation of being tired and the physical soreness of hiking and fighting, but as soon as the Iron mentioned rest, it took hold of his muscles like spiderwebs made of steel. He risked a glance at Rellah, hoping she would argue, but she was already nodding her assent. With a resigned nod, he tightened the straps of his pack.

Rellah moved to the front, giving the Cern markings a glance that lingered as she passed them until she made it further than her neck could turn. Hyatt watched her and tried to imagine what she was feeling, but before he could dwell on it, Delores nudged his arm and nodded after Rellah. His choice to follow her wasn't a conscious one, more jumpstarted by the Iron's urge, but he found his feet carrying him forward all the same. The Iron fell into step beside him with the same lackadaisical quality to her stride that seemed to apply to how she viewed everything else.

Her closeness to Hyatt brought back visions in waves – the memory of her beheading Sawmet in the Low flowers, the blinding flash when she fought the Veshtrue that knocked him unconscious, and the way she stood amidst the raining branches of the Skarren without a flinch or hesitation. Rellah's words crept back in too, stories he hadn't heard growing up in Brathnee Garden that seemed as true and obvious to her as the Warnings were to him. It all made her feel alien to him, not the heroic and gifted human that his friends whispered about over cups in Hoenbeck's Assembly, but something else entirely – something apart.

As soon as he felt it, he couldn't shake himself free of it. He widened the space between them without meaning to and shoved his hands into the pockets of his Cern jacket, as if leaving them exposed risked her touching him. Hyatt caught himself doing it and tried to fight the irrational urge, but he couldn't overcome it. In the space between his actions and intentions, a tension built until it felt like it was straining his bone's ability to stay tethered to each other.

"How many people have you killed?" He blurted it out and the suddenness of it, realizing she wasn't a part of the tangled thoughts that led up to his question, but he didn't retract it.

Delores canted her head and looked up at the sky through the canopy of the Reclaimed, squinting with one eye as she searched for an answer. "Maybe... seventy?"

He didn't know what answer he expected, but the number jarred him enough to whip his head around and stare at the side of hers. "You've killed seventy people?"

She shrugged, her thumb absently sliding under the strap of her pack to smooth it against her shoulder. "Maybe eighty."

"How can you... how could you..." Hyatt trailed off, picturing eighty men and women collapsing lifeless in a barren field.

The Iron didn't answer for a moment as they followed Rellah through the woods. On their left, the beginnings of ruins rose beneath moss and branches but let light filter through exposed rebar that suggested the structure had been much larger once. Deeper in the woods, taller walls and better materials had stood better against the successive waves of near-extinction, casting a long shadow across the forest floor.

"How many people would you kill, to save two million?" Delores asked.

The question pulled his attention from the ruins. "Huh?"

"A hundred? A thousand? A million?" she prompted him. "How many people would you kill to save the remainder?"

The question felt like he was standing at the bottom of a cliff during a rockslide, chunks of its implications battering his thoughts with no way to deflect them. "I- I don't know. As many as I had to?"

"Exactly." Delores looked straight ahead and nothing changed in her posture, but there was a cold hardness in her voice. "As many as I have to."

A cool breeze slid between the ancient trunks and thick branches of the reclaimed, but it was the chill of her words that made goosebumps break out across the back of Hyatt's neck. He instinctively believed her – there was no question in her mind that she believed in her mandate from her deity and that she slept without the nightmares that plagued him despite the number of dead bodies to her name. A spike of alarm coursed through him as he wondered if she would kill him or Rellah if Sklodowska willed it, but it subsided with the simple certainty that she would.

"What happens if the Keeper is right? What if there's an Eighth Warning?" he asked.

Delores opened her mouth to reply but froze instead, her front foot planted and her rear foot stalled on its toe as if she'd become a statue of ice. Hyatt took one extra step before realizing she'd stopped and stood still too, that familiar flush of anxiety washing over him as he spotted Rellah ahead of them, crouched low.

The Cern skulked backward, staying low until she was close enough to whisper to them. "A branch broke."

"Cern?" Delores asked, her hand drifting to the grip of her weapon.

Rellah shook her head, her eyes scanning the depths of the Reclaimed ahead of them. "Cern don't break branches. It wasn't —"

The loud crack of a weapon being fired cut off her word and beside Delores, the trunk of a softwood tree exploded outward with a shower of finger-length slivers. Hyatt and Rellah flung themselves to the ground as a second shot rang out, the bass report echoing off trees around them. Delores took a single, graceful step as she pivoted, her back to the tree that bore the scar of the first shot. The silence that followed was heavy with the threat of another attack and Hyatt searched frantically for the source of the rifle fire, but saw no one between the stands of trees and low brush.

"My name is Delores, Iron of the Eastern Reach." Her voice was clear and loud, and she paused as another shot blistered the tree at her back, then continued as if nothing had happened. "If you keep shooting, you'll attract Skarren."

"You're not going to stop us, Iron!" a man's voice called from somewhere beyond Hyatt's sight. "Kill her!"

Fuck, there's more than one of them! Hyatt gritted his teeth and struggled to free himself of his pack, shrugging out of it so he could crawl across the forest floor on his stomach.

Ahead of him, Rellah moved like a bear on her hands and feet to scurry to the base of a large tree. Her pack dropped from her like water running off her shoulders as she moved and by the time she reached the safety of the tree's trunk, her knife had appeared in her hand as if it had always been there.

"You didn't say anything about fighting an Iron!" another man's voice replied, laced with panic and closer to Hyatt than he expected. "This wasn't part of the deal!"

He watched Rellah jump and grab a branch, then pull herself up onto it as the roar of a flechette gun ripped through the air. The metal shards were close enough for Hyatt to hear them whistle as they flew by and he pressed himself flat to the ground, then redoubled his crawl towards the relative safety of the brush.

"Turn over the Keeper, and everyone else can go," Delores promised without a hint of concern or ulterior motive. "Your story doesn't have to end here."

In response, another salvo of flechette carbines and the punctuating crack of another weapon filled the forest. Hyatt tried to count the number of carbines based on the sound of the roar but he could only guess there were more than four, and trees on every side seemed to spray wooden shrapnel as their trunks were torn apart by the volley. He tried to fight the terror expanding in his chest and searched the branches above for Rellah, but she'd moved from where she'd climbed to and he couldn't find her.

Delores stepped from behind her tree and drew her thick-bladed weapon with a singing sound. "It can, though."

Another shot rang out, the distinct sound of the rifle not firing metal shards, and the Iron turned towards it. Hyatt watched her walk directly towards where the shot had come from while two more flechette carbines fired, slashing apart the branches and leaves around her but leaving her unscathed. To his side, there was a sudden crash and a scream of pain, then silence. He shoved himself to his feet and ran towards it, hunched over to take advantage of the low brush, and broke into a clearing just in time to watch Rellah rip her knife free of a man's face and spatter Hyatt with the arc of hot blood.

The wet warmth of red droplets on his mouth and cheek made Hyatt's tongue taste metallic but he didn't slow down, sliding to a stop beside the dead man and picking up his flechette carbine. He tipped the weapon to the side to let the light from above reach it and saw it still had ammunition, then tugged the strap up over his shoulder. As he pulled the stock to his shoulder, he caught Rellah's dark eyes through a full face of dripping blood and the sight of her smile of unmitigated approval felt like it might blind him, but she turned and was gone through the barrier of brush before it could explode his heart.

On the other side of the brush, the sickening crunch of bone preceded a geyser of blood by the space of a breath. Hyatt stepped towards it and another form bolted like a partridge taking flight, and he tracked the running man for twenty degrees and fired. The gun kicked harder than he expected and he winced as the stock did its best to bruise his shoulder, but he forced his eyes open just fast enough to watch the runner crumple forward and hit the ground face-first. Hyatt took four quick steps closer, pointed the flechette carbine at the back of the man's head, and pulled the trigger. A dozen metal spikes shattered the prone man's skull and his leg spasmed, then lay still.

Before Hyatt could process what he'd just done, a violent downdraft buffered him and almost ripped the carbine from his hands. He jerked it upward and pointed it up at the sky as a giant shadow bathed him in darkness, and the temperature seemed to drop instantly as the flying form blocked out the sun. From another stand of trees, someone let out a wail of fear and despair as another savage gust shook every branch in sight.

Hyatt stared up through the sights of the carbine at the fanned tail of the Skarren as it spiraled like a hawk and started another pass over the skirmish. "Oh, fuck."

EIGHTEEN

Hyatt had just enough time to fire the carbine pressed to his shoulder before branches, sheared from the treetops by the flying beast above them, started raining around him like a volley of spears. He dropped the weapon and the sling caught against his shoulder, bashing against his arm and hip as he ran towards the biggest tree nearby. Shattered limbs with points like pikes buried into the ground around him, cracking and snapping as the impact raced through stress fractures in the wood and blew them apart like bombs. He felt fist-sized chunks of trees pelt his shoulder and back.

Somewhere nearby, another carbine fired. Hyatt had no idea if it was one of the men with the Keeper or if Rellah had wrested a weapon from someone, but he hoped whoever held it was shooting at the Skarren and not each other. His lungs were searing and he gulped for air, trying to fill them. The shadow of the Skarren dragged over him again as the Heir circled, searching for them through the gaps in the canopy.

Through the clatter and crash of falling branches, Hyatt saw Delores walking with the same easy stride that said she was invincible and unconcerned. He watched her blade arc overhead and come down with an almost casual swing that cut away the brush in front of her, clearing the path towards an enemy he couldn't see. Rellah was nowhere to be found, but Hyatt was certain that somewhere amidst the trees and bushes, she was alive.

Another deafening roar filled the Reclaimed as the diving Skarren shattered more trees and Hyatt pressed himself against the tree trunk in front of him, waiting for the agony of being impaled by a plummeting branch. When it didn't come, he spun so his back was to the tree and fumbled to get his weapon back into his hands.

If this fucking thing is going to kill me, he thought as he raised it to point at the sky, *it's going to remember me for as long as it lives after.*

Nearby, one of the Keeper's hired workers reached the same conclusion and fired again. Hyatt pointed his weapon and stared through the carbine's sights, looking for the outline of the Skarren through the branches and surprised in the moment by how much his grim determination fortified him. When the creature passed over again, he aimed just in front of it and leaned into the anticipated recoil of the gun as he pulled the trigger. Noise and fire burst from the end of the barrel and he visualized the metal shards punching into the body of the Skarren, and grit his teeth against the smile that threatened to form over his tight lips.

Hyatt expected a roar or pain or the whooshing thrash of wings as the Heir drove itself higher and out of range, but the next sound Hyatt heard was like the thwap of two dozen clotheslines being snapped tight. It seemed to come from all around him, not loud enough to deafen him but pervasive enough to vibrate through him like he was a string instrument. Suddenly, the leaves of the canopy above him were on fire. He instinctively flinched as the flashfire blazed to life and spread, igniting every branch in every direction for twenty paces. Nearby, Rellah's voice raised in a triumphant and jubilant sound that had no words but said everything good and victorious, and Hyatt lowered his weapon in secure confusion.

A flaming droplet fell towards Hyatt and he stepped back just before the pitch-like substance landed, watching as it splatted on the ground and burned out in a coil of black smoke. He looked up to the canopy where the burning pitch fell from and saw no sign of the Skarren circling. The immediate danger averted, he searched the forest for his friends. Delores came into view, blade coated to the handle with blood and a serene expression on her face. Further to his left, Rellah staggered from the brush, her jacket and face spattered red and a wolfish grin on her features.

"What happened?" he asked as he stumbled towards his companions before his eyes focused on the answer to his own question.

Through the brush, a dozen Cern raiders closed on them with bows in hand. They seemed to melt from the forest without being revealed by any particular moment – Hyatt was alone with his friends in one breath and surrounded by Cern in the next. He didn't remember reaching for the stock of the weapon slung over his shoulder but suddenly his fingers were white-knuckle tight around it, ready to pull it up and use it.

"Easy, raider," a man's voice said behind him, punctuated by the pressure of an arrowhead pressed between his shoulder blades. "Put that weed weapon down... it's over."

The surprise of someone so close behind him was drowned out by the assumption he was Cern, and he had no explanation for the flush of pride and belonging that ripped through him like lightning before the threat of the arrow point took hold. Hyatt nodded and lowered his shoulder so the strap of the carbine could slip free, and the weapon hit the forest floor barrel-first with a muted thud.

"Get that arrow out of my back, or I'll feed it to you," he growled without turning his head, a spike of fear chasing the words from his sternum to his throat. *Where the fuck did that come from?*

The man behind him chuckled. "You're a long way from home, Moss Wall."

Hyatt started to wonder why the raider thought he was from Rellah's pack, but his surprise as the man withdrew the arrow from his back was stronger than his curiosity. He stood a little straighter, squaring his shoulders and flexing his fists. His attention moved across the Cern raiders in front of him, assessing their weapons and their expressions, but he felt no wash of fear – something colder and cleaner moved through him. Hyatt felt something he didn't have a word for but wondered if it was what Rellah felt, or how Jenna felt when the ambush broke out at Vohk Bridge.

Ahead of him, Rellah stepped into view, flanked by Cern raiders. The differences between her jacket and the ones worn by the men on either side of her answered his question about the nearby Cern's assumption, and it made him aware of everywhere that his own jacket touched his shoulders and arms and hips. He searched the rest of his field of view for Delores, but the Iron was nowhere to be seen. The canopy overhead continued to burn, charred remains of leaves plummeting to the earth in blazing cinders like a thousand red-orange falling stars.

"Nine dead," a raider on his left called out. "All Haleu."

Hyatt tracked the man's gaze across to who the report was meant for, a short and stocky Cern holding a pair of Cern blades. Other raiders turned to him too, waiting for his response to the count, and Hyatt could see why – the man radiated authority from every step and every shift of his weight. He glanced at Hyatt, then fixed his attention on Rellah like one of Brathnee Garden's searchlights.

"Not enough Haleu in Moss Wall territory, becquerela? You need to come all the way to Cleft Rock to hunt them?" The man's voice was bemused, but the undercurrent of danger was like a riptide.

"I'm Rellah, and I'm Claimed," Rellah replied, causing both of the raiders beside her to visibly lean away from her, "hunting a runaway Keeper. The weeds were just a bonus."

The leader of the raiders continued his walk towards Rellah, unaffected by her statement, and handed one of his blades to a raider. As he drew closer, the Cern around her stepped further away, and Hyatt tried to gauge whether he could cross the distance to help Rellah if the man attacked her. He hadn't realized he'd done anything to telegraph his thoughts, but the Cern behind him put a hand on Hyatt's shoulder.

"You wouldn't make it three steps, becquerel." Rather than a threat, the raider's tone sounded like helpful information, like he was warning Hyatt that fire was hot.

Through the blazing cinders that fell and drifted like snow as the canopy fire burned out, he watched the man reach Rellah. He stopped too close to her, daring her to take a step backward, but her boots were planted firmly and it looked to Hyatt like she actually leaned her shoulders forward a little bit to steal the limited space between them. The sounds of the Reclaimed seemed to quiet and the raiders stood still, watching.

With a sudden motion, the man grabbed Rellah's forearm in a welcoming grip. Her fingers curled around his, and it felt like the whole forest exhaled to expel the tension of the moment. Rellah stepped towards the man until her right shoulder connected with his, their clasped arms trapped between them, and they both stepped back.

"I'm Ehtred, second to Pack Master Grehv. Your day begins now." He let go of her arm and turned to regard Hyatt. "And you? Are you Claimed too?"

Hyatt's mind was cascading through terms he'd only heard once or never before and why Rellah didn't mention Delores, leaving his thoughts unready to be the subject of Ehtred's attention. "What?"

"He's not," Rellah answered for him, stepping forward to stand beside Ehtred and shoot Hyatt a look that weighed a thousand pounds. "He saved my life, so I have been traveling with him and an Iron until the favor is settled."

Ehtred glanced sharply at her, then looked at two of his raiders, but the Cern shook their heads. His lips tightened and he took a deep breath in through his nose, releasing it slowly. Watching him made Hyatt more aware of his own breath, the fading scent of smoke from the charred canopy, and the smell he was beginning to associate with newly dead bodies.

"Where is your Iron friend now?" the Cern leader asked, soaking Rellah's acquaintance with Delores in enough vinegar that her cheek twitched in the ghost of a wince without breaking from his gaze.

"If you didn't find her body, she probably went after the Keeper," she replied.

Ehtred's features were perfectly still and he said nothing for a moment, staring into Rellah's eyes like he was burrowing into her soul. His eyelids flexed, as minor an expression as her wince had been, and then he shrugged and looked back at Hyatt who nodded to confirm Rellah's explanation.

"Then we'll give you supplies and send you after her." Ehtred raised his voice to talk to his raiders, but he kept his eyes on Hyatt. "Collect the bodies and burn them – scatter the bones."

He walked toward Hyatt without looking around to ensure his team was following his orders, and Rellah followed. As the man grew closer Hyatt could make out more of the details of his jacket, stitching in muted colors on Ehtred's sleeves and patches sewn over his chest and shoulders. It made Hyatt want to examine his own jacket again, to find a moment to ask Rellah what each symbol meant, but he couldn't bring himself to look away from Ehtred while the man was staring at him and walking towards him.

The leader stopped in front of Hyatt, as close as he had stood to Rellah, and Hyatt fought the overwhelming instinct to take a step backward. The strength of the urge surprised him, and he was grateful that he'd approached her first, or he was certain he would have. Instead, he felt his stomach tighten and his shoulders flex with the effort of standing his ground. Ehtred hooked his thumbs in his belt and looked Hyatt up and down from sternum to crown, then met his eyes with the potential energy of a tree about to fall.

"Where's your weapon, raider?" he asked.

"He-" Rellah started, but Ehtred lifted his hand and her sentence stopped as if he'd cut it in two with the gesture.

"I'm talking to a Cern, Rellah." His eyes stayed fixed on Hyatt. "Where's your weapon?"

Ehtred's tone had been mild but in Hyatt's periphery, it punched through Rellah like one of her own arrows and the color drained from her face. In his head, the assumption he was Cern raider and the implication Rellah wasn't felt like twin explosions, and in the clouds of dust that spread through his mind, he remembered the Untethered Communicator in his pack. He didn't want to lie and didn't know what answer would be expected of a raider, but he knew there was no way Ehtred was going to move on until he got an answer.

"We fought a Veshtrue," Hyatt replied with a shrug.

Ehtred nodded as if it answered his question and gestured over his shoulder, and the raider with his second blade appeared beside him. He took the weapon and hefted it alongside the one he still held, looking back and forth between them, then turned it over and held it up handle-first towards Hyatt.

"Here. I won't have Moss Wall saying we left one of theirs without a weapon out here." When Hyatt hesitated to grab the handle, Ehtred shook it at him. "Take it."

His hand closed around the weapon's grip and before he could thank the Cern leader, he'd stepped past Hyatt and begun walking again. Around them, the rest of the team dragged dead Haleu into a pile in the middle of the space that pale gray ash from the burning canopy had coated like frost. Their arms snagged twigs and the curled edges of fallen leaves, leaving disturbed trails on the forest floor in their wake. Hyatt turned and followed Ehtred as the scent of an accelerant drifted through the air.

On the thirty-minute walk to the Cleft Rock encampment, the Cern leader stayed beside Rellah but said little. Hyatt kept pace with them on Ehtred's other side, searching the canopy for signs of the Skarren's return and taking in the changes in the Reclaimed. The trees were slenderer, with paler bark and higher branches than the forest that surrounded Brathnee, and the low brush seemed to have more density and less sprawling vine. The few flowers that grew had elongated blooms like teardrops, and scattered clumps of berries were pearl-white. He wondered as he moved beside Ehtred if he would have noticed the differences when he left the Garden, and started at the realization it had been only days ago when it felt like months.

Two Cern sentries stepped into view from behind larger trees as Ehtred approached and he led Hyatt and Rellah between them. Hyatt felt their silent gaze track them as far as they could without turning their bodies, curious but unwilling to interfere in Ehtred's business. Beyond their posts, shelters shaped like three-quarter domes and made from gray and tan canvases dotted the forest, nestled between clumps of pale brush with sharp, matte leaves. Members of the pack moved between the tents, their voices low and smooth so they seemed to blur with the ambient noise of the Reclaimed. Those in Ehtred's way stepped more quickly to clear his path, nodding in recognition and murmuring acknowledgments as the three of them moved towards the heart of the camp. Hyatt heard a hawk's brittle call somewhere overhead, made louder by the contrasting quiet of the camp.

"I'll see you to Grehv, and get some rations and arrows together for you. How long is your draw?" Ehtred asked, his voice softer than it had been at the ambush site.

Rellah lowered her voice as well. "Twenty-seven inches."

Together they crested a small rise and in the depression beyond, Hyatt saw a man sitting on a stump with seven other Cern gathered around him. Ehtred lingered at the height of the terrain until the seated man noticed him, then made his way down the gradual slope towards the group. Behind him, Hyatt stepped closer to Rellah.

"Why is everything so quiet?" he asked, his voice barely a whisper.

"We're in the middle of working hours." Rellah gestured absently at the camp behind them and stepped closer to Hyatt as she did until their shoulders brushed. "Three hours in the morning and three in the evening when we focus on getting things done."

Ehtred noticed they hadn't followed him and gestured for them to keep up, and Rellah started after him. "Now that they think you're Cern, you'd better keep it that way."

"Why do they think I'm Cern?" Hyatt hurried to keep pace with her, whispering louder to make sure she heard him. "Why does he think you're not?"

Rellah just shook her head, and then they were too close to Ehtred for her to answer privately. He started walking again as soon as they reached him, and together they broke the circle of Cern surrounding the seated man. He nodded to Ehtred and then studied each of them, and Hyatt felt like he was already picturing the glyphs he would carve into Hyatt's bones. Beside him, Rellah nodded to the seated man and slowed to a stop.

"She's Claimed, and he's Moss Wall." Ehtred was succinct and gruff, and Hyatt wondered if he skipped their names because the Cern leader didn't know his, or because they were irrelevant to the man he assumed was the Pack-master. "Her day began an hour ago. There's an Iron in our tract, somewhere north of here."

The man on the stump planted his hands on his knees and launched himself upward in a single, sudden motion. The explosiveness of his movement surprised Hyatt – the man looked worn by a hard life and unforgiving winters, but shifted with the quickness of a much younger man. The surrounding Cern men and women turned their attention to the three newcomers as the older man walked between them, and Ehtred stepped aside, leaving the path clear to where the older man stopped two arm's lengths from Hyatt and Rellah.

"I'm Grehv, and these are my Cern. Do you have everything you need?" he asked, studying her face.

Rellah put her hands in her pockets and nodded toward Ehtred. "He's getting arrows and food for us. Other than that, yes."

Something was hanging in the air between them that Hyatt couldn't place, an unspoken sentiment from Grehv that settled somewhere between fascination and concern, and deference blended with stubborn independence in return from Rellah. It made the span of feet between them feel full and vibrant in a way that Hyatt felt like he hadn't experienced before, but then he recognized where it was familiar from – he'd felt it when the Veshtrue had burst from the brush outside the Cloi, and again when he'd realized Delores was about to behead Sawmet. The connection in his mind ran through him like a static charge.

Satisfied with her answer, Grehv turned to Hyatt and raised an eyebrow. "And you, raider – what kind of deal did Moss Wall strike with an Iron?"

"No deal." Hyatt shook his head with determination, buying time to dig through his memory and smash together fragments into an answer the Pack-master would accept. "Some weeds from Brathnee got ahold of a Turning Weapon and pointed the Iron at us. Jethrek sent me with her to prove it didn't come from us and we've been hunting a Keeper pile of compost ever since."

Grehv stood silent, staring at Hyatt's eyes without blinking until he was sure the pack-master didn't believe him, but just before Hyatt opened his mouth to double down on his explanation Grehv spoke. "Heirs love ruining hunts."

While the Cern gathered around them traded opinions with each other in low tones, Rellah nodded in agreement. A woodwind instrument's warbling imitation of a bird call sang out from somewhere deep in the camp, and when Grehv continued, he spoke at a normal volume that added gravel to his voice.

"Are you going after the Iron, or headed back to Moss Wall?" He nodded at Rellah without looking at her. "There are six Heirs for her to hunt in Cleft Rock tracts."

The idea of Rellah facing any of the monstrous masters of the Reclaimed by herself made the marrow in Hyatt's bones turn to frost and he felt his face tighten, but fought to stifle any other reaction to the Pack Master's words. "Jethrek will want that Keeper dead before I go home. I'll head after the Iron."

"Then go kill him," There was a begrudging pride in Grehv's voice that drizzled into sardonic humor, "and the Iron too, if the chance comes up."

NINETEEN

When the Cern raider with the knife buried in her neck staggered towards him across Vohk Bridge, she wasn't alone. Behind her, a man shambled forward, wicked shards of flechettes glinting in the moonlight where they protruded from his forehead and cheekbone. On the far end of the bridge, Sawmet's corpse lay slumped against the Line Junction, his severed head on the broad boards between his knees. Under the cloudless sky, Hyatt noticed two more differences from his dreams before – he wasn't terrified, and he was holding a Cern blade.

His hands came together around the weapon's long grip, choking up on it until his thumb met the oval handguard, and he took a step forward. "It's Shelara, right?"

The hungry grin showing her red-spattered teeth and wet lips faltered at the recognition before curling into a snarl and she limped forward, and cascades of blood welled up around the knife behind her clavicle to spill over her collarbone. The man behind her wrapped a hand around the largest metal shard in his chest and pulled hard, and it made a sucking sound as he wrenched it free of his body. His eyes, glassy and vacant, fixed on Hyatt and he staggered forward.

"That's mine," Dark red blood dripped from Shelara's lower lip, stringing out until it met her filthy shirt and absorbed into the rough material.

"You're dead. You both are." Hyatt took a hurried step closer and shifted his weight to his back leg, knuckles turning white against the leather-wrapped handle in his hands. "You made choices that got you killed, and I'm done feeling bad about it. This time, you're staying dead."

Shelara grabbed the handle of the embedded knife as she closed the last step towards Hyatt, pulling it free with the sound of ripping meat and holding it low. "Give me back my jacket."

"It's my fucking jacket." As soon as she put weight on her front foot, he swung the Cern blade as hard as he could.

The blade bit through her flesh and vertebrae, and she crumpled to her knees as her head fell to the bridge with a thud. Hyatt was surprised at how easily the wicked, curved blade beheaded her but had no time to dwell on it as the standing man lunged with the jagged metal in his hand. Hyatt sidestepped the slash and pulled the Cern weapon up and back, swinging it down like a woodsman's ax and driving the curved edge into his skull. The man spasmed and the flechette fell from his open hand, burying point-first in the bridge by his feet. He lifted both hands and wrapped them around the blade stuck in his head, blood leaking from the corners of his eyes.

"You..." he coughed, his fingers failing to work as if they were trapped in mittens.

"Yeah, me," Hyatt replied, ripping the blade out of the man's skull and watching him collapse onto the flechette before laying still, "again."

He woke, not with a spasm and start, but like he had eaten well and slept a full night. The gray canvas of the Cern shelter Grehv had directed him to shifted and rolled in the light predawn breeze. As the fog of unconsciousness receded, he felt the warmth and pressure on one side of his body was greater than the other and looked down to see Rellah curled against him, her head on his shoulder and her thigh slung over his. A knit blanket, apparently shared at some point in the evening, stretched over and tangled between their calves where one of them had kicked it free.

His body reacted to the realization that she was the source of the weight and heat, and Hyatt's pulse in his throat threatened to cut off his breathing. Recognizing his own reaction only accelerated and amplified it. He tried to cant his hips away from her to prevent her from feeling her effect on him, but the almost non-existent shift of his body was enough to make her eyes flare open. He froze without looking at her as he felt her pupils focus on his cheekbone. Unwilling to move and unable to move with the way he was half-pinned under Rellah's body, his blood rushed to the only place it could and he swallowed hard to prevent himself from making a sound.

"Hyatt..." Rellah's single word was loaded with every flavor of warning and determination she could pack into two syllables.

Irrational words squeezed through the cracks between Hyatt's rising anxiety and his growing need to be anywhere but where he was, sounding insane even as he heard himself say them. "Am I still dreaming?"

Rellah was as still as stone against him and her tone was too neutral for him to read. "Why would I be in your dreams, Hyatt?"

"I... well, it's –" Hyatt cursed his morning brain for using all his energy on apparent bravery, and none on helping him extract himself from Rellah's half-mounted position. "No reason. I mean – you're not."

In the process of Rellah uncoiling herself from around his side, she dragged the inside of her thigh across the top of his, and Hyatt held his breath to stop himself from making a sound until she'd risen to her knees. She ground her palms against her face to scrub the sleep from her skin and in the moment her eyes were covered, he rolled to a seated position with his back to her. The rustle of canvas folding and cotton sliding against skin behind Hyatt told him Rellah was changing and getting ready to leave, and the realization propelled him forward onto his hands and knees to crawl out of the shelter and into the pale pre-dawn light.

"Where are you going?" she called after him.

"Be right back." Hyatt pointed his reply at the shelter's opening and hoped she didn't realize it didn't answer the question.

Around the encampment, beds of cooking coals dotted the ground beneath low tarps that blocked their light from the sky. Hyatt shoved his hands in his pockets, taking in the Cern moving between their shelters and their fire pits, and scrunching his neck against the collar of his jacket to block out the cold morning air. He stamped his boots against the hard forest floor, willing the blood from his hips to flow towards his feet to warm them and simultaneously alleviate the evidence of his reaction. One of the Cern noticed him and gave him a brief nod, just his nose jerking upward, before returning his attention to the meat and vegetables he was skewering on a metal rod.

The shelter rustled behind him as Rellah emerged, her pack on her shoulders and his dragging behind her. "You good?"

"Uh-huh." He nodded and raised his hands just in time to catch the pack she shoved into his chest, then slid an arm through one of the straps. "You?"

Instead of answering, she turned to take in the camp. While her gaze wandered from one cluster of Cern to another, Hyatt's attention shifted from the full quiver of arrows on her hip to the extra bulk of her pack from provisions Grehv had given them. His eyes finally reached the profile of her face, a tension in her cheekbones and a distance in her eyes that he couldn't quite place and felt wrong interrupting. Instead Hyatt waited, pulling the other strap of his pack over his shoulder and checking the buckles to ensure they wouldn't bind or give way.

"I'm good," she replied with a single nod like she was nailing the answer home for herself. "Let's go find that Keeper."

They walked together between the coal pits and the shelters, and as the Cern sentries at the perimeter came into view, Hyatt looked back at the sprawl of the encampment. "And idea how we're going to do that?"

"Hy-att." The way she said his name was two-syllables of exasperation and he realized to her, he'd just asked her how a river was going to make it to a lake.

"Right. Sorry." He nodded like he knew the obvious answer, and hoped she believed him.

As they approached the sentries, Hyatt recognized Ehtred lingering nearby with a Cern blade in hand, and saw Ehtred see him too. He glanced at Rellah who merely shrugged, then headed toward the Cern leader to meet him halfway. Ehtred reached out as he drew close and Hyatt remembered their greeting at the ambush site just in time to grab the man by his forearm, stepping close so their shoulders could connect. He let go when Ehtred did and fought the urge to immediately step back, though it felt too close to have a conversation.

The Cern leader spun the weapon once like he was checking the balance, then handed it to Hyatt. "It's not as good as mine, but it will get you where you're going."

A thank-you rose in Hyatt as an instinct but he bit it off, accepting the weapon and flipping it over once like Ehtred had done though he had no idea what he was checking for. "It will work."

"Raiders found another weed north of the ambush site, cut apart with a serrated blade." The Cern leader nodded to the side, like the general gesture was a straight line to the place he was talking about. "Looks like the Iron is ten, maybe twelve hours ahead of you. Good hunting, becquerel."

Hyatt felt another wash of gratitude for the information and suppressing it felt like he was trying to be somebody else, someone different than he'd always been. "Take care, Ehtred."

He started walking and felt the solid impact of the Cern's palm against his shoulder, clapping hard enough to rattle his lungs in his chest. Rellah had lingered in the periphery while they spoke but caught up as he passed between the sentries, and by the time the Cern guards receded and disappeared into the shade of the trees, she was walking beside him. Neither spoke until they'd walked far enough for the brush and foliage to obscure the Cleft Rock encampment entirely.

"I have so many questions," Hyatt said, breaking the silence first, "about so many things that just happened."

"Okay," Rellah replied, surprising him. "Ask them, all together, all at once."

Faced with her terms, he had no idea where to begin. "Why aren't you Cern? Is it because you're Claimed – and what does that mean, anyway? What's a becquerel? I thought Cern and Irons had a truce, or a deal, or whatever – did Grehv really think I was going to kill Delores? Did you? Why don't Cern thank each other? What did they mean, about you only having a day? How... no, that's it."

Rellah didn't answer for ten more steps, letting the rhythmic shift of branches in the morning air and the eerie quiet of the Reclaimed contrast with Hyatt's salvo of questions.

"Well?" he asked.

"Those aren't your questions," she replied, looking away from him to track a sound she heard but he didn't through the forest. "That's you being a weed, trying to get all the information you can and know as much about everything you can before you ask the question you really want to ask. I'm not going to waste my time on weed questions."

Hyatt tried not to look shocked or offended by her statement. "What's my real question?"

"That's another weed question." Rellah shook her head like she couldn't believe what she was hearing.

Rather than risk a third admonishment, Hyatt abandoned the conversation and walked quietly beside her. He was unused to the way the Cern weapon swung against his belt and thudded against his thigh, and he rested his hand idly on the grip as they made their way through the Reclaimed. Daylight spread across the forest floor around him like spilled paint, driving the shadows back under the low brush and closer to the pale trunks of the slender trees.

When he felt like enough time had passed, he tried again. "Do you think Delores caught the Keeper?"

"How would I know that?" Rellah's started with a barbed tone but caught herself and when she continued, it was more conversational. "It's okay not to know things. We'll find out when we get there."

He nodded, wondering if he'd upset her again or if something else was going on. Rather than ask, he took her cue and instead dug an herb-twist from his jacket, quietly peeling away the wax paper and nodded and took a bite before handing it back. Something in the exchange made him feel better about her unwillingness to talk.

They walked for an hour under the slowly rising sun and interlaced branches of the canopy before Rellah stopped, cocking her head to listen. Hyatt couldn't hear anything but froze as well, turning only his head to search as far as he could see in the forest. The trees had grown thicker and closer together without him noticing, and the brush was taller, but he couldn't find whatever had made her pause.

"What is that?" Rellah asked.

Hyatt couldn't hear anything, and shook his head, confused. Rellah squinted one eye and turned slowly like she was being led by her ear until she was facing the opposite way, then pivoted towards him.

"It's coming from your pack." She took a step backward and her palm hovered over the knocks of the arrows in her hip quiver. "What the hell is that whine?"

He jerked a strap off his shoulder and spun free of the remaining one, and the bag hit the ground with a thud. "I can't hear it – what are you hearing?"

She shook her head, searching for words as he knelt down and tore at the fasteners that held the top flap of his ruck closed. "I don't know, it's – it's like when you're too close to a really loud explosion, and your ears sing after. But high – really high."

He poured through the contents of his pack, dumping shirts and towels and socks onto the floor without a second look. He picked up the ration packs Cleft Rock had given him and tossed them aside plunging deeper through fabric and tools, unsure what he was looking for, and suddenly froze. In the bottom of his bag, the device from Iron Sawmet's hold was flashing a bright blue pulse through the death markings on its lid.

When he uncovered it, Rellah's squint became a wince and she took another step backward. "What the fuck is that?"

"Uhhhh..." The noise came from Hyatt's throat as his brain refused to reconcile what he was seeing with the possible meanings. "It's... you know that thing I found at the crater?"

Rellah kept backing up and Hyatt started to follow her example, but he suddenly realized he could hear it too, a high-pitched whistling whine that made the bones in his neck hurt.

He gritted his teeth and picked it up, watching the azure light from the device's lid ebb and flow.

"Get away from it, you fucking weed!" Rellah shouted at him and reversed direction, breaking into a charge toward him.

He was so engrossed in the little metal box that her words washed off him. He felt around the edges for the ribbed edge he'd found before and pressed on it, trying to slide the two halves apart. As he did, the lights on the lid stopped blinking and stayed on. Fascinated, he pressed the lid a little bit further – and Rellah slammed into him like a battering ram.

Her shoulder connected with his sternum as she speared him with her body. The device popped out of his hand and flung skyward like a shooting star, tumbling end over and gleaming in the early morning light. His lungs emptied from the impact and locked, refusing to fill with air again, and he hit the ground on his shoulders with nothing left to expel. Rellah wrapped around him as their momentum rolled them over each other across the dirt until they tumbled to a stop ten paces from his discarded pack. The device hit the ground with a thud.

"You're such a rotten pile of compost!" Rellah shouted at him, struggling to free her arm from under him where his weight was trapped.

Hyatt opened his mouth to protest, but his body was still remembering how to breathe and his words came out as an incoherent wheeze. He sucked air in with a sound like it was raking its way down his throat to reach his lungs, and he swallowed hard as his chest tightened to reflexively push the air back out.

"What if it killed you, you dumb weed?" Rellah roared, as mad as he'd seen her since the Moss Wall encampment. "You're all I have – you stupid dumb fucking rotten compost! I'd be alone! Don't take stupid fucking risks like that, do you hear me!"

Hyatt hadn't been ready to be tackled, but the raw emotion pouring out of Rellah made him wish she would have hit him again instead. His eyes welled up and he moved his lips, willing them to tell her he was sorry, but he couldn't. The feeling of hot tears burning trails down his face embarrassed him and he shook his head to try to clear them, taking deep and shallow breaths and rising to his knees.

"Okay. I hear you," he choked out, rubbing his throat where the syllables took their ounce of flesh on the way through. "I got it."

She hit him in the arm, hard, and then decided it wasn't enough and flailed with three more poorly aimed punches into his chest and shoulders. "You're a real idiot, Hyatt."

"It couldn't have killed us. I don't think so anyway." His choice of defense ignited Rellah's rage again and her eyes widened, and Hyatt brought his arms up to defend himself from another barrage. "It's not a weapon! It's used to –"

"It's called an Untethered Communicator." Delores broke in as she emerged from behind a larger tree's trunk a dozen paces away, her weapon drawn. "But you knew that, right Hyatt?"

TWENTY

Hyatt forced himself to his feet and as Delores walked towards him, he realized his hand had found its way into a death grip around the handle of his Cern blade. The Iron saw it too, her whole head turning with the shift of her gaze to his whitened knuckles before looking up to meet his eyes with an expression that chilled him to the core.

"So the artist found a sword... still swimming, Hyatt?" she asked, the edges of her words rounded with a satin touch.

"Still swimming," he replied evenly.

He wondered if he could get the weapon free of his belt in time to stop her from cutting him in half, or if it would even matter. The smooth, careless, confident way she moved unnerved him and he flashed back to her cutting Sawmet's head off, and he was certain he lacked the skill or practice to keep himself alive if she planned to kill him. Beside him, Rellah rose with an arrow in hand and shifted away from him, creating space for them both to fight.

"Do you want to see the end of your story, Hyatt?" Her tone turned up like a question, but there was no curiosity in it.

"That's close enough, Iron," he answered as he drew his weapon and gripped it with both hands, hoping he sounded braver than he felt. "You're not ending my story here."

Delores continued forward, lifting her blade at arm's length to point it at Rellah and track along with her movements without taking her eyes off Hyatt. "I'm not ending your story at all. Only two forces have that power – Sklodowska's will and your bad choices. Put that thing down – now."

"Don't do it, Hyatt," Rellah called to him. "She'll kill you."

Delores ignored her and took two more steps, stopping just far enough apart that their weapons could touch if they reached toward each other. "I know Sklodowska's will. Don't let your bad choices get you killed. I won't ask you again, Hyatt."

He darted his eyes to Rellah and then back to the Iron, who was staring him down with an intensity that felt like it was burning his retinas away. Her face was locked in that same expression she'd worn when they'd left the crater, awash with her fanatical faith in her divine patron and ready to do anything she believed Sklodowska asked of her.

"Not happening, Iron. You were gone before I found the Untethered Communicator, and I'm not letting you kill me over it. Let's get this over with." The leather wrapping around his weapon's handle creaked under the pressure as Hyatt adjusted his grip, and he whispered to himself, "It's my fucking jacket."

As if his last word was a signal, Rellah charged Delores. Hyatt watched it happen in slow motion as Delores pulled the pommel of her blade to her chest, wrapped her second hand around the grip, and spun in a full circle.

"No!" he screamed, breaking into a sprint towards the Iron.

The flat of Delores' blade smashed into Rellah's head at full extension with a sickening crunch and the Iron turned through the strike, ending with her weapon at arm's length and the point leveled at the bridge of Hyatt's nose. He jerked himself to a stop just before he would have speared his face on the gleaming tip.

"She'll live." Delores' words were carved in ice. "You might too, if you put that sword down. Put it down, Hyatt. Now."

He stared at her down the length of her short, broad blade and saw nothing in her direct gaze that implied she would hesitate to lean forward and drive the tip through his head like a tent-spike. Behind her in Hyatt's periphery, Rellah lay motionless but not bleeding with her arrows half-expelled from their quiver across the ground.

She could have killed her and didn't. I hope that means something. Hyatt released one hand from the leather wrap of his Cern weapon and extended it away from him with the other one. He uncurled his fingers from around it and it dropped, the weight of the blade pulling it towards the ground and embedding at an angle in the earth. Disarmed, he kept his hands out and away, waiting for the Iron to respond.

"A week ago, you were terrified of your own shadow." Delores lowered her blade but kept it between herself and Hyatt as she moved in an equidistant arc around him until she stood between him and the abandoned device. "Now you're willing to fight for a Cern raider and hide an Untethered Communicator from an Iron. You must see Sklodowska's hand in that."

As the Iron backed up towards the pack, Hyatt moved forward, keeping the distance between them. "Is that why you came back for us? Did you dream that I still have a part to play in this plan?"

Delores knelt beside the Untethered Communicator and scooped it up in her palm. "They're not dreams, Hyatt, any more than your desire to protect Rellah is a whim. And yes, you still have a part to play."

His eyes darted to the unconscious Cern, but she hadn't moved. He was glad to see there was no blood pooling around her head, but it did nothing to relieve the tightness in his stomach. As the Iron slid the device apart and moved her thumb over the keypad, he made his way around her with careful steps towards Rellah.

"Where's the Keeper?" he asked as the whine from the device faded until he could no longer hear it, the blue light from the lid ebbing and dying before the Iron pocketed it.

Delores nodded back the way she'd come. "He's almost to the ruins. We won't catch him before he arrives."

Hyatt reached Rellah and knelt beside her, placing his hand over her mouth and nose. Her warm, wet breath was shallow but stuck to his hand, and he rolled her onto her back. Her eyes were closed but her chest rose and fell, so he looked up at the Iron who was sheathing her weapon.

"Coming back for us was more important than catching the Keeper?" he asked, suspicious. "Isn't catching him the whole point?"

"Where did you get the Communicator?" she asked.

"Answer my question first – why did you come back for us instead of catching up with the Keeper?" he replied. "This would all be over by now if you'd killed him like you planned! That's why we're here!"

Delores waited, letting Hyatt's frustration hang in the forest air between them until the sheer vastness of the Reclaimed sapped its vehemence. She picked up his abandoned pack and casually rifled through the handful of possessions not already scattered across the ground, then dropped it.

"Don't play with me, Hyatt, first of Brathnee," she warned, returning her full attention to him where he crouched beside Rellah. "Where did you get it?"

The edge in her tone caught against something inside him and he rose, his tongue coppery with the anticipation of confrontation. He curled his hands into fists and squared himself with her, regretting in a flash that he'd dropped his weapon. Delores didn't move except to turn and fully face him, her thumbs hooked through her belt.

On the ground beside him, Rellah rolled onto her side and pressed her hand to the side of her skull where Delores' weapon had left a thick, swollen knot. "Ask your god, Iron – or doesn't she know either?"

While Rellah climbed to her knees and collected her arrows, Delores kept her eyes on Hyatt like a hawk searching the forest floor for mice. "Hyatt?"

"The Cleft Rock Pack Master gave it to me after you disappeared," he replied. "They were going to send it to an Iron but I said I was headed to find you, and I'd bring it to you. Now you have it."

"I have it." She stared at him with a piercing look that made Hyatt feel like she knew he was lying, but he stared back without a word. "Put your gear back in your pack and get your sword – we have a lot of ground to cover."

He moved towards his pack at the Iron's feet as she walked away from it, headed towards Rellah, and he cast them a sideways glance as he shoved his belongings back into the bag. The Iron spoke in a low tone and he could read the tension on Rellah's face, but was too far away to make out her words. By the time he'd closed the straps over the top flap of his pack, the Cern was on her way to gather her own. Without waiting for either of them, Delores started in the direction she'd appeared from.

"Are you okay?" he asked as he reached Rellah. "Anything broken?"

She shrugged. "I won't die."

They followed the Iron through the Reclaimed, keeping five paces behind her as she navigated over the rolling terrain. "What did Delores say?"

"She said she and I can finish our fight after we get you to the ruins, but that's more important." Rellah's reply ended on a deep breath and after a moment she added, "and I agreed."

Her tone was matter-of-fact, but the meaning raced through Hyatt like an electric jolt anyway. "You're going to fight Delores after we kill the Keeper? That's insane – she has to go find Sawmet's replacement, and you'll never see her again. We can all just walk away."

"And go where, Hyatt?" It wasn't quite a snap, but the edges of her words were jagged.

He didn't have an answer for her and so he walked in silence, staring at the Iron's shoulders and focusing on moving quietly. The ground was dry but the scattered leaves were damp with morning dew and made no crunching noise as they walked, and avoiding the brush and branches that reached for his pants and sleeves had become second nature. The sun had risen high enough against the horizon to filter through the canopy more downward than across, carving long and dark shadows from the trees to vanishing points in the dirt.

The earth began to slope downwards and the trees began to thin as they made their way down the embankment. Ahead through the brush, the stone walls and moss-covered pillars of a ruin began to peak between the low brush, rusted metal rods extending from broken brick and mortar at angles too straight to appear in nature. The sight of it still made Hyatt's spine tingle, but he knew they hadn't traveled far enough to reach the circled space on the map. He glanced at Rellah, but she hadn't glanced at him since her rhetorical question and didn't return his apprehensive gaze.

Watching Delores angle toward the structure instead of choosing a route around the outside did nothing to calm his nerves, and as they drew closer, he realized she was headed for the open door in the wall. Her blade sang free of its sheath as she reached the doorframe and she lingered outside for a moment, glancing back to see how far behind her they were, then stepped over the threshold.

"What is this compost..." he muttered.

Getting close to the outer wall of the ruin made Hyatt's skin crawl, a kind of primal aversion to the place that he'd never felt before. He almost hesitated, but the sound of Rellah unslinging her bow from her pack behind him steadied him some. As he popped the restraint around his weapon's handle, the stillness of the place struck him – it was different than the rest of the Reclaimed that seemed to sway and shift with a thousand inaudible sounds at all times. The broken and overgrown structure seemed to drain not just sound but life itself, making the moss that grew on it feel hollow and the saplings closest to it vacant and unresponsive to sun. The shadow of the doorframe felt foreboding as it passed over Hyatt in a thin band, dividing the world beyond from the world within.

Ahead of him, Delores had moved to the center of the large square room and was turning slowly, taking in the metal rafters and crumbling walls held together by vegetation and rust. Light streamed through the gaps but carried no warmth with it, bleak and pale, but it made Delores' eyes shine brighter as she stared up into it. The scene was otherworldly to Hyatt, the Iron bathed in cold light amidst the ruins from an earlier History.

"This is not a good place," Rellah said quietly, appearing by his side without the sound of a footfall. "We shouldn't be here."

Hyatt didn't answer – it needed no answer. He could feel it. Instead he watched Delores complete her slow turn, looking upward at the sun, until she lowered her head and nodded to the long hallway exiting the room from the far side.

"This way."

By the time Hyatt and Rellah caught up with her, Delores had left the enveloping light of the large chamber and made her way into the growing shadows of the hall. A complete ceiling let no light through and made the ivory and pale green walls seem sinister as they faded to black on either side, and Hyatt had to close the distance to the Iron to keep her in sight. He could feel Rellah behind him and clung to that sense to steady himself.

Open doorways on the left side of the hall opened into unlit rooms, each filled with darkness that made Hyatt cling to the right edge of the corridor. He'd never seen Keeper marks in person, but he recognized the sky-blue splashes of paint on the doorframes that said the cloistered researchers had explored the rooms in years gone by. As Hyatt followed Delores through the broken sunlight that poured through the ceiling of the ruin, he imagined the robed researchers sifting through the rubble for manuscripts from the Histories and dangerous artifacts while a Skarren circled in above them and a Veshtrue stalked around the exterior, waiting for them to emerge. The image pulled every muscle in his body taut and he curled his fingers tighter around his weapon.

Ahead, Delores stepped out of the hallway and into a stairwell, light pouring in through collapsed side wall. Vines and moss tinged everything green over layers of amber rust, and the metal edge-guards of the steps that ascended to a missing second floor were bent as if a monumental force had slammed into them. The Iron instead turned toward the canted staircase of tin metal steps that descended into the floor and the waiting darkness below, protected from oblivion only by a thin metal rail that veered away and broke four steps down.

"There's no way..." Hyatt began, but trailed off as he realized the unthinkable was about to become the inevitable.

Delores spared him a bemused look over her shoulder before descending the first step, and he watched her move down the stairs as if she was descending into a pool of pitch-black water.

Rellah caught up with him as the Iron reached the first platform and turned the corner, and she leaned over the railing to look down at the top of Delores' head.

"This is an even worse idea," Her voice was heavy with certainty. "Let's go."

Hyatt felt his agreement with her like a fist-sized rock in his stomach and as he descended the steps after the Iron, it felt like the shadows were wrapping themselves around his calves and dragging him under. The rusted metal creaked under his boots and he didn't know if it was flexing beneath his weight or if he was imagining it, but he moved his weapon to his off-hand and clung to the railing bolted to the wall between each step. The Iron rounded a corner in the square stairwell and he lost sight of her. With a grimace, he hurried down the ancient steps to catch up to her.

"Go slow, Hyatt," Rellah warned him. "Test each step. She'll wait at the bottom."

Lingering on each step as he tested the next one was counter to every survival instinct in Hyatt that screamed for him to keep moving, but he locked his jaw and slowed down. Every new step down groaned as his weight stressed the metal and his knuckles turned white against the railing, listening to the rapid clang of Delores hurrying down the stairwell below. He focused on the sound of Rellah behind and above him, moving with purpose and caution. As they descended, the light from above became thinner and thinner, until he could barely make out the steps as a different shade of black against the darkness.

"Do you know this place?" Hyatt eased himself down onto the broad landing and worked his way along the wall to the next flight of stairs without looking back at her.

"I know places like these," she replied, further behind him than Hyatt. "There is one in Moss Wall. Cern die there every year.

Delores' steps sounded unconcerned and fainter as she stretched the space between them, and Hyatt tried to guess how many landings were between them and the Iron. "Great. Thanks, Rellah."

"We're probably going to die too," she added in a tone that might have sounded casual but carried a taut undertone as she reached the platform and Hyatt stepped onto the next stair. "Anything you wish you'd done first?"

Her grim, candid question jarred him, and he hesitated. His thoughts turned to Gorman, making up nonsense to add excitement to an ordinary day, and to Jenna who started his trip unimpressed with him and ended it treating him as something like a friend. He envisioned Stella, who had never known his name but touched his arm and fawned at him to sap some of the temporary fame he'd been washed in. He flashed to Moss Wall camp, a thousand tiny moments on their journey since then, the death-defying ride on the Rail, and the way the Cleft Rock packmaster had mistaken him for Cern.

"I wish... I think I wish that I'd talked to Shelara's sprouts," he replied as he stepped down onto the next step, listening to it groan as the metal strained in protest, "and I wish I'd gotten to the Veshtrue first, so you could go home after all of this."

Rellah took so long to answer that Hyatt had descended four more steps and wondered on each one if he'd said the wrong thing, failed a test he hadn't recognized. Every new stair attacked his answer from a new angle and he could no longer see the next one, feeling his way downward and wondering why he always felt like he was missing Rellah's meaning when she spoke and giving the wrong answer to questions she asked.

"That's all?" Her indiscernible tone did nothing to let him off the hook.

Hyatt let his hand on the railing carry more of his weight as he felt for the next step, racking his brain for what other answer she might have expected. His thoughts flashed to Rellah in the reading room of Iron Sawmet's hold, legs stretched out and crossed in front of her, and for the first time he was grateful for the darkness that hid the heat rising to his face. He found the next platform and worked along the wall again, glancing back at Rellah and catching the single sliver of daylight drawing a pinpoint line along the bands of her braid as she passed through it on the stairs behind him.

"That's all." He tried to sound gruff and certain. "I lived an easy life, and then an exciting life. I'm set."

Again, the silence that followed his statement seemed to gain mass until it almost crushed Hyatt's lungs and anchored him in place. He found his way around the corner to the next flight of stairs and realized the sound of Delores' descent had stopped. Hyatt could no longer make out the steps as a variation of the darkness. Four more platforms spanned the distance between him and Delores, and Rellah didn't say a word as they climbed down. Four of the steps wilted under his weight but stopped short of collapsing, and he made it to the last platform after what seemed like a year of carefully placing every step.

As Hyatt rounded the corner and reached the top of the last flight of stairs when he heard Delores below. "I'm going to make light – watch your eyes."

He closed his eyes and turned into the wall, recalling the blinding flash of green and violet that had knocked him unconscious, and didn't know if he was disappointed or relieved when he heard the familiar sound of a magnesium flare igniting. Whatever feeling it caused, it was washed away on a tide of frustration as he squinted to let his eyes adjust and hurried down the last flight.

"You had flares the whole rotted time?" he shouted, incredulous.

Delores shrugged, unimpressed by his outrage. "We didn't need them for that part."

The blinding light from the stick in Delores' hand doused the large, square room in red-orange light and drove the shadows to the corners and the creases between the off-white bricks where the mortar had been eroded by time. As she raised it over her head, it lit up the dark and yawning opening to another long hallway with no doors or windows on either side, with metal bars bolted to the floor that reminded Hyatt of the Rail from Ceojic.

"We need it for that," she added as Rellah reached the bottom step and appeared beside Hyatt.

He felt himself nodding before he realized he was doing it. *Of course we're going down the long, dark, underground hallway. Great.*

Rellah unslung her bow and checked the tips to make sure the string was set evenly on the tracks of the wheels on either end, and Delores started down the corridor with the flare in her hand driving the darkness back before her. As the Cern pulled an arrow from her quiver and curled her fingers around its shaft, Hyatt started after the Iron, but Rellah reached over her shoulder with the arrow and used the tail end of the broadhead to pull him backward. It caught him by surprise and the twin points pricked against him, forcing him to stumble as he tried to keep his footing until his shoulders were against her chest and her hips pressed against the back of his pants.

"You missed something," Her words next to his ear had that indecipherable tone again, coated with a sticky meaning he couldn't read. "Try not to die yet."

He opened his mouth without anything to say, and her closed fist between his shoulder blades propelled him forward down the hall after the silhouette of Delores framed in bright, foreboding light.

TWENTY-ONE

The underground corridor from the stairs within the ruins was longer than Hyatt had imagined a man-made structure could be. It seemed to go on forever, with no breaks or discernable features to show how far they'd walked except a thick, metal support ran up the walls and across the roof every fifteen paces. Hyatt counted the first fifty before abandoning it, convinced the hallway would go on forever and they would die of starvation following the Iron into oblivion. Only the sound of Rellah's footsteps behind him and the lingering confusion on her cryptic remark stopped him from pausing to rest and reconsider his choice to follow Delores.

"How do you know this place?" He tried to be quiet, but the way it reverberated against the unforgiving walls of the hallway made it louder and sharper than he wanted.

"The Keepers found one of the Warnings here," the Iron replied, as if she was commenting on how mild the weather was.

He was glad she was walking in front of him, so she couldn't see his back stiffen or his jaw fall open. If she felt any change, it didn't show – her stride stayed purposeful but unperturbed at the center of the pool of light that drove the darkness back before them and stretched her shadow past him on the hallway's floor. He shook his head at her.

"Okay, but you weren't alive then. How do you know about it?" He thought he heard Rellah snicker behind him, but couldn't be sure it wasn't a spot of dust caught in her throat.

Delores half-turned to catch him in her periphery, a smirk tugging at the corner of her lips. "There is a field of Low Flowers near here. The Iron that trained me was born there."

Her statement about the origins of one of the Warnings had caught Hyatt off-guard, but the mention of her Calling struck him as well. He tried to draw up anything he knew about her before she became an Iron, but beyond her youth in Ceojic, he couldn't summon any meaningful detail. As he followed her down the corridor, he wondered how he'd spent a week in her company and had no idea what trade she'd committed to or if she had any family. He wasn't sure if he was disappointed in himself or impressed with her for the enigma.

"Where does it lead?" The dam was broken and Hyatt felt compelled to fill the silence with more questions.

Delores didn't answer for a moment, but Rellah picked up the thread. "We're headed northwest. She's trying to get ahead of the Keeper, and if he's injured, fighting through the Reclaimed... we might."

"We will," the Iron replied, absolutely certain, "and he is."

Ahead, the corridor changed for the first time in what felt like hours. It widened into a long room with raised platforms on either side and as they pressed forward in the lower level, Hyatt looked up at the faces of square pillars that appeared at the edges of the flare's glow. Some had pieces missing and others were broken through entirely, chunks of column and the roof they had supported scattered around their bases. Others bore fragments of glass that might have once been a full sheet, bolted to the column by rusted pins and edges glittering wickedly in the red-orange light.

The air tasted stale and damp, and Hyatt licked his lips to clear the feeling of it clinging to them, He tried to guess how far underground they were, but he'd lost track of the flights of stairs they had descended into the terrifying darkness. The space of the room relieved him of a claustrophobia he recognized within himself but replaced it with the danger of anything else that could occupy the black shadows that encroached on them from every side. With a shudder, he quickened his pace to close the distance to the Iron ahead of him.

"Stop." Rellah's word behind him was just above a breath, but perfectly clear.

The muscles in Hyatt's body locked before he consciously registered its meaning. As soon as he froze, he heard a whispering hiss and knew she must have picked it up in the background of their footsteps. Ahead, Delores dropped to her knees and ground the flare into the corridor's floor. They were plunged into sudden darkness, save for the lingering embers of the flare's tip that refused to surrender to the blackness.

His pulse began to quicken and he took a deep, slow breath to try and fight it, but his hands turned clammy anyway and he had a flash of panic that they might sweat too much to keep his grip on his blade. He wanted to ask what it was, but in the moment that it took for his voice to fail him, he realized he should be as quiet as he was still. Close to him, he heard the barely audible shift of the wheels on Rellah's bow rotating, and the hissing he couldn't place was joined by the whisper of Delores' strange weapon coming free from its sheath.

The foreign sound moved and he turned his head to track it, willing his pupils to expand and soak up light that wasn't there so he could see the threat. Rellah's prediction of their deaths rattled around in his skull and his Cern weapon suddenly felt both less useful and more important than it had been when he was carrying it moment before. As he tried to track the sound of the danger in the dark, he caught himself missing the Reclaimed, with a thousand places to hide but daylight or starlight to find the things that tried to kill him and plenty of space to run if he needed to. As the belated realization that it was the wilderness he missed rather than the high, safe walls of the Garden, Rellah's bowstring twacked and snapped him back to the moment that life-or-death circumstance made infinitely small and granular.

Hyatt knew that the flight time of Rellah's arrow couldn't have been more than a second, but the space between the sound of her shot and the shriek that followed seemed to last for six breaths. When the piercing howl of agony reached him, it was like it came from everywhere all at once, high-pitched and saturated with surprise and pain. The roar of it made him crush his eyes closed as if it could rupture his retinas and he staggered backward, but Rellah's palm between his shoulder blades stopped him and propelled him forward towards where he'd last seen Delores.

"Run, Hyatt!" she shouted, and her bowstring sang again.

The force of her shove left Hyatt no opportunity to argue, and he stumbled into a sprint as he tried to keep his feet. Running in the pitch black was terrifying and he expected every step to trip him or slam his knees into something immovable. He crossed the space where Delores had extinguished her flare, but wherever she had moved to, she was no longer in his path. Behind him, the speed at which Rellah poured arrows from her bow into the darkness made him wonder how she was moving that fast. He ran from the screeching howl of whatever terror lived in the corridor's depths that changed pitch and direction in a grisly rhythm with Rellah's bowstring, sending arrows into it and driving it between the pillars in the dark.

A blinding flash and concussive roar exploded behind him and knocked him flat, and the air left his lungs as he slammed into the rails that ran the length of the hallway. As he planted his hands on the cold metal and forced himself to his knees, another sound reached him and with a start, he realized Delores was singing. Before he could react, a hand coated in something warm and wet was curling into his collar and hauling him bodily to his feet.

"Go!" Rellah shouted, her breath close enough to his face for him to smell the mint and thyme of an herb-twist on her breath. "We have to go!"

She shoved him again and he was moving before he could will his legs to obey. He couldn't stop looking backward at the flashes of blinding light that filled the room behind them, blinding bursts of violet and evergreen that lasted less than the space of a blink and left veinous glowing patterns behind his eyelids when he closed them against the unbearable brilliance.

"What the fuck is it?" he yelled as they ran, the need to know one of the hundred fractured thoughts in his head trying to escape his ears and nose and mouth.

"It's a –" Whatever Rellah was about to say was drowned out in another ear-splitting roar that shook the floor and walls of the corridor.

As the deafening sound faded, Hyatt realized he could no longer hear her running behind him. With a growl, he planted his foot to stop his own sprint and raced back until he felt her, then pulled her to her up by her shoulders to her feet.

"Drashvoy!" she gasped out on a breath not yet fully formed from her fall. "Pack-slayers. We have to get out of this rotted tunnel."

"Is Delores—" he started.

"Fucking run, Hyatt!" she screamed at him, and then they were running again.

When his lungs began to scream from the exertion, Rellah outpaced him, but he chased after her. When she got far enough ahead to turn around and knock another arrow to cover the hall behind him, he demanded more from his legs than he thought they had to give. As they put more distance between themselves and the Drashvoy, the flashes and blasts in the long room with the columns stopped. Rellah didn't let him stop running until silence settled over them, and Hyatt doubled over with his hands on his knees as he fought the urge to vomit.

"We are okay," Rellah said.

Nothing in Hyatt felt okay. His blood was rushing in his ears, and breathing felt both magnificent and agonizing. The contrast of the strobing green and violet light with the repeated roar of blasts he couldn't place and the darkness that saturated the corridor made his head swim, and the desperate sprint through the dark made him certain he would vomit at any moment. The silence in the wake of near-death felt like the ground was made of water and he leaned against the wall to feel something solid and stable.

From the direction they had come, Delores' footsteps were unmistakable in their cadence, lackadaisical and unhurried as if an Heir hadn't nearly killed all of them moments before. Through the rushing in his ears and the tightness in his sternum, Hyatt listened to her approach until the hiss and brilliance of a flare freed her from the darkness, and when he saw her face and hands streaked with blood it pushed him over the edge to retching in the corridor. Blood spattered her face and clung to her hair, dripping in stringy trails from her jacket and the blade of her weapon, and something about the way her lips were pursed in an idle whistle made seeing her all the more horrifying.

"Still swimming, Hyatt?" She wiped her hand against her jacket, smearing gore across the leather.

He straightened himself despite another spasm in his sternum that threatened to expel bile, spitting the warm, metallic saliva from his tongue. "How... how did you..."

"I just did what Her plan required," Delores replied as she passed him, slapping him on his shoulder and leaving a clear handprint in blood. "Whatever it takes."

As Delores continued through the underground tunnel, Hyatt glanced back at the room and recalled the roars and flashes as the Iron had fought the Heir. Memories of Rellah's version of Iron history intermixed with the raw, unbridled power that had allowed one woman to stand before a Drashvoy and survive, and suddenly it seemed more plausible that someone with so much power could obliterate a Garden. Rellah passed him and became a silhouette between the flare and Hyatt, her fingers adjusting the arrows left in her hip quiver and the profile of her features turned towards him to make sure he was following. When he did, she focused on Delores' back and matched her pace.

By the time they reached the end of the corridor two hours later, Hyatt had traded the adrenaline and terror of encountering the Heir for the more familiar exhaustion in his legs and shoulders of traveling with Delores. The room that the hallway emptied into was square with an ascending staircase and two more corridors that led left and right, but the light from the flare showed impassible debris that blocked both hallways. Hyatt wondered as he watched Delores mount the first step and start her ascent if she had known the end of the passage would be clear, or if they might have come to a cave-in like those that blocked the other corridors and been trapped. He stared after her until she reached the first platform and turned the corner, siphoning the light of the flare from his view, then started after her but stopped when he felt Rellah's hand close around his shoulder.

"Hyatt, I need to tell you something about the Keeper we are hunting." Her words, clipped and direct, felt like getting pelted with fistfuls of ice.

"We can talk about it when we–" Hyatt pushed the words through a growing tightness in his chest, an indescribable aversion to hearing whatever Rellah was about to say.

"No." Her hand tightened over his collarbone as he tried to pull away, anchoring him in place. "It will be time to kill him soon, and then Delores and I will do what we have to do, but it matters that you didn't think I lied to you. Before."

He turned around, and in the pitch-dark absence of the flare's glow, he could feel something dreadful filling the space between them. Hyatt wished for a flicker of light so he could see Rellah's irises and the scar almost invisibly nestled in her hairline, anything to ground the moment in the woman he'd come to know and trust instead of whoever she might be about to become.

And love, he realized, so clearly that there was no defense for it. *Know, and trust, and love.*

"Tell me." He thought he would choke out the words but they were flat and direct, and the wild, uninvited thought came to him that in another moment, Rellah would have been proud of him.

"The Eighth Warning he's looking for... it might be real."

TWENTY-TWO

Hyatt couldn't answer Rellah, because the air in his lungs had turned to concrete and refused to pull any more in or push any sound out. It felt like the darkness itself was suffocating him while the Cern's words slammed into him again and again. The sound of Delores' footsteps above them had faded to a distant whisper of resonant metal as steps flexed and protested under her ascent.

When he didn't reply, she kept talking, her voice low and her cadence quickening as she went. "There's a Cern story, something pack-teachers tell sprouts –"

"What..." Hyatt muttered, the only sound he could make.

"—about the end of the last... what do you call them, Histories? Right before the Iron Accords. While the Irons were meeting with the High Rangers and the Pack Masters, nine Cern raiders hit a group of Keepers at a ruin. Everyone died, on both sides –"

"What?" Hyatt interrupted again, his word gaining volume and a steel core.

"Except two Cern raiders, who left the Reclaimed with whatever they took from the Keepers. Their pack recovered seven bodies and the binding of a book with the pages ripped out, new tears – "

"What the fuck are you saying right now, Rellah?" he shouted into the darkness between them, loud enough that he heard her take a step backward. "Are you saying – "

Her voice was tight but calmer than his. "It doesn't change anything, Hyatt! We still have to stop him from breaking the other Warnings! I just – "

"Just what? Just said nothing while we hunted him across the Reclaimed?" Hyatt turned to follow Delores up the stairs, but his anger wasn't spent and it whirled him back around to face Rellah again. "She thinks he's fucking insane, but he's not, is he? He thinks he's it's real!"

"What would it have changed, Hyatt? Nothing!" she snapped at him, closer than he expected. "She's going to kill him, because that's what Irons do!"

"That's rot, or you wouldn't be telling me now!" Hyatt started climbing, feeling along the handrail in the dark as he stomped his anger and hurt and betrayal into the thin, rusted metal. "Why the fuck would you tell me that now?"

Rellah's boots hit the stairs six steps below him, climbing faster than he was as he turned the corner onto the platform so she could plant two hands on his pack and shove him into the wall ahead. Hyatt caught himself on the railing and spun in the dark, one hand around his Cern blade and the other clenched tight, but couldn't react in time when she shoved him again. He instinctively brought his hands together in front of his chest where she'd pushed him, and something hard rapping against his wrist caused his fingers to spasm open and drop his weapon with a clang.

"In case it's not her, you dumb weed!" she snarled at him, so close to his face that he could see the intensity gleaming in her irises, even in the pitch black. "In case it ends up you and him, you deserve to know! So you can make a choice, no more swimming just to stay alive – a real choice!"

Her hands bashing him and her words slamming into him felt like a full sensory assault and he stood stunned, chunks of his anger breaking and falling away as he tried to understand what she was saying. He'd stopped noticing her accent, but in the dark and full of emotion, he could hear the rounded edges of her consonants and flat sounds of her vowels again. As if to drive the lesson home, she shoved him one more time and then started up the stairs. Hyatt rubbed his chest, picked up his weapon, and followed her more slowly, using the sound of her footfalls on the flexing metal to keep track of her in the dark.

As he felt his way along every step, he wondered if Rellah thought he'd been just staying alive, and that made him wonder for himself if that was what he'd been doing. The hollow clang of the stairs and the cold metal of the railing under his hand were unsympathetic, and he tried to figure out how many choices he'd made along the way and how many times he'd done as he was told. As he reached the next platform, he didn't like the conclusion he was reaching.

"You should have told me earlier," he murmured, certain from the sound of her steps that she was too far ahead to hear him.

Even as he muttered it under his breath, he knew why she hadn't. *Before, she was Cern and I was a Haleu, temporary allies and lifelong enemies. What does she think I am now?*

The first light into the stairwell from above was more of a glow than a ray, so soft it barely partitioned the outlines of the steps from the black depths below. He froze and gripped the railing as one of the steps groaned and buckled under his weight, creaking as the metal rended and threatened to break free. Hyatt gingerly eased his boot back off it, then pulled hard on the railing to propel himself over it to the stair beyond. The tug was too much for the closest anchor of the railing and it broke from the wall, three dislodged screws clanking with erratic, tinny noises as they bounced off steps and plummeted into the dark. His pulse racing, Hyatt quickened his step and didn't exhale until he reached the next platform.

For the rest of his ascent, he expected structural failings to try to kill him again, but the light grew brighter and no more ancient architecture collapsed as he climbed. His thighs burned from exertion and the wild, irrational urge to chuck his pack into the stairwell just to be free of it gripped him, but he settled for grinding his teeth and focusing on the sound of Rellah's footsteps on the thin metal stairs two flights above him. Their muted rhythm gave him something to lock his mind around and when they stopped, he knew she'd reached the surface and he was almost there.

The violent and amber twilight that slid under the canopy of the Reclaimed to wash Hyatt in cool evening light told him that he'd lost track of time in the underground corridor. He squinted into it before spotting Rellah off to the side, her backpack resting against a tree as she pulled her fingers through her hair to free it from its braids and pull the dirt and blood from her locks. She caught his glance and nodded for him to join her, and Hyatt's whole body relaxed with relief as he slid his pack's straps from his shoulders and tossed it next to hers. It hit with a careless thump and Rellah's eyes narrowed critically, but being free of the bag's weight felt too good to care.

"The Iron is down the hill, washing gore off." She nodded over a nearby knoll. "There's a little watershed pool. She thinks the Keeper is close."

Hyatt's glance in the direction Rellah nodded was half-hearted and he shrugged. "What do you think?"

The question caught her by surprise, but she squinted and looked across the forest beyond the ruins in the direction they'd come from. "It's an uphill climb and the Reclaimed is thick, but I don't know how far ahead he was when the Iron turned back. She said he was injured... it's hard to say."

"Do you think she knows?" He eased himself onto the forest floor with a groan as his legs and shoulders protested against bending, then settled back against the broad trunk beside his pack. "I mean... really?"

Rellah walked in front of him and he thought for a moment she was about to start pacing, but instead she jumped so she could grab a low branch to hang from. Her spine cracked in four places and as she rolled her head around her shoulders, the sound of crunching gravel reached him. Hyatt winced, but as she dropped back to the ground and windmilled her arms, she looked refreshed.

"I've never seen ... what she did down there." Rellah tipped her head back and forth, her ears almost touching her shoulders on each end of the motion. "Don't sit long, your muscles will become like rocks. Stay moving until we sleep."

Hyatt scowled at her, but planted his hands in the rapidly cooling earth and forced himself to his feet in a staggered movement. He could already feel the truth of her warning, the long cords of muscle in his back and the sore places between his shoulders and neck taut and refusing to extend without a fight. He mimicked her movements, swinging his arms and twisting at his waist.

Delores crested the nearby knoll like the rising sun, her hair still dripping but most of the Drashvoy's blood and intestines gone from her clothes and skin. "We can reach the site on the map by nightfall if we leave now."

Hyatt couldn't stop himself from groaning out loud. "We can't wait for him here?"

The Iron smirked but shook her head. "He could go around us, or sneak by us. The only way to be sure is to make him come to us at his destination."

He trudged back to where his pack sat at the base of the tree, scowling first at Delores and then at it as he bent down to grab the closer strap. "You could ask Sklodowska to have him come to us here. It's Her plan, right?"

Delores laughed, a sound discordant with the layers of carnage that had coated her moments before. "That's not how it works. I ask Her what the plan is – I don't make recommendations."

"Have you tried?" He gritted his teeth as the pack weighed down the places on his shoulders still tender from carrying it before.

The Iron shook her head and started walking, her hand on the grip of her weapon and an unnerving spring in her step. Hyatt picked up his weapon, instantly regretting that he hadn't collected it before putting on his pack, and by the time he started after her Rellah was moving too. They fell into step side by side, passing through the light of dusk behind Delores' silhouette.

The sounds of the Reclaimed were a persistent whisper, the rustle of leaves across the ground and the unplaceable shift of the miniature fauna that made their home in the wild. Hyatt listened to them as they walked in silence, remembering when every one of those notes would have terrified him. Instead, they were comfortable to him, a soundtrack to their journey that was unbroken but never overwhelming.

"If she can do that to a Drashvoy, maybe you shouldn't fight her." He tracked a bird breaking from its perch and darting through the branches on his left in a humming furry of short wings. "We find the Keeper, Delores goes her way, and we go ours."

"I'm not afraid of her," Rellah replied.

"You're not stupid, either." As soon as he said it, he started to say something to soften the statement, but stopped himself.

The ground began to slope upward, one more insult to Hyatt's aching legs, and more dead branches littered the forest floor. They walked without saying anything until they crested the small hill. He caught his breath as the terrain leveled again, wondering how Rellah never seemed to be out of breath or out of energy.

"Our way," she repeated, fishing an herb-twist from her pocket.

"Yeah." He couldn't read her tone but hoped she was warming to the idea. "The Iron goes back to hunting Warning violators or brokering deals between the Gardens –"

"And you?" she interrupted, a surprising bite to her tone.

"I..." he began, but his words dried on his tongue. "I don't know."

She nodded as if it was the answer she expected. Low clouds drifting in from their right conspired against the last of the daylight and all at once, the shadows deepened around them into darker pools. She quickened her stride and Hyatt stretched out his steps to keep up, and ahead the ground began to slope back down again.

"My way is Claimed. I spend the rest of my life wandering alone, hunting and killing Heirs until one of them kills me first." She took a bite from the herb-twist and talked through her teeth gnashing it. "It doesn't usually take many seasons."

Hyatt stepped over the slender, dead trunk of a fallen tree. "That rule is compost. You should be able to go home."

She shook her head. "You're missing the point."

He wasn't, but he didn't want to admit it to himself or to her. They made their way down the gentle incline and when it turned steeper, Rellah turned sideways and used the edges of her boots to control her descent. Hyatt tried to copy her and left longer grooves in the earth as he sent rocks and chunks of dirt tumbling down the incline, but he managed to keep his balance and caught up with her at the bottom of the slope.

"You don't..." he started, but trailed off again as he noticed that the rustling leaves no longer carried the current of little wings and claws throughout the Reclaimed.

Rellah nodded wordlessly and turned outward, her eyes narrowing as they swept the depths of the forest. Hyatt recognized the familiar tension in his chest and tingle in his knuckles where his fingers met his palms, and he hoped for the chitter of a chipmunk or the call of a confused songbird, but none came. He could feel every seam in the wrap of the Cern weapon he carried against his palm. The air became thinner with every passing heartbeat as he searched for whatever had silenced the animals.

As suddenly as they had stopped, the second layer of noises resumed. Rellah exhaled slowly and lowered her bow back to her side, and Hyatt rested the flat of the blade on his shoulder. He took one last look across the Reclaimed and then met Rellah's gaze, surprised to find her looking right at him.

"You don't have to wander alone." The rest of the thought left his lips without giving his mind time to mitigate it. "You can't go home and I don't think I can either. We can do it together."

"We'll die." Rellah sounded certain and resolute, but she didn't blink and she didn't look away.

Hyatt clapped her on the shoulder, the leather of her jacket warm under his hand as it contoured to his grip. "Not today."

He turned and started walking, spotting Delores further ahead between two slender trees, exhilarated by the feeling of Rellah staring a hole through his shoulders with that unreadable expression and determined not to ruin the one time he knew he'd said the right thing. By the time she fell in step beside him again, he'd recovered his composure, but nearly lost it again as she bumped her shoulder and elbow into his without a word.

The low ground was short-lived and as Hyatt began to climb again, it felt gradual at first, but fifteen minutes later it was steep enough that he needed to hold onto branches and vines to pull himself upward. Rellah climbed beside him and above them, Delores crested the steep slope and disappeared from view.

"There is no way the Keeper is going to climb this if he's injured," Hyatt gasped out between held breaths, pulling himself up to the next place he could find stability. "We could just stand at the top and put an arrow through his head."

"There you go saying 'we' again," she replied, passing him as she found complimenting handholds and pulled herself up. "Did you pick up a bow somewhere?"

He rolled his eyes and focused on climbing, planting his boot in the fork of a small tree and leveraging himself onward to the next outcropping of rock he could grab. The conversation collapsed under the strain of their ascent and they made their way over the last pitch of the hill that had become a cliff. Hyatt rolled over the top edge and lay on his back just long enough to catch his breath before crawling back to offer his hand to Rellah. She lunged to grab his arm, her fingers locking around his forearm like a vice-grip as she pulled herself over to flat ground. When she let go, he knelt and stared up at the canopy, gulping another lungful of air before struggling to his feet.

"Okay," Rellah said.

"Okay?" he echoed.

"Okay. Yes. We can go together after this, until we die." There were fewer trees at the new altitude for her matter-of-fact tone to bounce off, and it made her words sound even more nonplussed than usual. "It will probably be only a couple weeks anyway."

TWENTY-THREE

When Delores stopped ahead of Hyatt and Rellah, he thought for a moment she'd reached the edge of the world. The trees stopped and the ground fell away, and stars stretched across the midnight blue horizon of the evening sky like a mural. The twenty paces left between them had little undergrowth between the older, thicker trunks of the gnarled trees with broad canopies. Patches of gray rock dotted the forest floor as if the absence of the low brush gave them a needed chance to rise from the depths.

Delores glanced at him as he approached her left, but Hyatt barely noticed as he took in the plunging depth before him. He wondered if it was the encroaching night that made the yawning chasm look bottomless, or if it would have swallowed daylight the same way. Only the blotted-out stars told him the world continued on the other side, an uneven line carving across the sky in jagged peaks and valleys.

"I guess we're not going that way," he said, hooking his thumbs under the straps of his pack. "The good news is, neither is the Keeper."

Rellah reached his other side and leaned forward to stare down over the edge, then stepped back from the brink. "Not without wings."

He expected Delores to reply, but she just studied the ravine ahead as if she hadn't heard them. The crisp moonlight added angles to her face and pushed her shadow away at an odd pitch, and the stars above the far side of the chasm were bright but tiny in the clear sky between wisps of high cirrus clouds.

"No... that's not right." Hyatt winced as he set his pack down, happy to be free of it. "He broke Warnings, collected workers, traveled this far... he had to have a plan."

"Or wings," Rellah replied with a shrug.

Without the protection of the trees, the evening wind was cold. Hyatt hunched his shoulders to pull his jacket closer to the back of his neck. A thrush bolted from the edge of the Reclaimed behind him and soared a dozen paces over the depths, turned, and flapped hard to make it back to the woods before it ran out of endurance. Nearby, Rellah unslung her pack and set it down gently, then took a seat on it.

"He's coming here, and he has a plan." Delores turned to face them, certainty pulling her cheeks and her irises glowing in the moonlight. "We'll wait here."

"That is a very bad idea," Rellah replied, shaking her head. "We're beyond the forest and trapped against a cliff. This is not a place to fight."

Hyatt looked around, trying to see what Rellah saw – the open space between the cliff and the forest felt good for seeing the Keeper coming in any direction, but her resistance seemed to change the light and made him feel vulnerable to dangers from any direction. The cliff was no longer an obstacle to their journey but an enemy all its own, a way to contain them. The realization sharpened in his mind how comfortable the Reclaimed had become, that the unsubjugated land and dense canopy was preferable to open skies and room to move.

"She's right, Iron." Hyatt nodded toward the forest's edge. "Let's back up."

Delores studied him for a long moment and Hyatt wondered what she was reading on his face. He tried to avoid reacting, unwilling to let her believe her penetrating gaze had made him backpedal or dig in, but wondered if not reacting had the same effect. Caught in her sight, he felt unable to look away. It broke when she shrugged and looked back at the forest with an approving nod.

"Okay. We'll wait for him there." The Iron gestured toward the forest. "After you."

The idea of picking up his pack again made him regret the decision to move, but he stifled the grunt of effort as he picked it up. Rellah fell into step beside him again and did her shoulder-bump that told him she appreciated him, but after the flash of warmth it spread through his core, he wondered if he'd agreed with her because of how he felt about her or because it was the better choice. The question clung to him as they passed over the dividing line between shadow and moonlight, the branches of the Reclaimed spreading over them to welcome them back. He looked up at the stars in the patches of sky between the leaves and vines and wondered if their pinpoint brilliance was celebrating their journey or lighting the way to their funeral.

"Here." Hyatt stopped abruptly, determined to make a choice that was all his own without Rellah's influence or Delores' guidance. "This is a good spot."

He didn't know why he expected resistance from one or the other, but Rellah nodded and Delores just shrugged again and tossed her pack towards a tree like it was filled with air.

"Okay. I'll start a fire," the Iron replied, kicking a fallen branch towards the center of the clear space in the stand of trees.

Rellah's voice was stern and reproachful, and Hyatt was glad it wasn't pointed at him for once. "A fire will show the Keeper where we are."

Delores crouched to collect a bundle of kindling and dropped it in a pile on top of the first branch. "When we meet the Keeper, there is a fire and a carrion bird. No reason to fight it."

Hyatt had just dropped his pack again, but her words snagged his attention like a fish hooked on a line. "What are you talking about? How can you know that?"

Instead of answering, the Iron struck her Firestarter and started loose tinder ablaze at the center of her pile of sticks. The red-orange light drove back the shadows in every direction in an instant, then began the battle at the outer edge as darkness tried to reclaim the ground and slowly igniting wood struggled to push it outward. Rellah shook her head but didn't say anything, choosing to count the arrows left in her quiver instead.

When the fire had started to consume the larger branches, Delores took a seat cross-legged beside it and unsheathed her weapon. She lay the thick, short blade across her knees and rested her hands on the flat of it, tipping it forward so the firelight pooled in the blood groove down the weapon's center.

"More visions from Sklodowska," Rellah answered for her, derision tinging her words. "What does She say about you and me, Iron?"

Where the moonlight had turned Delores' features sharp and angular, the firelight made them molten and fluid, like something primitive and elemental. Her eyes traced designs between the hilt and the tip of her blade, sloshing lazily in their sockets as her gaze shifted. Rellah moved around the fire to sit across from her, leaning back against her pack so the straps went slack over her shoulders.

The Iron looked up at Rellah through the flickering tongues of flame, a faint smile at the edge of her lips. "We both end up dead in the end."

Her voice had that same unnerving certainty, devoid of anger or fear, and it sliced through Hyatt like Jenna's blade had decapitated Shelara. The Iron's belief in the outcome of all of it, the Keeper and the journey and Rellah and herself, seemed unassailable. The fire crackled and one of the branches split in two with a loud pop, as if it was driving home her answer.

"Everyone ends up dead," Rellah replied, less impressed with the Iron's prophecy. "More smoke and flash from Sklodowska's blade."

Hyatt wondered if they were going to kill each other before the Keeper showed up and leave him to deal with it, but Delores only sat quietly. He rifled through his pack for a wrapped ration until he felt the wax paper and hemp string, pulled it free of the rest of the hastily stuffed contents, and sat down on a side of the fire between the two of them. The thieves' hitch came apart in his fingers and he tossed the string into the fire, where it twisted like a worm on a fishing hook as the flames consumed it. The sound of the wax paper crinkling as he unwrapped it blended with the crackling of the campfire and the rustle of the wind through the branches above.

"Your mother was a raider, but your bow was a gift from your father. Your arrows are fletched blue because your first love wore a blue beaded anklet," Delores said, trailing a fingertip along the groove in the side of her blade and pausing for a moment on its path at each statement before continuing toward the weapon's tip. "You dream over and over of black birds in a flock, flying over ruins, a place you've never been. You don't believe in Sklodowska but you do believe in Irons, and you worry that Hyatt won't choose you when –"

"Enough." Rellah's eyes flared in the firelight.

Delores stared her down for a moment as her fingertip paused an inch from the end of the groove, then lowered her eyes to the blade again and slide her finger over the remaining distance to the angled tip of the weapon. "Enough."

Hyatt hadn't realized he'd stopped breathing until he couldn't breathe in, and let the air escape from his lungs as slowly as he could manage to avoid the heavy sigh he wanted to release.

Before the quiet could thicken into something impenetrable, he turned to Delores. "You said you've been to this place before, but there are no ruins here."

She nodded, rocking her fingertip on the point of her weapon so it pressed into the pad of her flesh without drawing blood. "It's across the chasm."

"How did you get across?" he asked.

"There was a bridge." Delores pressed harder, and a drop of crimson burst from the pinpoint prick. "We destroyed it."

"We?" Hyatt furrowed his brow but Delores didn't answer, so he pressed on. "If the bridge was the only way across, maybe the Keeper didn't know it's gone – he thinks he'll be able to cross the ravine. What's on the other side?"

"Earlier Histories called them Laybrairs – dangerous places full of secrets and untethered communicators. We destroyed everything we could, threw the debris into the chasm, and severed the bridge –"

"—but he doesn't know that." Hyatt finished for her, feeling the conversation quickening like a river narrowing into rapids. "Wait – that means... you know what was there. What did you destroy, Iron?"

"There was no Eighth Warning," she replied, guessing at what he was asking.

Hyatt felt his chest tighten and fought to keep his face neutral, resisting the almost overwhelming urge to look at Rellah who was studying the fire's bed of coals. *That's not entirely true... it was gone already. You didn't destroy it in time.*

"That doesn't answer the question... what was there?" he asked, hoping it would propel them past the omission before it gained mass. "What did you and whoever was with you do here?"

Hyatt was so focused on getting answers and avoiding giving any up that the growing sense of dread creeping through him was belated and took him by surprise. Visions of Delores flashed in his mind, covered in gore like her fight with the Drashvoy but distinctly human with her unique blade in one hand and a pulsing human heart in the other. An image of her face, eyes lit with fanatical zeal and lips broken and stained, came to him so vibrantly that he flinched. He looked up and saw her looking at him, that stare that drove through his pupils like Iron spikes while saying nothing at all.

"I did as Sklodowska required," she replied without blinking. "Whatever it takes."

There was a horror in her placid confidence that flushed ice through Hyatt's veins, but he believed her wholeheartedly and hoped they would never find their way across the chasm to whatever she had left behind years ago. He averted his eyes first and hated himself for doing it, but the flicker of the fire was preferable to her direct attention, unbearable present and vacant at the same time.

"When it's done, where will you go?" he asked, picking up a stick and prodding the coals to send a burst of errant sparks skyward.

"Ceojic," she replied, as if they hadn't just been talking about an undescribed horror. "Iron Sawmet said Adeben was the name Whispered to replace him, so I'll find them if another Iron hasn't done it yet."

The alarm Hyatt felt at the idea of another Iron starting their commitment to Sklodowska surprised him, a knot in his throat and a metal taste on his tongue that made him struggle against the desire to spit warm saliva into the dirt to clear it. "Then?"

She shrugged and pulled her weapon from her where it rested across her knees and in Hyatt's periphery, he saw Rellah tense as the Iron's hand wrapped around the grip, but Delores simply slid it back into its sheath on her side. "If Sklodowska's plan includes me after Ceojic, She hasn't chosen to let me know."

"We should sleep," Rellah spoke up at last, rocking her shoulders to push her pack further back across the ground so she could recline against it. "No sense in dying tired. I'll take mid-watch."

"Hyatt?" Delores asked.

He thought about it for a moment, not ready to let go of the conversation and wrestling with the feeling it was their last night before their lives changed forever. "I'll take the early morning, I guess."

The Iron nodded in agreement. "First shift is mine, then."

Hyatt considered crawling across the ground to his pack, but instead, he forced himself to his feet. His legs were tight and his arms felt heavy, and he hoped that the ration would restore his strength before the morning. He glanced at Delores' pack without meaning to and the idea of herocaine flashed to him, chased by a dull ache in his stomach and a sharp feeling in his head, but he shook free of it as he unfurled his bedroll across the forest floor. *That stuff is dangerous.*

He settled onto the sleeping pad, but propped himself up on his arm as Rellah dragged her pack and bedroll closer to him. She laid it out without a word, inches from his, and set her bow and quiver on the ground between them. Something about it felt like a gesture of trust and a hazy warmth spread through Hyatt even against the dominating chill of the night. He rolled onto his back and stared up at an accidentally perfect view of a star cluster between branches that framed it in, letting the warm feeling linger and drive anxiety from his body.

"Sleep good, Hy-att," Rellah murmured, just loud enough for him to hear. "Tomorrow matters."

TWENTY-FOUR

"Tomorrow is today, Hyatt, once of Brathnee," Delores said gently, shaking his arm. "Watch is yours."

He opened his eyes and flinched at how close the Iron was, but if she noticed, she gave no sign. Dragging his palm down his face from his hairline to his chin, Hyatt nodded his understanding and watched Delores recede into the darkness that had overtaken them in the absence of the fire. He yawned and stretched, feeling his muscles come to life, and sat up to take in the almost nonexistent glow of the remaining embers and the way that beyond the edge of the Reclaimed, the sky was one shade lighter than the land. With no wind, the silence of the wilderness was broken only by the sound of Delores settling onto her bedroll for a few hours before the day began.

Hyatt picked up his Cern blade and struggled to his feet, grateful that the soreness in his muscles had changed in the night from a dull agony to the warm acknowledgment of work from days before. He stretched again and looked down at Rellah, half-fetal on her side facing him with an arm outstretched and her fingers splayed across the leather quiver between them. In the dark, the blue of her arrow's fletchings was indistinguishable from the ground but he could make out the shape of them.

Your first love wore an anklet with blue beads... he shook his head to clear the prickly feeling of that memory from the night before and shifted his weight from one foot to the other, willing his circulation to resume, but the lingering sentiment brought Stella's golden hair and heart-shaped face to mind. He looked down at Rellah again and superimposed the Brathnee woman's face over hers, struck by how different they were – Stella had been delicate and feminine with hair treated in oils and nails painted, while Rellah's nails were bare and chipped with half her hair shorn tight to her skull and braids under mahogany bands pulling the rest back along the contour of her head.

With another shake of his head, Hyatt moved away from her in case the weight of his thoughts had the power to wake her when she needed sleep. *Except Rellah is Cern, and I didn't love Stella.*

He started a slow patrol in an arc around their camping space, far enough in the dark to lose the benefit of the coal's dying glow but close enough to wake the sleeping women if he needed them. His thoughts turned to Gorman, and Jenna, and the companions who left Brathnee Garden with him to escort Delores to the Cern camp. As he wove between the trunks of the ancient trees and stepped over fallen branches, he wondered if Tayo and Pippa and Aleks had found something to hunt on the way home, stories to tell when they gathered at the Hoenbeck's assembly. He imagined Gorman telling stories about his crazy friend Hyatt who left with an Iron and never returned, probably gored horribly by an Heir or a Cern raider, as he tried to become important by proxy and pair with a pretty Journeyman Provisioner like Vamerie. He tried to fathom if Jenna even remembered him, if she talked about him to other weeds who thought they wanted a life outside the walls of the Garden.

Weed? That's uncalled for. Even as he realized he thought it, he could only offer token resistance to it. Recognizing that came with another confession he was only ready to hear in the dark alone while Rellah and Delores slept – he didn't miss any of it, not Gorman's exaggerated stories or the social competition of Assembly or making art in the workshops of Brathnee. It all felt distant, and foreign, and trite, and those feelings tangled in a ball of conflict and confusion in his gut as he started his second pass around the campsite. *Is that what Delores meant about never going home again?*

Unlike the morning before, daybreak came without grace or warning. The sliver of sun that rose over the horizon carved savage paths through the Reclaimed and turned the vegetation a million shades of green and brown all at once, bleak and blinding. The light came first without warmth alongside, razors of illumination that turned even the shadow beneath fallen trees gray instead of black. It made the edge of the forest look closer than he remembered, and Hyatt took a single, indecisive glance at Rellah and Delores before walking towards the empty swath between the trees and the ravine. Crossing the line from the Reclaimed to the grass beyond felt like having his clothes stripped off him and he looked back again, no longer able to see the embers of the fire, but pressed on toward the chasm's rim.

With the dawn, Hyatt could see what had been hidden before, a concrete pad and anchors broken at jagged angles where a bridge had stood. Rising from the depths of the ravine, evenly spaced pillars with broken tops spanned the distance between the near edge and a large pair of doors set into the rock face on the far side. He looked from one destroyed support to another, trying to guess at the space between each one and what kind of force must have been required to decimate the bridge that stretched over them. The memory of Delores emerging from the dark covered in gore entwined with her statement that she'd done what was necessary, and the rising daylight was not enough to extinguish the chill that tightened the spaces between the vertebrae in his spine.

He took another step forward, looking over the edge. The walls of the ravine were steep and unclimbable, ending abruptly in a river that moved with a current he could see even from his vantage point. His gaze swept up slowly along the closest pillars and across again to the opening in the earth on the far side, then higher to the horizon line of peaks and valleys with no trees atop them.

"The edge of the Reclaimed," Rellah's voice startled him, but she didn't comment on the way he started as she appeared beside him. "The northern limit of humanity... I never thought I'd see it."

Hyatt nodded, unable to find the words to express the feelings roiling in him. Instead, he turned away from her and swung the Cern weapon, turning it over like he'd seen its last owner do before handing it to him.

"You're not going to kill anyone like that, Hyatt," she said behind him, a hint of amusement in her voice that drove needles into his shoulders.

"Haven't you heard? I've killed lots of people. Tons." As soon as he said it, he worried that his sardonic joke was out of bounds and turned to face her, but her smile had grown even as she crossed her arms and he couldn't help smirking himself.

"Hold it higher, right next to the hilt," she said with a bemused shake of her head. "It's a quick weapon, not a heavy one."

Hyatt choked up on the blade's handle until he could feel the cold metal hilt resting on top of his thumb and index finger. He gave it a test-swing, feeling the difference.

"Your other hand goes low, just above the pommel, the round part at the bottom –" she continued.

"I know what a pommel is," he interrupted, but closed his other hand around the very bottom of the handle as she said.

"If you need power, you can slide your top hand down to use the whole length of the weapon. Most of the time though, fight with your hands apart – it will give you more maneuverability and use the scallop of the blade the way it was intended," Rellah said.

"Thanks," Hyatt replied, dropping his false confidence. "Maybe I won't die right away."

"A few weeks, at least," she agreed with a wink, a simple gesture that slammed into Hyatt like one of her arrows and left him wordless.

The moment stalled and he turned his attention to the pillars again for something to focus on. As the sun finished breaking the horizon, a crisp morning wind rose, and Hyatt watched four of the pillars sway dangerously as it funneled through the chasm.

"The Iron did... this?" Rellah asked, something tense in her tone.

Torn between reassuring her and agreeing with her, Hyatt split the difference. "She did say she had help."

She chuckled, a dry sound with little humor in it. They stared across the chasm together, watching the sunlight catch on exposed rebar at the pillars' breaks and the barely visible rended metal in front of the door on the far side. Hyatt ran his fingers through his hair and tried to imagine the bridge that had covered the distance between based on the near anchors, wide enough for twenty people to walk shoulder to shoulder across and high enough to guarantee death to anyone who fell over the edge.

"Skywalks and underground tunnels," Rellah muttered, echoing his unspoken thoughts. "Whoever lived in the Histories had an obsession with going where they didn't belong."

"Says the Cern nomad," Hyatt added, watching in his periphery until she laughed again to confirm she'd taken the joke well.

Rellah looked over her shoulder at a sound Hyatt missed, and he followed her attention to see Delores crossing the edge of the forest into the grassy expanse between them. Her easy stride was gone, replaced by a purposeful gait and a firm grip on her weapon's handle. The sun caught in her hair, blinding strands of platinum traced through her locks that Hyatt had somehow never noticed before. She waved as she saw them see her, a simple raise of her hand before letting it fall back to her side. Hyatt felt the change of a dozen little things in Rellah, her weight shifting to the balls of her feet and her back straightening as her shoulders went taut.

"The fire didn't bring your Keeper here," Rellah said as the Iron came into earshot.

Delores shrugged. "Maybe it wasn't the right fire."

Her rebuttal made Rellah narrow her eyes, but she didn't offer a retort as Delores joined them at the edge. She passed between them, walking to the lip of the ravine and looking out along the broken pillars to the door beyond. Something distant crossed her features, but it was gone in a moment, replaced by her placid determination. The wind rose to meet her, climbing the wall of the canyon to drive against her face and whip stray wisps behind her like pennants before dying off and letting her hair settle.

A thousand unanswered questions churned in Hyatt, but the answers daunted him, and he wrestled with his uncertainty until one broke free. "Why did the Keeper need a Turning Weapon? Why risk getting your attention?"

Delores crossed her arms and for the first time since Hyatt met her, she looked indecisive. Her gaze shifted to Rellah, who stared her down without flinching, then back to Hyatt who did the same. With a cock of her head, she stared up into the pale morning sky like she was weighing options, then nodded more to herself than to him.

"So far, you have had choices, even though it might not have felt like it. You could have fought Sklodowska's plan, but came willingly," Delores said, her voice becoming strangely and unnervingly formal. "You could have allowed yourself to die, but chose to live. She is grateful for your service. Hyatt, once of Brathnee, first of Cleft Rock pack, you are called to Her service—"

"Wait – what the fuck?" Hyatt tried to break in, dumbstruck surprise carving grooved in his forehead and around his eyes as they widened.

The Iron continued, ignoring him. "—bound by the Iron Accords of the Seventh History to protect this site and execute the Keeper for violations of the Third Warning—"

"I'm what the rot now?" Hyatt could hear his own voice rising, but could stop it.

"—in the event my life is ended before this task is complete. The penalty for failing to carry your role in Her plan is hunt by Irons for the rest of your days and execution, for violating the Iron Accords by concealing an untethered communicator and refusal to abide your Charge."

"Fuck you, Delores!" he shouted at her, taking an involuntary step backward towards Rellah as his fist clenched around the handle of his blade. "That is some compost! I have done everything you asked me to do, with no explanation!"

The Iron set her pack down and turned towards him, lifting her weapon an inch from its sheath and staring into his eyes with her dominant, penetrating gaze. "Are you refusing service?"

The question weighed a million pounds and took up all the space between them, each moment granular and explosive. Hyatt felt something new in him, black and mephitic and hateful, rising through his torso and spreading down his arm to his fingertips pressed into the handle's wrap. He tried to judge the distance between Delores and him, if he could bring the weapon slashing down on her faster than she could get hers free of her sheath, and envisioned her rended form enveloping the scalloped blade amidst a river of dark red blood. The upward tug at the corner of his lip was unfamiliar to him, but felt right.

"Hyatt." Rellah's single word was quiet but layered with a thousand meanings, the strongest of which was caution.

The Cern's word sounded distant, like it was trying to reach him over miles and through fog, but it was enough. He clung to it, rolling and forming the two syllables in his mind until he recognized his own name, and stealing the energy from his black desire to do it.

His fingers fought to stay vice-gripped as he consciously loosened them, but he didn't look away from Delores. "Keep swimming, Iron. I'm not looking forward to doing your job for you."

She held his gaze a moment longer, like she could read everything he felt through his pupils, then settled her hilt back against her sheath. As she turned her back and knelt beside her pack, that feeling surged again and he knew he could bury his blade in her back. *No one knows she Charged me but her and Rellah, and Rellah would never say anything... she might even approve...*

The urge reached a crescendo, but Rellah's hand on his elbow broke it and brought it crashing down like shattered glass. In its wake, a mortifying wash of shame crashed over him and he almost dropped the Cern weapon, unable to believe what he'd been rationalizing.

"She's right." Rellah was distracting him and he knew it, but he was grateful for it. "You took a Cern jacket, you were given a Cern weapon, you slept in a Cern camp, and were given a raid order from a pack master. You're not Haleu anymore, and you're not Claimed... you're Cern."

Hyatt was overwhelmed and wished for everything to stop for a moment so he could untangle it, but Rellah's hand fell away from his arm as Delores stood and turned to them, a brass and leather spyglass in hand. She extended it until the one section became three and held it out to Hyatt.

"If you're going to protect the site, you need to know how," she said when he didn't immediately take it, giving it a shake for emphasis. "Look."

He took the spyglass from her at arm's length, looking it over before turning towards the chasm and pointing it across the gap. "What am I looking for?"

"In front of the door, on the right, near the edge of the inset. There's a gray box, the same color as the stone. Do you see it?"

The magnification was disorienting and Hyatt lowered it to look across at the door, then brought the narrow end back to his eye. Every shiver from his body soaked with tension and unspent adrenaline made his view spasm and jump, and he took a deep breath to try and steady himself. It took him a moment to figure out how slowly to move so the view would track evenly, but he caught the handles of the door blurring by and used them as a reference to find the face of a box with a hole in the middle and a glistening metal tip at the center of the hole.

"I see it," he replied. "What is it?"

"Look at the top edge. Do you see a red, horizontal handle?" Delores' voice seemed disembodied, outside the magnified view of the telescopic lenses.

He nodded, then cursed as it made him lose his view, and tried to pull it back into place. "Yes."

"Pulling that handle releases a spear, launching it to us. The spear tows a spun-metal cable." Her hand closed around the center of the spyglass and pulled it from his hands. "We didn't know what it was when we destroyed the bridge – Keepers uncovered another one of the mechanisms in ruins to the south."

"So if the Keeper could reach the handle... it would span the ravine with a cable? That's not much of a way across," Hyatt replied.

"But it is a way." The Iron collapsed the spyglass and returned it to her pack. "We can't let that happen."

"It's on the wrong side of the ravine," Rellah joined in, stepping closer to the edge and holding up a single finger as she closed one eye, sighting through her fingernail. "It's thirty paces between pillars, and there are more than ten pillars."

Delores nodded her agreement. "A Turning Weapon can shoot that far."

"That's not possible," Rellah protested.

The Iron didn't argue – instead, she stared at Rellah for a long moment before turning back to Hyatt. "That can't be allowed to happen."

He could feel the missing piece, but it hovered just out of his periphery as he tried to grasp it. Everything she and Rellah had said in the last hour whirled in his head, soaked by the new, dangerous feeling that receded but refused to dissipate entirely. He studied the span across the chasm, trying to imagine a weapon that could hit a handle he could barely see that distance, and his question broke free like a bird from its nest.

"You said you destroyed everything in the – what did you call it? The laybrair? You destroyed it all before you collapsed the bridge." He turned to Delores, his eyes narrowed. "Why does it matter if the Keeper gets inside? What's left?"

Delores opened her mouth to reply, but her words were swallowed up in the loud, staccato crack of a gun being fired, and Rellah screamed.

TWENTY-FIVE

Rellah hit the ground with so much force that she flipped over, landing on her back. Crimson blood soaked through the left shoulder of her jacket and blood burbled between the torn leather around the exit wound. Her back spasmed and she instinctively clamped her hand over it, as if she could stop her body from hemorrhaging vital fluid.

Hyatt dove flat in the grass and crawled towards her, but panicked as he realized he had no idea what to do. He pressed his hands over hers, the warm red blood leaking between his fingers and covering them in the space of a breath. Rellah's face was taut with anguish and she shoved him away with her shoulder as she rolled onto her side, clawing a fistful of earth and grass into her hand and packing it into the wound.

"Go, Hyatt! Fight!" she snarled, her eyes ablaze with something molten and primal.

Rellah's order lit on fire the thing inside Hyatt that the Iron's proclamation had created. He felt it unfurl as he turned towards the woodline and started running in a skulking crouch, weapon low and ready as he searched the trees for their attacker. Another shot fired, a flat cracking sound, but it only made him run harder toward the Reclaimed. A growling roar, foreign to his own ears, broke from his mouth as his legs pumped hard against the soft grass and his grip tightened around his blade.

"Keeper!" Delores' voice called from behind him, confident and clear in the open air. "You have violated the Warnings and the Iron Accords! Come forward – it's over! Let's end this!"

Another shot rang out and Hyatt heard a whirring sound, like metallic hummingbird wings shearing the air beside his ear. He caught a flinch of movement near a broad tree ten paces into the forest and willed himself to run faster, changing his angle to charge at the motion that didn't belong with the gently shifting branches of the Reclaimed. Exertion turned his arms to lead but he pumped them anyway, moving as fast as he ever had and fueled by the blood drying on his hands. He'd just reached the first pair of trees when the man peeked from his hiding place with his weapon up, and the trunk on Hyatt's left blew apart in a shower of splinters amidst the roar of another shot fired. His vision narrowed to a tunnel, darkness blotting out the trees on either side and focused on his attacker's hiding place.

Hyatt raised his blade up over his shoulder in the last two steps between him and the man behind the tree and brought it arcing down with all the power he could drive from his shoulder, through his arms and hands, to the curved edge of the blade as he rounded the trunk. The stranger panicked and recoiled, trying to keep the barrel of his rifle pointed at Hyatt, but Hyatt was already inside its reach and the blade sliced down through the side of the man's throat until it met breastbone and stopped. A geyser of hot blood sprayed them both. The stranger dropped his rifle and wrapped his hands around the blade in a futile attempt to dislodge it from his body.

"Kill him!" someone shouted behind him.

Hyatt felt like he was two people in one body, the first registering the panicked realization that there was someone else close who meant him harm, and the second a colder, more dangerous thing that told him to plant his foot on the dying man and rip his weapon free. His boot connected with the man's sternum and he yanked on his blade, sending radial splatters of blood arching up through the overhead branches as the metal let go of bone with a grisly cracking noise. He spun to find his next enemy, and the impact of a bullet slammed him back against the tree's trunk.

Being shot hurt, but not the way he expected it to. His legs wobbled and gave out, and the tree's bark tugged and snagged at his jacket as gravity pulled him towards the forest floor. His vision swam at the edges but stayed clear in the center, and he watched the kneeling woman with a rifle six paces away from him rise to her feet. She pointed her barrel down at his face and he lolled his head to the side, as if the little movement would let the next bullet pass harmlessly by his ear and bury in the dense wood behind him.

I wonder if that's what that whirring sound was... The realization that he almost died before the fight began seemed funnier than it should, adding momentum to the dry chuckle that escaped his parted lips as the woman pulled the trigger but was rewarded with only a tinny clacking sound. Somewhere nearby, metal was meeting flesh and bone and it tugged at Hyatt's periphery, but all he could do is stare up at the woman trying to get her weapon to work.

She cursed and pulled a lever on the side of the gun, then snarled as she worked it back and forth with half a dozen rapid jerks, trying to fix whatever had stopped it from firing. When she didn't get the result she wanted, she pointed it up at the treetops and shook it violently. Her focus was so intent on the breach of the gun that she never saw Rellah appear next to her. The Cern spun and eviscerated her with one savage slash that opened her abdomen and exposed her spine, and as she completed her turn, Hyatt caught the hungry expression on her face with lines of blood dashed from her cheek to her eyes. Behind her, emerging from the cover of low undergrowth, the Keeper limped into view.

Hyatt lunged forward and caught himself on his hands, crawling like a bear as he tried to close the space between them. "Rellah!"

She realized too late what he was trying to shout and only half-turned as the attacker swung a rifle by the barrel. The stock connected with her cheekbone and spun her like a screw as she crumpled to the ground, her shoulder and temple bouncing as she landed. The force rolled her onto her stomach and she lay flat, motionless. The reverberation of the connection staggered the Keeper and his right leg almost gave out, but he straightened it and steadied himself.

Hyatt got his feet under him and dragged the tip of his blade through the earth as he tried to lift it, his left arm refusing to obey him. His hand was throbbing and as hard as he tried to grip the weapon's handle, he could feel his fingers loosening around the cloth wrap. The space between them was six paces but felt like a thousand, but he struggled forward even as a cold gust threatened to unbalance him and knock him back to his knees.

The Keeper turned his rifle over in his hands and pointed the deadly end at the back of Rellah's head, only inches between the battered metal and her blood-soaked braid. "I'll kill her, Haleu. Drop it."

Hyatt's tongue tasted bitter and acidic, and his eyes stared hate through him, but he stopped his advance. A wave of dizziness swirled in his head and he felt a slick, wet trickle roll over the crest of his elbow and race down the back of his forearm inside his jacket. With the best shove he could manage to take his weight off the weapon, he switched it to his right hand and leaned against the tree beside him for support.

"You don't know what's at stake," the Keeper said. "We could be ending the world and not even know it!"

"There's no Eighth Warning," Hyatt growled. "There's nothing in those ruins. The Iron destroyed it all... years ago."

"Then why are you here?" He thrust his rifle towards Rellah's unconscious form to drive his question home. "You're lying. I'm going to do whatever it takes to reach it. Drop your weapon, or I kill her. I won't say it again."

Hyatt had no explanation for the question he'd asked but Delores had been unable to answer. Through a gap in the canopy above, a silhouette of oval wings and the slender head of a carrion bird made a slow clockwise turn against the azure sky. Another wave of dizziness washed over him, and his fingertips on his left hand felt like they'd gone to sleep.

"It doesn't matter if you kill her, Keeper." Delores' voice came from behind him, a moment before she stepped into Hyatt's view on the other side of the tree, her strange blade drawn. "Your workers are dead and the bridge is destroyed. Your story ends here."

"No, Iron – yours does." The Keeper snapped his rifle up to his shoulder and fired.

The flash from the muzzle was red-orange and blinding as Delores' head snapped back, taking her off her feet and slamming her shoulders into the ground with a grisly thud. The sound radiated through Hyatt and hollowed him out until everything in him felt like an empty cavern, his bones ready to disjoin from each other.

The Keeper lowered his rifle just far enough to look over it at Delores' still body, then started to arc his point of aim back down to Rellah. Mid-motion, he turned and brought it back up to point it at Hyatt. A second carrion bird joined the first in large, lazy circles over them, appearing in the openings above and vanishing again behind the branches, marked only by their shadows dancing across the forest floor between the two standing men.

"I just killed an Iron," the Keeper said, a quaver in his voice that did nothing to dispel the raw determination that ran through his words, "so you know I'll kill you too – but you don't want me to kill the Cern breedstock, and I can't get what I need from the ruins without help."

"Fuck you," Hyatt growled, pushing against the tree and fighting the tide of nausea that hit him as shooting pain lanced up his left arm from his elbow.

"What is that accent? Brathnee Garden?" the Keeper asked, pulling his rifle tighter into his shoulder and gripping the stock tighter. "You would be a hero to the High Ranger, to your family... the unskilled worker who found the Eighth Warning. You could pair with anyone you wanted."

In his periphery, Hyatt saw Rellah's leg move. It was little more than the flex of her thigh through her pants, an almost imperceptible change in the bend of her knee, and her eyes were still closed. The air had gone still and with it, the staleness of death drank the moisture from the world, not a branch swaying or leaf shifting. Hyatt locked his teeth to keep himself focused as he took a single step toward the Keeper, the tip of his blade dragging a score through the dirt beside him.

"There's no bridge, and no Warning," he said again, resisting the compulsion to look down at Rellah.

"Don't make me kill you." The Keeper's finger slid between the trigger and the metal shell that protected it, the pad of his fingertip pressed against the metal.

Hyatt uncurled his fingers from around his blade's handle, and it fell to the earth with a muted, flat sound as he took another labored step forward. "I'm not unskilled. I'm a journeyman artist – a sculptor."

The Keeper's eyes darted to the dropped weapon and then back to Hyatt's face, and his brow furrowed in confusion. "You're a rotted artist?"

The carrion birds had ceased their circle, their shadows no longer shifting on the ground between them. Hyatt took another step, and then another, listening to the deafening sound of silence through the Reclaimed as if it held its breath to watch the moment play out. Blood dripped from his middle and ring finger, droplets and then a stream and then droplets again, drawing a dotted line across the leaves and broken twigs in his wake.

"She's not breedstock, and she'll cut your throat for saying it." Hyatt was close enough to see Rellah, her head turned towards him and her cheek motionless against the dirt, open her eyes. "Won't you?"

A look of realization flashed in the Keeper's eyes and he jerked his rifle downward to point it at Rellah, who burst into motion with a roll and thrash of her legs that connected with his right calf and thigh. Hyatt threw himself forward as the Keeper's leg gave out under Rellah's savage kicks, and he ripped his knife from his sheath as he came down on top of the Keeper's collapsing form.

Under his weight, the Keeper snarled and thrashed with the desperation of a wild beast caught in a hunter's snare. He drove his left hand into the side of the fallen man's face, smearing his cheek and nose with blood as he shoved it up and to the side to bare the Keeper's neck. Gnashing teeth and spasming legs made him seem more animal than human, but Hyatt didn't hesitate. He drove the knife into the Keeper's neck and shoulder over and over, ripping it free and stabbing again and again as blood flooded and sprayed from the dozens of wounds he was inflicting. The Keeper stopped moving but Hyatt continued to stab him, over and over again, mulching the flesh between the dead mans' esophagus and the point of his clavicle until the short blade of the knife could no longer find resistance or purchase.

He felt hands on his shoulders, trying to drag him off the mutilated body, but the rage in him refused to be harnessed. Hyatt thrashed his shoulders to shake them off, raising the knife and burying it through the Keeper's cheek. Ripping it free tore flesh and chunks of tongue with it, but at the height of his stroke to bring it slamming back down again, an arm curled around his wrist to pin it back and a hand found purchase on his jacket again.

"And I'm not Brathnee!" Hyatt screamed at the dead man, fighting to close the distance between him and the Keeper as two determined arms dragged him backward off him. "I'm Cern, you fucking compost rot!"

His resistance wasn't strong enough to match the force from behind him and he fell backward, landing on his rear in the dirt. He looked up to see Rellah looking down at him, her arms grappling with his to pin them out and away as she pulled him back against her thighs. His whole body shook and he looked up into her eyes through the masquerade mask of blood and dirt that covered more of her features than it left bare.

"Let it go!" she shouted at him. "It's done."

The rage draining from him and the loss of blood threatened to rob him of his consciousness, but her voice plunged through to the part of him that could understand. He opened his hand and let the knife drop from it, spasming and unable to stop staring up at her framed in the late morning light.

"It's done, Hyatt." She lowered her voice. "It's done. You killed him. He's dead... it's done. It's over."

Hyatt nodded, let out a breath he felt like he'd been holding for days, and passed out.

TWENTY-SIX

"Hyatt... Hyatt, wake up." Rellah's voice seemed distant and slid through the darkness like smoke from a fire, twisting and twirling through his mind so that it was nowhere in particular but everywhere at once.

He hadn't known he'd been unconscious until he wasn't anymore, and the space between utter black and awareness was thick with fog and unwilling to let go of him. Hyatt tried to focus on the rise and fall of her words, but as he rolled his head towards their last lingering note, it vanished and came from behind him instead. Turning that way made him realize that his thoughts were rotating but his body was still, which told him he had a body even if he was detached from it. Adrift, Hyatt let his mind chase the spindles of Rellah's voice through the vast open darkness with no ground or sky.

"Hyatt..."

Hands closed around his awareness, pressing it into a ball and holding it still. He tried to thicken his thoughts to twist free, but the palms and fingertips that contained him refused to let go. In front of him, the darkness rippled like a fish rising to the surface of the pond and at the center, features emerged – first nose, then lips, then empty eye sockets that let pupils and irises blossom from their depths like roses. *Shelara.*

Hyatt winced, and he knew he winced. He could feel his eyes narrow and his nose crinkle through the barest spiderweb strands of connection between his mind and his flesh, but some of the threads pulled free as he tried to wrest himself from her. Shelara's face mouthed words he couldn't make out and a feeling washed through him, warm and crisp like baked apples tinged with autumn spices. He relaxed, her face receded into the dark, and he opened his eyes as sunlight directly overhead reduced his pupils to pinpoints.

His body spasmed and he swung his arm, but Rellah leaned back and it passed by her without connecting. "Easy, Hy-att. You're okay - you're fine."

Sensation came back with a vengeance -his head pounded like he'd been hit with a falling tree and something wrapped his upper arm tight enough to bite. He was cold, his jacket stripped and his sleeve cut away. The daylight was offensive and relentless. Every thought that tried to surface shattered like glass and he pulled his uninjured arm across his face to block the blinding light, rolling his head to the side. As the lesser aches of his body flared to life, he wished he was still unconscious.

"No more sleep. Get up." Rellah's tone was brusque, but concern tinged the edges of her words. "No point if winning if you die of brain-blood, weed."

With a groan, he lowered his arm to slide it behind him and brace himself against the ground. "How long was I out?"

"Five hours." She stood and dusted the dirt from her knees, then reached out a hand to help him up. "Your body woke up twice, but your brain wasn't inside."

He sat up and grabbed her forearm. The strength of her pull surprised him as he lurched upward, and he barely got his feet underneath himself before she let go. As he swayed, trying to get his bearings, Rellah walked toward a nearby tree where she'd piled their packs and weapons collected from around the site. Beyond, the bodies of the Keeper and his workers were stacked like logs.

"Five hours? Why did you –" As he staggered after her, a bolt of realization caught him and he did a double-take at the corpses in the pile. "Did you plant the Iron?"

Rellah crouched by her pack but looked over her shoulder at him with a confused squint. "What are you talking about?"

He stopped and turned left and then right, frustrated that reality was lingering just out of his reach as he searched the forest floor. "What did you do with her body?"

"Hyatt, she didn't die. She was gone when I pulled you off the Keeper." Rellah stood, an herb-twist in her hand, but the crease between her brows deepened and she dropped it in the dirt. "Let me look at your head."

She closed the space between herself and him, and he didn't resist as she grabbed his head and jerked it to the side with a rough yank. Rellah drove her fingers into his hair to the roots and pressed her fingertips hard into his skull like she was trying to crack it open.

"The Keeper shot her in the head," he protested, grimacing as her fingernails caught a scab and broke it free. "Hey – take it easy! Stop it."

"Not unless her face is made of metal." Satisfied, she pulled her hands free of his hair. "No mush-bone, no fractures. Just blood loss."

He opened his mouth to insist he knew what he'd seen, but it hung open and the mid-day air dried his tongue as he tried to recall what happened. The bullet wound in his arm throbbed, a radiating heat that slid along the bones in both directions, and his head still thudded. Hyatt remembered the Keeper raising the rifle, firing, and Delores knocked backward, but he couldn't remember if he'd seen the wound or the Iron's blood.

A flash of irritation flickered in Rellah's eyes and she crossed her arms. "I'm not lying to you, Hy-att. She was gone by the time I got you laid down."

"No, I didn't think—" he started, but his fluster joined forces with every part of him that hurt and killed the sentence, so he took a deep breath and tried again. "I believe you. I just don't know how."

"Maybe she faked it, so you'd have to fulfill her prophecy and kill the Keeper yourself. Maybe she did get shot, but it wasn't bad. Maybe Sklodowska resurrected her little butcher." Rellah just shook her head she bent down to pick up the herb-twist, dusting specks of dirt from the tacky surface of the snack before tossing it to him. "Who cares?"

He caught it and as he looked it over for clods of earth she missed and then bit the end of it off, he realized she was right – how didn't matter. The Iron was gone, the Keeper was dead, and Rellah and he were alive. He was Cern, and for Cern, it was allowed to be that easy. The mint of the herb-twist brought his tongue to life and made his throat tingle as he swallowed it, and for a moment the flavor and sensation drowned out the throbbing in his arm and the wrenched muscles in his back. The daylight seemed less harsh, and for the first time since waking, he could hear the sounds of the Reclaimed again.

"Now what?" he asked with his mouth full, grinding the snack like taffy between his teeth.

She looked over at the pile of dead bodies, sunlight filtering through the canopy to cast long illuminated stripes over them at odd angles. "We should deal with those. They're not ours, so we don't need their bones. Do you want to plant them?"

He thought about it for a moment, then shook his head. "No. They tried to kill you, me... they don't get to grow and live again."

"We'll leave them for the death-birds then." Rellah picked up the three rifles from the pile and slung them over her shoulder. "Now, we take these Turning Weapons apart and throw the pieces in the ravine. Come on."

His hips and knees protested every step as he followed Rellah toward the edge of the forest, but he forced them to obey. He trudged after her, more shuffling than striding as a concession to the condition of his body, but she walked slow enough that he caught up with her as they reached the edge of the forest. The calf-high grass wilted and matted under his boots as he made his way with her toward the destroyed anchor of the bridge by the chasm's edge, and the scattered cumulus clouds seemed to shy away from the overhead sun that washed them in light as it descended from its apex.

Rellah unslung one of the Turning Weapons and handed in Hyatt, then took hold of another one and worked her fingers against a pin ahead of the trigger. The metal whined and popped free, and the weapon came apart in two pieces. She flung the stock of the rifle over the edge of the ravine without looking out after it, and it disappeared from view as it plummeted to the chasm's depths. Hyatt studied the forbidden weapon and found the same pin, pressing hard against it with his thumb until it came apart. He wondered as he flung the rear half over the edge, why Delores hadn't taken them with her to see them destroyed.

"You can go back to Cleft Rock," Rellah said, interrupting his thoughts before they could finish forming into a spiral, "but I can't."

"Do I have to?" He watched her twist the nobs that mounted the sight to the top of the remaining half of the Turning Weapon, and started to torque the ribbed edges of the matching knobs of his.

"You don't have to do anything," she replied. "You can do whatever you want."

"Anything?" he asked.

Rellah rolled her eyes. "Yes, anything. Join a pack. Go back to the Garden. Wander the world alone. It's up to you."

The sights became wobbly in Hyatt's hands as the knobs loosened and then came off entirely, and he lobbed it underhand into the ravine. Rellah bashed hers against the barrel and the sound of cracking glass filled the air. She tossed it gently and punted it with the laces of her boots, sending it soaring out over the gap before gravity pulled it down to the rushing water far below.

Hyatt turned the barrel in his hands over and saw no other pieces that could come apart. "What if I went with you, and we found other Claimed Cern, and made a pack of our own?"

Rellah grunted with effort as she threw her barrel over the edge, then crossed her arms. Hyatt felt like it took her forever to consider the question, and he tossed the remaining part of his Turning Weapon into the ravine as he waited for her to answer. At last she turned toward him, hooked her thumbs behind the buckle of her belt, and cocked her head to the side.

"That's not a bad idea, Hyatt." Rellah squinted at him, that same indecipherable look in the way the corners of her eyes crinkled and one side of her lip raised almost imperceptibly. "We could hunt Heirs all through the Reclaimed, like the first Cern did. We might even live through the cold season."

"Might sounds good," Hyatt replied with a smirk.

Rellah unslung the last weapon and looked down at it, hefting it as if she was deciding how much it weighed, as she looked back toward the forest and then out across the tops of the broken pillars at the door on the distant side. Her eyes shifted back to the weapon in her hands, then back to the door, before she looked up to meet Hyatt's gaze.

"Want to know what the Irons left behind in the laybrair?" Her question sounded more like a dare than a curiosity.

Hyatt's heartbeat climbed slowly, from the strained pulse of a body recovering to the beat of a giant drum above his sternum. His attention drifted down from Rellah's face, along her open jacket, to their last Turning Weapon, and he thought it would only take a moment to push apart the pins and unscrew the sights, to be done with the thing they came to do. He took a deep breath in through his nose as he looked back up at her, then over the unthinkable distance across the chasm to the almost invisible pinpoint of glittering metal on the gray box by the door. His eyes tracked down over the depths and he counted the compound impossibilities – that they had survived the fight in the open where they shouldn't have been, that Delores had been shot in the head and lived, that Rellah could hit the red knob to fire the javelin and pull the spun-steel cable across the ravine before she ran out of bullets, and that they could cross that cable to reach the door on the other side. It reminded him of a story Gorman would have told, and he wouldn't have believed a word of it. He exhaled slowly.

Hyatt turned back to Rellah and took the Turning weapon from her, pressed it into his shoulder, his injured arm sending bolts of fire through his shoulder and elbow as his muscles tensed. He looked through the magnified sights across the expanse - the red handle looked closer than it seemed through Delores' spyglass, and the crosshairs of the sights bounced and danced on the metallic surface as he tried to hold it still. The longer he held the rifle up, the more his arms began to shake, and the more the sights jerked and jumped.

He lowered the rifle, turned back to Rellah, handed it back to her, and smiled. "Yes – yes, I do."

THE SEVEN WARNINGS

No individual sources of power

No untethered communications

No turning weapons

No individual transportation

No captivity

No inheritance

No everlasting commitment

ACKNOWLEDGMENTS

One of the greatest moments for a writer occurs in the space between the final chapter of a novel and the back cover, where we are afforded the opportunity to express our thanks to those close to us who contributed in one way or another to our process or draft. Like most milestone-moments in life, despite consuming a wealth of written advice and oral tradition about Acknowledgments, I have no idea how to proceed. What follows are my best efforts, with the promise that I will write something more poignant in the final pages of future works.

I would be remiss if I did not begin by thanking Delene Kendrick, because there is no hyperbole in my admission that this book would not exist without her. She fell in love with what began as a writing exercise destined for my folder of unfinished works-in-progress, never to see the light of day, and knew before I did that I had created something others would love. Her enthusiasm for the world and the characters and her hunger and delight with each new chapter fueled my motivation and creativity in ways I had never experienced before, and I share a debt of gratitude to her with anyone who finds themselves curious about or captivated by any part of this tale.

If Delene is the soul of the Reclaimed, then the talented and amazing men and women who provided feedback on The Eighth Warning are the bones and organs of this book. It is the curse of writers that our words fail us when they are most important, and I have no words to express how important and valuable the contributions of Daniel Quigley, Rance Denton, Michelle Cruz, Davene Le Grange, Cindy Pike, Erika Falk, and Ruth Garner been to the journey of this book from a first draft to a completed tale. They donated time from their lives and personal projects to read an unpolished edition of The Eighth Warning and infuse it with their contagious excitement about their favorite characters and scenes, and I cannot express the encouragement and validation that came from friends and fellow writers becoming invested in the story. Their feedback shaped this book in important ways, and I am humbled by their efforts on my behalf.

My friends and family who propelled this work forward by intermittently asking about my progress also deserve my humble thanks. There is an extraordinary moment for writers, not often discussed, when our friends begin to append 'writer' to the ways they identify us. "This is Sam – he writes books!" and "Hey, you're a writer – would you go over my paper?" carry a form of fulfillment, both low-key and profound that is impossible to put into words but invaluable to us. I am so happy that Ariana Pike, Chris Larson, Kate Hines, Majad Alawi, and Christi Opresko know me as their writer-friend and were endlessly forgiving as I skipped social engagements and disappeared for weeks at a time to focus on completing my draft. Their fingerprints are not on the pages or paragraphs of the Eighth Warning, but their support and encouragement are very much a part of its existence.

I enjoy writing most when I have inspiration, encouragement, and place outside my home to be awash in ambiance without becoming involved in it. Significant sections of this book were written in Misha's Coffee Shop and Murphy's Grand Irish Pub in the downtown district of Alexandria, fueled either by hot chocolate laced with lavender shots or pints of Kilkenny, and on the chance that the staff or owners of either establishment are readers of my genre, I felt it important to thank them here. Whether or not they realize it, the welcoming warmth they provide to all manner of patrons have ripple effects that reach unexpected consequences, of which this book is only one.

I'd like to end these acknowledgments by thanking you, the reader. Creating a book begins with a writer, but the story takes on texture and meaning in the hands of those who enjoy it – the images my words conjure in your head and the attachments you form with my heroes and villains are yours, guided by my descriptions but given life by your imagination. I sincerely hope that as you close the back cover of this novel, you are left imagining everything left unsaid about the backstory of a character, the unexplored reaches of the Reclaimed, and the lives and adventures of everyone you met for only a moment before their own stories took them from the pages of this book destined for tales untold. Thank you for being the part of this book that is beyond the soul and skeleton of the story, the color and contrast that makes it real in a way that only you can.

COMING SOON

Desolate Garden

Book Two in the Reclaimed Saga

ABOUT THE AUTHOR

Sam Odiorne was born in New England to a compassionate mother and a logical father, and by all accounts, he has never recovered.

He dislikes talking about himself but when pressed, will tell you that he loves old whiskey, new cities, baby rhinos, and you.

Sam can be found on all the usual social medias under his somewhat unusual name, through his website.

www.samodiorne.com

Lightning Source UK Ltd.
Milton Keynes UK
UKHW010648290921
391374UK00002B/283

9 781737 875901